I0819125

SOMEWHERE SOFT TO LAND

BALLANTINE BOOKS

NEW YORK

SOMEWHERE SOFT TO LAND

A Novel

kai alonté

Ballantine Books
An imprint of Random House
A division of Penguin Random House LLC
1745 Broadway, New York, NY 10019
randomhousebooks.com
penguinrandomhouse.com

Hardcover ISBN 978-0-593-72679-2
Ebook ISBN 978-0-593-72680-8

Printed in the United States of America on acid-free paper

1st Printing

First Edition

Book Team: Production editor: Annette Szlachta • Managing editor: Pamela Alders • Production manager: Samuel Wetzler • Copy editor: Sara Robb • Proofreaders: Hope Clarke, Dan Goff, Nicole Ramirez

Book design by Elizabeth A. D. Eno
Title page background stock art credit: PNG Kingdom/AdobeStock

The authorized representative in the EU for product safety and compliance is Penguin Random House Ireland, Morrison Chambers, 32 Nassau Street, Dublin D02 YH68, Ireland. https://eu-contact.penguin.ie

for the space cadets

SOMEWHERE SOFT TO LAND

PROLOGUE

ELMWOOD COLLEGE, MASSACHUSETTS | THE YEAR OF SOMEBODY'S LORD TWO-THOUSAND-SOMETHING-SOMETHING

Despite my long-standing disdain for organized religion and, in particular, Christianity, the first Sunday of October at eleven, I shuffled my way to the school chapel. The fingertips of my left hand pressed firm against a disquieted spot on my chest, the home of a caught breath more than a decade old.

I sat toward the back, hoping this would spare me from any compulsory social interactions. Just as the service started, I caught movement in the corner of my eye, heard someone slide into my row. I glanced at the opposite end of the pew. She settled in, crisscrossing her legs on the varnished wooden pew bench. Not exactly standard church etiquette and also a move that if I tried I would topple over, smack my head on the next pew, and bruise my knees into permanent hyperpigmentation. Something about her seemed familiar, but long, 1B/27 box braids blocked my view of her face. I moved my eyes back to the front of the church; I wasn't trying to actually know anyone here.

I just needed, for two hours—or however long this was going to last—a reprieve from my increasingly problematic non-belonging. I hadn't found my place on the rest of campus, so if I had to say *amen* and *hallelujah* a few times to get it, that was a price I was willing to pay. Elmwood had the standard liberal arts Black people quota, but until now, I hadn't worked out where they were hiding. Probably because I was hiding, too.

At the very least, church could be the one place I, an older-than-I-should-be sophomore, didn't feel self-conscious about having the wrong wardrobe for an upper-middle-class hipster paradise. Having been raised by a mother with expensive tastes and a frequently empty wallet—due, mainly, to her expensive tastes—my style was comprised of my sister Esther's hand-me-downs, though she was shorter, smaller, and more evenly proportioned than I was, and a hodgepodge of shirts and sweaters I'd found at Goodwill over the two years I lived in Oakland. At my height, it was impossible to find pants that fit properly for less than fifty dollars, so I didn't wear pants: I wore whichever of Esther's old skirts had elastic bands, with black convertible ballet tights and black Payless ballet flats I'd worn out within weeks of buying them.

I chanced another sideways look at the girl in my pew. She was wearing not the hipster uniform but a burgundy peacoat over a herringbone skirt, black tights, and un-scuffed ballet flats.

"Welcome, my flock!" Pastor Shirley proclaimed, airing out the collar of her voluminous monotone shift, the costume jewelry resting atop it jangling with each movement. A muffled snort drew my attention back to the opposite end of the pew. The girl examined her nails—painted an iridescent blue—and smirked, her head shaking from side to side. Eyebrows drawn together, I prepared to look away; she looked up before I could. Whatever she saw on my face made her laugh fully, then cover it, unconvincingly, with a cough.

The rest of the service passed in a blur. As I sat, medium-zoned-out, I wondered how many of the—mostly melanated—women gathered here were actually religious back home and how many, like I, could only find a semblance of home in this artifact of forced conversion.

I muttered, "Amen," when the pastor paused; I let my eyes glaze over as I watched the more dedicated churchgoers act as acolytes. I avoided the hugging segment by skulking at the other end of the church, pretending to be engrossed in some dusty Bibles in the farthest-from-everybody-else pew. When the service ended, I made a beeline for the exit.

The next week, I saw my ballet-flats compatriot at church again. Again, she spent the service masking her laughter with coughs and throat-clearing, and I tried my best, occasionally failing, not to join in. But we didn't speak until a week later.

Since I was a preteen, I'd harbored a rose-colored, soft-lighted fantasy about attending a—preferably Italian, because once delusional, why not really lean into it—dance conservatory. I was so sure of the impossibility of this dream that I never took any serious action toward it. Instead, I thought to find a compromise I could live with. A college prestigious enough that my parents would only have to lie to their *most* judgmental acquaintances about where I'd ended up, with a strong-enough dance program that I could—at least for a couple of hours a day—pretend I was at a performing arts school.

The master class was on a Wednesday at noon. I arrived at the big studio medium-early so I could find a spot in the far corner. In front of the mirror, the teacher, an Ivorian adjunct professor, stretched, chatting with the drummer who sat behind her, warming up beats on the taut canvas of a tall djembe. She looked up from her conversation when I walked in, winked. I smiled and looked away, wishing I had the courage to strike up a conversation. The only thing that came to mind was *Help!*

On the far side of the room, five or six white girls I recognized from the Modern Languages building sat in a cluster. They looked up, too, but did not wink; they scanned me from head to toe, returned their eyes to the group, and whispered with scattered snickers and glances back in my direction. One stood, approached. Petite and palpably energized, she had close-cropped brown hair, wore Lycra booty shorts and a cheetah-print sports bra.

"Heeey." She glanced back at her group and smirked, then returned her gaze to me. "Do I know you? You look really, really familiar. Oh my God, I *love* that you wore a leotard to this. So formal. Aren't you gonna overheat?" She had a high, chirpy voice.

My brain short-circuited; it took me a moment to sort out which questions she'd asked and whether any were worth answering. "Uh. Maybe." I picked at the ruched hem of my pilled warm-up pants. I should have lotioned my feet more thoroughly. "I think I've seen you in the language lab."

"Oh my God, *yes*!" she crooned, ruffling her brown hair and raising a fist in victory. "That is totally it. I'm taking French this semester. My grandmother was French, so. You know. What are you—oh wait, I've *heard* about you! Yeah, you're taking Italian, right? So random, but like—you go, girl! Wait, do you identify as a girl?"

"What?" An eyelash crept into my right eyeball. This wasn't the first time someone expressed confusion about my choice of foreign language. Even if I felt like explaining that my mother grew up in Italy, I refused to indulge the notion that there was anything aberrant about a person of my complexion speaking a language white people thought belonged to them. If their ancestors truly wanted to keep their languages to themselves, why had they gone to such great lengths to colonize absolutely everybody? I blinked until I could no longer feel the stray eyelash.

The girl continued, "I am sooo excited for today. You have no fucking idea. I mean, one of the reasons I came to this school was actually for the opportunity to take this class. I mean, obviously, I'll take the full-on course as soon as I'm eligible, but I'm *so* grateful for the workshop option. My family and I used to go to New York *all* the time—we're from Greenwich? I *love* Alvin Ailey."

"Sorry—is that—this isn't an Ailey class?"

"Oh, no." She tousled her hair. "But I just mean. You know. So I heard your family's from Africa. I'm so jealous!" She laughed a little manically. "Didn't you learn to dance like this when you were, like, five?"

I blinked, stunned. For one, that anyone on this campus noticed I existed. An oversight, on my part. "I don't know." I shrugged. "Did you do the quadrille with your grandma when you were five?"

"Sorry?" She laughed.

"She's French, right?"

"O . . . kay. Not sure I catch your drift, but whatevs. Anyway, I'm gonna get back to my girls, but see you around. We should get coffee or something. I'm Sam, by the way." She stuck her hand out.

I kept mine on my thighs. "Great to meet you," I said without any conviction. "I'm actually gonna run to the bathroom before class starts." I pushed my drawstring bag and water bottle closer to the wall and stood. The room was nearly full now, of emaciated, pale bodies in glorified bikinis. Some wore sarongs that looked straight out of a Tahitian airport kiosk. Others, like that girl Sam, went with the animal print theme. I could get my bag and water later.

I shuffle-ran to the doorway, my calluses chafing against the floor. When I reached the threshold, a head made sharp contact with my breastbone. "Ow, shit, sorry." I winced, even though I was pretty sure the collision hurt me more than the other way around. I looked out, then down. It was the girl from the opposite end of the church pew. She wore black leggings and a loose marigold tank top, her braids pulled back into a ponytail. I said, "Sorry," again and moved to pass her.

She grabbed my arm. "Don't you dare," she said. Her voice was more resonant than I'd have expected for someone so small—and filled with humor. "Leave me here with all of these Caucasians."

I laughed, then cleared my throat. "Oh, I was just—"

"You were just making a break for it. I know that look. You had that look in church, too, and so did I, girl. I have waited too long for the opportunity to dance to a non-EDM beat, and we are not about to let a bunch of hipless hipsters ruin this for us."

I hesitated. She tugged on my arm and pulled me back into the room. "Come on. If nothing else, this is gonna be hilarious. And by the way"—she smirked—"the quadrille? Epic." She tugged me to a spot in the middle of the room. I never, ever danced in the middle, not even when I danced alone.

"Okay, people," the teacher began, projecting her voice over the drummer's medium-tempo rhythm. "Get off your behinds and move those behinds to the floor. Let's get warm!"

As I lifted my arms at the teacher's cue, a nudge—a punch, really—jostled my left shoulder. "Oh, by the way," the church girl whispered between drumbeats, "I'm Tatiana."

I hated talking in class; breaking rules made me visible. But given that Tatiana had spared me the bother of being the "only" here, I decided to make another exception. "Hey. I'm—"

"Dzifa, right?"

I nodded, frowning. My invisibility cloak, effective for twenty years, was apparently losing its efficacy. It hadn't been easy, cultivating a personality that was unappealing enough to normal people that they left me alone, but not so unsettling they'd remember having interacted with me and initiate further, usually mean, interaction. Though I hadn't become myself on purpose, I lamented the loss of anonymity.

I had another name—a Christian name, as my mother called it—but I didn't like it and was too afraid to ask why I'd been given it in the first place. Knowing my mother, the answer would not be flattering. Calling a child *Mercy* was either, in the context of my family, a bad joke or a curse. "Yeah. Dzifa. That's right," I answered.

She smiled, returned her gaze to the mirror. We brought our arms down to our sides, bent our knees, stretched our torsos down to the floor.

After class, Tatiana invited me to the dining hall to debrief. On our way in, I waved at Angela, the salad bar supervisor.

"You a regular here or something?" Tatiana laughed.

"Oh." I lifted a shoulder, my eyes lingering on the large plastic tubs of romaine, arugula, mixed greens. "Kind of. I work here. Gonna work the dinner shift in a bit, actually."

"Oh, that's so weird. I'm here all the time and I don't think I've ever seen you. I work in the computer lab, but I usually eat over here 'cause the cafeteria on that side of campus doesn't have mozzarella sticks."

I nodded my understanding: sound logic. "I'm usually in the back. Dishwashing. But I got promoted recently to the burrito bar. So. Not to brag."

"Whoa." Tatiana raised her eyebrows. "And is it everything you ever dreamed of?"

I knew she was joking but answered honestly, my head cocked to one side. "Actually, yes. One of my favorite games as a kid was 'cafeteria.' You know, where you'd pretend to slop giant ladles of buffet foods onto an imaginary plate? And now I get to do it in real life, and honestly, it's weirdly satisfying. I mean, some of the customers are way too invested in the technique with which I fold their tortillas. Though, as a Californian, I can respect that." This was the longest I had spoken with anyone, probably since I matriculated. We reached a table in the far-back corner of the seating area.

"Okay, I don't know if it's a Boston thing—probably not—but I never played 'cafeteria.' I played 'future CEO' or 'movie star,' you know? But if you like it, I love it for you, girl; I'm happy for you."

Tatiana pulled out a black, low-backed chair with curved, metal armrests and slid into it, pulling her feet up onto the seat.

I sat diagonally from her; the angle was awkward, but I hated direct eye contact. "You're from Boston, then?"

"Yep." She shrugged. "Unfortunately."

"I never thought it was that bad, though I guess I wasn't actually in the city. Just sort of . . . around. Would escape there some weekends when I was in high school, if I was allowed to."

"What? You were in Mass? I thought you were California all day, every day. Where did you go to high school?" Tatiana perked up.

"Uh . . ." I grimaced. "Council Grove."

"Oh, okay, so you bougie." She laughed. When I opened my mouth—not to protest, because my parents' bougieness could not be disputed, but I supposed, to elaborate, as their bougieness was, with the most generous-possible branding, "layered"—she waved a hand dismissively. "Just messing with you. So am I. Prep school after prep school before after-school college-prep program, you know what I mean? My mom was *not* playing. And neither was I, come to think of it." She pursed her lips as if this had only now occurred to her. "You know . . . honor roll, debate team, dance captain, mathlete, blah, blah. What did you get into at good ol' Council?"

My eyes wide, I swallowed. None of that, certainly. "Nothing much. Like . . . I did dance also, but . . . I wasn't really very social. And honestly, my grades weren't that great. I didn't really know how to cope with the whole New England . . . thing."

Tatiana smirked. "Oh, you mean the white boys with the IV at the end of their names and the double-layered popped Lacostes? How their families had four houses but, somehow, regular-ass jobs? Yeah, believe me: I am familiar. Luckily, Mommy has been preparing me for that mess since I emerged—thirty-year-plan in hand, legend has it—from the womb." She mimed ticking off items on a checklist. "What's your family's deal?"

I offered a tight smile in return. "I don't know. I have four older sisters. The three eldest went to boarding school in the UK. But we weren't all close. Growing up, it was just me and Esther, mostly."

"Gotcha." Tatiana frowned. "Wow, five kids? Your mom must be, like, Superwoman."

I blinked. "Well, she's . . . a woman . . ." I trailed off, my eyebrows scrunching together.

She laughed. "Okaay then. Maybe not. I just mean, like? Five kids? You guys Catholic? Mormon? I'm pretty sure I'm not gonna have kids, so to be honest, having more than zero is kinda wild to me."

"No." I didn't resist the smile that crept up on me. "And—same. They're not religious. It's more like: The first one was an accident. My mom never even wanted to get married. But, I don't know. At that point, I guess you figure you might as well double down, convince yourself it was your plan all along." I shrugged, unsure why I bothered to defend—or invent, more likely—my mother's thought process.

"Uh—sounds like your mom quadrupled down, but I hear you. I mean, won't be me, but—respect." She drew her hand away from her forehead in a mock salute.

"Yeah." I grimaced.

"Okay, cool." Tatiana surveyed the room, then turned back to me. "Wait, so what do your parents do?"

"I don't know," I said.

"Girl, what?" She laughed and leaned back in her chair, pulling her knees up and draping her arms around them. "What are they, spies?"

"No. My dad used to be a professor—physics. Now I'm not sure what he's up to—haven't seen him for a while. My mom used to be a physicist, too, but then with all the kids . . ." I raised my eyebrows. "I don't know. Technically, she worked from home, but it's hard to say specifically."

"Dzifa . . ." Tatiana paused. "That is how you pronounce your name, right?"

I nodded.

"How do your parents pay the bills?"

I considered lying but figured this might be my one and only chance to make an actual friend. "Anywhere between . . . often and always, they don't."

Her eyes widened. "How are you here, then? Like, did you get a scholarship?" This was the first time anyone had asked and the first time I'd talked about it to anyone besides my high school friend Zeynep, and we hadn't spoken since I left the Bay. It wasn't personal; Zeynep's issues with object impermanence extended to other humans, but it stung nonetheless. Tatiana's inquisitiveness was a little unnerving, but it didn't seem malicious, just intense. Unabashed.

I chewed on my lower lip. "Loans. And I saved up for a couple of years—did a bunch of random jobs while I went to community college. I'm a year behind." I ignored the pang in my chest; this was the truth—well, the bare bones of it—but it felt like a dirty secret. To my family, it was.

"Word." Tatiana nodded. "I like your work ethic. I mean, my situation was a little different 'cause I'm an only child and Mommy was older when she had me. She planned the *shit* out of the whole parenting thing, so she was *ready* ready. No offense to your mom. Although thankfully, she didn't have to use all her savings; I got a little STEM scholarship, and I've been working since I was fourteen. People are forever telling me I'm doing the most. But while I am open to a whole range of life experiences, one that I am *not* open to, my friend? Being broke. You know?"

"Oh." My eyes darted toward my lap. I raised them and nodded. "Yeah. Um . . . that's cool." I filed away the twinge of discomfort at her anti-scarcity declaration, chalked it up to my lack of practice talking about my family. I was happy for her preparedness and apparent abundance, even if I couldn't relate. "Congrats on the scholarship," I followed up. "So, what about your parents? What's their . . . deal?" I borrowed her phrasing.

"Oh, Mommy's done it solo from the start," Tatiana answered. "On purpose. My uncle Aman helped out a ton, but Mommy really *is* Superwoman, so I never felt like anything was missing. Honestly, when I'd visit my friends who had dads, I'd be like: For what? For why?" She held her palms out for a few seconds. I wondered if I was supposed to answer, even though I'd asked myself the same question as a child and . . . her guess was as good as mine. "What about your parents, the spies? They still together?"

I regretted opening myself up to this line of inquiry. "Yeah, they're still married. But they haven't lived together in . . . I don't know, fifteen years? Twenty? My dad's in Accra; my mother sort of floats around between my sisters' houses these days." It seemed a comfortable enough setup for her, and most important, it kept a three-thousand-mile minimum between her and me: a prerequisite, I'd learned the hard way, for my sanity.

"Tale as old as time." Tatiana sighed. "Ah, upwardly mobile Black families and their precious image." Tatiana tapped her belly. "But I'mma need some snacks. For fuel. So we can get to the bottom of which government your spy parents work for."

I laughed, shrugged. My chair screeched against the floor as I scooted back, preparing to stand. Mid-ascent, Tatiana waved a hand. "Nah, you're about to start work anyway. Allow me. You like mozza sticks?"

PART 1

CHAPTER 1

NEW YORK | JANUARY | SEVEN YEARS OF ASSORTED LORDS LATER

I left his house at five. Tatiana refused to call him anything but "Chicago Shithead," or, in more gracious moments, "Bootleg Barack," because he managed to insert the fact of his being from the South Side of Chicago into conversations about tuna fish, graphic design, and Belize. This was true but unfair, I felt, to premium Barack.

Typically, I refused to call him anything at all, since I was in denial about repeatedly dating someone I did not actually like and who very much did not like me either. But he was tall, child-free, and insistently heterosexual, and he wore tailored suits to work; I reasoned that eventually, the sheen of these qualifications would supersede my dislike of him. And after an ill-advised phone call with my mother the previous afternoon, I craved the familiarity of any person who wasn't her. I could have called Tatiana, but wouldn't; I was not ready to own up to my poor decision-making of late. Therefore, I reasoned the best course of action was to make an even poorer decision.

Leaving his place before dawn was easy. I usually hit Snooze dozens of times, but not around him. It was a commonality between the men I'd been with that year—that they couldn't or didn't sleep. Instead, they lay alert on their sides, disrupting my sleep with the kinds of touches you'd give a pet you were about to put down. A tender goodbye in preparation for tomorrow's kill. It was a desperate and careful touch, a sad worship without overt sexuality, though it felt sexual in ways that rattled me when I remembered them.

With women, I felt safer and further away from myself. My preferences had always been more atmospheric than gender-based, and the first time—of three, in the six months we dated—that I broke up with Chicago Shithead, I set out for more thorough field testing. In spite of a prolific effort, I came away from each encounter feeling like I could have enjoyed myself if I'd cared to, if my birth control didn't dull my libido, if my sexuality wasn't merely the byproduct of adrenaline and terror, if I didn't wonder whether I had any sexuality at all.

I ordered a cab on my way out, passed the time pacing back and forth in the tiled entryway. If I walked to Eastern Parkway at such an empty, cold hour, I'd end up having to run; my head hurt as it was. I ached elsewhere, too, though I decided to chalk it up to the winter draft permeating the entryway, rather than the excess aggression of the previous evening. As I waited, I read, reread, and contemplated the deletion of the text my mother sent after our call yesterday.

The thing about coping with depression for any significant length of time was: While one could technically forestall premature unaliveness, the craving for a reprieve from active existence was at times so acute that it found creative ways to achieve its goals (e.g., "How about, instead of physiologically dying, you date a man with the emotional regulation of a toddler on high-dose steroids and the internalized racism of a Tyler Perry villain—that way, nobody will call you selfish for trying to off yourself, but you'll still get to *feel* like you've perished?"). Who said women couldn't have it all?

So at 5:38 P.M. the day before, leaning against the façade of a downtown Le Pain Quotidien, I unblocked his number. I felt justified: I'd endured seventeen minutes more than the self-allotted twenty of my mother's exceptional ability to scramble my psyche, without breaking a sweat, shedding an eyelash, or getting a snag in one of her spotless cashmere sweaterdresses. I couldn't see her reactions or her outfit over the phone, but I remembered them well enough—too well for my own good. While continuing to dodge Tatiana's texts so I would not feel compelled to admit to my colossal, double-pronged backslide, I found myself, just a few short hours later, being medium-terrorized in Bootleg Barack's musty apartment, once again.

I checked my phone; the taxi was still a few minutes out. Fidgeting with the neckline of my dress, I reread my mother's message.

> Hello Dzifa. I spotted this article in the Atlantic. By an acclaimed researcher. Harvard-educated. PhD. (Lost a bunch of weight, incidentally.) Per our conversation.

I could not initially view the link and should have taken that as a sign from the universe to skip it entirely. I reloaded the page and read the title: "Psychiatry Is the Only Mental Illness: My Fight to Bring Personal Responsibility Back to American Youth."

On a better night: For example, a night where the man I backslid with was not having a rage meltdown, I might have been better equipped to respond appropriately. To force myself to laugh it off, even as the impact of my mother's dig stung. To call Tatiana and wait for her to laugh at Mrs. Quartey's signature brand of rubbing salt in the very wound she'd opened. But it wasn't a better night. It was the night it was, and, as I waited for the cab, I read the entire article and let the flashbacks roll through me, clutching at my chest as if the memories were lodged there instead of in my head.

The sharp alert from my phone brought me back just enough to leave the building. I pushed open the door, stepped through. As the door swung back, I raised my leg to kick it shut, relishing the rush of cold air and the force of my boot against the thick slab of metal. When the door clicked—with agonizing ease—back into place, I released a short, grainy scream.

"Uh . . . is it . . . Mercy?"

I swiveled around, spotted the source of the low, timid voice. A black SUV idled at the curb.

I released the tension in my forehead, the tightness in my lips and cheeks. "Oh, hey!" I matched my voice to his, just above a whisper. "Yeah, that's me."

The driver was young and handsome. He played pop-friendly hip-hop and said nothing all the way back to my neighborhood; meanwhile, I fantasized about how I might feel if I'd spent the night with him instead. He was the sort of pretty, shy-seeming man by whom I might actually request to, rather than relent to, be touched. I said nothing either. When we were close to my place, I asked him to drop me at the corner store. "Thank you," I said too brightly, a smile nobody asked me to force straining my cheeks.

It was only three minutes from the store to the brownstone where I'd been living for the past six months. A small plastic bag slapped against my legs as I walked. A few steps from the house, I tripped, scraping my tights across the pavement, and righted myself with a flushed, shaking hand. The flesh on and between my thighs strained against the impromptu lunge. I winced and pulled myself up, checking my hands for dust and drug paraphernalia.

The house was quiet when I walked in. Three of my housemates slept on the ground floor, three of us upstairs. I closed the front door and nudged my flats onto a thick doormat. In our big, bright kitchen, I pulled a tall glass from the cupboard and tore open a packet of Alka-Seltzer. It fizzed for two minutes. I lifted it to my mouth, tilted it back, and drank it down in big, choking gulps. I took a couple of painkillers, a rare practice even though I had accumulated plenty of meds over the years, mostly long-expired antidepressants, and a couple for the heart palpitations I'd had since I was a kid. I'd be well within my rights to take them as I needed them, but it was my policy to convince myself not to need them most of the time.

Rooms being closets were not hyperbole in New York; my room had been a closet and now housed a single bed, a small desk, a blue exercise ball I used as a chair, no windows, and me. All five of my housemates were some variation of white, ranging from fifth-generation standardly white to second-generation ethnic white. I moved to the brownstone in July, six months after my Russian live-in boyfriend broke up with me because he was thinking of joining the priesthood. I resented being forced into the tired role of jilted girlfriend crying into a tub of ice cream, even if being jilted for a lifetime of asceticism gave me slightly superior branding.

Perhaps it was his newfound spirituality, or perhaps it was that a month after he broke up with me, I projected onto him the blame for the memorably unpleasant encounter I endured during my first attempt to date somebody else. I went for drinks, then home, with a Connecticutian man who lived in a Midtown high-rise, who had large veneers and Jason Bateman energy I clocked early enough to survive but a little late to avoid a resurgence of immobilizing panic attacks that made taking public transit a greater-than-usual safety risk. Either way, the Russian Who Dumped Me gave me first, last, and security, and drove me and my belongings to the whitest part of this part of Brooklyn, this place a twenty-minute walk from my workplace, with three big boys who didn't know me but who I assumed were hormonally predisposed to fighting should the Connecticutian show up for seconds.

I paid the Russian back with my next three paychecks, but that didn't assuage Esther's certainty, during our rare phone calls, that I was letting my role as the concubine of an Unmelanated Immigrant linger a little too long. To be fair to me—not that Esther was interested in that kind of exercise—I'd expended a not-insignificant amount of emotional labor to be with a man who denied having any childhood trauma, even though, having grown up in a country that operated at a postapocalyptic level of intensity, any story he reluctantly shared about his childhood was the most alarming I'd ever heard. He critiqued me for being openly damaged, but this was the very quality I appreciated most about myself. I did nothing to hide that I wasn't equipped with a standard operating system. That way, people were less likely to assume I was a fully functional adult, only to later be surprised by my propensity to psychologically collapse in the face of social and developmental expectations that were, to them, normal, and to me, baffling and untenable.

I dropped the bags in my windowless room, changed into a T-shirt and leggings, and dashed out to the gym around the corner, clutching my down coat behind me. On the way, I paused every few steps to raise my free hand and scratch at the edges of my scalp. In spite of my mother's assumptions, which she had so kindly reiterated over the phone, I went to the gym nearly every day. I just looked how I looked and felt how I felt.

There were half a dozen sweating bodies, mostly smug, spray-tanned men in tank tops, scattered throughout the first floor. I shuffled to the nearest treadmill, kept my head down, stuck my earphones in, and hit Start. I ignored the aches in my head, my body. I couldn't run anyway, never had the vitality to do so. Instead, I turned the treadmill settings to a brisk walk at a steep slope and tried not to trip.

My phone beeped. I wondered if it was Tatiana again. I'd been dodging her texts since two weeks back, when she was home in Boston and I was at a co-worker's Christmukkah celebration in the Bronx, avoiding eye contact and sneaking into the bathroom so I could google "non-painful ways to self-induce a coma." I'd blocked and dodged the communiqués of plenty of others before Tatiana; it was a lot easier than developing more conventional boundaries. But when it came to her, this was a first.

Tatiana was exactly the sort of person who'd say, "I told you so," when you did something that both you and she knew you shouldn't have done. Like, say, returning to the apartment of a man who wasn't *violent* violent but wasn't *not* violent. Or, say, answering calls from and opening links sent by a mother who wasn't *violent* violent but wasn't *not* violent. I might have resisted pressing the Block button on Tatiana, but I still refused to disclose either of these lapses in judgment, let alone both.

I relaxed; the text was from Maya, my direct supervisor.

hey mercy how's it going? sorry to hyu so early, but just a heads-up we're doing biannual reviews today. late notice, but . . . new management and shit.

There was always a split second when I saw this name I'd resisted for so long and felt compelled to say, *Sorry, wrong number.* On the other hand, having *Mercy* as my technical-if-not-actual name had proved useful for employment purposes.

When I moved to New York after college, I took two trains and a bus to the Upper West Side to clean white people's houses. Each night that year, I slathered my hands with shea butter to offset the daily doses of lye. With greasy fingers, I'd set my computer on my lap, open three or four job sites, and see how far my actual name, Dzifa, could get me. She got me as far as one train and a bus to the Upper East Side, where I raised white people's children. Mercy, along with Tatiana's encouragement/strong-arming, got me a marketing internship a year later, a decent-enough boyfriend, and a swift rise to the low-paid middle tier of corporate content creation. Maybe this was how I found my place, I figured. By becoming *basically* a different person without having to legally change my name.

I wedged the phone into an empty cup holder and turned up the incline so far it was painful. Routine burnout being my Achilles' heel and, possibly, entire personality at this point, I'd never worked anywhere long enough to undergo such a review. This job was a first in many regards; most important, it was the first time I was paid consistently, and without begging, to create something. Even if all I created was SEO copy for a fintech company. It was unlikely I'd ever get paid for the choreography I made up privately; I'd take what I could get. The review was probably because the new owners found out about the concessions Maya made for me, to accommodate my increasingly obvious inability to do anything but the actual work. This didn't bother her much, because when she interviewed me, I started telling her the usual lies about my being a team player and a go-getter and an all-American winner of things—basically, I channeled Tatiana—and she held up a hand to stop me. "I literally don't care," she said. "I've read your portfolio."

She let me work from seven to three instead of ten to six, and she let our team get fully drunk on Fridays at lunch. Maya's manager was also a woman of color, a chain of command I'd never encountered before but found to be optimal. It was remarkable how much work I got done when I didn't have to manage white people's egos or anxiety disorders. None of us had the final say on anything, but until the recent change in upper management, we were mostly left alone. Now meetings were a frequent thing, seating assignments were forcibly rotated every week, and lunch was timed.

Sweat poured down my face, soaked through my clothes, dripped into my shoes. The itch on my scalp and the sharpness between my legs amplified with every step. I would just have to walk it off. A couple walked in laughing. He had high cheekbones, a V-shaped torso, melanin-rich skin. She was pale, with narrow, downturned eyes, and a cropped BLM sweatshirt. She stepped onto the treadmill beside me and scanned me from toe to head. She smirked and turned her eyes back to her machine. I hit Pause and collected my belongings.

I was first to the office as usual and sat in my assigned seat in the middle of the open-concept space. While drinking cup after cup of diluted Keurig coffee, I spent an hour hate-reading discouraging stats about Black women and love, Black women and health, Black women and money, Black women and survival, toggling miserably between those gems and the equally discomfiting link my mother sent.

My colleagues trickled in, clutching plastic coffee cups and massaging their temples. "Hey, Mercy." The ones who were in the habit of talking at me nodded in my direction; the others looked at their phones and walked ahead to their desks.

Maya came in at ten forty-five. She threw her upscale purse onto the desk next to mine and rolled her eyes at the closed office door of her manager's manager. "I am just not into this whole setup." She pulled out her laptop and, with her free hand, gestured toward the massive, open-concept warehouse floor, full of long, white plastic tables and devoid of privacy of any kind. "Not into it at all."

I raised my eyebrows in agreement. She got to work, covered her ears with a pair of oversize headphones. I resumed my combination of working and hate-reading. At one, my phone buzzed. I pulled it out of my bag.

Heyyyy, Tatiana wrote, I think your phone has it in for me again; I haven't been able to reach you in ages! Rude. Anyway, wanna go to 55 tonight? We could get those mozzarella sticks first. I reaalllyy want those mozza sticks.

I darted my eyes around the office. Everyone was focused on their work or, at the very least, focused on looking focused on their work. But I didn't like the possibility of people reading over my shoulder. I slid the phone back inside my purse; I'd gotten the bag, a large, eggplant-hued monstrosity, from one of those knockoff big-box stores in Harlem, the ones whose aisles reminded me of a stolen-goods truck.

It buzzed again. "Sorry," I muttered to my own lap, reaching back in to retrieve my phone.

> I know you saw that text!! Come onnnn. I have some hot gossip for you. We have to catch up. And get those mozza sticks LOL

Hey, sorry! I typed back. My phone has been acting kinda weird and I've been busy with work. That project I started last month is taking foreeeverr. I would love to see you, but I'm super tired today and I might get off work pretty late.

A throat cleared behind me. I jolted upright, set the phone down. Peering back, I forced a smile. It was the new manager, an imposing man in his fifties who had a standard corporate résumé and little interest in his employees beyond the frequent memos scolding us for plotting to circumvent his hot-desking obsession. "Sorry," I said. He said nothing, his bespectacled face still and unreadable. He retreated into his office.

An hour later, Maya pulled me into a room with her counterpart in Sales. He'd been promoted to her level after the change in management, despite his relative lack of experience. He was Scarsdale-bred, had a square jawline, and belonged to one of those big, one-room gyms where investment bankers subjected themselves to unnecessary rigors for $750 a month. "We're really happy with your work," they said. I didn't speak or move my face, because I truly didn't understand. They handed me a packet of paper with multiple-choice bubbles and blue pen marks. "This is the format they ask us to use for reviews. We really don't have any complaints." I frowned at the packet.

"Really?" I resisted the urge to suggest a few.

"Seriously, Mercy." Maya's laugh was low and uncannily rhythmic. "I'm gonna give you a compliment and it's not gonna sound like a compliment, but it's actually the best kind a manager can give: You're so good at your job that I frequently forget you're even here."

"Sorry?" I flipped through the pages.

"It happens all the time, where I'm running through what I've got on my plate for the day, and I'm delegating all this sh—stuff, and it'll be like weeks before I realize I haven't given you anything. Like, that's because you make it incredibly easy for me to just get on with my other work."

"Wow." I waited, glancing at both of them with suspicion that the other shoe would drop; a few seconds passed. Maybe that was both shoes. I heard the compliment in what she said, but I suspected this was not an achievement I should take pride in. It wasn't the first time someone told me that their favorite thing about me was that they did not notice me at all. "Uh . . . thanks."

I spent another two hours sneaking glances at my perfect score. This was it, I guessed. The pinnacle of all those years scrambling, flailing, trying to become sufficiently tolerable to stay, at the very least, housed. And what was next? An eventual promotion? A different apartment I spent 90 percent of my salary on? A new partner who left me for a different religious order? I stared at the score, trying to feel something, waiting for the pride to hit. *I should feel proud*, I berated myself. I wasn't usually good at anything. Not by my family's standards, which involved going to Harvard and being a professor of astrophysics, which I had not and was not. Even as the child both of my parents invested the least energy in, I'd learned early that anything short of the highest quantifiable level of excellence qualified me for irreparable degenerate status.

A down-tempo ringtone started up; Tatiana's name flashed across the home screen. Clicking my tongue, I wiped sweaty hands on the thick fabric of my dress and muttered an apology to Maya. I contemplated hitting Decline and feigning ignorance if I ran into Tatiana in person—we did live within a ten-minute walk of each other—but instead, I half jogged to the barren foyer outside the office. Might as well get it over with. The glass-paned door didn't shut completely behind me. I nudged it closed with my free arm. "Hey."

"Well, thank God you're alive." There was crowd noise on her end; I wondered if she'd stepped out for a late lunch. The tech company where she was a junior executive had its own cafeteria, or "culteria," as she called it, but she made use of every opportunity to take a break from her coworkers. "I thought you'd been sex murdered or something."

The corner of my mouth ticked up against my will. "Not today. How's it going?"

"Eh, we had a shit ton of meetings this morning. The senior execs are acting all intense, and I am really tryna stay professional in the midst of all this whiteness. But sometimes you just look at these people like . . . wow, it must be nice to be so mediocre and not get demoted or shot in the face. Meanwhile, I'm over here with my 4.5 GPA and *literal abundance* of industry experience, but sure, Peggy, you and your University of Phoenix degree can be my boss, yeah, that's fine. You know how it is."

"Do I ever." I relaxed a little, against the door.

"Exactly." Her sigh lasted longer than it usually did. "Anyway, dream job and all that . . . so we're going to 55, right? Like, we'll go before anyone comes. We can cut it up and leave when the Caucasians arrive. As per ush. I'll meet you . . . yeah, let's just meet at Sola at like six forty-five for our mozza sticks, and then we'll go from there."

I always found it easier to say no via text. I was not in the correct frame of mind to watch men dismiss me in real time, but if I didn't go, Tatiana would be in a mood. When she was in a mood, she said all kinds of sly things that stung for years after the fact. After our last meeting at a sticky Gowanus bar with a jukebox in the corner, it took me, a world champion of delayed processing, four days to realize I felt stung by her many "jokes" about my concerted attempts to get Chicago Shithead out of my system by sleeping with as many other people as I could stomach, which was not many by New York standards, and an unforgivable number by my family's standards.

Meanwhile, I had shown what I felt was extraordinary restraint as she described, somewhat smugly, a pattern of alcohol-fueled recklessness on her part. I knew my anger came from a bizarrely metastasized self-shaming more than any righteous anger with Tatiana, but I had a strange pride in the fact that my sluttiness was calculated rather than impulsive.

I once spent two hours giving a Hinge stranger a rundown of the plot of *A Series of Unfortunate Events* before I felt comfortable getting undressed in front of her. I wanted Tatiana to acknowledge, if not applaud, the lack of ease with which I shared my body. But because my anger didn't materialize until way after the fact, it seemed, logistically, my best options were either swallowing it or ignoring her indefinitely.

My fear of being demonstrative in public won out. I did not want to have an argument ever, but certainly not where my co-workers could see. Plus, maybe her time with her mother over the holidays had refreshed her, imbued her with just a touch more sensitivity. Unlikely, but a girl could dream. "All right, fine. But I seriously need to get home early. And I'm capping it at one drink, max."

She whooped. "Yeah, of course. Done-zo. I'm so excited. I missed you! Okay, I'mma go back in so I don't get fired byeeee."

"Yeah . . . likewise. Bye."

CHAPTER 2

"Should we get a bottle? Why are you sweating so much?" Tatiana scanned the menu, though we'd already ordered and she memorized the whole thing months ago. Our favorite Chelsea bar sat on the edge of a long, clean avenue. I liked that it was low-lit and all the tables looked out at the sidewalk. Tatiana liked that the tall, European waiters served gourmet junk food.

"Mm. I'm fine. It's because of the subway; they turned the heat on full blast." I grimaced. "How much is the bottle? Probably not."

"Yeah, you're probably right. I really need to be paying off this credit card debt, ugh. I don't understand how I'm making the most I've ever made and my quality of life is exactly the same, if not worse. I'll just get a glass." She flagged down the waiter, a lanky Greek man in his thirties. He stood a few feet away from us with his hands clasped behind his back. "Hey!" She smiled at him; he smiled back. "Could I have a glass of Riesling? Or actually, I had your chardonnay once, but I can't remember what it tasted like. Could I maybe taste it again? And then I'll decide."

"Sure thing." He nodded. "Would you like to taste the chardonnay as well, miss?"

"No thank you. I'll just have the Riesling," I said to the table.

"You know, we'll both try the chardonnay. Thanks so much," Tatiana instructed in a stage whisper. I ran a hand over my eyes. The waiter nodded and walked over to the bar.

Tatiana reached her hands out and mimed wringing my neck. "Girl, you are the surliest of surlies sometimes. That man is *hhhot.* Why. Aren't. You. Getting. It. Look at you—you're serving weave and everything. Did you do that over the break?"

"I seriously doubt that," I grumbled. "Men like fun, peppy women. You're fun. And peppy. You date him."

She rolled her eyes. "Uh, I don't think so. Mommy did some quick braids when I was home, but they were only in for a hot second. So I shall be dateless until I get those extensions back in. I mean . . . *I* know I'm hot, but you know how men are. Their eyes don't work right; they really just see shapes. Like, faces? Never heard of 'em. You know that explains at *least* half the interracial relationships in Brooklyn."

I stifled a laugh.

"Last week, I walked by this man who looked like he was *literally* carved out of bronze. By Michelangelo. And the girl he was with? You already know."

I thought back to the couple at the gym this morning.

"Anyway, by their standards, you're the pretty one today. You're a whole gazelle, and you're acting like you don't know it. If I was a gazelle, my rent would be paid, no problem, every month of the year." She laughed and pulled at a few strands of her teased-out Afro.

"What are you even talking about? Men would flock to you even if you had a bowl cut. They see me and think I'm a pillar or something."

"Uh, *no*." Tatiana laughed. "You could have a whole harem if you tried." She lifted a tall glass of water to her lips. "Seriously, skip me with that low-self-esteem bullshit, Dzifa. That's for white girls." She mimed flipping her hair over her shoulder. "'Oh my God-ah, I ate a piece of cheese today. I heeate myself.' They hate themselves and they get everything anyway. So just try a little. I keep telling you to take advantage of this whole Nubian queen, Pan-African princess narrative you could totally play into, and you aren't listening to me. You *know* people love an Exotic Black; they're never gonna know or care you can't speak Ga. Like, you should really take a page from the Nigerian girls and act like you own the whole damn earth and everyone on it. You know how they are. Let's get you some Louboutins so you can go around stomping on all the peasants."

"Jesus." I shook my head, choking back another laugh. "You've got a lot of hot takes today."

"Yes, well, I don't make the rules; if I did, I can assure you we'd both live in manors. Not even mansions, girl—*manors*. With conservatories, drawing rooms, *and* stables. Stables, I tell you! In the meantime, we all just have to use what we've got. *I* have amazing bone structure, a body any of these girls *wish* they did but could never, a mind like a supercomputer, and a stellar personality. *You* have the opportunity to convince hot ignoramuses that you're West African royalty."

The waiter set two short-stemmed glasses on the table and poured a small amount in each. I had to admire Tatiana for never wavering in her messaging since college, both darting our eyes toward each other during praise dance rehearsals, church services, the increasing number of dance and language classes we took together. Even then, she'd been on a soapbox about the necessity for Black women to have unshakable confidence at all times, in any circumstance. To abandon the coddling, faux-socialist false promises our hipster classmates espoused. To take responsibility for our own destinies by standing, firmly and without the shadow of a doubt, in our innate magnificence. I wasn't sure any of that was realistic, but didn't say so when we met. In the absence of a rebuttal, Tatiana assumed I agreed. With that and all her other ideas.

This assumption wasn't unique to her; it was an occupational hazard of being a so-called quiet person. Extroverts and others with pushy dispositions took one look at my silence and projected onto me an entire personality, backstory, and social role I'd never explicitly agreed to. By the time I got to college, I was tired of fighting it, so I let people believe what they wanted. If they thought I was meek, so be it. If they thought I was a bitch because I only blinked at them after they delivered a monologue they mistook as a conversation, I could live with that. Tatiana, at least, projected onto me a version of myself that was far more stimulating than what anyone else managed to imagine. In her eyes, any friend of hers was just a touch of self-confidence away from being as fabulous as she.

Although I couldn't say I wanted to be her, exactly—I would never have the energy for that—I did admire that while I was the sort of person who spent up to six hours questioning all my words and actions throughout the day before I could fall asleep, Tatiana was the sort of person who assumed all her words and actions were both morally correct and brilliant, since they came from her. It scared me, a little, the possibility of living with a total absence of self-doubt—which of my meanest impulses would I act upon, then? But there was something about that freedom to be exactly as one was, without the slightest apology, that caught my attention in college. I hadn't been able to let go since.

Tatiana picked her glass up by the stem and swizzled the wine, her lips pursed. "Mm." She nodded. "Not bad at all! But you know what? I actually might want a red. Do you have a pinot noir? I would like to try that, please."

"Why." I turned my head toward the retreating waiter. "Could I please just have a glass of Riesling, thank you so much."

"By the by . . ." Another tall, European waiter set a tray of architecturally arranged cheese sticks on the table. They were good, but I suspected we both liked the bougie plating just a little bit more than we liked the taste. Tatiana took a bite. She chewed, dancing side to side in her chair. "Has Chicago Shithead called you again? 'Cause if he did, I will find him and kill him for you."

I nudged two sticks apart with my thumb and dragged one onto a side plate while I prepared to lie. "Of course not."

"Thank God. I was worried about you getting a li'l lonely over the holidays and backsliding into an abyss." She ate two more sticks and brushed her hands together to rub the crumbs off. "What an absolute nightmare. I still can't believe the things he said to you. And did! My God. My mom acts like Black men are the only men that exist, but guess who else acts like that? Black men. Ugh. I say let them have Peggy. I'll take my tragic mulattos, and you can go back to dating Russians and other weird, quiet dudes who look like they've been recently exhumed."

"I dated *one* Russian." I rolled my eyes and broke my lone mozzarella stick into three uneven pieces. "That's hardly a fetish. And I don't think you're supposed to say *tragic mulattos*." Despite my lack of attachment to most of my previous partners, I was oddly sensitive about my dating choices. Tatiana wasn't sensitive about much of anything, and if she was, I didn't really want to find out. While my tendency was to withdraw when someone saw me a little keenly, hers was to eviscerate.

Tatiana tipped the rest of the sticks onto my plate. "What is wrong with you? Eat. All you talk about is food. All of a sudden, you're not hungry?" She sat back. "And why are you still so PC? It's a waste of time. Keeping it real saves you energy, I'm telling you. Anyway, how much you wanna bet you meet a Russian tonight?"

I popped one piece in my mouth at a time. "How about let's *not* bet on that, since I do not want that." The waiter set down my Riesling and poured her a tasting of the pinot noir.

"Too bad." She laughed and bit off another piece. She was the size of a child, and all she ever ate was pizza and mozzarella sticks.

In middle school, we had to do this state-mandated fitness test, presumably to gauge whether we showed sufficient promise of future orthorexia: a legal requirement to be certified as Californian. I proved I could do twenty-five "girlie" push-ups and fifty sit-ups, though I'd have done hundreds if they asked me to. I could push my legs out into a middle split and lean my head onto my elbows, potbelly and all. But I couldn't run. I limped to the finish line twenty minutes after everyone else had finished, as a wall of my classmates awwed and cheered. Nothing could be more demeaning, I thought, than this little crowd of lithe white bodies cheering for me. I preferred their racist vitriol, as it suggested a hint of personhood to be diminished. Their pity clapping confirmed what I of course knew and did not want anyone else knowing, which was that I was fundamentally malformed.

Tatiana brought both hands to her heart and adopted an improbably thick Russian accent. "Saint Petersburg! *Do svidaniya!* Would you like to hear my theory?"

"No thank you." I pushed my plate to the side and crossed my arms.

"Okay, I'm gonna tell you." She crossed her legs, one high-heeled boot knocking a metal table leg.

"Great." I rested my elbows on the table and buried my face in my hands.

"You know how you're always talking about Americans being, like, completely obsessed with happiness? Like, you have to be optimistic at all times or you'll be excommunicated?"

I peeked an eye through my fingers. "Yup."

She leaned back in her chair, a slow and uneven smile spreading across her angular jaw. "Yeah, so, honestly—no offense, but good luck finding you an American guy and also why would you want one—but the Russians? Now, they like a surly woman. You could even be, like, *more* taciturn. If you can manage it. And all those shady things you keep in your head? You should just say them. I swear to God, if you do that, you'll be barefoot and pregnant in Moscow by the end of this year, max."

My legs swiveled to the edge of the seat on their own accord. "Wow, sounds like the dream. Should we go soon?"

She waved at the waiter. "I'll have one of these, please. Actually can I just get the bottle? Thanks."

"Uh, aren't we about to get drinks at 55? Let's just wait till we get there."

"Noo, they're overpriced and watery there. Here, I'll pay for it; in fact, I'll treat you for the whole meal. Just enjoy."

Two bottles later, the waiter laid a black leather checkbook on the table. Tatiana opened it and grimaced. "Okaay, so maybe I could treat you next time? Sorry about that. It's more than I thought."

"One sec." I checked my phone for my bank balance, glancing behind us to make sure no one was looking over my shoulder. "Um. Sure, yeah, no worries."

"Sorry." She frowned. "I'm such an Indian giver, I know. I'm working on it."

"I'm not sure if we're supposed to say *Indian giver*?" I muttered.

She laughed, continuing in full voice. "Oh, I'm basically an Indian; it's fine."

I slid my least maxed-out credit card into the plastic fold, closed my eyes, and swallowed the response that sat on my tongue.

55 was more of a bar than a club, but it was mainly used as a club. Wedged in a dismal side street on the Lower East Side, it bore no sign or notable façade. Every time we looked for it, we ended up circling the surrounding blocks at least twice.

"*Buongiorno!*" Tatiana announced to the room. She did two shimmying jazz squares until we reached the other side. There were only two other people there. The bartender waved without looking at us. The DJ stood at his corner booth, wearing his usual black hoodie and diamond studs and refusing to acknowledge our existence. We wedged our bags into the corner of a long, leather booth and draped our coats over them, tucking them in at the sides.

"I'm gonna get a G&T. You want anything?" Tatiana pulled out her wallet.

I sat stiffly at the booth. "We had so much wine. I don't wanna get drunk; I'm thinking of going to the gym tomorrow."

"Gross. That's exactly why you need a drink. Have you learned nothing from me?" She laughed and model-walked to the bar, leaning over it like an ingenue in an old-timey movie. If I tried that, I'd look like I was having a stroke.

My phone lit up.

Are you avoiding me?

I'm busy, I texted back.

I need to talk to you. Come over.

Do you have amnesia?

Text bubbles appeared and disappeared twice.

I said I was sorry.

"Okay, who are you texting? Your face tells me you are texting someone you should not be texting." Tatiana held out a cup of murky brown liquid. I dropped the phone back into my bag.

"Nobody. And thanks—what is this?"

"Your frat boy favorite. Jack and Coke. Don't change the subject."

I pulled the glass close to my mouth and sipped from a straw I belatedly realized was a stirrer.

"Hellooo. Who were you texting? Who were you textiiing? It had better not be Chicago Shithead."

I drank until the liquor hovered just above a lone, spherical ice cube.

"Dzifa, your phone is blowing *up*. That's Bootleg Barack. It has to be." She reached across me and threw her hand into my bag.

"Hey!" The majority of my drink sloshed over the edge and onto my lap.

"Sorry not sorry!" Tatiana swiped up to reveal the most recent messages on my screen. "Oh my God." Her freshly threaded eyebrows drew together. "Why, *why* have you not blocked this woman?" She shook her head at the text from my mother, which she could see I'd read, even if I hadn't responded. I watched her click on the link, her head still shaking as she read. "I mean, not gonna lie, I don't *totally* disagree with the content, but I disagree with her texting you on principle. She is for sure tryna fuck with your head."

I held my tongue—this would *not* be a good time to tell her I'd actually spoken with my mother for almost an hour—and held out my hand for the phone, but she resumed scrolling the text threads, her mouth agape. She'd read, I assumed, Chicago Shithead's litany of insult-ridden pleas for me to return his calls. Tatiana sighed. "So you really do wanna be sex murdered."

"That's not funny," I groaned. I set my drink on the nearest table.

"No, it isn't." She shook her head, scrolling down until she reached the last of today's messages. "Dzifa, this man is not a good person. Like, he's actually a bad person. You can do so much better. I feel like I've failed you as your friend and self-appointed confidence mentor. Is that why you've been ignoring me? Because you're—what even is this? An exercise in masochism?"

I scratched at an agitated spot near my hairline. "You haven't failed me. And I haven't been ignoring you. I told you my phone is messed up."

She handed it back to me.

I slid it into the bag without looking.

"It looks fine to me. Did I do something wrong? I know I'm not exactly tactful, but, like . . . if you don't like something I do, you should just tell me."

"You didn't do anything wrong." As I remembered our last conversation, the one that made me feel like she'd stuck little daggers underneath the surface of my skin, I realized she had never been anything but herself. It was my expectations of civility that got in the way, as they always did. "You didn't do anything wrong. I'm just stressed out. I've been a little depressed."

She leaned forward, resting her chin in both hands. "Yeah, I can see that. Do you think there's maybe a correlation between you being depressed and you dating an actual psychopath? You're sweating again. You okay, sis?"

"I'm fine." I wiped at my face. My hand came away damp. I wiped it on the slowly fading drink stain. "I'm not dating him. I was just . . . I'm getting another drink. You want one?"

"G&T." She extended her arms and gave me three seconds of ecstatic jazz hands.

I came back with two fresh, watered-down drinks and a resolve to change the subject. "Are you still with that Puerto Rican guy?"

"Uh, racist. He's from *Costa* Rica. And no, he kept going on these long diatribes about capitalism every time we went out for drinks, and you know I don't have time for that hippie-dippie liberal Kool-Aid they tried to force down our throats in college." Tatiana rolled her eyes. "No, remember the guy I ran into the last time I was home? The finance bro I met right after graduation?" She leaned back against the booth.

I shouldn't have blocked her. And I should have listened more carefully these past few months, or years, apparently; I had no idea who she was talking about. "Oh yeah."

"Right." She extended her arms and arched them back and forth to the beat. "Well, so when I first met him . . . that was what? Four, five years ago? Ages. Anyway, at the time, he was hanging out with this supremely basic sorority girl, so we were just sort of texting back and forth, but nothing really came of it. The last time we saw each other, it was just in passing, at this Italian place I'm gonna take you to one day; they have the best G&Ts. But this time, when I went home . . ." She dropped her arms to her sides. "I'm not telling it right." She squeezed her cheeks between both hands. "Okay, so I went out with Sarai . . . Have you met her? Oh, wait, I keep forgetting you haven't met anybody from home."

"Sorry. I keep meaning to visit, but . . ." But I never did. Maybe for the same reason I used to hate running into a teacher outside of class. Our friendship was the longest I'd had, and yet I wondered if its longevity was all down to context. Around other people, I could all too easily see the qualities in her that, in honest moments, unsettled me. One-on-one, she was just Tatiana.

"More's the better, my friend." Tatiana shifted in her seat and tucked her legs behind her. "Boston is a shithole. The actual worst. But anyway, Sarai is the one I told you about who kind of fucked her life up. Like, she got knocked up when she was seventeen?"

"Oh, right—her." There was a "Sarai" in my family, too. I suspected she was happier than the rest of us. About once a year, my eldest sister, Charity, called a videoconference of "the good kids in the family," a club I should not have qualified for. I suspected the rightful members simply forgot I was at the meetings. These virtual gatherings were opportunities to brainstorm how "we" could "get" our Sarai, a cousin on my father's side, on "the right track." On occasion, I suggested that she was perfectly fine and seemed to have way fewer mental illnesses than we did. Plus, I may have had a bachelor's degree, but waiting until I had the degree to have sex only made me into the whore my parents always warned me about. So who was winning the game, really? "But, um . . . so you were hanging out with your . . . Sarai when you ran into . . . this person? What's his name?"

"Mm-hmm. We went out dancing together." When I waved at her to continue, she smiled. I'd never seen her withhold information. "His name is B."

"B . . ." I held my hands out. "B what? Like Bumblebee?"

"Oh." She shrugged. "His name is dumb, so I just call him B. I think his last name is Ad . . . hm. Adler? Adkins? Ad-something."

"Wow, he sure left an impression. You sure you can just refuse to use the name of someone you're dating?"

Tatiana threw a jubilant "Heeey!" out to the DJ when he turned on "Ain't Nobody." "We're not 'dating.' And I can do anything I want."

"I mean this is true. But, like, I don't super love when I tell people my name is Dzifa and they're like, 'Oh, okay, nice to meet you, Darleen.' "

She held up a finger in protest. "Well, yeah, but you have a white name you can just whip out at any time. And nobody is named Darleen."

"It's called a *Christian* name, not a white name."

"It's a white name," she countered, drumming a hand on the table to punctuate each word. "I should know; my mom gave me one so I wouldn't get stereotyped to death. But that's not B's problem. The problem is his name is *too* white, and he's biracial as it is. And I just disagree with that on principle, you know? Like, maybe five, ten years ago, I'd have loved a tragic mulatto with a super-white name, but the new-and-improved me, reader of Queens bell, Toni, Audre, et cetera? Can't do it."

"If you say so." I shrugged. "So? What's the story? You're being kinda cagey about it—did he do something bad?"

She shook her head. "No. No. He was cool—he and his friends came up to us and bought us drinks. We danced, and then . . . he brought me back to his place around the corner."

"Promising." I took a sip of the Jack and Coke. She glanced at the door of the bar, then at her impeccably painted nails.

"And then, yeah! That was basically the situation." Her cheeks darkened. I frowned, taken aback by this uncharacteristic shyness.

"Cool—um. Did you have a good time?" I wasn't even sure what "a good time" entailed. Personally, managing not to traumatize me for life was good enough, but it seemed that different women had different standards.

"Well . . ." She set her drink down and scooted closer to me. "We . . . didn't, uh, yeah. Yeah! It was fine. It was . . . yeah."

"O . . . kaaay?" I gripped the edge of the booth.

"Yeah . . ." She pulled back and teased out a few strands of hair. "The thing is, things happened really fast. So I don't know if he's boyfriend material; he's not that interesting. Like, maybe if I had your abysmal math skills, no offense, I'd be wowed by the finance thing, but I feel like if I had as many years in the field as he does I'd be a multimillionaire, and he is not even close. But . . . you know."

I did and I didn't. "That's . . . good. I mean . . . so . . . wait." I nodded once, then again. "Oh. So, did you use . . . ? Or did you take the pill?" I said it as levelly as I could. Shame always rendered me useless, but resisting the urge to inflict it upon the people I loved was harder than I wanted it to be.

She grimaced. "Should I get us another round?"

"No thanks." I shook my head, setting down my not-yet-empty drink as I considered how to sidestep her deflection. "Well, whatever happened . . . I'm sure it'll be fine. I'm sure it'll be fine."

Her smile wavered. "Yeah. Probably. I mean with the amount of fibroids I've got going on, it would probably take a miracle for me to have a baby anyway."

"Right." I nodded, clasping my hands together efficiently. "I mean . . . not *right*, fibroids are the worst, but, like . . . you'll be fine. All you need to do is wait for your period. And maybe . . . take an STI screen. I'll go with you if you want? I take them all the time; it's not scary or anything. There's this doctor at the MinuteClinic on the Upper West Side—I think she's tired of me coming in every other week, telling her how I'm afraid I got smallpox from touching a subway pole. I'm sure she'll be happy to see literally any other patient. I have kind of a crush on her."

Tatiana extended a leg, the arch in her foot curved like a quarter moon, and stood. "So she's Russian, then?" She laughed. "Nah. You're right—I mean, you are deeply troubled, my friend, but you're right. It's gonna be fine. It's going to be fine. I'm on top of all of *those* tests, so all good there. I just need to swing by my gyno soonish. I am destined for greatness, not . . . suburbia." She smoothed down her skirt. "Okay, cool, this has been a super-fun therapy sesh, but men are trash and we should dance. People are starting to come in."

I let her pull me up from the booth. I felt sweaty again, my stomach achy and unsettled, that ancient chest pain present, heightened. As we made our way to the center of the bar, I resolved that my unease was a result of the drinks, or an extension of the anxiety that had been escalating for months. As we began to do our very best ballet warm-up to '90s R & B, I couldn't stop thinking that if I hadn't been ignoring Tatiana, if I hadn't held back on any of our numerous conversations where she stealth-shamed my choices and I said nothing about hers, maybe she wouldn't be in this situation. But she was probably right—it would all be fine. For her, it always was.

CHAPTER 3

"Sorry," I panted into my cellphone. My three-inch block heels slid through the winter sludge; I righted myself at the last minute. "I'm gonna be there in five minutes. Less. I miscalculated the route." It felt like days since I met Tatiana at 55, but apparently, I'd gone AWOL for three weeks.

The first week seemed justified enough; I took a sick day the Monday after 55. I did feel unwell; I was fatigued, panicky, with a side of spiked heart palpitations. Not unusual but worse than usual. By the second week, it was clear I was losing traction, shifting from what some people very misguidedly called *high-functioning depression* to what I could only describe as my soul having left my body prematurely. Of all the abandonment wounds I'd accrued to date, this was by far the most unsettling.

"Miscalculated—the fuck?!" Tatiana scream-whispered on the other end of the line. "Why are you acting like you've never been to Flatiron before? It's like, five stops."

"Just—hold on, okay? I'm around the corner. Okay, see you in a minute." It took seven. This part of town always confused me; in spite of the idiotproof grid system of New York, I could never remember whether to take a left or a right to get to Madison after exiting the train. "Fuck!" I yelled to anyone who'd listen; the city being what it was, nobody blinked an eye.

Aside from work emails and the unusually long call—ten minutes—I'd had with Esther two days ago, I'd been avoiding my phone again, including Tatiana's texts. I was lying on my bedroom floor, wedged between the ball I used as a chair and the single bed I now found unbearable to sleep in—feeling my back taut and solid against the uncarpeted wooden floor was the only thing that kept me sufficiently sentient to complete my work assignments—when her text came in.

> Dzifa, I know you're having a hard time but I really need you right now. Can you meet me at Madison Women's Clinic Wednesday at 1:30? It's really important.

I responded right away: Of course. See you there.

And here I was, at 1:50, letting her down. I finally located the building. Having ditched the gloves in my rush to leave the apartment for the first time in a week, my fingers ached from the cold. The doorman saw my sweating, sludgy distress and ushered me in. "Hi, sorry, I'm looking for Madison Women's—"

"Go to the fourth floor," he said, his Nigerian accent steady. I felt grounded by the familiarity of his cadence, even if my nerves were frayed by the lunchtime subway ride. I rushed out of the elevator and jogged down the carpeted hallway to the clinic's closed doorway.

Heaving a sharp exhale, I pushed the door open and scanned the pristine, wood-accented room for the front desk. "Hi. Hi—" I approached the receptionist. "I'm looking for a friend who has an appointment right now; her name is—"

"Dzifa," a quiet voice said. I darted my eyes around the waiting room until I found her. Tatiana sat with her legs folded onto one of the curved, wooden-back seats, her Burberry peacoat draped over her lap. It looked so oversized from this angle, it almost eclipsed her.

"Oh my God, thank God, you haven't gone in yet? I'm so sorry I'm late. I totally—"

"No, I'm done. I mean, the appointment is over already." She stared ahead at the stack of medical magazines fanned out on the table in front of her. Next to it was a plastic cup, nearly full with water, with a smudge of purple lipstick on the rim.

"Oh. Shit. I am *so* sorry. Shit. Sorry. Um." There was only one other person in the waiting room, a middle-aged woman staring intently at an outdated copy of *Women's Fitness*. I spotted an empty chair next to Tatiana and pulled it to face hers. "Are you okay? Do you have another cyst?"

She snorted. "You could say that." Her lips curved upward, but her eyes were blank.

"Shit." I wiped a hand over my forehead. How was I sweaty *and* cold? "Are you going to need surgery?"

"Well . . ." Finally, some life returned to her eyes. She swallowed and met mine. "That remains to be seen. Apparently, I'm pregnant. So."

I wanted to retract the sharp intake of breath that escaped me. For starters, I wasn't that surprised, even if I wanted to be. As distracted as I'd been these past three weeks, every now and again, usually when Tatiana sent a text it took me days to reply to, I indulged an intrusive thought or two about that night at 55: about how maybe, if she *wasn't* lucky, things would not turn out so smoothly after all.

But more important, I wanted to be steady. "O . . . kay." I nodded. I raised my hands, palms down, as if to place them on hers, but settled for the arms of her chair instead. "Okay. How . . . how do you feel? I mean, how are you?"

"Well." She clicked her tongue, her eyes widening. "This was not part of my thirty-year plan. So there's that."

I hesitated, waited for her to continue. She didn't. Better not to fill in the blank.

"That . . . yeah. Um, do you want to—I don't know. What do you want to do right now? Maybe you could take the rest of the day off work? I could go with you back to your apartment? Get you some takeout?"

"Dzifa." Tatiana rolled her eyes. "This is pregnancy, not the Black Death."

As little as I was enticed by the prospect of growing a fresh human, I wasn't sure I could tell the difference. "Gotcha." I nodded. "Okay. Then just let me know how I can support you right now."

"The thing is, and—you're gonna think I'm crazy, not that you don't already"—Tatiana cut a glare at me—"which, I don't know if that's why you've gone MIA again, but okay."

"That's not it. I'm—we can talk about it another time. I've just been—" I stopped, swallowed, tried again. "I didn't know. I'm sorry; I'm here." I returned my hands to my lap, my eyes drifting away from her. "Whatever you want to do. There's a Planned Parenthood—"

"No." Tatiana shook her head. "That's what I'm trying to tell you. I mean, I just found out and I don't know." She laughed wryly. "If you'd asked me, like, thirty minutes ago what I'd do, I'd have thought, *No way.* But during the appointment, I just . . . I have this feeling like maybe this was meant to happen. Like it was fate or something."

A dozen honest responses darted through my brain. Among them: *This wasn't fate. It was unprotected sex.* Instead, I asked, "How do you mean?"

"I don't know." She shrugged, beginning to put her coat on. "It's just like—okay, so I got the promotion this fall. And then what? Another promotion? And then what? I've already done, like, 98 percent of the things on my thirty-year plan. Okay, this wasn't on it, but otherwise, I'm actually way ahead of schedule. Remember that internship I did? Summer of junior year? That douchebag on the Engineering team bet I didn't have what it took to learn how to code, and now I could outmaneuver every last one of them in my sleep, and I don't even *like* to code. I don't even like *computers* that much. It's all just kind of—whatever, you know? Like, I was blessed to be born with a fire sun *and* ascendant; why am I still living this Capricorn-ass life?"

The woman hiding behind her magazine—did she even *have* an appointment?—snickered. We shot her a glare; she ignored it. I couldn't recall Tatiana's ascendant and didn't know enough about astrology to discern if fire signs were more partial to child-rearing. From the little I knew about my mother's chart, I doubted it. "I—what are you saying?"

"I might keep it." She adjusted the lapels of her coat.

"Tatiana," I said slowly. "You . . ." I took a deep breath, then started over. There were easier ways to switch careers or spice up her lifestyle—did she not know this? "Whatever you want to do, I'm behind you, okay? You want to . . . go through with this, I will throw you a baby shower. I'll . . . help you decorate the nursery. I don't know if I'll babysit, because you know babies freak me out. But I'll help however I can." She snorted. "Just—just think about it, okay?"

Her eyes narrowed. "You don't think I can do it."

No, I thought, didn't say. "That's not what I mean. But realistically . . . Esther and her husband have, like, the two incomes from really good jobs, and a ton of other support from her husband's family in Oakland, and babysitters, and Esther has been planning her family since she was like four years old and still—it's . . . she doesn't really have a life outside of that. Which," I added hastily, "is what she wanted, I guess. But is that what you want? Like, are you sure you want to raise a child with—this man?" I felt awful for forgetting his name, but to be fair, she'd never actually told me what it was. "Because until, um, pretty much now, you always said you didn't want kids."

She stood, adjusted her coat, then sat again to button it. "You're blowing this out of proportion. I'm twenty-six, not fourteen. This is not, like, a problem. I'm not destitute. I'm educated. I'm employable. *And*"—she held up a finger to shush me when I opened my mouth to respond—"regardless of how B wants to handle this, and . . . I don't even know if or when I'll tell him . . . my mother didn't have a husband or a boyfriend or anything, and she always said having a man in the house 24-7 would've been more of a hindrance than a help. 'It's just one more person you have to raise,' she always said. Which—was she wrong?"

I shrugged. Thought about my parents, who, on paper and from a very far distance with very poor vision, could be thought to have the Ideal Family Structure. Two parents, technically married decades, both obscenely educated, ever-having a big ol' house to not pay the mortgage on. I had to concede that having a two-parent household was mostly a value-add when you had two parents who . . . parented. And how many people had that?

Tatiana continued, "I'm not saying it would be easy, but I can do this myself if I want to. I can do anything I set my mind to. That's always been true, and it'll never change. PS," she added, a little more bite in her voice, "I never said I didn't want kids. I said I didn't know if I could have them and I could be happy with that. But here we are."

I racked my memory; maybe she was right. Maybe it was I who was so sure I didn't want kids, and I'd just heard the *no* in her answer and projected the rest. Somewhere along the way, I'd taken for granted that any woman with a choice, unless faced with the ideal circumstances in which to have a child—which, to me, only existed in an alternate universe where modern life was not, primarily, a reenactment of *The Hunger Games—would* choose an abortion.

"Look," she said, standing again. I abandoned my existential thought spiral. "I have to go back to work soon. So—I don't know. Maybe we can continue this another time. Thanks for coming. Eventually." She started toward the door. I stood, clumsily, and dragged my chair back into its original position, then rushed after her.

"Tatiana," I called after her as she stepped into the elevator. I managed to open the door at the last second and wedge my way in. "I meant what I said. Whatever you decide, I have your back 100 percent. Okay?"

She said nothing for the rest of the elevator ride down or the walk back out onto the street. An unpleasant blend of sleet, wind, and smog greeted us outside. New York's very own wintry mix, even though it was verging on spring. I hated it here, sometimes and increasingly. Tatiana looked up at me and narrowed her eyes. "All right," she said. "In that case, I'mma take you up on that lunch offer, but it has to be quick, and it has to be drunk man noodles, 'cause that's all I want to eat lately."

"Done." I smiled, clasping my hands together as if in prayer. "Lead the way."

A block from the nearest Thai place, Tatiana grabbed my arm and dragged me down a short flight of stairs, past a shop window framed by a flickering, fluorescent purple light strip. "Absolutely not," I groaned, realizing this was the same hokey-looking psychic shop she'd been begging me to accompany her to for four years, which I had successfully refused to enter that entire time. How was a business like this even able to stay open in this part of town? Mafia ties, probably. I did not want to be involved.

"You owe me." She glared, then shifted into a gleeful smile when I sighed, relenting. "And anyway, it's gonna be good. I told you; she's the real deal. We both need this. Trust me."

I avoided eye contact with the psychic, though I had to admit she didn't look like I was expecting. An older woman greeted us, her unbound silver-streaked hair grazing her shoulders. She wore jeans and a long, woven sweater, and seemed, at least from her even, casual tone upon ushering us toward a minimally decorated wooden table, reasonably present in this dimension. I tuned out most of what she said until nearly the end of her fifteen-minute reading. The words *your first child* jarred me from my skeptical space-out.

"Sorry, say that again?" I looked at Tatiana, then the psychic, for clarification. Tatiana was not noticeably pregnant yet, and though I'd only been half listening, I knew she hadn't mentioned her pregnancy either.

"I said," the psychic repeated, "that she's going to have a daughter."

Tatiana frowned and made a discontented noise. "I mean . . . okay. I love that for me, but I gotta admit, I always kind of thought if I had kids, I'd have a son. Like, I feel like we could mix it up a bit in the Bishop household, you know? There's only so many periods one wants to sync up, am I right? So? Do you see me ever having a son?"

The psychic sat back in her chair, regarding Tatiana without any change in her muted expression. "Yes." Tatiana breathed out a sigh of relief. "And no."

"Um, excuse me?" I interjected on my friend's behalf.

"I'm getting," she continued levelly, "that you could have as many children as you'd like. But a son? That's all I can say."

"But—" Tatiana protested.

"And that's fifteen minutes!" The psychic concluded with a clap of her hands. As much as I would have loved to judge the cruel efficiency with which she doled out her gift, I'd take any excuse to get out of here.

"Well, that's . . . different. Anyway, let's go eat?" Tatiana stayed in her chair another minute, frowning. I gently tapped her shoulder, and she finally rose. The psychic ushered us toward the dingy, glass-paned exit.

Just as I reached for the handle, she said to my back, "You a Scorpio?"

I kept my back turned. "No idea," I lied.

"Hm. Doesn't matter. I do feel called to mention, though, that I can see an unwellness in you."

I swiveled to face the shop interior, finally meeting the psychic's brown eyes. Her expression was focused, unsentimental. "No kidding."

Tatiana laughed and pushed past me to leave. I turned back to follow her. The psychic continued, nonplussed, "It isn't yours. The unwellness you're carrying. Might help you to read about Persephone. Usually good medicine for Scorpios. Or"—she shrugged, the corner of her mouth tilted up—"people with Scorpio energy."

I sighed, returning my gaze to the exit. "Cool, thanks."

"Enjoy the weather," she called behind me. I detected a hint of sarcasm in her tone but might've been projecting. I took in what now felt like a lifesaving inhale of chilly, smoggy air and shut the door firmly behind me.

The Thai place was packed when we arrived; under different circumstances, I'd ask Tatiana if we could go somewhere less crowded, but today, I'd do my best to deal. I could retreat to my hermitude soon enough.

"So . . . are you happy with . . . that?" I winced at my delivery. "I mean, was it helpful for you? The reading?"

"Yeah . . ." Tatiana picked at her noodles. I did the same with mine. "I mean, she's no-bullshit, as you can see. So, like, it's not the accuracy I worry about. I know you don't believe in this stuff, but, like, she's been right about everything else since I've started going to her. And like you saw, if she doesn't know something, she won't pretend to." I shrugged. It was the least judgmental response I could offer at the moment. "It's more, that wasn't really what I wanted to hear?"

"Why?" I asked, feeling strangely defensive of her possible-daughter. "What's the deal with having a son? You're always saying men are trash anyway."

"Yes, but exactly," she countered, eyes wide, letting her chopsticks clatter against the bowl. "Like, when they're trash, it's usually because they weren't raised right. I never told you, 'cause I knew you'd laugh, but . . . anytime I thought about if I would have kids, I just thought maybe I could raise a boy who was like—I don't know, only medium-terrible. Like your Russian." She laughed, but I could see she was sincere. "Or even better, like my uncle. He's solidly decent, somehow. Boring, but decent."

I forced myself to take a bite. It was good, probably, but my appetite had been gone for weeks. "Gotcha. Well—hey, she didn't say *no*, exactly. Also, she's not a doctor. You can have whatever kind of family you want."

Tatiana took a sip of water. "I guess. Anyway, that's a later problem. For now . . . looks like I'm gonna have to stealth-research maternity leave at my job."

"You're really thinking of staying here?" The bite I swallowed felt caught somewhere between my neck and my chest. I gently tapped the area with my free hand, then more carefully took another bite.

"As opposed to what? I didn't come all this way just to go back to fucking Boston. I mean, I haven't told Mommy yet, but I'm pretty sure she'll help either way. Maybe I can get her to take a sabbatical, stay down here with me for a while." When I opened my mouth to answer—or to take another bite; I hadn't decided—she continued, "Look—I'll figure it out. I'm just glad you'll be here."

I looked down at my plate, the remaining noodles having been anxiously precut and shoved to one side. "About that. I really meant what I said, you know . . . that I'll be there for you in any way I can. But—"

"No buts." Tatiana shook her head. "Today has already been waaay too much. I don't have space for any more buts."

"However," I offered, ignoring her eye roll, "I don't know how much longer I can stay here. I haven't been to the office in three weeks. I'm out of remote days, and I . . . just can't go back. I don't know how to explain it—but it's . . . do you remember, junior year at Elmwood? How I was?"

Tatiana stilled her chopsticks, leaned back in her chair. "Yeah, girl, I remember."

It was hard to forget—that was my roughest year in college; hers was the following. She got me through mine; I reciprocated the next year. I probably could never, though, truly repay her. She visited me every day after class, that month I skipped class because the nightmare cocktail of lethargy and self-judgment—what I affectionately termed *the Abyss*—

that plagued me through most of high school resurfaced, rendering me sluggish and reclusive, first, then immobilizing me completely. After what I'd been through with my mother, I couldn't fathom reaching out to a therapist or confiding in anyone official from the school or, God forbid, a hospital. I knew that while Tatiana had little more, practically speaking, than overconfident affirmations and Christian-coded self-help books to offer, one thing she would never do was call a therapist, or 911. What she offered, more valuable than any psychologist-sanctioned action step, was her presence.

I still wasn't sure if that crushing malaise simply wore itself out or if it was my friend's final pep talk that did it. It was so perfectly Tatiana that I couldn't help but laugh: "Look, girl—you can kill yourself if you want to, but just remember: One day, you are *definitely* gonna die. So, like, no need to force it." I felt, in her lack of sentimentality or hand-wringing, her lack of judgment—the corner of my hopelessness begin to peel back, give way to more space, if not for hope, then at least for breath. Once I could breathe again, I could move again.

"It's like that." I cleared my throat. "But worse somehow. I can feel it. I mean, I've felt it since all that stuff with my mom, since before that, even—it's just, I can feel I'm losing the energy to keep it at bay anymore. And if I lose this job, I don't have any savings, so . . ."

"Whoa, whoa, whoa." Tatiana gave up the ruse of continuing her meal and threw her crumpled napkin over the bowl. "Since you asked me, I'm asking you. Where in Jesus's name do you think you're going?"

I considered another bite, if only to avoid telling her the truth. "Esther and I have been talking more, lately. Well, not much, but, like, we talked once, a couple of days ago. And she said, if I really, really need to, I—"

"Are you high?" Tatiana laughed. "You are not going back to Oakland. Not only did I not come all this way just to go back to Boston, you sure as hell did not come all this way to go back to the absolute cuckoo for cocoa-puffery that is your batshit family, no offense."

I couldn't help the laugh that escaped me. "Esther isn't batshit. She's the sanest one out of all of us, actually."

Tatiana shook her head. "If it's not drugs, is it amnesia? Esther could be Mother Teresa for all I care. She is related to your other family members, and most importantly, she is related to your mother. Which means if you put yourself back in proximity to Esther, your mom could circle back at *any time*. Hard no, hard pass."

I shook my head, pulling at the strands of my dehydrated hair. I'd taken out the weave in a fit of itchiness a week ago. "Actually. I . . . didn't tell you this at the time, because I was just . . . I don't even know why I did it."

Tatiana sat back in her chair, crossed her arms. "I don't like this. What did you do?"

"My mother asked to speak with me, like, um . . . remember the last time we went to 55? Yeah, the day before. On the phone. I . . . I took her call."

"Dzifa, no!" She brought a palm to her face, dragged it down, let it fall to her lap. "What is going on with you? Oh my God. Oh my God oh my God oh my God. This is why you were acting so weird and cagey, isn't it? This is why you're, like, spiraling out, isn't it? Why would you speak to that woman? You've been doing so well since junior year! Do you not recall that *resuming contact with her* was the reason you fell apart then, too? Have we learned *nothing*?!" She groaned.

I stared at the table. "I have not been doing well, Tatiana. I mean, maybe it looked like that to you, but it never felt like that to me. I feel like an imposter all the time. Like I'm in a play of someone else's life, and I'm gonna forget the lines any moment, and I'm gonna be kicked offstage completely. And anyway, I only spoke with her for twenty minutes." I shrank beneath her glare. "Okay, closer to forty."

Tatiana shook her head slowly, kept moving it side to side as if the motion would shake some overdue sense into me. "Why would you *do* that? And what did she even want?"

I ignored her first question, still didn't have a definitive answer myself. "She bought a house in Maryland, and . . . she wanted me to know."

"What? The fuck?" Her eyebrows drew together as she processed this. "I . . . Am I having a psychotic break, or are *you* having a psychotic break? We know your mom is having a psychotic break. For f . . . Does she even know anybody in Maryland?"

"No." I shrugged. "I mean, that's where her dad was from. But he hightailed it outta there when he was a kid so, like . . . not a place with happy memories. I don't know. I guess she suddenly got nostalgic about her ancestors or something. She kept talking about tobacco for some reason."

"What is happening?" She tugged at one of her braids, grimacing.

I leaned my head into my hands. "I don't know. I think she's talking about these, like, weird barn thingies we saw when we visited my grandpa once. She kept calling them *tobacco flats*."

Tatiana stared at me, blinked. Shook her head. "No. Just, no. Dzifa, you know I don't put much stock in the whole concept of mental illness and all of that. But, like, there are exceptions. And your mother is . . . I shouldn't even have to tell you. I should not have to tell you this. How could she even afford to buy a house? Isn't she always broke?"

I swallowed, braced myself to share this next part. "My . . . my college savings? That Esther and I always thought our dad took for . . . whatever he's doing? Yeah, I guess she had it all along." I rushed to continue as I watched her fume. "I'm actually weirdly impressed she managed to save it for that long. But, um, yeah—that's how she paid for it."

Tatiana scratched a spot behind her ear, shook her head again, regarded me with a mixture of pity and bewilderment. "All right, girl. I"—she stretched an arm out wide, brought it back in, set her hand on the table with painstaking care—"truly do not know what to say to any of that. Except it proves my point even more. You cannot. I repeat: Can. Not. Put yourself back in the mix with your family. I forbid you."

"Esther isn't like my mother. She's—I mean, okay, she doesn't like me and she's really judgmental, but, like . . . she's overall a decent person. Steady. She's steady." When Tatiana opened her mouth to protest, I rushed on. "I'm not like you. You're gonna be fine. I know that, you know that. But I'm already. This is already—" For the first time that day, the adrenaline subsided, and the true weight of my fatigue caught up with me. I slunk down in the chair. "I just can't. I can't do it anymore. This city is too fucking intense. I'm losing it. I thought I could . . . I don't know. Be normal. Be fine. Like . . . okay, Dzifa didn't work out. I thought—let people call me *Mercy*, even if I can't fucking stand it . . . it's an easier name, maybe I'll have an easier time. But it's just . . . something is not right. Something is always . . . just not right. I just can't."

I watched a thousand protests pass through her, watched her battle with herself in a rare show of restraint, to keep them inside her mind, behind the fiery intensity of her eyes. "We'll see," she finally said, and I could tell she'd settled on her favorite position, excessive confidence—this time, not for herself but for me.

Knowing she was not to be outwitted, even if, in this case, she was wrong, I shrugged. "Yeah." I nodded. "I guess we will."

CHAPTER 4

OAKLAND, CA | AUGUST | ONE AND A HALF (UN)GODLY YEARS PASSED

"Heey!" I waved at the phone screen propped up on the dashboard of my car. "Happy almost birthday!" I greeted Tatiana. In the corner of the screen, her daughter guided a purple teddy bear up and down the middle of B's living room. "Hey, Maddie."

"Thaaanks," Tatiana offered back. She called out, "Say hi, Mads!"

Maddie continued quietly tending to her teddy bear's journey. Her faint humming substituted a reply.

Tatiana sighed. "Well, we're still working on it."

I shook my head, waving a hand to dismiss my friend's concerns. "I'm pretty sure she's fine."

"Mm." Tatiana shrugged. "At least she's healthy. I guess that's all that matters. Maybe her Bishop spirit and any associated loquaciousness will kick in in time. I feel like all my confidence training is finally starting to work on you, like, belatedly, but better late than never. Look at you! Organizing covens and whatnot."

"It's not a coven." I laughed, rolled my eyes. "It's just a group of women, a movement collective. And I didn't organize it, I'm just hosting tonight."

"Um, sounds like witchcraft to me. Like, what even is a 'movement collective'? Nope, it's either a class or it's a coven, my friend. You Californians . . ."

"A movement— Never mind." I shook my head. I'd already explained this. Also, a person who attended a church called the Divine Temple of Esoteric Christianity needed to not judge my monthly dance group. "Anyway, I'm pretty sure Maddie is just, like, happy to keep to herself, you know?"

"Jury's still out." Tatiana shook her head, watching her daughter's movements. "I love her, but—we have *got* to work on her social skills."

I decided to let it go. As far as I was concerned, socializing with a stuffed bear was more than sufficient. Also, Maddie was barely one; it seemed a little early to subject her to a Sixteen Personalities quiz.

"Oh, well," Tatiana said, walking over to the kitchen to pick up Luca. He squealed, squeezing his little fists in delight. "Like I said, she's healthy, and that's the main thing. Plus, this one is definitely gonna pull her out of her shell. He is giving big-time Bishop energy. Right, sweetie? Right?" She beamed at him, lifting one of his hands to wave at his big sister. The video shook each time she bounced him in her arms.

"I'm still kinda iffy about if not getting him the surgery was the right thing," she continued. B's mother, who was vehemently against anything "unnatural"—synthetic fabrics, processed foods, baby formula, Tatiana's sizable collection of premium Kanekalon braiding hair—had protested the possibility of Luca getting a neonatal operation to repair a mild heart defect. I felt a little responsible for my friend's reluctant acquiescence. "Don't you have a heart thing?" she'd asked. "And you didn't get any surgery, and you're fine, right?" I reminded her that my heart palpitations were insignificant compared to Luca's condition and that, in any case, nobody who knew me would consider me a poster child for wellness. I wasn't expecting her to glean reassurance from my response.

Tatiana heaved a long sigh. "I can't say I'm comfortable with the decision. But the doctor said we can always revisit that option later, so . . ." She kissed his cheek. "You sure you don't want one?" She turned back to face the camera, the top of Luca's head peeking through the bottom of the frame.

"No, I'm good," I said immediately. I winced. "Sorry. They're super cute. But I can barely keep a cactus alive, and I am from a state full of cacti, so you'd think I'd know how."

Tatiana laughed, circling the apartment. She bounced him in one arm as he squealed and laughed with her. After making two rounds, she set Luca into a big fabric playpen in the corner nearest the door. "Well, yeah. I get it. Like, I'm happy to have these little munchkins, but it is *not* for everyone, and I do *not* plan on being one of those moms who's pushing everyone else to have kids. I'm kinda desperate to put Maddie in daycare already, but at the same time, I do not want to be part of the Boston mommy brigade. No thank you."

I had no idea what the "Boston mommy brigade" was, but I could envision it, if I thought of the prep-tastic girls I went to high school with, aged them up ten to fifteen years, and imagined them with even more money and less compassion. Probably not a fun scene. "Yeah, that does not sound . . . great. But hey, I'm sure you'll find your people. You always do."

Tatiana cocked her head to the side, eyes narrowed. After a moment, she grinned, nodding. "True. I *do* do that. Okay, I gotta go, 'cause I'm about to make a potentially ill-advised financial decision? And I need to do it before I chicken out."

"Um . . ." I laughed. "What?"

Tatiana walked to the kitchen counter and began preparing a bottle of formula. "Yeah. So get this: This really weird kid from my high school, right? Like, total loner. Not exactly 'upward bound,' as Mommy used to call it. But guess what? He actually became, like, really, really famous. He's the front man in this, like, crazy, trippy alt-rock band. It's really well regarded among the artsy-fartsy elites here. So anywho, there's a concert next week, and I think I'm gonna go!" She closed the tall, narrow bottle and dropped it into an electric warmer.

I sat back in my seat, checking the window for traffic cops. Though outside of my apartment, I was technically illegally parked at the moment. All clear. "Well, that sounds . . . random. But whatever floats your boat."

Tatiana brought the phone close to her face and stared me down. "Dzifa, I have to get out of here." She laughed, but the smile didn't reach her eyes. "I'm kidding. I just mean, I need to get out more. I love these kids, but, like . . . I am not a housewife. Mommy and I have already been talking about me moving back in. And I haven't *officially* officially told B, because his mother is *always here* these days, and she cannot be trusted with, like, literally any information. I swear to God, she won't be happy until I go full *Handmaid's Tale*, ugly-ass bonnet and all," she joked. I didn't laugh, or respond. I didn't know what to say anymore. I'd come to the conclusion that matching the lightness she forced into her tone when B's mother came up was the most supportive thing I could do. But it took considerable effort, biting down the things I really wanted to say. *Run* being the primary thing. It seemed like she was finally getting there herself. Maybe this time she'd really do it.

Tatiana handed the bottle to Maddie, who accepted it quietly, set it down on the hardwood floor, and resumed her game with the teddy bear. "But as long as she doesn't get involved, I don't think he's gonna mind. I mean, it's not like I'm asking for sole custody or anything. I'm just thinking we don't need to cohabitate anymore. He definitely isn't life-partner material." She raised an eyebrow. I offered a grim smile and nodded. "But he's a pretty good dad. I wouldn't have had Luca if he wasn't. I just think I'll be at my best if I have a little more space and like . . ."

Her head snapped toward the front door. Keys rustled in the distance; old wood creaked open. "Fuck, gotta go."

"Okay, got it. We'll talk l—"

The call ended. My hand hovered over the phone for a moment. I thought about calling her back, but this wasn't the first time that had happened. I shook my head. Not my business. I'd check in with her later. I reached over to the passenger's seat, retrieved the grocery bag full of now probably half-melted frozen goods, and went inside.

—∾—

It took a year of living in Esther's spare bedroom, working at whichever cafés, factories, and boutiques hadn't fired me when I was nineteen, for me to start getting back on my feet.

Esther's disgust of my lethargy was palpable, but she tolerated me because of lingering, though unnecessary, parental feelings toward me, and also because her kids didn't mind. I wasn't the auntie that Esther once shared she'd dreamed I'd be, the eccentric but lively and responsible one who'd initiate painting activities and read *Harry Potter* to the kids, or who would offer free babysitting with glee and without the sigh I couldn't help that escaped me sometimes. My days as a New York nanny had not awakened a latent maternal instinct.

Instead, Esther, her three sons, and her gently homophobic husband got Elusive Recluse Auntie, who appeared for nightly dinners—always preplanned and preassigned on a family whiteboard—and the occasional dance party. If my presence was requested to read a book or play a game, I'd oblige with considerably less dread than I felt about hanging out with the adults in the room, but I was shamefully inept at initiating further engagement. I loved my nephews and was proud of Esther for creating the controlled, functional-seeming family she'd always wanted.

It was my gift to her to keep my distance whenever I could. I didn't at all fit the Future Obamas vibe she was cultivating. And my lack of enthusiasm for child-rearing was sacrilege in our culture. My age, gender, and childlessness should, conventionally speaking, have predisposed me to become a de facto house girl for the more established family members. Yet I'd learned the hard way that when it came to my family, it was better to be faulted for being scarce than for sullying their image with the inconvenience of my individuality.

I scrounged together two good-enough references and talked myself into a job, six months after I left New York. Another fintech company. The title was lower than what I'd had in Brooklyn and the white people significantly more irritating, but the pay was more or less the same.

Another six months later, I'd saved up enough to leave Esther's house.

I moved in with one of her sorority sister's younger sisters, a medical coder named Naya who was three years younger than I was and kept to herself as much as I did. We found a two-bedroom walk-up in Cleveland Heights.

Now that I lived in a place that was at least half mine, the fog of my abruptly terminated New York trajectory began to fade away, giving way to a more predictable existence. Something about my life still felt performative, but this time, I didn't delude myself. I acknowledged, at least privately, that I was making another, albeit more convincing and warmer-climated approximation of the person I thought I should be. It was good enough, I thought; as close as I was ever likely to get to getting away with being myself. At least these days, I felt sentient and more or less intact, not so much like I was slowly, violently self-imploding: my disposition on a good day by the time I left Brooklyn.

I did not enjoy my job but valued the steady paycheck, the feeling of renewed personhood it imbued me with, and I got pretty good at putting on noise-canceling headphones and lightly dissociating for eight hours a day. Slowly, I decorated my room with items I bought on sale from HomeGoods or found on the sidewalk and deep-cleaned. I opened a savings account, a concept that was never mentioned in my family of origin but which, it turned out, some people swore by. The gesture felt like growth, even if I rarely managed to keep more than fifty dollars in the account due to the exorbitant rent, my HomeGoods purchases, and because—in my recognition I needed emotional support even if a therapist was off the table—I'd discovered the very expensive world of holistic healing remedies. Sound baths, salt baths, Reiki sessions, singing circles, even—to my absolute horror—occasional hikes. The latter didn't cost any money, but it did cost me my dignity.

The unease I'd felt in New York, at Elmwood, in my teens, as a child—despite best efforts to bury it under a mountain of crystals of dubious origin and jumbo packs of off-brand collagen water, sometimes spiked—crawled out from under the surface. So I supplemented the holistic modalities, which insurance very much did *not* reimburse, with other things a California-born person trying to heal in California might do. I went to new moon rituals and Saturday-morning farmers markets. I pretended to give a shit about the beauty of a fresh spaghetti squash, even as I craved, and continued eating, when alone, cheeseburgers and mozzarella sticks. I started dating a mantra-loving polyamorous femme who did not exhibit any obvious signs of psychopathy. I considered this to be one of my healthier relationships, because I rarely saw her, did not know her well enough to become attached, and she, a half-Laotian, half-Polish environmental activist and recreational protest attendee, was terrified of accidentally breaching her devotion to nonviolent communication and therefore spoke in a psychedelically positive word bath of affirmations about my "cosmic energy." This dynamic was endlessly entertaining to Tatiana, who interrogated me after I first described it to her. It was our first video chat in months, a week after I moved to Cleveland Heights. "Are you serious with this polyamory shit? But you're not even poly yourself? So you're, like, a side-piece everybody knows about, but with no actual benefits? No gifts? Trips? You're still not able to shop at Whole Foods? Have I taught you *nothing*?"

I even reached out to my high school friend Zeynep. We'd barely spoken since I went to Elmwood, and in the years that passed, I convinced myself we were never really that close. If we were, wouldn't we have stayed in touch? It crossed my mind to text her when I left New York, but I didn't feel like getting into the details of what happened. "I was very sad and took a call from my mother" didn't seem compelling enough a reason, even if it was the truth. Plus, I didn't want Zeynep to think I needed anything from her. When I returned to Oakland, I was in a penitent mood. I had failed, I figured, to take root and stay rooted, and here I was, slinking back to the same state I'd taken such great pains to leave in the first place.

But once I moved in with Naya, I felt I'd hidden enough, atoned enough after a year enduring Esther's palpable disapproval of me, felt I could afford to make myself a little more visible. I texted Zeynep: Hey, back in Oakland. How's it going? Do you still live out here? Since then, we texted sporadically, exchanging macabre memes about neurodivergence, mainly, but also catching up on the life updates we'd missed. I now knew Zeynep had been dabbling in graphic design, that she had a partner who was ace like she was, and that they cohabitated in the apartment her parents had bought for her.

Sleep, or the lack thereof, was the one area of my life completely impervious to my resolve to sage it away or tai chi it better. I'd been dreamless, surrendered to hopeless practicality, for years. Since I moved out of Esther's, though, a longing I thought I'd quelled, if not killed, returned. In what little sleep I got, I started having dreams, at first occasionally, then nearly every night. Sometimes the dreams were linear: narrative, peculiar recountings of a possibility I never lived, a life I might have had. Nightmares, I branded them when I woke, because it was too late for all of that.

Other nights, the dreams were abstract, nonverbal: just movement, the feeling or remembering of it. I gave myself an inch, let myself look for a way of indulging, just a little, that part of my child brain that still bore this absurd attachment to an occupation that was no longer an option. The way I'd been raised, if you weren't headed to ABT, there was no point in dancing. Maybe I'd resisted this belief at Council and Elmwood, but I tried to let it go while I lived in New York. To get real.

While waiting for the dryer to finish at the laundromat a few blocks away, I saw a poster on the bulletin board advertising a local WOC movement circle. I took a picture, thinking that following my curiosity about it would give the dreams an outlet, and then—with any hope—they'd dissipate.

Though I wouldn't admit it to Tatiana, we did gather on or near the full moon, there was journaling and intention-setting involved, sometimes there were even candles. Mostly, we danced, free-form. Whoever hosted chose the music. I'd been twice so far and had volunteered to host tonight's meeting. I invited Naya, but she said she wasn't really into spaces where people who routinely consumed edibles unearthed whatever was lurking in the recesses of their imaginations, and I respected that. She left to stay at her sister's place for the night.

These women seemed, so far, well-meaning, creative, and friendly enough. Still, they felt unknown, or I felt unknown to them. In a moment of panic at the newness of it all—actually requesting that relative strangers come near me rather than fleeing from them at the first available opportunity—I invited Zeynep. She said she'd come, but from what I remembered about her, it was unlikely.

In involuntary homage to my mother's fastidious hosting habits, I deep-cleaned the faux-marble kitchen countertop and arranged a platter of Costco mini quiche, some chips and salsa from down the block, and the vegan strawberry cupcakes I made and frosted earlier.

The group trickled in. Eighteen people signed up, but only half a dozen showed up to the last two meetings. Today would be similar, it seemed. The women got as comfortable as they could on the hard, beige pullout couch I pushed against the far wall, or the pillows I set out around the perimeter of the room. We were just about to start when Zeynep knocked, then pushed open the door. She closed it behind her.

I stepped away from the counter and waved. "Come in! Hey! Uh . . . hi!" I wasn't sure whether to hug her. We stood across from each other with our arms half-extended like we were getting ready to do the robot.

"Hi," she said with a half smile, peering around at the group of people already settled in the living room. She looked so much as she had before, I was startled: more grown, certainly, but she was even wearing the same sort of oversize '80s band T-shirt and patterned palazzo pants she used to wear back in the day. The only difference was her lack of hijab; she'd twisted her thick black hair into a bun at the base of her neck. She laughed, a short, bright laugh I remembered clearly, and stepped in to hug me fully. I'd forgotten we were the same height. She stepped back and waved toward the living room, setting a bottle of wine I hadn't realized she'd been holding on to the counter. "Hey, everyone. I'm Zeynep?"

Once met with a scattered chorus of *Hey, Zeynep*, she grabbed a plate, balancing it precariously on the edge of the counter, and began filling it. "Oooh, mini quiche, come here, ye sweet li'l cheese buckets," she whispered to the quiche. The other women laughed; I shook my head, surprised by my own smile. Zeynep whispering sweet nothings to hot snacks had been a mainstay of our house-sharing experience back in the day.

My smile lingered as she joined the group, piling three stray cushions on top of one another and squirming around until she found the optimal angle. Three quiche fell on the floor in the process, to which she said, "You know what? I think these are fine. Dzifa, you still a clean freak? These are fine." She reached out and tapped the knee of the person next to her, a Sierra Leonean woman named Dee. "That's not slander, by the way. Living with Dzifa was God's gift to the overall hygiene of my living environment. Though now my partner and I have surrendered to full squalor. Okay, sorry, sorry, I'll stop talking."

"Oh, y'all lived together?" Henrietta was a community organizer and one of the group's two cofounders. An Oakland native, she used to dance in videos for local artists and wanted, as she'd written on the group description, a space to "literally set her ass free from white supremacist heteropatriarchy." So she created it. "Dzifa, I forgot you lived in Oakland before."

"Yeah, Zeynep totally saved me." I nodded. "Up until then, I was couch surfing—"

"Can we *please* retire that term? White people made that up like they make up all them bullshit exercise cults. Couch surfing." Sarah, the other cofounder, was seated beside me on the couch. She rolled her eyes. "Tryna make a recreational sport out of homelessness."

"How about: *housing insecure*," Henrietta suggested. And then laughed at Sarah's playful glare. "But yeah, if you were 'couch surfing' and you didn't wanna be . . . I think we can all agree you weren't on vacation."

"Well . . . yes." I nodded, pushing away the memories of that time. "It was definitely not a vacation. But anyway, Zeynep let me stay with her for, like, over a year, I think."

"It was *awesome*." Zeynep clapped her hands. "We had so much to catch up on. In high school, we both used to hide out in the health center instead of going to STEM classes. Our report cards were *very* uneven."

"Baller," someone whose name I didn't catch affirmed from where she was curled up against the side of the couch, the fabric of her chiffon maxi skirt grazing the carpet.

"Thanks." I laughed. "Uh . . . should we start with intentions? Who wants to go first?"

Zeynep lingered after the others went home, ostensibly to help me put away the dishes. But since "the dishes" were paper plates I threw into a jumbo trash bag, it didn't take long. She hovered by the front door. "So!" she started. "I'm really glad we could finally meet up. It's been so nice getting back in touch. And again . . . I'm really, really sorry I kinda fell off the face of the earth when you moved to Mass. I didn't forget about you, I just . . . you know how I am. But I'm glad we connected again. This was fun. Like a coven. I've always wanted to join a coven."

I looked down at my bare feet, the toenails I'd painted midnight blue earlier in the afternoon. I never painted my nails when I stayed at Esther's house; I felt uncomfortable putting any effort into my appearance there, since she prided herself on a utilitarian professionalism when it came to her style. My style, if I really wore what I wanted these days, was more woodland-nymph-in-a-dungeon chic. I sensed that Esther would find it agitating to cope with this aesthetic on her property. "It's okay," I reassured Zeynep. And it was. Well, it had been painful. But the thing about Zeynep was: She was forgetful, disorganized, and did, in fact, disappear off the face of the earth for enormous swaths of time. But at least back then, when she did show up, she *really* showed up. That counted for a lot. "I get it," I added. "And about the coven thing . . . I know." I laughed. "I wasn't 100 percent sure you'd come, but I thought . . . this might be something you'd be into."

"True facts." She beamed. "Okay, I'll leave you alone. It's late, and unless things have changed drastically, I remember you were not at all a night owl like me. But don't be a stranger, 'kay, Dzif? 'Specially now you're back in the Bay, we can do those eight-hour hangs like old times. My partner's only over half the week, 'cause we both like our space. And they're like 80 percent nonverbal anyway, so we can all introvert in peace."

"Sure, I'll take you up on that." We hugged again. I waved as she stepped out into the hallway, balancing a loosely Saran-wrapped plate of leftover mini quiche.

CHAPTER 5

Once I came down from the afterglow of the gathering, the night started like any other: I jolted awake every other hour, snapping my head toward the window, toward the bedroom door, bending my torso over the edge of the bed and checking for shadows underneath. It was a child's fear, but it came from adult things. I tried to remember the last time I'd slept without fear the ground underneath me would be ripped away—that my body would be, one moment, safely ensconced beneath the sheets, and the next, torn away and sequestered somewhere unknown, unsafe. My mind couldn't, or wouldn't, travel that far back. In those short bursts of sleep, my dream self danced through water thick and black as oil, limbs heavy as lead, neither drowning nor afloat.

At 3:00 A.M., the phone rang. I ignored it, keeping up the pretense of sleep. It rang a second time. I unstuck the T-shirt from my skin and rolled over, peering at my phone on the bedside table. I saw Tatiana's name, rushed to grab it. By the time I swiped to answer, she'd hung up.

As my finger hovered over the callback button, a voicemail notification popped up. Before I could listen, a text came in:

Call me when you can. I don't know what to do.

I hit Call once, twice—no answer. There was something leaden, just as in my dream, weighing on my heart, on my hands, even, holding me back from pressing Play on the voicemail. I tried to steady my breath, still my shaking fingers. I pressed Play.

"Dzifa," Tatiana pushed out, her voice thick, "Luca's dead. Can you—I can't—" She broke off. The voicemail ended. I called again. Again. No answer. I dropped the phone to the floor and sank back into the bed.

A chasm opened wide in my chest and shriveled back in a rapid spiral. I tried to erase its wreckage by forcing my eyes closed and retreating underneath the duvet. I hid there, half-asleep and willing the truth away, wishing the fabric around me were heavier, sturdier, Teflon. I hid until a few hours later when the sun started peeking through my thrifted curtains. Later, I'd deny the time it took me to act, to myself and anyone who asked. The hundreds of dollars it took to get a next-day, one-way flight from San Francisco to Boston were à start, as far as atonement went.

I'm on my way, I texted back when the five calls I attempted at 6:00 A.M. went unanswered. I could make up the rest of the atonement by submitting myself to the requirements of Tatiana's grief, which I suspected—hoped—would be numerous and strange.

I went to work numb, my mind flashing back to Luca's face yesterday, grainy and serene on the other end of my phone.

I'd never met him. I'd never met him or Maddie, I reminded myself, added to my list of infractions to atone for. And while Tatiana had asked me to visit, she never pushed. Not since Maddie's baby shower, which, in New York, I had promised I'd be there for, that I'd help organize, which another of Tatiana's friends had instead organized, and for which I was completely absent. Perhaps Tatiana suspected—and I hated that she was right, added it to the list of infractions, too—that even though I cared about her, I was plainly disinterested in the daily minutiae of parenthood. I supposed she knew that, because until a couple of years ago, she'd felt the same.

How did this happen? I puzzled on the BART ride to work. *How did we get here?* I busied myself with ruminations, as if I could unravel the problem, reverse the tragedy, by figuring out the math of it.

In the office that morning, I turned up the volume on my headphones and avoided the penetrating stares and Invisalign smiles as everyone else streamed in for work. I didn't want to be here, but I couldn't get an earlier flight.

At 1:00 P.M., I stood abruptly and told my manager, "I have to go." I said it loudly, without apology, while I fielded Tatiana's frantic texts. When you couldn't take it anymore, she asked in her third and final messages, what did you do? What do I do? It felt oddly affirming to know that if nothing else, I was a subject-matter expert on suicidal ideation.

After work, I stopped by Esther's place. I'd left my weekend bag in her guest room closet. The moment I got to her two-story house in the Oakland Hills, the gut punch of this morning's news hit me in a second wave. I would only ever know Luca, now, as an idea, could never know him as a person.

When my heart ached, whether from a fresh event or the memory I most wanted to forget, I found it best to let gravity drop me to my knees, to let myself wail. Emotions this big needed a physical outlet, I found, or they'd find a way to eat me. I'd been rediscovering in the movement circle how giving feelings too tangled to articulate someplace to go, some momentum through which to be released, stopped them from getting stuck. I wondered what Tatiana would do when she processed what she had seen, what she knew, what she believed, what she had lost. Would she fall and wail or hold still, stuck and numb?

Esther stood behind the granite island in her custom-built kitchen, chopping vegetables and sliding them neatly into a Pyrex bowl. Probably the makings of vegetable muffins for her sons. Even before she had kids, she always made everything from scratch, including the three-course dinners she prepared for her husband every day. I thought she was setting an unhealthy precedent for modern women. "Hey," she said, not looking up. "Do you actually work? It's, like, two."

"Do you?" I countered, cringing at my own nonsensical comeback. Esther hadn't been unemployed a day in her life. Not since she was fifteen and started working because our mom, at that point, decided to parent us intermittently. Things were less contentious between me and Esther then, when she switched roles from My Elusively Cool Big Sister to Guess You're My Mom Now. It was probably hell for her; I could feel the resentment wafting off her when she made opaque references to her lack of a childhood. Still, our dynamic had been clear, at times peaceful, before she left for college and I was alone, again, with my mother, until I went to boarding school at fourteen. In her period of isolation, which could have been months but felt like years, my mother managed to shift the balance of her mood swings from 80 percent rage blackout / 20 percent sorry-for-throwing-cutlery-at-you-let's-go-see-a-ballet to something more like 40 percent rage blackout / 40 percent total disengagement / 20 percent inspired, if slightly edgy, parenting. Since Esther left for college, things between us were too amorphous. In several thousand miles of distance, our individual identities shifted and codified in viscerally incompatible directions. She'd taken up the more virtuous trauma response: becoming the pious, perfect opposite of our mother. Since that trauma response was taken, I made the most of what was left.

Esther let out a short, derisive laugh without breaking focus from the bowl in front of her. "Yes, *I'm* employed, full-time, at the company where *I* have worked, for years. That's how I was able to buy a house. A fairly common milestone, for some."

I fought a decades-deep urge to silently walk away, right out the door, and keep walking. "Jesus. I'm not even staying here anymore. And you're the one who told me I should come back to California in the first place. If you didn't want me here, you could have just said so."

"I didn't say I didn't want you here." She rolled her eyes. "You're my sister. I just wish you would . . ." She lifted her hands, palms open, and parted them swiftly, like she was smoothing down a fitted sheet. *Be someone else*, I filled in the blank for her. No need to say it; we both knew it. Were in agreement. "Whatever."

I waited for further, better explanation; it didn't come. "Cool. Well, I have to go to Boston tomorrow, so. Enjoy."

"Why?" She spooned almond flour into a measuring cup.

"To support a friend of mine. Family emergency."

Her eyes went wide for a moment. She blinked and resumed her task, cracking an egg into the flour. "Oh. That sucks. Which friend? The one who got pregnant by some rando?" She smirked, barely, but I caught it. Esther likely planned her own pregnancies seven years beforehand, no doubt on one of the multitude of spreadsheets she pretended to be embarrassed about. Despite harboring similar judgments deep down, I felt some kind of secondhand sting from Esther's slight.

"He's not a rando." I sighed. "They live together. And it was her newborn, who passed away."

"Oh." Esther set her hands on the counter and looked up. "That's terrible." She glanced blankly into the growing pile of muffin mix, then blinked back up at me. "I can't even imagine. Well . . . give her our regards."

At dawn, just as the darkness receded, I threw shirts and underwear into the bag I retrieved from Esther's and dodged potholes on my way from Cleveland Heights to the West Oakland park and ride. A few bested me, so I had to cross my fingers and hold my breath while I waited to see if these wheels, long overdue for changing, would make it out whole. Even for a vehicle this broken down, the monthly payments were pushing impractical, but I needed to be a person with a car. I got out at the park and ride and walked for five minutes, then came back, sticking my worn key into the driver's door lock and twisting it forcefully to the right.

On the BART ride to SFO, I ignored the preponderance of odors, the unsettling stains and jagged lumps on the carpeted seats. I focused instead on puzzling out the odd combination of heaviness and relief I felt. Heaviness, I told myself, because of why I was headed to Boston. Relief,

I reasoned, because I was always relieved to leave California, no matter the occasion. Even yesterday, when I dropped by Esther's, I felt it acutely: that unreleasable breath I held most bracingly around my family. I wanted Esther to be exempt from this, immune to it, felt she'd earned me feeling relaxed, easeful, grateful around her. But it was impossible to achieve such full-breathed presence, as it had been when we were kids, even though I could no longer pinpoint the exact moment things shifted, the moment I inhaled, and the air got stuck. I could only see, when I concentrated, how things were sometime after the shift.

—ᵚ—

The year before Esther left for college, I was in fifth grade. It was October, and I could feel it was going to be a doughnut day. I'd seen Esther at our mother's bedroom door, speaking in a low tone. I couldn't hear from where I stood at the other end of the carpeted upstairs hallway, but I saw my sister's neatly tweezed eyebrows draw together, her hands, clasped behind her back, clenching. She would never cross her arms in front of our mother, but I could tell she wanted to. "Yes, Mom," Esther said a little louder than she probably meant to, then sucked in a breath when the door slammed in front of her. She released her tightened grasp and brought both hands up to smooth her already perfectly flat-ironed hair. "Stop lurking, Dzifa," she teased. I slunk out of the entryway to the hall and waved.

"You okay?" I asked.

"Yeah." She shrugged as if there would be no possible reason not to be okay. "What are you holding?" She pointed at the wrinkled white printer paper I was gripping.

"Mm . . . a picture." I stared at the floor, feeling somewhere between defiant and embarrassed.

Esther crossed to me, gently removed the paper from my hand. She took a long look at it, though she'd seen dozens, maybe hundreds, like it before. "Another cat family? You're a weirdo."

"She likes cats." I shrugged. "And this one is *Phantom of the Opera*–themed. See?"

Esther exhaled slowly. "You know she just throws them away, Dzifa."

I darted my eyes toward the closed bedroom door. "'Kay. Meet you in the car."

"Whatever." She moved past me. Once she'd disappeared, I tiptoed toward my mother's room, knelt, slipped the drawing underneath her doorway. I raised my hand to knock, thought better of it, tiptoed backward.

I missed my mother. I missed her laughing as she mimicked Sarah Brightman's onstage affectations, her acerbic takedowns of the tacit white supremacy of my elementary school teachers. I missed her long diatribes in Italian, which she'd learned growing up on an air force base. I missed her style, the time she put into it. A statuesque woman, she adorned herself like the queen she experienced herself to be. It was hard to tell if she felt any particular affection for the designer brands she bought or if it was a matter of principle: that she *should* be able to buy them, wear them.

At least things were more even with Esther at the helm. She became my default caregiver almost immediately after she got her driver's license. I no longer felt my heart racing with the sound of Mom shouting, "Rise and shine!" two hours before our alarms went off, was no longer unsure if it was going to be a regular day—manageably chaotic and anxiety-ridden—or one of *those* days. I orbited, since I could remember, around our mother's moods—pulling back when the water appeared to be boiling over, letting myself be drawn in when she was craving connection, holding my breath when she hugged me and it felt, somehow, like someone reaching beneath my skin, sliding their fingers under the bone, grabbing hold of my veins and tugging.

Sometimes Mom's car, a sleek, slate-blue Mercedes she'd bought with money Dad sent for our school tuition and general upkeep, was gone from the garage when we got home from dance class. Most of the time, it was still there, and any groceries Esther bought that week were still untouched in the pantry and the fridge. That Mercedes made me uncomfortable, like the impractically large house we lived in; I didn't like being seen in it. It was tasteful, like everything my mother had selected and meticulously cared for, but beyond our means, like everything my mother had selected and meticulously cared for. Neither Esther nor I could ever quite discern what our means were. They came from our father to our mother and seemed to disappear in the vicinity of her palatial shoe closet before they got to us. Whatever the case, we sensed we weren't allowed to mention the disparity between the façade of the house, the car, the schools, the manners; and the disorder we actually inhabited.

It took a bit of a jump to get myself into the passenger's seat of the Ford Explorer that Dad bought Esther for her sixteenth birthday on one of his increasingly rare trips through town. It was the happiest I'd seen her, ever. Of course, her happiness faded once she realized he'd bought her the car so she could shuttle me around.

When I finished school, I waited for her to finish, then went with her to work, then dance, or the other way around. While my sister claimed to be a "keeping to herself" type, I suspected she only wanted to keep to herself when she was around our family. She'd always displayed such an ease making friends. I didn't get it—how she managed to be her perpetually unenthused self *and* have friends. For me, the two had always been mutually exclusive.

Esther turned on the engine and reached up to press the garage door opener. As the heavy wooden door lifted behind us, she perused the options in the six-disk CD player. "Did you steal *Lucy Pearl* again? It was here last night."

"No." I swiped a smudge of dirt off the window with my thumb. "I'm back on *Prince of Egypt* right now, so I don't have time for other music. I'm making a ballet version of it. You know that part in 'Deliver Us,' where it's like, 'Deliver uuuuuuu—' "

"You know," Esther cut me off, "it's unhealthy to listen to the same song over and over again on a loop like that. It's also very annoying for me, who has to live next door to *you*." She held up a hand to silence me when I opened my mouth to defend myself. We rolled down the driveway and into the main road. "Guess it's gonna have to be Trina Day today. It's also gonna have to be a doughnut day; I forgot to eat breakfast."

"Yesss." I shook my fists in victory at both of these revelations. "Trinuu, doughnuuut, Trinuuuu—"

"Oh my God," she cut off my improvised song. "Never mind." She pressed the rounded, black plastic button beside the CD drive several times, selected *The Nu Nation Project* instead.

We turned onto the freeway just in time to recite the words to "Revolution."

After Esther paid for her chocolate-glazed and my maple bar, she checked her watch. "We have, like, five minutes. Want to sit outside?" She nodded toward the stone benches outside the doughnut shop, which was located in a nondescript outdoor mall two exits down from our school.

"'Kay." I shrugged as if nonchalant. But it was always a treat, getting to spend extra time with Esther.

I sat cross-legged on my side of the bench. She kicked one leg over the other and bit into her doughnut. "How's your Barnard application?" I asked.

Esther stopped chewing, raising an eyebrow. "What Barnard application?" she said between bites.

"Yeah, I know you said not to tell Dad yet, and I didn't." I said it as if there would be an occasion to do so anyway, but our dad hadn't been in town for over eight months, and we no longer got calls in between. Well, *I* didn't; Esther got biweekly phone lectures about her progress getting into Yale. "But you're still applying, right? I mean, you have the grades and everything. And they already got to see you dance. You still have to apply."

"Dzifa," Esther sighed. "There is no way on God's green earth Dad is gonna pay for that."

I considered whether to say what I wanted to say. Finishing my bite, I took a deep breath. "You know who would help you convince him if you asked . . ."

"No." Esther finished her doughnut and crumpled up the paper bag, throwing it behind her into the trash can. I tried the same move, and the bag fell a full foot away from the can. I scrambled up from the bench to deposit it properly. Esther stood. "I mean, I can cover the application fee myself. But I can't go if I don't get a scholarship. And they're not gonna give me a scholarship, because look where we live? No one's gonna believe I need it. So, oh, well."

"Esther." I headbutted her shoulder, and she shoved me away. "Just ask Mom. She's the one who put us all in dance. She gets it. At least try. See what she thinks."

"Dzifa." Esther looked down at me. "Mom is an *insane* person." She raised her eyebrows and stretched out the vowels. "I don't care what she thinks. You should not care what she thinks. And you know who *really* doesn't care what she thinks? Dad. Let's go."

"Okay." I shrugged. "But you should still send in your application. Just in case. Also, can I please have another maple bar? I'm still hungry."

"You're the worst." She sighed, grabbing my arm and gently, but firmly, pulling me away from the doughnut shop. "And it's *may* I please." It was something Mom would say. I thought, but didn't say, *So you do care what she thinks.* I rubbed at a spot in the center of my chest, pretending to brush off doughnut crumbs, when really, it just hurt a little.

—∾—

As the BART screeched to a halt in Millbrae, I forced myself to let go of the search for when, and why, it all started. Impossible to know: Even on that particular doughnut day, the caught breath was already there, had long been there. It was just: I had enough hope in me then that the bracing subsided more often. I stood, dropped my palm from my chest. Hoisted the bag over my shoulder, sidestepping a man who smelled like Jolly Ranchers and urine, and exited the train.

PART 2

CHAPTER 6

I'd never been to Tatiana's house before. I'd been to Boston many times, though, all those years ago when I was shipped off to boarding school like the troubled child of an oil baron. The mid-August heat was heavy, nasty, but I could breathe better than in Oakland. I considered it a gift from the weather gods, their way of saying, "Don't worry, nobody can breathe this time of year." I found my way to Dorchester through a combination of technology and direct questions to strangers. Those who fielded my questions, standing about the T or on street corners, answered me with slight smiles or none at all, their energy somehow both focused and frenetic. It was strange how good it felt to be back around people this hard. The Californians I grew up with—and my current co-workers—were softer, sweeter, routinely disingenuous.

I loitered outside her mother's cul-de-sac, scanning the block full of mismatched, traditional single-family units for thirty minutes before her text came in. What would I even say when I saw her?

We're all at B's house.

I copied the address into my phone. A forty-five-minute ride on the T. I sighed, backtracked to the station I'd just come from. She texted me B's number and instructions to call him when I arrived.

When I made it to the Back Bay, sweaty and sluggish, the fatigue from the six-hour plane ride set in. From the outside, B's place looked like a pretty standard two-story building. An unkempt brownstone on a sterile, nondescript block. This was where the big banker lived? I had no doubt it was an expensive purchase, but aesthetically, it was modest, at least compared to the grandeur Tatiana attributed to it. But she was, astrologically speaking, prone to embellishments.

I called, practicing appropriately somber greetings in my head. "Hello; I'm sorry." No, too abrupt. "Hi, how are you?" No, too stupid. The phone rang six times. Nothing. I decided not to call again. I didn't know the etiquette for this type of situation. I sat stiffly at the edge of the stoop.

A *GQ*-pretty white boy emerged from a black BMW and walked up. "Hi," I said, waving. He struck me as the kind who courted skinny blondes with rich daddies and fantasized about disrobing Black women. He probably didn't know it yet. Something about the blankness in his eyes, the steadiness in his step. Impressionable. Bored. Boring.

He said nothing. I introduced myself, waved again. One wave too many. He remained silent. "I'm . . . Tatiana's friend? From Oakland? So." I needed a script for this.

He nodded tersely, not meeting my eyes. *Should I not be here?* He produced a small bronze key from his pocket and opened the heavy door to B's brownstone. For a second, I thought he'd let it slam behind him, but he held the door open with his foot. I walked in and tripped to the side when a young white woman nearly my height pushed past me with a mumbled *excuse me*. Righting myself, I offered a nonsensical *sorry* to her swiftly retreating form and proceeded up two flights of steep, narrow wooden stairs. I'd already forgotten what B looked like, but it was hard to imagine a man who wore custom-tailored suits tiptoeing down these stairs with a stroller in tow.

The pretty boy was B's half brother, I later learned. His name was probably Tad; it wasn't clear what I heard while shouldering my way through the front door of the apartment. I was distracted as it dawned on me that I was partially responsible for the spectacle I saw inside. Tatiana called me a week after our post-sonogram lunch, to ask one last time if I thought she was making the right choice. I was still at the tail end of my Cautious Feminist phase and two weeks out from leaving New York for good. I reminded her, my feet slipping off the lower rung of a Park Slope barstool, "I meant what I said. I support whichever decision you make." I didn't say, and should have said, "Get a fucking abortion, you idiot."

The apartment was cramped, a one-bedroom with decently high ceilings and indecently tight walls, mismatched brick on one wall, sickly olive paint on all the others. The heaviness of the outside air was not so forgiving in this space, devoid as it was of fans, air-conditioning, or Tatiana. *Where is she?* I fought the urge to tilt my head upward when I walked in, to see if the air that felt stuck sideways would circulate better if I caught and released it skyward.

Keeping my head tilted down was a matter of safety, tradition, avoidance, defiance. An act of apparent submission I didn't mean as such whatsoever, certainly not in this crowd. The bedroom was stationed at the very back, hidden from view by a tall, industrial sliding door. A small, square bathroom sat beside the bedroom, covered in cracked white tiles, mildew creeping in between the cracks, clusters of soap-caked product bottles obscuring the porcelain rim of the tub. There was a modest kitchen corner guarded by a three-foot marble island. Atop the island, three dented foil trays of untouched food.

I couldn't find a natural angle in the folding chair I sat in. I was too big for it, so I adjusted my hips, contracted my torso forward and back every two or three minutes. *When you're onstage, make sure you always have something to do.* I pulled my flimsy shirtsleeves down over my tattoos even though the most relevant people in the room had already clocked me; I could tell from their eyes, which I could feel but not see. *Outsider, Negress, slut, strange, somebody hide the cash.* Those eyes felt like my childhood.

At these kinds of gatherings, after a recent death was discussed or alluded to, I'd feel an impulse to burst out laughing. None of it was funny, but something in my gut said there needed to be sound, any sound, for any of it to make sense. I wanted to laugh now. I crunched my toes inside my sneakers and pressed them hard into the soles.

B was regular-looking and regularly statured. He sat stiffly, surrounded by half a dozen white people and an infant whose face I couldn't see but whom I assumed to be Maddie. She was a few weeks shy of one, now—at least, according to me, who lacked the mathematical precision of a mother, counting every day, week, month of a child's being. Having only seen her before through the screen of my phone during video chats, I was startled by the scale of her. When one of B's relatives took a turn holding her, I saw her brown eyes, alert, scanning the room. I didn't know why I'd expected her to be crying. I didn't know if she knew what happened, or, if she did, if a person who'd had so little indoctrination into what adults decided life was supposed to mean, how long adults expected it to last, would feel the same indignant flavor of grief an adult would.

Maddie shifted, silent but decisive, away from the pale hands that held her. B retrieved her; I moved my gaze back to him. I'd thought, when I saw B in a blurry phone picture two years ago, that he just wasn't photogenic. Whenever Tatiana called me on FaceTime, he was never in close view, if he was there at all. And in recent months, if he was there, so was his mother, and then our calls were cut short, Tatiana's rushed *Shit! Gotta go*, reigniting my dread about the nature of her dynamic with B's family.

If I were a shorter, craftier woman, I could see the appeal of B's small head, undefined features, and expensive shoes. Before I moved my eyes away from him, his gaze snapped sideways toward me; the rest of his face was still, downturned.

It was then that the memory came back, one I hadn't remembered forgetting. Me, sitting stiffly in a plastic chair in the waiting room of Council's health center, as I did so many mornings while I was a student there. Him, sitting in the row of chairs perpendicular to mine, his legs stretched out in front of him, a bag of ice covering his wrist. Or his elbow. Or whichever part of him was, on that particular visit, bruised. He wasn't there nearly so often as Zeynep and I were. Maybe once every few weeks. We never spoke, though Zeynep attempted to talk at him several times. He only ever grunted a noncommittal reply. If he got seen before we did, Zeynep made a habit of turning toward me and stage-whispering, loudly enough for the entire health center to hear, "You know he's a *day* student, right?"

This could not be the same person, could it? I had textbook face blindness so could not be relied upon to recognize people I didn't interact with regularly, but that memory of the waiting room wouldn't leave me, now that I could see his eyes. They'd been the same then—a grayish brown, hollow and sharp at the same time. I'd text Zeynep later. It was a little unconventional for a follow-up text given we'd only just reconnected, but I needed to know, and her memory was photographic.

Slowly, B panned his eyes back to his little Protestant semicircle. I flushed, sneaking a glance at the lone representative from Tatiana's family, an elderly auntie, sitting by the oven. She kept her eyes trained on the tray of jerk fish to her right—clearly, her contribution—no secret head nod or sympathetic wink offered.

I looked back at B's family. You wouldn't know the Adams were originally considered white trash unless they told you, which they wouldn't. They spoke softly, if at all, and never about the obvious. Apparently, real estate in the Poconos was riveting these days.

B had the misfortune of being the biracial, fatherless stepson of Northeastern Republicans. Not the Martha's Vineyard types with the pastel polos. These were Confederate Flag types who hid their true colors in military green. B's mother, Brigitte Adams, was a career marine. As was her husband, B's third stepfather, a tall, broad man with sunburned skin and a predictable crew cut. As were her three blond-haired, blue-eyed sons, each one from a different marriage. Brigitte—as Tatiana told me on multiple occasions, rolling her eyes across the screen during our sporadic video chats—grew up in rural Connecticut, not the idyllic kind of rural, and enlisted when she was twenty-one, and B was five. She took the liberty of changing her name at that point, though Tatiana had no idea what it was originally. All B ever said about his father was that he was from the Continent, he'd been gone long before B was born, and that Brigitte never spoke about him. If B brought it up, Brigitte was prone to clicking her tongue and reassuring him, "You have a father, darling," referring to Stepfather Number Three.

The Adams weren't eating anything now, and I suspected they never ate. Having grown up in a sea of spray-tanned WASPs myself, I learned early on that my people had no language for affection, so we fed each other incessantly. Theirs would never do anything so crass as enjoy themselves, so the best you could hope for at Krissy's or Sara's house was a pile of baby carrots and a lukewarm Coke Zero.

After looking from exposed brick wall to uneven floorboard and back again, I fixed my gaze on Brigitte, the deliberately meek matriarch. She was the only one who introduced herself to me directly, though she held my hand like it was a dirty rag and flinched when I said my name, the real one. I was obsessed with women like her, women with frail bones and soft voices, who were inarguably pretty but impossible to sexualize. Women who could commit murder, if they wanted to, and have the man standing nearest them gladly take the fall for it. It was exactly my attraction to exactly this sort of woman that made me wonder if I really was queer or just colonized.

Tatiana shuffled out of her bedroom with a petite, alabaster-skinned friend in tow. I swallowed, smiling timidly at them both. Reevaluating the solemn faces around me, I shrank my smile to a grimace. Solidarity.

"Hey, you. Long time no see!" Tatiana's companion crossed the room, her straight, platinum-blond hair flapping about with every stride. I tried to place her properly before she realized I didn't recognize her as readily as she'd recognized me. If this was the same Sam from our year in college, and I hoped she was not, she had brown hair before, didn't she? And it was shorter. She hugged me tight; I fought the urge to flinch. I wondered how long it would take to shake her happy-go-lucky energy from my skin. I preferred to avoid affection from short people, because their faces ended up in my chest when we hugged, which made me feel like Aunt Jemima.

"Yep. Great to see you!" I lied. It struck me as duplicitous that Tatiana would invite her here, but I knew that wasn't fair. I didn't do things like baby showers and births, and I was notorious for distancing myself from people who were likely to request my services as a bridesmaid. Sam, on the other hand, had been proactively helpful throughout a pregnancy I was so indiscreetly baffled by that I stayed three thousand miles away as it unfolded. Still, I wished I could be the designated best friend in life's darker moments.

Tatiana hugged me next. "Thanks for coming," she whispered as she pulled away. When she stepped back, I nodded, surveying her expression—for what, I wasn't sure. I couldn't conceptualize the enormity of her grief, tried to envision it the whole plane ride over, and though a montage of rended garments and piercing wails of sorrow came through as possibilities, I couldn't quite place them on my friend. Though her voice was quiet, I tracked the signals of an inward unsettledness: the way her eyes flitted every few seconds to Maddie, closed too firmly to be a casual blink, the way her hands clenched into half fists, knocking sporadically against her legs.

We retreated behind the heavy bedroom door. I stood inside, tall and stiff, as the two of them resumed their level, familiar friendship pose. The bed was a California king, but the frame was so low to the ground it might as well have been a floor mattress. I did not understand this choice, nor did it strike me as something the Tatiana I knew would put up with. Why buy a mattress that large and expensive, and then put it on a frame that required you to either roll onto the floor or deep-squat out of bed every morning?

"I'm not crazy, right?" Tatiana spoke in a whisper again. I forced my eyes to drift back toward the bedroom door, where the two hovered, Sam with hands on her hips, Tatiana's arms crossed over her chest. Unsure of what to do with mine, I crossed them behind my back and leaned my hips against the door.

Sam shook her head, strands of her bleached or un-browned hair falling across her face. "Oh my God, no," she assured. "She's totally watching Maddie like a hawk. You want me to grab her?"

"No, I—" Tatiana looked up at me and blinked as if she'd forgotten I was still there. I wondered if I should be. "Sorry, Dzifa," she said. "Since this all—since it happened, she won't leave me alone with Maddie. That's why it took me so long to come out and see you. We were trying to figure out what to do about her."

I closed my eyes for a moment, hoping to disguise it as a slow blink. I'd come here to make myself useful, to plug myself into whatever funeral proceedings the Bishops and Adams had agreed to set up. I'd been to enough funerals to know there were steps that needed to be taken, that there was a time limit for taking some of those steps. But there were no proceedings here, no plans. There was only the thick stillness I walked in on in the living room, the way the Adams sat, stoic, as if nothing had happened, as if they were sitting on an expansive lawn waiting for someone in a crisp apron to bring them tea and the newspaper. Then there was this: clandestine chitchats behind sliding doors, the anxious urgency of my friend and our former classmate. "Sorry, who are we talking about?"

"Brigitte?" Sam said it like a question, but her impatient tone indicated I shouldn't have needed to ask.

"Right." I nodded. "Um, is . . . So—" I stopped, shut my mouth, decided to quit while I was behind.

Sam and Tatiana returned their attention to each other. "Okay," Tatiana said through a deep sigh. "I'm just gonna go tell her I'm taking Maddie for a walk. There's stuff I need to talk to you guys about. I haven't had a single second to myself this whole time. I feel like I'm in an observation room here. I feel like I'm losing it." She shook her head, nudged an errant braid away from her eyes.

"Gotcha, Tati." Sam nodded, eyes wide. She laid a small hand on Tatiana's shoulder and squeezed. "Let's do this."

Nobody moved. I held my breath. Sam and Tatiana stared at me. Tatiana raised an eyebrow, and I realized I was blocking the exit. I jolted to the side, as if electrocuted, and stumbled when Tatiana lifted the door latch and slid open the heavy wood. Sam glided out after her. I followed, at a lag, and tried to close the door behind me but couldn't figure out the latch. Dropping the curved metal bar I'd been struggling with, I turned to find B frowning at me, arms folded across his chest.

"I didn't catch your name," he said, his voice devoid of accusation, devoid of anything. I grimaced, my eyes tracking the room for Tatiana and Sam. They were in the kitchen nook, where Brigitte had migrated with a sleeping Maddie.

"Um . . . I should—sorry. I'm Dzifa?" So he must not be the person

I thought he was, after all. Either that, or I was exactly as invisible in high school as I thought I was, and he just didn't recognize me. "I should really—"

"I see. And you're a friend of Tatiana's, are you?"

I blinked, looked at my shoes, then chose a spot just above his eyes to fixate on. There was a tiny dot of hyperpigmentation, just above his left eyebrow. "Yes. I'm . . . Dzifa?" I repeated, as if his hearing were the problem.

How was it possible that a man who lived, had had two children, with my best friend, could not know that I was her best friend? But when I looked at Sam and Tatiana at the edge of the room, the way Tatiana's voice rose in volume, the way that Sam stood, steady and protective beside her, I wondered if that was still true. Maybe it was untrue enough that I hadn't been worth mentioning. Or if I was, if Tatiana had mentioned me, then it hadn't been often enough I was worth remembering. I cleared my throat; this was ridiculous. A child had died. Who cared if he didn't know my name?

B's frown deepened. I dropped my eyes to the neatly pressed collar of his polo shirt, dragged them back up to the spot near his eyes. "Sorry, but . . . I should probably—" I gestured toward the spectacle percolating in the kitchen. "We'll be back in less than an hour," I heard Tatiana snap at Brigitte.

"What were you guys talking about?" B asked levelly. He kept his eyes on me as if there was nothing else going on in the apartment.

"What?" I shook my head. "I don't—we weren't—we were just catching up. I mean, I was getting caught up. On everything. Sorry. Tatiana and I didn't really have a chance to talk in detail since . . . everything happened. I'm going to just—" I stepped away from the door.

"And what is it that she told you happened, exactly?"

Two steps past B, I turned back to him, my eyes narrowed. "What do you mean?" Was this a test? My heartbeat picked up. I bit down on my tongue a little, trying to stabilize.

"I'm asking—" He shook his head. For the first time, I saw a flicker of change in his eyes. A very quick clouding over, then back to normal. "I wasn't there when it happened." He held my gaze—or tried to; I kept darting my eyes away—as if some clarity about events I wasn't here for either was to be found inside my pupils.

My head half-turned toward the kitchen, I swallowed. "That must be . . ." I had no idea what it must be, for any of them. "I'm really sorry," I said to the floor, "I need to . . ." I shuffled the few remaining paces into the living room, then found a spot in the standoff. Brigitte stood on the side of the kitchen island closest the wall; Sam and Tatiana stood on the living room side, facing her. The trays of neglected food were still sitting on the counter, but the auntie who'd been there when I arrived was nowhere to be found. I looked around the room when I didn't see Maddie. She was in the corner of the living room, I finally saw, sitting on Probably-Tad's lap, playing with a big cardboard book. There wasn't really room for me on Sam and Tatiana's side of the island, so I positioned myself on the narrow edge of it, closest the front door. It was a bad choice, the position of a mediator, or a judge, able to see each side of the argument out of one eye, still oblivious to the full picture.

Sam mouthed something at me, with a confused gesture toward B's direction. I shrugged. We turned our attention back to Brigitte, who was staring down Tatiana with even more intensity than her son had leveled at me. Her gaze, though, wasn't blank; it was my first time seeing someone sneer through their eyes. "Oh, I am only here to help. As I have been, all this time. I'm sure all of us who have Madeleine's best interests at heart"—she scanned the living room, where her family members conversed quietly, inanely, their poses as stiff as they'd been before—"would agree that the best thing for her. And for you, of course, dear"—she nodded at Tatiana—"is for you to take some time to rest."

Without bothering to fake a smile or any warmth, Tatiana replied, "I'm sufficiently rested. So, as should *always* be the case, as—perhaps you've forgotten—her legal, primary guardian, since—as you've pointed out five thousand times, we are not married—I will decide what's best for my daughter. Thank you so much for your concern, though."

Brigitte blinked. She stepped back against the kitchen wall, crossed one foot over the other, and crossed her arms over her chest. Her lips ticked up into a soft grin. "I haven't forgotten," she said quietly. "And I'm sure you have not forgotten that, since you are not married, this is my son's home. Legally speaking."

"Oh, you have got to be out of your f—" Tatiana started.

"Sweetheart," Brigitte interrupted. "We are all here for you through this. I took leave from work"—she paused and darted her eyes toward me, and I was unsure of the response this apparent cue was supposed to elicit. A quick *Thank you for your service*? A salute? A bow? I offered an involuntary eye twitch. She returned her gaze to Tatiana—"to support *you*. You must know that. I understand you may feel a little defensive given the events of the last—"

"Defensive?" Tatiana's hands tensed beside her. Sam laid a steadying hand on her shoulder; Tatiana shook it off. "I don't have anything to be defensive about. You, on the other hand, were the—" She paused, looked toward the bedroom. I followed her tear-filled eyes and could no longer see B. Had he left, somehow, or was he hiding? Tatiana took a breath and continued. "You were the last one with him. Are *you* feeling defensive, Brigitte?"

Brigitte's jaw tightened, her barely there smile dropping. I watched her pass her natural response through a silent—though judging by the fury in her eyes, extensive—filtering system. With a short, sharp exhalation that could have been a laugh, Brigitte pushed herself away from the wall and placed her hands on the edge of the island. The curve of her narrow fingers over the marble surface reminded me of my mother's hands. Elegant, as relaxed as they were controlled. Her fingernails were neatly filed, impeccably clean, and bare. "We will continue keeping an eye on Madeleine. While you catch up on some sleep, give yourself a chance to recharge."

"Um," Sam interjected, voice wavering. "Maybe . . . Tati, we could take a walk and come right back? Maybe, like, regroup or . . . ?"

Tatiana stepped away from her side of the counter, hands still tight in fists beside her, then stepped back, skimming the side of her body until she was opposite me on the other narrow edge of the island. She shifted back and forth from one foot to the other, her cheeks a canvas of dried and fresh tears, and clenched and unclenched her fists. Her head tilted toward Brigitte, but her eyes stayed on the marble. Brigitte's fingers tightened, ever so slightly, on the countertop.

"Ook! Ook!" We snapped our heads toward Maddie, almost in unison, where she drummed on the cardboard book, now on the floor, Probably-Tad cross-legged beside her. Maddie's eyes were on her mother, her sparsely toothed grin eager.

"That's right, Mads, that's a book!" Sam cheered, clapping her hands. "Tatiana, is that her first word?!" In another time, on some other occasion, we might all have built on Sam's abrupt enthusiasm. I wondered if it was the kinder thing for a child, to play like Sam: to ignore the heaviness of the moment, to attend to the child's joy. Or if it was kinder to teach her earlier that joy happens in the midst of a million other things, that the celebration of it will not always be affirmed or accommodated.

Tatiana turned toward her daughter, a weary smile bypassing her prior scowl. "Good job, sweetie. You wanna go for a little walk?" She moved away from the island and crouched down, extending her arms. "Come take a walk with Mommy."

Maddie dropped the book and crawled toward her mother.

Brigitte cleared her throat, regarding Probably-Tad with a tight smile. "Sweetheart, would you do me a favor and put Madeleine back in her crib? I think she's ready for a nap."

Probably-Tad darted his eyes toward Tatiana, toward Maddie, then back at his mother. "Um—I'm not really sure if—"

"Darling," Brigitte clipped. "Today, please."

A throat cleared near the back door. B stood there, clutching a cellphone. He looked as if he'd aged a decade in the past few minutes. "Mom, can I have a word?"

"How nice of him to drop in," Sam muttered.

Tatiana rushed to Maddie's side while Brigitte deliberated. Gently, she picked her up, nuzzling Maddie's little head against her cheek. "You're okay, honeybun," she said, perhaps as much to herself as to Maddie, who became fixated on retrieving the book. Probably-Tad handed it to Tatiana; she held it up so Maddie could continue playing with it.

"Can it wait?" Brigitte clipped. "We were in the middle of a discussion."

B looked between his daughter, Tatiana, Sam, me, his brother, the seated members of his family who silently stayed out of the fray, opting instead to look at their phones or remark on the weather, and finally back at his mother. "Look: How about this. Tatiana, I will watch Maddie, okay? If you could just give me and my mom a couple of hours to sort things out."

Tatiana and Sam shared a glance I couldn't decipher. I tried to anchor myself more steadily, feet planted on the floorboards beneath me, hands pushing against the marble. I waited for what I was sure was coming, what I was shocked hadn't come yet. The Tatiana I knew did not capitulate to anyone, for any reason. "There is nothing to sort out." Tatiana scoffed. "She's acting like I'm not allowed to take my own daughter outside."

Brigitte raised an eyebrow. "I did not say any such thing. I was simply making a suggestion. For your benefit. You're practically a daughter to me, dear."

"And yet, I'm not your daughter." She said it through gritted teeth, her voice level. Maddie dropped the book again. Tatiana bent, retrieved it, set it on the counter. "Hang on one second, Mads," she whispered. Maddie continued grasping for the book but stayed firmly in her mother's arms. "I didn't have to move in with you," she said to B, shaking her head. "I didn't even have to tell you. Are you serious with all of this?"

B approached his mother and the mother of his remaining child. When he was standing closer to both, he extended his arms toward his daughter. "Tatiana, please. I'm just thinking of what's going to be least upsetting for Maddie right now. Please give me and my family some space. So we can try to . . . process. It's been a lot for them, too. I promise, when you come back, we will give you and Maddie some space, as well. Okay? Right, Mom?" He glanced sideways at his mother.

Brigitte preened. "Of course, sweetheart. Just as I said."

Tatiana kept her arms around Maddie, her breath so heavy it moved her daughter away and toward her in a strange little dance.

"Tati," Sam offered tentatively. "I know this is super stressful. And unfair." She glared at Brigitte. "But I do think it's gonna be good to get some fresh air. You don't need it," she rushed to clarify. "But let's go for a drive or something. Get you something to eat. My car is right out front."

Tatiana kissed Maddie's cheek and hesitated. An eternal-feeling half minute later, she handed Maddie to B and stepped back. "To be clear," she said in a low voice. "*You* will watch Maddie." She tipped her head toward B. "Not her."

"Yes."

"And when I get back, there will be no more of this absolute nonsense."

B frowned, looked at his mother, then back at Tatiana. "I meant what I said. We just need a minute."

"Yeah, yeah." Tatiana cut him a glare. "As a family. Got it." She stalked past him, retrieved a large leather purse from where it sat just outside the bedroom, and motioned to me and Sam to follow her out the door.

CHAPTER 7

"So. Where to?" Sam patted her thighs, once situated, seatbelt on, in the driver's seat of her SUV. Tatiana sat beside her, one elbow on the window ledge, her head leaned into her hand. I defaulted to the back seat, trying and failing to see if, given the heat, my body would go ahead and melt into the leather.

I pulled at the fabric of my jeans where it stuck to my legs and suppressed a rare and pressing urge to fill the silence that followed. I was afraid I'd fill it with a contextually inappropriate reflection. Unless this was the only appropriate context for it.

On the plane, I kept thinking about Luca's name. How it was Tatiana's decision to call him that, how B never agreed—because Brigitte disagreed—and they'd therefore yet to record his name officially on the birth certificate. I didn't know why this stood out to me, except that names were so important in my family's culture. Outdoorings, held on the eighth day of a child's life, marked the child as an official person in the world. Until the naming, the child was considered inhuman—a spirit passing through.

I knew this even though, or maybe because, I was the only one in my family who had not received an Outdooring, a fact of which my eldest three sisters never hesitated to remind me. Even though I was neither religious nor in regular contact with my father, I always found those old ways generous, intuitively true, if technically unprovable. Instead of all the rigmarole about heaven and hell, there was primarily the wisdom that, living or dead, we were never truly lost. It was only ever a matter of where we were and in what form, not whether we were. It reassured me that all beings, living or dead, were equally real, could be felt, connected with, whether they were ascribed personhood or not.

The old ways offered an explanation as to why my family treated me as if I were not technically a person, not quite whole. Perhaps to them, since I'd never been properly named, I'd never been properly born. My given name—"peaceful one"—might have had a nice meaning, but it wasn't the correct one. The Ga traditions gave me hope that even if I was not whole, even if my name wasn't even Ga, I could still be real. That I still had the chance to be felt, cherished, even if only as a spirit temporarily passing through.

I had this impulse to dispense with the condolence card platitudes and instead say something about the Ga naming traditions. I was wanting, perhaps, to get at the bit about no one ever being lost or gone, just changing locations.

Tatiana spared me from making a possibly catastrophic faux pas in the realm of death-related social norms. She reached down into her purse and extracted a shiny rectangle of white paper with black typed print. She handed it to Sam. "Here."

Sam studied the paper. "Uh . . . Tati, are you sure?"

I leaned forward over the center console. It was a printed concert ticket. For the concert she told me about on our last call, I assumed. It should have seemed ludicrous that, this monumental tragedy barely a day passed, Tatiana still wanted to go to an event that she hadn't seemed that enthused about in the first place. Then again, it could be a chance to do something so loud, unfamiliar, and distracting she'd be unable to think about this Back Bay apartment and everything that had happened in it.

Now that we were outside, free from the stifling silence of B's brothers and stepfather, of B's emotionless gaze, of his mother's calculating one, I could better digest the unease I'd felt inside. It was the same unease I'd felt that third-grade spring when my mother, in one of her not-infrequent Moments, abruptly took Esther and me out of school and drove us from California to Baltimore to visit her father's grave. My mother never explained why we had to drive instead of fly. As we dipped through and across the South, she stopped several times on the side of the road to observe—and demand that we also observe—these creepy little wooden barns abandoned in the middle of dead cornfields. "Tobacco flats," Mom would say, her tone grave and wistful in a way only she could manage. We sat parked, for hours sometimes. On the drive to Maryland, we spent more time than I felt was necessary in Arkansas, where it seemed that every other driveway and church was decorated like a racist fever dream. Crosses and flags—those crisscrossed flags that said, "Get out." Boston was a different place with different problems, but B's house felt familiar all the same.

"I'm sure," Tatiana answered. "Why not? I'm not allowed to see my own daughter right now, so . . . what am I supposed to do? Go for a jog? Get an ice cream? Sit and bake in the sun while my thoughts try to eat me? No thanks."

The paper rested in Sam's open palm. "I don't know, Tati—it might seem . . ."

"What?" Tatiana released a caustic laugh. "Don't tell me you're on Brigitte's 'Tatiana's a shit mother' train. It might seem *what*?"

Sam handed Tatiana the ticket. "If you really want to go, we'll go. But I'm just a little bit worried about Brigitte's comments. I wonder if we should maybe be a little more careful. What do you think, Dzifa?"

I wasn't expecting her to ask. Tatiana, who possibly wasn't either, clicked her tongue and turned toward me, eyebrows raised. Like Sam, I thought, with a woman like Brigitte involved, going to a concert a day and a half after your son died looked bad. I thought, with a woman like

Brigitte involved, anything Tatiana did or did not do would look bad. I thought, if I were in Tatiana's shoes, I'd want to do anything to make myself forget what happened, what was happening. I thought that if the rigid display I'd witnessed inside B's house was the way his family grieved, then I didn't think they were in a position to judge. "I don't know." I shrugged. "It's not my call. I . . . do see how Brigitte could twist this into something it's not."

"Twist what?" Tatiana stuffed the ticket back into her bag and kicked it away from her. "I didn't do anything wrong. What—because I had a glass of wine? Don't be fooled by Brigitte's whole Puritan prairie wife act. If she wasn't a party girl, B wouldn't exist. Which, let's face it, would've done us all a favor." I offered a shrug in reply and, to some extent, apology for having offered my opinion.

"Nobody thinks you did anything wrong, Tati," Sam reassured her, reaching out to squeeze Tatiana's hand. "But we know Brigitte is . . . challenging. Just trying to save you the trouble of having to deal with more of her judgment."

Tatiana turned her face away, burying it in her hand again.

"Okay." Sam swallowed. "You know what? Let's do it. Brigitte doesn't have to know about this."

We dropped Tatiana at Paradise Rock Club. She climbed down from the front seat and lingered there, eyeing the band name on the large, black marquis, the door half-open. As she hesitated, dozens of concertgoers brushed past the car and toward the entrance, laughing raucously, seemingly already inebriated.

"You sure you want to go, Tati? We can still go back. Or somewhere else. Or you want us to wait for you here? We can park right nearby if you want, and then if you want to leave, you just call me and we'll come."

Tatiana blinked, her eyes now fixed on the car radio, which she'd fiddled with the whole way over, changing from one track to another, mostly songs from her curated list of international cool-girl tracks. "No." She shrugged. "I'm already here, so. I just can't be in my own head, you know?"

I said nothing. Sam flashed a sympathetic smile and nodded. "Yeah, I hear you, Tati. Okay. We'll just hang out near here anyway, 'kay? Your phone is charged, right?"

Tatiana didn't smile back. "Yeah. No, you don't need to hang out here. Just . . . I'll let you know when it's almost over." She had nearly closed the door but wedged a foot in it and pulled it back open, leaning forward to look at both of us. "Actually, can you guys get me something to drink?"

"Uh." I darted my eyes toward Sam. "Don't they have a bunch of drinks here?"

Sighing heavily, Tatiana shook her head. "No, like, for home. Can you guys just get me something from the liquor store? Like, get enough for the week."

Sam, who was still wearing her "everything will be fine" smile, let out a small, halting sound like she was going to speak and decided not to. Clearing her throat, she tried again. "Sweetie, are you sure that's a good idea? I know everything probably feels pretty raw right now, but—"

"Oh, you know how this feels?" Tatiana snapped. She slammed the door and stalked away.

"Okay, no problem!" Sam called after her. "Do you know what you—actually, don't worry about it, I'll text you!" Tatiana was lost in the crowd by then.

I never asked the questions I wanted answers to. I wanted to ask how exactly Luca died, and whether B and Tatiana still had sex, and why B showed up to the infirmary with bruises in high school, and who was going to plan the funeral.

I wasn't going to ask those questions. On our way to the liquor store, I tried a tactic I'd learned from women like Sam: I went around and under. "So . . . when did you get here?"

Sam turned down the radio. "Right away, of course."

"Of course," I echoed, matching the piousness of her tone as closely as I could manage.

"It was awful, as I'm sure you know." She glanced over at me, her blue eyes widening with every word. "I mean, I didn't even pack. I just got right in the car and I told Jon—that's my boyfriend, have you met him? Oh, of course not, you weren't at Luca's baby shower, or Maddie's . . . or at the NICU. I told him, 'Sweetie, I'm so sorry, but I have to go right now and I'm really not sure when I'll be back,' but he was so understanding. He loves Tatiana; like, we've all spent so much time together since before the kids were born. We haven't spent that much time with B, though. Every time we came, he was working or out with work friends, or with his mom. Their vibe is a little weird because they never really talk to each other, but also B barely ever talks at all."

"Oh." He did not seem particularly chatty at whatever that gathering was earlier. "So does he—"

"Sometimes," Sam continued as if I hadn't spoken—maybe I hadn't?—"I just can't even figure out what Tatiana saw in him. Like, she has a personality, and he . . . well, I just don't see it. People like that who refuse to open up—you really have to wonder what they're up to. I have a few theories, because I took psych in freshman year, so I'm really good at understanding people emotionally. You didn't take psych, did you? So informative. Anyway, Jon and I drive over all the time from Providence. Jon is such a good guy; he's a chiropractor, you know?"

She looked at me again. Her eyes narrowed, so I hazarded a smile. "Cool. I mean . . . I'm glad you were able to get here so quickly." I waited for whatever was next. Sam was the type, I was quickly discovering, to talk fast and often, whether or not anyone was listening to her.

Sam broke the silence I had just begun to enjoy. "I didn't realize you and Tati were still, like . . . close. I'm kinda surprised you're here, to be honest. Since you never met Luca."

I frowned, opened my mouth to respond, but she powered on. "But I get it, like . . . what happened to him is just . . . I can't even. I honestly still can't believe it. That was basically my nephew, you know? I can't believe it. Life is so cruel sometimes." Sam lifted a hand off the steering wheel and dabbed her knuckles beneath her eyes. "Oh, can you hand me a tissue? Right there in the center console."

I fumbled with the plastic black top of the center console. Finally, it snapped open. I spotted the full box of tissues, handed one to Sam.

"Thanks, girl," she said. I didn't enjoy white people calling me *girl*, *girlfriend, sis*, or any variation thereof, but given the circumstances, I'd let it slide.

"It's just so crazy." She wiped away her tears, blew her nose, held out the used tissue. I raised an eyebrow, reopened the console, and motioned for her to drop it in. "I mean, an innocent little baby." She glanced at me. "And there's something so weird about how everything went down, you know? Like, I know he wasn't the strongest, but still . . . he was doing okay, I thought. We all thought that. I don't know. What do you think?"

"Um . . ." I stalled. "I actually . . . I don't really know any of the details."

"Oh." Sam held a hand to her chest. "Well, there's just something weird to me about Brigitte. Like, she's so controlling. And she was the last one who saw him. And I don't know. I don't even know what I'm talking about."

My eyes narrowed; I took in her words. I was the last person to have outsize trust in hospitals—or in white women, for that matter—but infanticide, if that's what Sam was suggesting, seemed like a stretch. Not because I believed Brigitte incapable of it. I imagined, like most people who were that kind of Christian, she could justify any action she deemed righteous. But I couldn't imagine how or why it would benefit her to do so.

"Never mind. Forget I said that." Sam shook her head, then her shoulders, like her bold notion was crawling, possibly contagious. "This is okay, what we're doing, right?" Her hands tensed on the wheel. I arched my back in the leather passenger's seat; the resulting crack calmed me down.

"Um." I cracked my back again. "Maybe. I'm not sure, honestly . . . You should probably get off at the next exit." She turned her blinkers on and deftly switched lanes. When I changed lanes, I usually caused an incident.

A tight smile appeared, disappeared. "I see. Well. I'm not sure either." Her high-pitched voice was unsteady. "Like, alcoholism runs in my family, and I can tell you—seriously, *let me tell you*—alcoholics will find a way to drink, whether you bring the alcohol to them or not. They really will. Every time. And if they can't find it, they'll just start drinking mouthwash or something. So actually, it's better that she's not wandering around in her state, looking for a drink. We're probably actually helping her. I mean, she told me she just had a glass that night. Maybe two, max, and it doesn't matter anyway; she's not breastfeeding. So we're probably helping her."

I pulled my head to one side until I heard another crack. "Okay. So . . . okay. Are you saying . . ." Tatiana's request seemed reasonable enough to me, in a way. But I did think, as she walked toward that colorful throng of alt-rock enthusiasts at Paradise, about senior year at Elmwood. How twice, I'd escorted her to and from the emergency room. But that was college—occasional overindulgence was part of the learning curve. And any concern I held in New York, the handful of times she mentioned wanting to cut back, never stuck; Tatiana didn't actually drink more, quantity-wise, than most people I knew. In New York, you had to be a terrorist-level threat to humanity to be considered an alcoholic. Based on its reputation, I doubted Boston was any different.

When we got to the liquor store, we debated the merits of this pinot noir over that sauvignon blanc. I had no business pretending I knew anything about wine or attempting to give my input to someone who already knew everything there was to know about everything. But I said, "Yeah, that one looks nice," and "I think she likes merlot," and "Probably any of them is fine." Sam pretended to listen to my interjections as she waxed lyrical about cedar notes.

"Let's just get them all!" She handed me two bottles and skipped to the counter with two more. The total was over fifty dollars, which was approximately thirty dollars more than I was typically willing to spend on anything in one sitting. I considered my options: Sam had a car, a boyfriend, a dog, and a job teaching special needs children. I, being special needs myself, could not compete with these accomplishments. I insisted on paying for the drinks and watched the cashier stack them gently, side by side, in a brown paper bag. He slid open and squared up a plastic bag, then placed the heavy paper one inside of it; he said, "You have a nice night, now, ladies." I tasted bile in my throat.

On the way back to the venue, Sam turned down the music again. "Question for you," she began, and I worried that we were going to have another non-conversation about alcoholism or murder. "Do you have much experience with babies?"

Does it matter now? In my head, I chanted, *Don't say that, don't say that*, thinking of Maddie playing with the oversize book earlier. I tried to force a deep breath without audibly exhaling and choked. "I used to live with my nephews, um, at my sister's house."

"Oh." She sounded disappointed. "Well, I personally love babies. *Love* them. I can't remember if I told you, but I'm a teacher. Primary school. And my students are so troubled, you know? I work with inner-city kids, and most of them are really, really severely autistic. It's super tough."

I smiled at her, hoping she could see I didn't mean it. "I'll bet it's tough. Good for you. Such an important job."

She hummed her approval. "Well. It's what I went to school for. I mean, I didn't actually want to work with these kinds of kids, because it's so dangerous and they're always so difficult, but you don't really get a choice. You just get placed wherever." I would have liked to slap her. Instead, I retrieved my hands from beneath my thighs and dug my fingernails into my palms. "What is it that you do again?"

I should have opened the door and thrown myself out onto the highway, but there was too much traffic. "I work in marketing."

She gave me the same smile she probably gave her students when they managed to glue two pieces of paper together. "Oh, that's so interesting. I would love to work in the for-profit sector myself. It sounds so . . . fun. But I'm such a bleeding-heart, you know? And fortunately, I'm a hard worker, so I've already paid down my debt." It was a pleasure to work hard, I supposed, when you didn't have to work at all. That had to be why white-guilty trust fund kids like Sam fetishized grit the way they did. To them, it was a choice. A punishing yet completely voluntary exercise, like SoulCycle.

Grit was overrated, I felt, and I'd happily forfeit most of mine. "I actually work for a nonprofit." I regretted saying it. What was I trying to prove?

"Oh, how nice!" she cooed. "Though I'm surprised you're not, like . . . on Broadway or something. You were always so creative!" She wasn't wrong, but in college, my creativity felt less like a benign character trait and more like a dirty secret, no matter how public-facing it may have been. I choreographed with the desperate energy of a compulsion, and when I was finished, I could never stand to face what I'd made or see other people seeing me face it. "Why is that? I mean . . . like, what happened?" Sam followed up when I didn't respond.

"Nothing." I shrugged. "I'm living the dream."

We collected a frowning, disoriented Tatiana. On our drive back to the house, I learned the answers to most of the questions I didn't ask. Luca died in his sleep, sometime between when Brigitte fed him and when Tatiana woke up, B and Tatiana hadn't had sex since Luca was conceived, B's Stepfather Number One had Hulk-like tendencies, and nobody had said anything about planning the funeral. While I listened, hands clasped tightly in the back seat, I tried to imagine what it must have felt like, to pull your life apart to be a mother, to double down on your choice, and to wake up one morning with . . . this. Pushing my mind like I'd be tested on it later, I envisioned the apartment I'd now seen in person. I tried to reconstruct Luca's face, his eyes, which Tatiana said were just like his father's. But it was like I'd never seen him; blurred shapes moved sluggishly from room to room in my mind, never materializing the way I needed them to.

By the time we returned, B was sleeping—or at least, lying—in the bedroom, Maddie in her crib, the door closed. After checking on her daughter, Tatiana shuffled back out to the living room, closing the door behind her, and shook her shoulders as if to steel herself. Brigitte sat cross-legged on a makeshift sleeping pallet across the living room, just by the front door, mending one of Luca's old beanies. She'd kept a sublet nearby for the past year but didn't seem to have any intentions of going there tonight.

We opened the pinot noir in B's kitchenette and commenced a grief ritual more familiar to me than the tableau of civil stiffness B's relatives performed earlier that day. I recalled, as we watched Tatiana alternate between sipping, sobbing, laughing, and staring out into the abyss, the homegoing of my father's eldest brother. I was five then. I never forgot the sound—resonant, endless—of his wife, daughters, sisters, wailing. A show of respect, sanity. His brothers—my father included—and his sons held his coffin on their shoulders, carried him in open, straight-backed procession, letting the heft of his body be felt as everyone present co-signed, with prayer, song, untempered emotion, the release of his soul from it. The day's supplementary mourners—professionals, customary—held and amplified the frequency of familial sorrow.

In the years since, I'd wondered, as I scanned the dry and sterile California landscape, searching in vain for its graveyards and grief rituals, why death, in the West, was viewed as an aberration. A breach of contract. Were we, who descended from white people's idea of Elsewhere, primitive in our surrender to death? Was it civilized, really, to hold still and hold one's breath when devastation hit?

I doubted it, even as I sensed that the scene we played out was being willfully misunderstood by Brigitte. In each of Tatiana's shifts, from crying, to drinking, to cajoling me and Sam into reenacting our ballet warm-ups from college, to—at one point—singing the theme song from *The Last of the Mohicans* until we all broke down into laughter, then tears, I felt Brigitte's gaze: first watchful, then calculating, filling with something bright, something I worried was glee. I watched the judgment she bore with such pride crystallizing into something I feared we'd have to deal with long after tonight.

I said nothing. Didn't dare disrupt these proceedings that, however chaotic they may have appeared, I understood as rightful. Sacred. I channeled my five-year-old self—the good African daughter, the full-breathed mourner. I joined in the ritual, let myself be pulled in, carried with, as we did plié after plié, let ourselves laugh, let ourselves wail, let ourselves be witnessed: wild, lost, broken, inconsistent. Brigitte's eyes never left us.

CHAPTER 8

Falling asleep in places I wasn't comfortable was a skill I resented having learned. That night, once Tatiana got tired enough to attempt sleep, she suggested we all share the pullout couch. She and Sam were small enough to fit; I knew this wouldn't work for me. I shrugged off their protests and lay on the floor, instead, beside the couch.

"But you've traveled such a long way," Tatiana mumbled through a yawn, already drifting off on the mattress above.

"I like the floor, actually," I insisted. "I'm used to it."

This was true and not true: I was used to it. I didn't particularly like it, but I disliked it less than sharing a bed with anyone. Solitude signaled safety to my body in a way that even a softer plane than old hardwood couldn't manage. I'd felt alone all day but had been surrounded by people the entire time; tomorrow, I'd have to find an excuse to get some time to myself.

Brigitte lay still on the other end of the room; I did not believe her to be asleep. I felt confident, in fact, that as long as we were awake, she would be, too. I had no desire to call her bluff, lest I set off another argument.

I adjusted the thin fleece blanket underneath me and forced my eyes shut. I thought to count the seconds until I got sleepy enough to stop counting. I got to eighty and gave up, relented instead to tapping impatiently at the tightness in my chest. Couldn't say if I was trying to self-soothe or if I was trying to bore a hole through the layers of cloth, skin, and bone, till I got to the organ underneath, till I could see and contend with the guilt that had been growing in it since Luca died.

I slowed the pace of the tapping. Imagined the guilt a granary, full to the brim, spilling over, seeping between ventricles, seeping in or spilling out. Next, I imagined my heart the granary, the guilt buried inside a single grain. Eyes closed, I sifted through, picking out grain by grain, ascribing source-ness to each and every one, letting it go once I confirmed, *Not that one.*

Unlike Luca, I was lucky, I thought, and knew: This is the one—the grain that holds the guilt. Here I lay, a full-grown person who had, since childhood, contemplated un-aliveness constantly, compulsively, not wanting to think about it, unable to let go of the thoughts. Trying to calculate my worthiness of living, or—more likely—already having calculated myself as unworthy and trying, failing, to figure out the math. If I wasn't worthy, why was I still here?

My fingers stilled. This wasn't about worth at all; somewhere in me, I knew that, too. My longing for a reprieve from life had not disqualified me from nearly thirty years of it, just as Luca's infancy and innocence hadn't qualified him for more than three months. I let the grain of guilt slip back into place, lodge itself inside my heart, let it enmesh itself with the next caught breath. My hand slipped from my chest to the cold ground beside me.

At 4:00 A.M., my body relented to sleep. At 6:00, I woke to rustling in the kitchen. I pulled myself up; Tatiana and Sam were still asleep on the couch. Brigitte's sleeping pallet was neatly folded, and vacant. I retrieved my duffel bag and stopped by the bathroom, declining to shower in case it woke up the rest of the house. Absent the opportunity to wash without making a noise or a mess, I changed my clothes, brushed my teeth, aggressively deodorized.

I stepped out of the bathroom and into the kitchen. Brigitte was there, holding Maddie in her freckled arms, feeding her from a squat purple bottle. "Good morning," she said, nodding, eyes narrowed. I wondered if I'd already done something wrong; marveled at my productivity.

"Morning," I parroted back. "Um . . . I think I might go for a quick walk? If Tatiana wakes up while I'm out, would you mind letting her know I'll be right back?"

Brigitte pursed her lips. "Hm. Why is that?"

"I'm sorry?" I frowned.

"Why are you going for a walk?"

I looked at Maddie, who, occupied with her breakfast and also eleven months old, offered no explanation or suggestions. "Um," I hedged. "For . . . To experience the . . . outside? Is that okay? Or?"

Brigitte shrugged. "I just think it's interesting; that's all."

I struggled to think of anything less interesting than an adult person going for a walk in the morning, but different strokes for different folks. "Okay." I nodded, brows drawn together. "Um . . . can I get you anything while I'm out? Coffee? Or something?"

"Oh, I don't drink coffee." Brigitte shook her head. "Your friend drinks it like it's water." Brigitte met my eyes, an unkind little smile teasing at the corner of her mouth. "I was never like that. Well"—a frail shoulder ticked up—"I'll admit I was young, and learning on the go, with my first. I was practically a child myself. But with my second, I completely turned things around. Started eating clean, no caffeine, no alcohol, nothing processed, nothing addictive. Anything I put in my body, I knew I'd pass to my babies, so I was always very careful."

"Okay," I said, wondering if now was a socially appropriate time to exit this conversation and also this apartment.

"But by then, I'd enlisted," she continued. "And it completely changed me. I found a real family when I joined. People with actual values. Discipline. Responsibility. You know: American values."

"Well—" I tried very hard to keep my face neutral.

"I'm told," she interjected, "your family is from abroad?"

I pursed my lips. "Yep." She waited for me to continue. I didn't.

"Are you Christian, dear?" She followed up, glancing down at my bare arms, her eyes scanning the tattoos. I'd brought a sweater; though it was sweltering, I'd make sure to put it on before I met Tatiana's family.

"Well," I started again, then paused. What could I say, without lying, that would agitate her the least? "Actually," I changed tacks, "I did go to a Christian school growing up. Yeah, and our teachers kept telling us if we didn't accept Jesus as our Lord and Savior, we were all going to hell. They made it sound really scary, so I converted when I was, like, nine." I did not add that a few months later, at a daily chapel service, I spontaneously deprogrammed while singing, "You are the resurrection."

Brigitte's eyes narrowed further. "I see," she said.

I forced a smile. "Mm-hmm."

Brigitte removed the bottle from Maddie's grasp and set it on the counter. Maddie coughed; Brigitte rubbed her back until she settled.

"Okay." I took my chances with the pause in conversation. "I'm gonna head out. I will definitely *not* bring you a coffee, then, um . . . okay, be back soon."

Once outside, I allowed myself a half hour only. It wasn't enough to get a coffee myself. That was probably for the best; I wouldn't want to bring back a takeaway cup and trigger Brigitte into another breastfeeding sermon. Instead, I wandered the blocks surrounding B's apartment and tried not to get too lost. I paused at one point and found that grainy photo of B that Tatiana sent me years ago. I sent it to Zeynep with a cryptic: Random question: Do you recognize this person? Also hi—how's it going?

When I circled back to the block B's apartment was on, I backtracked a little and found a shady spot under a planted tree at the edge of the sidewalk. I wouldn't dare sit on somebody else's stoop; this seemed like the kind of neighborhood that absolutely called the cops on unknown Black people existing near their houses. The planter was a bit of a risky location, too, but I needed to sit, and it would only be for a few minutes.

I checked my phone again. There was a short text from Esther: You get there okay? I replied with a thumbs-up; she didn't enjoy extensive answers to her questions. Over the years, I'd learned that while she did not particularly like me, she was hugely preoccupied with the physical safety of her blood relatives. This meant she was prone to randomly checking, via curt texts like this, that I wasn't dead, but ignoring any further or more detailed communications from me. I studied her profile photo: She and her husband stood in their college sweatshirts, looking pleased, but not excessively so, at the edge of Lake Merritt. I grimaced, my eyes fixed on those sweatshirts as if the name printed on them rose from the fabric and reached out a taunting, wagging finger to remind me of my substandard track record as a sister.

—∞—

Esther did apply to Barnard, and she got in, as I'd known she would. I intercepted her acceptance letter and needled her with fantasies about her potential, near-future life in New York. When that failed to move her, I resorted to warnings about how Yale, while fancy, was located in Connecticut. Even in fifth grade, I recognized Connecticut as a suboptimal state to spend four years in. I was never sure if it was that or her own—albeit dwindling—hopes that did it. But somehow, she agreed that we'd try convincing Mom, to convince Dad, to let her go to New York.

We chose a rare evening when Mom was out of the house. Dad had just sent her money to upgrade our school uniforms; she'd gone for a massage. It was perfect; she'd be uncharacteristically relaxed and uncharacteristically available for the ambush we were planning. When Esther pulled up the PowerPoint we'd prepared on our dad's ever-sleeping desktop computer, I put the finishing touches on the poster board she'd asked me not to bring. As I traced a sweeping, pink, glitter-glue *R* around the end of Esther's name, Esther released an agitated sigh. "Dzifa, I thought we agreed: No poster. It's childish."

"It's glitter." I shrugged. "We're gonna need glitter."

"I cannot believe I let you convince me to do this. This is not going to work."

"Esther." I rolled my eyes. "Stop distracting me. You just make sure you didn't make any typos. Mom hates typos."

"I don't make typos," Esther snapped. "You make typos."

"No, I don't," I countered. "Mr. Barkley said I have 'exceptional vocabulary and superb spelling.' He said I'm 'hyperverbal' and could take a test that proves it. So."

She rolled her eyes. "Mr. Barkley is a creep. Stop talking to him outside of class. You are so naïve."

"Whatever." I shrugged. Esther usually wasn't this mean. She was never nice, in terms of her demeanor, but she was kind in terms of her actions. Like keeping me fed and taking me to school and sharing her money from Claire's with me so I could have doughnuts and In-N-Out burgers instead of expired tomato paste, which was all I would have had to eat without her help. I knew she was just being mean because she was nervous. It wasn't like my mother's meanness, which was more of a fixed personality trait and, possibly, a hobby.

Esther's presentation was thorough, but on the off chance that (or the glitter) didn't tip the scales, I was willing to resort to calling our father directly. I would do it for Esther, but only in case of emergency. Our father was personable enough, but talking to him felt like talking to a benign stranger, with the acute awkwardness of both of us knowing, as we strained to find anything to say to each other, that it really should not feel that way.

Esther and Mom were the only ones around whom I was discernibly myself. Around everyone else, I felt as if I'd been dropped onto Earth from another planet, programmed to think and speak in a language with incompatible characters and syntax.

Esther and I tensed at the slow, steady groan of the garage door opening. "It's showtime," I whispered, rubbing the tight spot on my chest.

"Why are you whispering?" A smile teased at the edges of Esther's bow-shaped lips. She erased it as quickly as it appeared, but I preened. She caught my triumph and glared. "This is a horrible idea. I truly don't know how I let you annoy me into doing this."

I thought about making a joke, playing my usual role of the pesky, inferior sister, saying, "Because it's fun being annoying." But I saw, when I panned the skin above Esther's eyebrows, a drawn-in tension in the middle and noted the stiff set of her typically lithe hands above the keyboard.

I reached out a glitter-glue-stained finger; she swatted my hand away before I could smooth out the tension between her brows. I collapsed my hand and haphazardly stuck six Chorus Line stickers around the perimeter. "Because," I said instead, "you're a good person. And a really good dancer. Mom and Dad already have their straight A, Perfect McPerfecton kids. And okay, maybe they're really good at math. Whatever. But they're not good. Not like you. Like, good on the inside. You have to do this."

I watched Esther squeeze her eyelids shut as moisture welled up in their corners. "You have to," I repeated for good measure, because this was probably the first and last time she'd let me get away with anything approaching earnestness. "If you don't try, I'm not gonna try. 'Kay?"

As Mom's footsteps approached, I dabbed the corner of Esther's still-shut eyelids and then gently, tenderly, poked her in the middle of the forehead. "Ta-da!" I cackled. Esther snapped her eyes open just as Mom swung open the pristine, white-painted door to our father's office. Esther wiped at her forehead, which only smudged the glitter farther.

"Dzifa, may I ask what the—" Mom stopped, taking in the PowerPoint pulled up on the computer screen, titled "Why Barnard," and the glittered, Chorus Line–stickered poster board that lay across my lap, the outer edges tipping down on either side. "I see." She nodded as if this were a scheduled board meeting. She pulled up a low-backed chair on the other side of the ample mahogany desk. I exhaled as much as my lower belly would allow.

—∾—

I knocked on B's door.

"Hey," Tatiana said, rubbing her eyes. "I'm so tired I can barely think straight. When did you get up? You can't have slept much either."

I followed her inside and sat in one of the folding chairs that was left in the living room the day before. Maddie played with her favorite book and a squiggly plush toy, where Brigitte's sleeping pallet was neatly folded. Tatiana leaned on the kitchen island. "Sam's in the bathroom, by the way," she said. "And you-know-who stepped out with B. While I would like to be optimistic, I am personally bracing for a fight. Even though I gave them *plenty* of space yesterday, when I really did not owe that to them."

"Yeah." I nodded. "I really hope they . . . I don't know. Not really sure what her deal is. Have you had a chance to talk to B?"

"About what?" she scoffed. I ran through the possibilities in my head: the funeral arrangements, the argument yesterday, some reassuring explanation of why we'd come back with wine, or, perhaps, why Mrs. Adams watched us like a hawk?

"Uh." I waved at Maddie, who held up her toy in my direction and laughed. "I don't know. Just like, how you want to handle things? Like with, um—"

Sam emerged from the bathroom in a fresh pair of clothes, her hair wrapped in a towel. Since she hadn't packed before she came here, the clothes must have been Tatiana's. Apparently, Sam did not suffer the same hesitations I did about guest etiquette. A moment later, B and Brigitte emerged from the back door, Brigitte eerily calm, B stiff and disengaged as ever.

Tatiana walked over to where Maddie played and sat beside her daughter. "So we're gonna head to my mom's now. All four of us."

"That's fine." B nodded.

Tatiana frowned. "I wasn't asking, but thanks." She paused to survey Brigitte's expression, perhaps waiting for her to interject. When Brigitte stayed silent, Tatiana continued, "So how do you want to do this? Did you want to come pick up Maddie tonight? Or . . ."

B approached; Brigitte stayed by the back door, hands clasped behind her. Tatiana tensed as he drew near. I couldn't decipher their dynamic. They didn't seem to like each other, and there was no discernible attraction between them. The way she'd deferred to his suggestion yesterday made me nervous, made me think about how he'd managed to change her position about staying in Dorchester, how our communication tapered off the longer she lived with him. How, though she was still Tatiana, the light she'd had in New York was noticeably dimmer since I last saw her. She looked softer, sadder, more adult. Could have been grief, could have just been time.

Despite her tension around B, there was an unspoken communication between them, a familiarity impervious to the fickleness of affection. Probably, it was something only a parent could understand.

B sat on the ground, on the other side of Maddie. Maddie turned to him and plopped the toy onto his lap. "I'll see you in a little bit, little bit." He drew her into his arms and hugged her, kissed her cheek. He then transferred her to Tatiana's arms and stood again. "I'll text you in an hour or so. It's been complicated with work. I have to figure out my time off."

"You don't get bereavement leave?" Sam asked, leaning against the kitchen island.

He shrugged. "Technically, yes. But this happened at a . . . complicated time." I wondered what would have constituted an uncomplicated time for this to happen. "In any case, once I'm able to sort that out, I'll reach out and we can talk about arrangements for the . . . arrangements."

"All right." Tatiana stood, too, struggling momentarily to right herself, given she still held Maddie. "Later, then. Just gonna collect a couple of things." She passed by the counter; Maddie waved at Sam, and Sam blew kisses back at her. Tatiana paused at the sink. The squat purple milk bottle bobbed in an empty yogurt tub filled with foamy water.

"What is that?" Tatiana looked at B first, then Brigitte.

Brigitte ambled forward. When she saw what Tatiana pointed to, she said, "Oh, that's Madeleine's bottle, dear. I fed her this morning, when you were sleeping."

Tatiana exhaled slowly, through her nose. "As I have told you many times, Brigitte, please *only* use the bottles I have supplied for you and which I have prepared myself."

"Oh, I'm sorry," Brigitte said, a palm to her heart. "I heard you, of course. It's just helpful to have some extras on hand. Rest assured: The ones I purchased are the very best."

"If you—" Tatiana started, her breathing getting louder by the second.

Brigitte held up a hand. "I really apologize, dear. I only meant to be helpful. Only the best for Madeleine, right?" She reached out to squeeze Maddie's hand. "And I thought I'd pitch in since you were indisposed yesterday evening."

Sam cleared her throat. "Tati? We should probably head. Traffic's gonna be a nightmare." Tatiana stepped back, eyes hard. She nodded, absently patting Maddie's hair.

"Okey dokey!" Brigitte stepped back. "Please give your mother our regards."

Tatiana spared B one last, inscrutable look. She retrieved a few of Maddie's things from the bedroom. We went on our way, out the back door this time.

CHAPTER 9

I used to think all Black families had the water rule, the one where if you didn't offer your guests a glass of water and a three-course meal the very instant they entered your house, you had indisputably been raised by wolves.

Tatiana's family wasn't like most of the Black families I knew. Her mother's people could've lived in a "shinier" neighborhood, Tatiana once shared, but held fast to the principle of investing in the community they were already in. As a result, Ms. Bishop came from money—cash on hand—she owned property outright, and no one had ever threatened her with foreclosure. Accordingly, everything in their house was uneven, from floorboards to furniture. The surfaces were visibly dusty, the space high-ceilinged and narrow-floored. And due to the inevitable gentrification, it was worth a fortune, though they'd never sell it.

The more familiar-to-me model were the families like mine—new-money Blacks who grew up under the weight of their parents' PTSD, the parents who as children dragged cloth dolls along neatly packed dirt floors and listened, very carefully, to their daily respectability lessons. It was these families, newly shiny and ever shame-ridden, who spent their children's college savings on mini-mansions and deep-cleaned their refrigerators every day. "What if white people see?" was their driving pathology, even as they lamented white people ever crossing the thresholds of their homes, which actually were not quite, not yet, not ever theirs. The disdain that Tatiana's family had for interior design almost certainly took more than one generation of capitalist approval to cultivate.

I wedged my bag in a grayish corner and turned to face the living room. Tatiana's mother was working on a crochet something on the couch, and two of her great-aunts, including the one I'd seen at B's house yesterday, sat in slouching, uneven armchairs, grimacing with their arms crossed. Sam and I found space at the other end of the couch. It was my first time meeting Ms. Bishop in person, though she looked exactly like the photos Tatiana shared over the years: She had the same voluminous cloud of curly black hair; assessing, though not unkind, eyes; and loose-fitting, colorful clothes. I always thought, when Tatiana shared those photos, that if I didn't know her mother had such an extensive corporate résumé, I'd have guessed she was an art teacher.

Tatiana paced around the room, filling her family in on the goings-on at B's place. Her arms flailed as she paced, her frustration and vitriol filling the room. It was the sanest thing I'd seen since I got here. "I just don't get it," she fumed. "I mean, he's always been a pushover with her, but, like, is he *kidding* letting her kick me out of my own house yesterday? And the things she was saying! Does she think I don't know what she was insinuating? It was bad enough dealing with him freaking out every time I had a glass of wine."

"Maybe he's blaming himself," I offered quietly, "and projecting his guilt onto you. I mean, he . . . he was out that night, right?" I silently congratulated myself on remembering this detail through my fatigue and jet lag, though I felt unsettled by the memory of B questioning me while Sam and Tatiana were in the kitchen.

"Yes." Tatiana nodded. "Yes—thank you! This is what I'm saying. He was gone the entire weekend! He left me alone with *that woman*, who clearly hates me and listens to absolutely nothing I ask her to do. Like, at a certain point—mind you, I've told B again and again I don't want her there—but at a certain point, I was just so f—I mean, I was so exhausted, I just relented. She'd practically moved in with us by the time . . ." She trailed off, froze mid-pace, then shook her head and kept moving. "I can't *believe* her."

"I hear you, Tati," an auntie affirmed. "We hear you, we love you, we are holding you in this. Know, my brave girl, that God is holding you in this, too. And"—she hesitated—"you will not want to hear this. But having lost a child myself . . ." She paused again, took a breath. "I'd be negligent if I didn't tell you: You need to do your best not to pay any mind to anybody who's not in your corner. You need to focus on doing everything you can to stay positive. For Maddie."

"Positive?" She clenched her fists. "Where are you seeing the *positive* in any of this?" She stormed out of the room and made her way up the creaking, narrow steps. A door slammed.

"Um . . . sorry," Sam broke the silence. She turned to the aunt who'd spoken. "I'm so sorry for your loss." Her blond hair was stringy and damp against her neck, from sweat or her shower earlier; I couldn't tell. I'd never heard her sound hesitant, but I'd also never seen her in a room full of Black people, so maybe that was what it took. "And, also . . . did . . . um . . . did you want some help with the funeral arrangements? Because . . . um . . . we are happy to help. Not happy, but . . . like. Yeah. Let us know."

Ms. Bishop smiled, but her eyes stayed on her hands, which looped fluidly above a large bundle of purple yarn. "Thank you, Samantha. That's kind of you. It's a little complicated, though. I've been told the Adams prefer cremation. That is not something we do in our family. So there will need to be a discussion."

Sam nodded and fixed her eyes on her demurely folded hands. She opened and closed her mouth three times. "Okay. I totally understand. Just, um . . . Tatiana had mentioned wanting to follow her spiritual traditions?" She blew out a breath. "I know some people in Boston who are affiliated with Tatiana's faith; we met last year when she brought me to a service. I'm sure they'd be happy to help. I can make a call if you want that. Just if you want."

Ms. Bishop's smile tightened. "Thank you, Samantha. That's very generous. As Tatiana has only been of that"—she paused and took a deep breath—"faith since last October, we will decide how best to proceed, for both of the families." I felt a little defensive on behalf of Tatiana but didn't have a right to be. She'd started taking classes in Esoteric Christianity in New York the summer before everything changed. At the time, I couldn't figure out how to convincingly feign understanding, and I was pretty sure the DUMBO-based spiritual center that hosted the classes was a cult. But she said she was just exploring, the same way she'd once explored Judaism (no tattoos), then Buddhism (too much stillness), then Islam (too much ritual), then Jainism (no mozzarella sticks). I'd always nodded along through each of these explorations, because I could see the allure of joining what seemed, at least from the outside, like a cohesive community.

Tatiana may have been leagues more social than I was in college and afterward, but we were both perpetual outsiders, never having found a space where we effortlessly fit. Not in that campus church with all its pious young Black women, not in the communities we grew up in, where our personalities, peculiarities, and dreams were deemed aberrant, and certainly not at work. But it took me weeks to work up the courage to ask her what I really wanted to know, which was whether she realized that joining any of these religions wouldn't guarantee an end to her otherness.

For any of us others, our best bet, I figured, was cobbling together a community of misfits rather than trying to plug ourselves into a preexisting group with rigid, long-standing guidelines. When I shared this, Tatiana looked at me with such wounded disappointment, as if I should have been the one person in the world who understood her quest for belonging. I never brought it up again. When she moved on from her foray into Jainism and, a year later, began waxing lyrical about her classes at the Divine Temple of Esoteric Christianity, I didn't comment, nor did I pry.

"Right. Of course. No worries. Of course." Sam brushed clammy hands on her jeans. We could hear each other's breathing in the silence that fell.

I cracked my knuckles a little too hard. "So sorry." Heads snapped toward me. "Do you happen to have any water?"

Two hours later, Tatiana came down from her room, her energy less frenetic but now almost scarily focused. Her aunts having returned home, it was just Ms. Bishop, Maddie, Sam, and me now. Sam played with Maddie on the far end of the couch. Ms. Bishop worked on her laptop. I stared at my phone, pretending to check messages.

When Tatiana entered but didn't speak, we all looked up. She held her phone in her hand, tight, like it was glued to her skin.

"How you holding up, sweetie?" Ms. Bishop asked.

"I need to get my stuff from B's house," she said flatly.

Ms. Bishop's eyebrows drew together. "Didn't you bring a couple of things for tonight?"

"No," Tatiana corrected. "I mean, I have to get *all* of my stuff."

"Sweetie, what is going on?" Ms. Bishop stood, setting her laptop down on the side table.

"I don't know." She shook her head. "I don't know." Her voice broke a little. "I just got a really weird call. From, like, the police or—"

"*Excuse* me?" Ms. Bishop interjected. "Let me see."

"Mom, just—"

"Let me see it." Ms. Bishop held out her hand.

Sighing, Tatiana surrendered her phone and stepped back, crossing her arms over her chest and plopping down into one of the armchairs opposite the couch. "Give me Maddie?" She nodded to Sam, who acquiesced, holding Maddie's hands up while the little girl took slow, wobbly steps across the uneven floorboards. Tatiana scooped her up, setting Maddie down in her lap.

Ms. Bishop examined the number on Tatiana's phone screen, then lifted her eyes to her daughter's. "Tell me exactly what the person said."

Tatiana swallowed. "It was a woman, I think. I can't remember the name now. I wasn't expecting it, so. She said her name was . . . Detective . . . like, somebody Stevens? Stephans? Something like that? And she just asked if I had a minute to talk, to get some final details on some paperwork related to Luca. I—" She looked down at Maddie, out the window, back at us. "I didn't know what to do. I just said now wasn't a good time, that I'd appreciate if she'd contact me later, or I could call her back."

"Did you say anything else?" Ms. Bishop's voice held steady, stern.

"No." She tugged at the ends of her braids.

"Are you sure?" Ms. Bishop followed up.

"Now *you're* interrogating me, too?" Maddie protested with an irritated murmur at her mother's volume. Tatiana lowered her voice. "No, that was it. That was it. She repeated her number, the same one on the caller ID, and that was it."

Ms. Bishop frowned. Sweeping an errant curl back from her forehead, she paused for a moment, then spoke again. "Portia Stevenson? Was that her name?"

Tatiana mirrored her mother's expression. "I . . . Maybe. I think so. Maybe. Wait, how do you know that?"

Ms. Bishop closed her eyes, took a deep inhale, exhaled slowly through her nose. "If it's who I think it is, she was at the hospital the night of—the night of. Do you remember? She took a statement from you? Brown skin? Chin-length hair?"

Tatiana shook her head. "I don't know. I don't know. Everyone took a statement from me that night. It—I don't know. It was—I couldn't focus on anything anybody was saying. I— "

"It's okay, Tati." Sam stood and placed her hand on Tatiana's shoulder, squeezing. "I can only imagine."

"It's no matter," Ms. Bishop said. "She was only there as standard procedure. That's the way it goes whenever . . ." She paused, set Tatiana's phone on the side table. "Well. That's just the way it goes. But this . . . I don't like this. Luca's cause of . . ." She shook her head. "It was clear. They said so at the hospital. I don't like this."

"Yeah, exactly." Tatiana tilted her eyes skyward. "That's why I said I need to get my things from B's. Obviously, this is his doing. Or more likely, *her* doing. I mean, why else would this be happening? I cannot stay there anymore. I cannot trust that woman. Not around me, definitely not around Maddie, not even around my stuff. I'm going." She stood and handed Maddie back to Sam. "I'll be quick."

"Oh no you don't," Ms. Bishop countered, eyes wide. "This is not a time for impulsiveness, my love."

"I'm not being impulsive." Tatiana's eyes narrowed. "I'm just—"

"My love." Ms. Bishop held a hand up. "I know you. You'll go over there, you'll tell that man exactly what is on your mind, and while I would not normally fault you for doing so, this is not a normal situation. Mm." She shook her head. "No. You're going to stay exactly where you are, and I'm going to make some calls."

I glanced at Sam. She stood between the armchair and couch, wringing her hands. I looked down at my own hands, clenched together so hard the knuckles were getting sore. Tatiana stared at her mother, her chest rising and falling with each heavy, audible breath, then stalked back up the stairs.

After half an hour—during which Tatiana paced outside with a cigarette and Sam and I scrambled after her, trying to get her to put it out—a tall, solemn man introduced as her uncle Aman pulled up in a spotless, olive-green sedan. He and Ms. Bishop spoke outside the front door. Ms. Bishop held Maddie in her arms. Tatiana, Sam, and I lingered at the edge of the cul-de-sac, pretending not to listen. Well—Sam and I pretended not to listen; Tatiana stood, stubbed-out cigarette peeking from under the sole of her sparkly Converse, glaring at her mother and uncle.

Uncle Aman was a well-respected audio engineer. In college, she'd described him as having been kind, quiet to the point she wondered if he *could* speak, and reliable when there was a problem with the house. He was not a blood relative of the Bishops but an old family friend who grew up on the same block as Ms. Bishop and her two older sisters. His family settled in Boston in the '60s, after what sounded like an arduous journey as Ethiopian immigrants. He lived fifteen minutes away in Milton now, and came by on occasion to visit Ms. Bishop and her sisters.

"I think we should give them a call," Ms. Bishop said, her expression stern. "To let them know you're going to stop by. We don't want to appear . . ." She sighed. "It's important we tread carefully."

Uncle Aman nodded. "Agreed. If they're okay with it, I can be back in a couple of hours with Tatiana's belongings."

"*Or*," Tatiana interjected, kicking the cigarette butt away as she stalked to face her uncle. "I can go with you. Like I said, it's *my* stuff. And it's my apartment, by the way."

Uncle Aman looked at Ms. Bishop, then at his niece. "Your name is not on the lease," he said quietly, as if in apology, though what he said was true.

Her glare intensified. "Regardless, that is my children's—" She swallowed. "That is their home. And," she continued, before Ms. Bishop could chime in, "you don't even know what I have in there. Brigitte could be rifling through my things as we speak. I'm allowed to go inside my own home, whenever I want."

"You must listen, Tatiana." Uncle Aman kept his voice level. Tatiana pressed her lips together; I wondered if she was literally biting her tongue. "If you go inside that apartment, you could jeopardize an already delicate situation. You cannot let your emotions get the best of you."

Sam fidgeted beside me; I was frozen, my hands clenched to the point of numbness behind my back.

Tatiana turned to face us. "This is ridiculous. You guys, you *know* I have to go. All of Maddie's things, Luca's, everything is in there!" She stalked toward Uncle Aman's car, opened the driver's-side door, and got in.

I didn't feel my own feet move, not until they ground to a halt beside the open window, and my hand reached out to stall Tatiana's wrist as she turned on the engine. "For fuck's sake, Tatiana—stop it!"

Sam's mouth dropped open. Ms. Bishop and Uncle Aman drew back. Maddie swatted Ms. Bishop's collarbone. I blinked, wide-eyed, just as startled by my own movement, the volume of my own voice, as everybody else was.

"*Language*," Sam whispered, darting her eyes toward Ms. Bishop as she rushed to stand beside me.

Tatiana removed my hand from her wrist and gave me a look I'd only rarely seen slip behind her trademark smirks. Sharp and gaunt, her eyes narrowed and drained of their usual spark.

"Sorry." I swallowed. "Sorry. It's just—they're right. That call you got . . . you have to be really, really careful." When she snapped her head toward me, I held my hands up. "You didn't do anything wrong. We *know* you didn't. But B's family might think that you did. Brigitte is . . ."

I recalled the intensity of her gaze, that pious sneer as she waxed lyrical about her all-American values. "You can't go."

Uncle Aman cleared his throat, regarding me with an indecipherable gaze. He opened the driver's-side door and waited for Tatiana to step out. "I will go and collect your things, and you will stay here with your friends."

Elbow on the front console, Tatiana leaned her head into her hand, which I saw now was dry, the skin on the surface pulling off into gray flakes. "This is ridiculous," she muttered. "You are all treating me like I'm a child. I'm a mother. I'm their *mother*."

"Yes, my love." Ms. Bishop stepped forward to guide her daughter, gently by the elbow, out of the car, still holding Maddie against her chest. "And that's why everything you do now is very important." Tatiana shrugged out of her mother's grasp and strode down the block, drawing a fresh cigarette from her pocket.

Once Uncle Aman returned, a mismatched assortment of bags in tow, he and Ms. Bishop spoke in hushed tones in the kitchen. In the living room, Tatiana fed Maddie. When Ms. Bishop came back in, Uncle Aman headed out with a solemn wave and muttered, "Take care, girls."

Ms. Bishop squeezed her daughter's shoulder and sat on the couch. "I'm proud of you, sweetie. For not going to B's." Tatiana's only response was a deep sigh.

"Aman also filled me in," Ms. Bishop continued, "that B suggested we take the helm with the funeral arrangements. In addition"—she narrowed her eyes at her daughter—"he shared that comments were made regarding your attendance at a concert, Tatiana, as well as your alcohol use."

Tatiana protested; Ms. Bishop continued.

"This is a lot more serious than we anticipated. I've already reached out to a colleague from my old firm. She mentioned it will be important to preserve the appearance of cordiality and collaboration with the Adams, to prevent things from escalating further. That said, if you will agree to it, Tatiana, as much as it pains me, will you consider the cremation? Since the Adams have allowed us to plan the funeral, this would be a meaningful gesture. The hospital has finally cleared us to retrieve the . . . to collect . . . to bring Luca home. We could do so as early as tomorrow."

Tatiana looked at each of us—Sam, me, then Maddie—perhaps waiting for any of us to come to her defense, but Sam stared at the floor, eyebrows scrunched together. I chewed my bottom lip. Maddie played the drums on her favorite book. Tatiana shook her head, opened her mouth, closed it. Let out a brief, caustic laugh. "I need some air," she said. She retrieved her bag from its spot beside the front door and walked out.

She came back an hour later, smelling of smoke, and retreated to her room. On the way in, she ignored Sam's half-whispered, "Hey! Wanna vent? We can just listen!" Unease sank deeper with each passing hour B didn't call or make an appearance, as he'd suggested he would that morning. We took shifts with Maddie so everyone could get at least a little bit of sleep.

At two, Sam woke me from the living room couch and handed me Maddie. She had to leave for Providence before dawn, to get back to work. As Ms. Bishop escorted her to the front door, Sam promised to be in touch to help plan the funeral and to come back on the day.

Presumably, I'd have to get back to work soon, too. I told my supervisor I'd be gone a couple of days, but at the time, I had no idea what I was walking into. I held my breath and brought Maddie's head to my shoulder, cradling her with one arm, then the other just to be safe. I ascended the stairs one at a time, pausing and inhaling sharply after each one. In the nursery, I sank down into a rocking chair and let my breath out.

Later, I jolted awake and looked down at my stiff, numb arms. I was still holding Maddie. Panicked, I tried to listen for her heartbeat, but my own was blocking out the sound.

The nursery door squeaked open. I forced a smile.

"You know you don't have to hold her all night, right? She's getting way too big for that anyway." Ms. Bishop leaned against the doorless frame. She wore loose black sweatpants and a long-sleeved T-shirt.

"Sorry. Um, Tatiana said . . ."

"Tatiana is in shock," Ms. Bishop said. "Maddie's a good sleeper, and she's going to be fine. You just put her in the crib and you can go to sleep." The corner of her mouth lifted.

"Oh. Well, okay." I shrugged.

"Mm-hmm. I'll take it from here." She took Maddie, who stirred and whimpered, and she whispered, "*Shh*," as she transferred her to the crib.

I walked down the stairs and put the kettle on to boil.

CHAPTER 10

We left at nine that morning; Tatiana wanted to get Luca's remains as soon as possible. "I don't want him to be alone," she said as we set off for the suburban crematorium. Ms. Bishop offered to work from home so she could watch Maddie and watch out for a visit from B.

We stood in the parking lot, leaned against Tatiana's massive SUV. I snuck a glance at the entrance to the building. I must have been to a place like this before, but I couldn't remember. "People die in threes," I recalled my mother saying when she lost her father. She didn't say it with any kind of grief, just as though it was a fact that everybody knew. I took her word for it at the time; we had gone to three funerals that year. In retrospect, it was clear that people died all the time.

In any case, a building in which the bodies of your loved ones got incinerated really needed a waiting room. I imagined a tastefully lit foyer with cream walls and inspirational quotes. Maybe a watercooler on the side, with those paper cones they used as cups at tennis courts. As a kid,

I stood by those coolers on summer days, letting the wet paper linger on my tongue as ice-cold water trickled down my throat. I felt the water run all the way through me, wincing while I watched lanky boys I'd never know saunter across the court. Tennis was one of the activities my mother enrolled me in, in the hopes that either her class aspirations or my potential as an African child of good repute would take. Unlike the team sports my father commanded, via phone, that I attempt, in which I inevitably ended up crying and confused in the middle of a crowded field or court while my classmates yelled at me to move, I was naturally gifted at tennis. It was straightforward enough, and there were typically only two people involved, my preferred maximum number of people in any social situation.

Unfortunately for both my parents, once I figured out I was good at it, I threw almost every match. Winning made me feel exposed, out of sync with what I'd already internalized as my more natural state of disappointing ineptitude. I may have had the talent to win, but unlike the Tatianas of the world, I lacked the disposition to enjoy it.

The door creaked open; we snapped our heads up at the same time. A formally dressed man approached us.

"Yes?" Tatiana looked at his empty hands and let out a breath.

"It will be a few more minutes. We are almost . . . uh . . . finished."

I stared at him with wide eyes. Had he never received any training in bedside manner? "Fine, fine, just—that's fine. Thanks, bye." I nodded too many times and waved my hand to dismiss him.

He nodded back and said, "Sorry about that. Thanks for your patience." He walked back through the door.

"For fuck's sake," Tatiana bit out.

I reached a hand out, drew it back, then finally placed it on her forearm. Such gestures weren't really part of our friendship, but desperate times. "It's going to be okay," I lied.

"Thank you," she mumbled, adjusting her sunglasses and rolling her shoulders back. "I'm really glad you're here." Her voice wavered. "Thank you for being here."

"Of course."

"I'm . . ." She broke off, shifting one riding boot over the other, scraping the gravel as she went. "I didn't want this for Luca. I wanted him to be buried. He deserved to be . . . whole."

"I'm sorry." I squeezed my hand where it rested on her arm. "This is . . . this is really the worst. The absolute worst. And you don't deserve it. Nobody does."

The door opened again; the man returned, this time with an object in hand. My throat dried up; I kept my hand on Tatiana's arm.

"I'm so sorry for your loss." He nodded so deeply it could have been a bow, then handed over a bag—small, crisp, white—the type of bag you might gleefully swing from one hand after a Sunday visit to a luxury cosmetics store. I wondered where he kept them, if there was a stockroom adjacent to the furnace where a high stack of bags just like this fought their way out of industrial-grade plastic wrap.

Tatiana's hands hovered low, too low to grab the handles; I feared for a moment that the ashes would fall. He saw her struggling and gently placed it in her shaking hands. When he walked away, she finally broke.

She'd cried yesterday, but not like this. As she sank to the ground, I wrapped my arms all the way around her. I couldn't think of a worse job than crematorium director—except, apparently, mother.

For the first few minutes, we both stayed silent, crouched to the ground. When she could take full breaths again through the deluge of tears, Tatiana looked up at me. "I will never sleep again," she said. "Not really. When my eyes are open, I see him. When my eyes are closed, I see him. And I feel it, all over again. I knew it, as soon as I woke up. Even before I saw how still he was, I knew it. I wanted to convince myself I was wrong, that he was sleeping. But I knew it. And I can never unsee it. Not awake, not asleep. Not ever."

There were no words for me to say; I knew this, knew that even my earlier "Sorry" was inane and unhelpful. That to say anything at all now would belittle the weight of something unspeakable.

She stayed on the ground for another ten minutes, wiping away tears that seemed unending, even after the active sobbing had stopped; I checked my watch. We had an hour to get from the suburbs to the city center if we were to make it to the appointment Sam had set up at Tatiana's church. I braced my hands on my knees to stand, then moved them to the top of my skirt. "Come on," I said, pulling her up as gently as I could. "I'll drive."

I was a terrible driver and failed the test four times before passing by the skin of my teeth. Tatiana knew this about me, though she was the opposite. This time, she let me get in the driver's seat of her shiny black SUV. B got it last year, but unlike his apartment, they were both on this lease. I hit a few wrong buttons before I found the right one. The seat moved back a foot, and I stretched out my legs.

"Just a minute." Tatiana grazed a shaking hand over her face. She brushed away tears, and I realized she wasn't wearing any makeup, that the last time I'd seen her do so was the last time I'd seen her in person, a year and a half ago.

"That's okay." I checked my phone for the time again. We needed to go, but I let the car idle in the parking lot for another ten minutes.

Tatiana looked out the window and said, "Okay."

During my shift that night, I sat in the tiny nursery, rocking Maddie back and forth. I'd put her in the crib like Ms. Bishop suggested, but she'd woken and started crying. Now she faded in and out of sleep, resting against my chest, in between my folded arm and my chin. If she fell asleep or I did by accident, I tried to pause my racing heart to listen for hers.

I hadn't slept properly since before Elmwood, so I was used to the jittery mania fatigue gave me. I never told Tatiana the whole story, but I was sure she'd pieced it together from the fragmented anecdotes I shared about my mother, the pain of them masked by my joking tone but potentially still obvious to her. She was smarter than me, sharper than me, always had been.

I trusted her intelligence, even as I struggled to reconcile her religious choices. At least, after today's visit to her church, I was more confused than skeptical. Based on the name, I'd envisioned a building of palatial proportions, flanked by Greek columns and marble statues of biblical figures, floor-to-ceiling stained glass windows, and gold filigree all over the place. When we entered the nondescript, brick-and-concrete building, I realized my imagining of it must have been some sort of daymare fusing a Mormon temple and the Parthenon. The Divine Temple of Esoteric Christianity was structured more like a conference center than a church, and the room being prepared for the service was mostly bare: no wooden pews or giant statues of Christ on the cross, hair tousled, blood dripping down his six-pack.

I felt ashamed as I walked through the carpeted room, grazed my fingers across the books on the two massive bookcases against opposite walls, full of texts of spiritual inquiry from faiths around the world. I didn't, I was realizing, even know what Esoteric Christianity was.

Maddie stirred, babbling, "Ama, Ama." I stood from the rocking chair and did a lazy two-step until she fell back asleep.

My throat dry and aching, I cleared it as quietly as I could manage. It didn't help. The door creaked when I pushed it with my free hand. I paused, checking Maddie's face. Still asleep, still breathing. I edged my way out of the nursery and started down the uneven wooden steps.

"Shit!" I tripped on the second-to-last step and righted myself, holding my breath. Maddie's breath hitched, then resumed its normal rhythm.

"Can you be more careful with my daughter?" a low, terse voice spoke from the living room. I yelped, shuffling back against the staircase.

The fluorescent lights flickered on; B stood in a dust-caked corner of the living room, wearing sweats and a scowl. When I saw him before, I'd thought his hair was the same texture as mine and Tatiana's. Now that he was right in front of me, I noticed a layer of short, thin black strands looping sideways across his scalp, rather than zigzagging up and away from it.

"Jesus, what are you doing here?!" I secured my hands around Maddie, planting my feet at the foot of the stairwell and shifting from side to side unevenly. The wooden ceiling creaked above me. I ballet-walked to the edge of the living room.

"I have a key. What are *you* doing here?" He gathered the blankets in one fist and tossed them onto the long, patched-up couch. "I thought you lived in California."

I was too confused to muster up any vitriol. He *just* saw me the other day. We *just* had this same conversation. "Uh . . . yeah. Yes. I do. I flew here. On JetBlue. I was at your house yesterday morning? And the day before? We spoke?"

He raised an eyebrow. "The flight must have been expensive for you." What did he think he knew about me, if he didn't even know me?

Maddie twisted against my chest, making a noise I couldn't decipher. I pulled her up higher, her head farther over my shoulder, just in case. I didn't want her looking for food that wasn't there. "Sorry, did Ms. Bishop let you in?"

"Look. Remind me of your name? I'm afraid I can't remember how it's pronounced."

I frowned. Zeynep and I had arranged to speak the next day, so I still wasn't sure he was who I thought he was. If he was that same person, did he not remember me either? Maybe I should keep it that way. "It's . . . that's fine. You can just call me Mercy."

"Mercy? Hm. That's not what I remember." He reached out to stroke the side of Maddie's face. "In any case, I know you've known Tatiana for a long time. I don't know what stories she's invented about me, but I'm a nice guy, okay?"

I refrained from twisting away from him and running back up the stairs, holding on to Maddie for dear life. In my mind's eye and in the most horrifying nightly news stories, the Venn diagram of men who self-identified as nice and men who lost their shit, wrote a manifesto, and committed large-scale femicide had way more overlap than I was comfortable with. "I just want to hold my daughter. Look: She's starting to fuss. I'll hold her for a little while; you go back to sleep. You must be so tired."

I was exhausted to the point of incoherence, but refused to admit it. I secured my hold around Maddie. "No, I'm fine. I had . . . coffee. Earlier. So. Sorry, should you be here right now?"

"Yes." He nodded. "I should be where my daughter is. My mother didn't want me to—never mind." He shook his head. "I just wanted to see her."

This isn't my place. This isn't my place. This isn't my place. I couldn't help myself. "Then why didn't you show up yesterday? Tatiana wasn't stopping you."

He swallowed and looked down at his plain black socks. "You don't understand," he mumbled.

"I understand that you and your family have not been particularly kind to her. I understand that." I kept my voice low, level, trying not to disturb Maddie.

He looked up. His lips lifted in a brief smirk, then returned to neutral. "Well, since you know Tatiana so well, 'Mercy' "—he raised a hand to put air quotes around my name—"do you imagine she was kind to me and my family? Hm? I'm sure you know by now she's not shy about her opinions, no matter how uninformed or inappropriate they are." He narrowed his eyes. "Do you think I don't catch all her snide little 'tragic mulatto' comments?" I tried to conceal my wince. "Or how she calls my family 'backwater WASP wannabes'? You think that's kind?"

My arms strained with the effort to keep holding Maddie. I shifted on my feet and pulled her up a little higher. "Just, please stop . . . whatever you and your mom are up to. This is . . . The Bishops do not deserve this. Your daughter does not deserve this."

B took a decisive step toward me, lifted Maddie from my arms, and sidestepped my attempt to gently retrieve her. She woke up with the movement and began to squirm and whimper. "My daughter deserves a responsible parent," he said, low and quiet. "Ask yourself honestly if you think she's capable of that." Maddie's cries escalated. An upstairs door creaked. We looked toward the staircase.

"Tati?" Ms. Bishop's even voice called down from the top of the stairs. I planted my feet hips-width apart like I was prepping for a workout. Typically, my closed expression and naturally frowning lips were enough to keep people I didn't know away from me.

I stared at a freckle underneath B's left eye as the steady sound of her footsteps got closer. His down-turned eyes were bloodshot and vacant.

"What are you doing in my house?" Ms. Bishop stepped into the living room and crossed her arms over the thick brown robe that was tied securely over her high-necked pajamas.

"Kalisa—" B shifted his face from me to her, the light coming back to his eyes as the sides of his thin lips released their tension. "I just wanted to see my daughter." He held Maddie closer to him. I wondered, as if it was the most pressing issue, if Ms. Bishop had given him permission to call her by her first name. Under no circumstances would my mother, or any other Black mother I knew, permit that kind of behavior, and I couldn't see Ms. Bishop being an exception. "Can I please just spend a little more time with her?"

"How did you get in my house?" She held out her arms for Maddie.

He sighed and moved toward Ms. Bishop, handing her the baby with unmasked reticence. He kissed the back of Maddie's head before letting her go and stepping back.

"Tatiana gave me a key a while back. Please, I can stay here and watch her tonight. Or I could take her with me. Just until the funeral." B smiled and took two steps forward.

"Get out of my house." Ms. Bishop said it slow and steady, bouncing Maddie lightly with little *shh*s between each bounce. Maddie started to cry, balled fists kneading at her half-open eyes.

"Maddie?" Tatiana bounded down the stairs.

"Kalisa—" B held steady in his supplication. "Madeleine is my daughter. I just want to spend some time with her, okay? I'm sorry I couldn't make it yesterday."

Tatiana muttered something, many things, her volume increasing as she reached the landing and took in B's outstretched hands, her mother's guarded stance, my usual cowering in the corner.

Ms. Bishop handed Maddie to Tatiana. "Go back upstairs. You both go back upstairs. Now."

Tatiana's eyes were narrowed and sharp. I laid two shaking hands on her back and steered her up the stairs. Maddie cradled in her arms, Tatiana turned back every two steps and glared, hissing, "I hope he dies in a fire."

"Ookaaay," I sang back.

We paused on the last few steps.

"Tell me what's going on or I'm going back down there and I'm gonna fight him myself." Tatiana cut her eyes toward the living room.

"Uh." I sighed, turning to go back down the stairs, then swiveling my head back up, grimacing at Tatiana. "I don't really think it's my place to—"

"Get the *hell* out of my house. Now. And don't forget to leave the key." Ms. Bishop's voice rang out loud and high.

Tatiana and I jolted at the slam and echo of the front door.

I skittered down the stairs, tripping again on the second to last step and righting myself with a grimace. There was a divot in the wood, I now saw. For the first time, I wished Sam were still here. Ms. Bishop was standing in the same spot, arms crossed, as though that voice hadn't come from her. Headlights beamed through the sheer curtains, and a car's roaring engine sent me back against the wall, hands braced to either side.

"Are you okay?" I didn't know why I whispered it.

Ms. Bishop's shoulders lifted, paused for three seconds, lowered. "Would you girls like some tea?" she asked.

We stared at the table while the water boiled. I checked my phone for the time. It was 1:00 A.M. I didn't know what to say, so I said nothing. If Sam were here, she would have said something. Tatiana stepped out to use the toilet, handing Maddie to Ms. Bishop without a word. I wondered if I would ever have that caliber of nonverbal communication with my mother. I wondered if she would ever help me raise a child I hadn't originally meant to have. Probably not, given that she hadn't been that keen on raising me.

Ms. Bishop opened a sticky cabinet door, still cradling Maddie in her other arm. "Let's see what we have. Chamomile? Orange . . . orange ginger. Come here, sweetie: Pick out what you want." The folding chair creaked and tipped precariously when I stood. I surveyed the stacks of open tea boxes, looking for the one that was least empty. Green tea with honey. I didn't like green tea, and caffeine at this time of night was a bad idea. I pulled a bag out. "Which one would you like?"

Tatiana bounded in. "Green teaaa, please!" She laughed. It wasn't gleeful; it was uneven, giddy, and I knew she had to be battling an inhuman level of fatigue. "Unless you've got any wine."

"Tatiana, there will be no alcohol in this house." Ms. Bishop narrowed her eyes at her daughter, pouring hot water into three mugs. I avoided eye contact with them both. She handed Maddie back to Tatiana. "And put her to bed. You don't need to hold her all the time. Or let me be more clear: *I* don't want to hold her all the time. I don't like missing this much sleep."

Tatiana sat down, singing a made-up tune. "Mm-hmm, thanks, Mama."

I tore open the paper flaps and stuck one tea bag in each cup.

Ms. Bishop and I both sighed as we sat. I probably could have asked to step away to a pharmacy to try to get an emergency supply of medication, but it never felt like the right moment.

"Tati, I just don't think this is healthy," Ms. Bishop continued. "Sleep is very important. And you need to get Maddie back on a routine."

She rolled her eyes. "Don't you think these are kind of like extenuating circumstances? Also, you said you would help me."

Bobbing the tea bag up and down slowly, I closed my eyes for a moment and tried to block out the image of the full-force slap I imagined I would receive if I ever said that to either of my parents.

"I'm helping you by keeping my job and my sanity. Can you help *me* with that? Speaking of which, it might be a good time to start applying for jobs. That'll look good with everything we're dealing with now. Will your old job take you back?"

The tea was still too hot; I brought it to my lips anyway and grimaced as the mossy liquid scalded the roof of my mouth. I choked, spewing more than a few drops of hot tea on the back of my hand.

Tatiana reached out and patted me on the back. "You okay, sis?" She laughed.

"Yep. I'm fine, thanks."

Ms. Bishop raised her eyebrows. "You need to wait for that to cool."

"Right, thank you."

She played with the string of her tea bag. "How are things going with your job, sweetie? Tati told me about your job in San Francisco."

"Yes, it's um . . . it's a job." Usually, I lied with a barely convincing half smile and said, "I love it. It's so nice to work for people who care," or something comparably meaningless and false, but doing so felt corrosive in this context.

"Boy, do I know what you mean." Ms. Bishop looked down at her cup.

"Mommy is the hardest-working person I've ever met. She's only ever taken one vacation, and that was only because *I* paid for it." Tatiana twisted in her seat to face me. "That's where I get it from." She circled a hand around her smiling face.

"Well, you're not working at all at the moment, sweetie, so I'm not sure what you mean." She said it gently, in her measured way. I supposed she was one of the few people who could get away with such directness where Tatiana was concerned.

"Um, helloooo. I made two whole humans, okay? That *is* work. And I wasn't expecting . . . this. To happen." Her angled eyes widened at *this*.

"Nobody could, lovely. But this is why I have always wanted you to always be as prepared as you can be. You should not have quit your job."

While I agreed, since I'd quit far too many jobs at exactly the time I most needed the money, I was in no position to judge. It seemed like Tatiana was feigning relief when she said she quit, but sometimes I wondered if she really was relieved. If maybe she'd been looking for an out for a while. Not consciously, but consistently enough that the desire seeped into her subconscious, affecting split-second, life-altering decisions, like the ones that brought Maddie, then Luca, into the world.

"Okay! I mean, what's done is done, so." She shrugged. "Haters gonna hate." She winked at me. Maddie started pressing her tiny palm against her mother's chest. Tatiana stood and opened a cabinet on the other side of the kitchen. "Where's the formula?"

Ms. Bishop pointed at the next row of cabinets. Tatiana pulled out an empty bottle, a giant canister of powdered formula, and a blue plastic scoop. She filled the kettle with water again. "What are you guys gonna wear tomorrow?"

Ms. Bishop looked heavenward. "Black?"

CHAPTER 11

I stood in the back of the carpeted gathering room of the church, where the nondenominational—or was it interfaith?—service was to take place. Though Tatiana had attended this church many times, it was Sam who organized the service, coordinating via phone with the head reverend, some contacts from a local synagogue, about a dozen congregants from Ms. Bishop's Baptist church, and Uncle Aman's mother, who was active in the local Beta Israel community and offered to supply the food after the service.

Two young men, one pale, wearing a yarmulke, the other brown, with shoulder-length locs, dragged low, metal chairs into two sets of rows. A middle-aged woman with freckled skin, a chic bob, and low heels, who Tatiana explained was Sam's rabbi, instructed the young men on the placement of chairs. A young Japanese woman, who Sam explained was Tatiana's pastor, examined a sheet of paper beside the podium at the front of the room. She looked to be eight or nine months pregnant. While this was undoubtedly good for her, I wondered if it would heighten the anguish of the day, somehow.

I longed to make myself welcome even though I wasn't sure if I was, in this space or with the people who occupied it. I hadn't been to church since Elmwood. Not only was I afraid I'd open my mouth and accidentally say something sacrilegious—uncomfortable on any occasion but probably unforgivable at your best friend's child's funeral—I didn't fully trust my imperfect science of discerning which kinds of non-Black people were the most invested in their anti-Blackness.

"Okay, I don't know where Tatiana is." Sam strode up to me, wringing her hands. She wore an A-line skirt and blouse; both were black and patterned. "And I'm not sure how else to be helpful? I mean, the celebrant from the Esoteric Church is here, and—oh." She nodded toward the entrance, where a swatch of black-attired white people stood, assessing the seating options with unmasked confusion. I couldn't blame them, really. I wasn't sure about the funeral etiquette here either. Was there assigned seating? Was it like a wedding, where B's people sat on one side and Tatiana's on the other? "I'm gonna guess those are B's people, soo . . . looks like everyone's guests are accounted for. And my friend—the rabbi? She actually graduated from Elmwood way back. Anyway, she did an amazing job getting everything together, so yeah. I don't know what else to do."

"You and me both." I shrugged, leaning back against the wall.

She sighed as she joined me. "Yeah, and I talked to my mom this morning. About"—she dropped her voice to a whisper—"the detective. Tatiana asked me to." She preened a little, or maybe I imagined it. "I'm sure she's told you, my mom is a really good lawyer, and she has a bunch of contacts who deal with this type of thing, so she poked around a little to try to help us figure out what B's whole angle might be."

"Oh? And?" I was dying to know but fought to keep all traces of eagerness from my voice.

"And . . . look, my mom is not prone to hyperbole. The exact words she used were 'Make sure your friend has an excellent attorney; she's gonna need it.' So, if she says we should be worried, we should be worried. Mom went to Harvard *and* Yale. Wait, you never said what your mother does? What does she do?"

I coughed over a surprised laugh. Did she ever give herself whiplash? "No, I didn't," I said. "Although, she certainly didn't go to Harvard *and* Yale." She stayed at Harvard for all three of her degrees, and met my father during a fellowship at Oxford. "So, what exactly does your mom mean by 'we should be worried'?"

Sam squeezed her hands together, eyebrows furrowed. "She said, if it really was the Adams who got the detective to start asking Tatiana questions—and who else would do that? It's—she said we shouldn't assume it's purely reactive. As in maybe they were planning something like this before . . ." Sam dropped her hands to her side and looked around the church. "Well, before. In any case, she agreed with Ms. Bishop's call to reach out to a lawyer. And said the Bishops should cease all nonessential contact with the Adams, like, stat."

"Yeah . . ." I digested her words. "Yeah, that makes sense. But, like . . ." I scanned the room, fixating on a lone piece of lint on the ground in front of me. "I don't know. I just . . . Why? Like, what would be their endgame?"

Sam shrugged. "Your guess is as good as mine." I doubt she believed that; I hardly did, even if any number of guesses were floating around in my brain. While it was clear B had a genuine connection to his daughter and a genuine distrust of Tatiana, it didn't really seem like he was the one pulling the strings. Was this just the way some people responded to shock? Or were they, as Sam's mother had suggested, somehow not shocked at all?

My calves ached, and I realized how long we'd been standing.

"God, it's been a strange day. Strange week. I mean, not that strange, I guess. You have no idea how many times I've had to support friends through stuff like this."

"Stuff like . . . what exactly?" I looked at my shoes. I'd only brought one pair and had to borrow this loose black ensemble from Tatiana's mother. We didn't wear black in my family, not for funerals. On my father's side, elaborate burials were the tradition. On my mother's, we cremated everybody and threw them into the sea. My mother expressed how unsettling she found this—"as if we're throwing ourselves right back into the Middle Passage." She used to shake her head when yet another relative's preference for cremation was revealed in their will. Either way, on either side of my family, we wore white or bright colors.

"Just, you know, having to scramble and figure out how to protect yourself—or your friends—because a man suddenly starts acting mental. Being a woman is so intense."

I found that tapping one toe and then the other was a good way to avoid eye contact. "That it is."

Sam's eyes darted toward me. "Huh . . . It kinda surprises me you'd agree. You seem so . . . you know. Like, are you a Pisces? You seem like a Pisces."

The laugh that came out of me was as caustic as I wanted it to be. "Well, you don't really know me, so. Anyway, I need to . . . Do you know where the bathroom is?" I walked away.

When I came back, Ms. Bishop and Sam were huddled close together. "Is everything okay?"

Ms. Bishop turned away from Sam. "No one has seen Tatiana. I'm going to look for her down the hall. Can you girls come and find me if you see her? She was supposed to write something, and the pastor—your friend who helped organize this, Sam? She was asking if it's ready. We're going to start soon."

"Rabbi." Sam cocked her head to the side and smiled.

"Excuse me?" Ms. Bishop mirrored the movement.

"Oh!" Sam pulled her back off the wall and pushed her hands to the side. "I just meant . . . my friend is not a pastor, she's a rabbi." She looked nervous but kept talking anyway. "I just know how grateful Tatiana was to be able to incorporate so many of the traditions she holds dear, and since my friend is technically associated with a synagogue rather than a church, the terminology is—"

"Let me know if you find her." Ms. Bishop nodded curtly, strode out of the room.

We looked outside, inside, and down the street. After circling the building a second time, we found her sitting with her knees folded into her arms underneath a concrete patio just outside the side exit, smoking. She stared at a damp note card, tears streaming down her eyes and streaking the top of her tea-length black dress.

"Tatiii," Sam groaned, rushing to meet Tatiana. "Are you okay? Everyone is looking for you!" She enveloped her in both arms. "Also, I'm so sorry, but you can't smoke here. There's a sign, see?"

I walked slowly down a ramp attached to the patio and stood apart from them. I tried to stick my hands in my pockets, but there weren't any on this skirt. So, I crossed them behind my back. It hurt, and I kept them there. "Um, do you have . . . whatever you were supposed to write?"

Tatiana left the cigarette in her mouth and flapped the note card in both hands. It was one of those lined, rectangular ones we used to buy for school projects. Her elegant, looped handwriting was scrawled all over it in black pen, with thick slashes across several lines. "I can't do this."

"Can I see? Maybe we can help?" Sam squeezed her shoulders. She took the card from Tatiana's extended hand, read it, then handed it to me without looking at me.

"It's gorgeous." Sam moved to face Tatiana. "You have nothing to worry about. These are beautiful things to say about Luca. I mean, the line about his name is a little shady, but I don't blame you."

I kept scanning until I found the lines she referenced.

> *Luca means "bringer of light" in Italian. And though not everybody accepted the name I gave him...some people thought it was "culturally misaligned"...When I saw him for the first time, I immediately knew who he was.*

This was clearly a dig at B, who had only reluctantly agreed to the name Maddie and who thought Luca sounded too white. He thought Tatiana acted too white, too, even though he was only half-Black and all his known relatives were Tea Party fanatics.

"I need mine to be better than his," Tatiana said. I was startled but kept my mouth shut. "I need that," she repeated. Her tears had stopped, were drying.

"Well, it will be. I mean, he may be rich, but he's really not that smart," Sam reassured her. The two women stood, Sam supporting Tatiana, and the latter stamped out her cigarette on the pavement.

The room was full when we got back. More of B's people had arrived, and for whatever reason, the median height of his friends was about seven foot zero. I wanted to ask Tatiana why, but she was already seated in the front row, watching the reverend celebrant examine her note card. Maybe they were his colleagues at the wealth management firm he worked for. I stood two yards from a group of tall men and gaped.

"It's starting," Ms. Bishop whispered to me and Sam. Though the crowd still chatted in a low rumble, she shuffled to the front like she'd interrupted something. Sam and I sat in row three, in the two seats nearest the wall. Uncle Aman sat farther down the row, next to two older women in long skirts, their hair covered in simple cloth wraps. I sat as I always did with this many people around: legs pressed together and tilted to the right, back contracted until the middle of my spine bruised the plastic of the chair, chin down as far as I could without losing my sight line. It was a sorry attempt at hiding, but the habit was so long-standing, I didn't bother trying to relinquish it. Now I hid in the third row when a dark part of me wanted to have been invited to the first.

When the service was over, the two young men who set up the chairs took them away. Everyone else milled about the foyer as the repast was set up. Ms. Bishop held Tatiana tight, rocking her side to side as Uncle Aman took a phone call.

"Do you think I won?" I heard Tatiana whisper. Her mother rocked her silently.

My tears had stopped and so had Sam's, but she hugged me twice in a five-minute span. Both times, my arms were stiff at my sides. I chewed on my bottom lip and waited for it to end.

Tatiana's cousin Sarai came over to pay her respects, her inquisitive ten-year-old daughter in tow. Sarai had a pierced nose and wore a long, white scarf loosely draped over her curls. Before heading out, she asked Tatiana, "You want to step out for a quick—" She extended her right hand and mimed bringing a cigarette to her lips. "I have a couple minutes, then I gotta get back." Her Boston accent was the thickest I'd heard in Tatiana's family so far.

Tatiana blew out a breath and glanced at Ms. Bishop. "I wish," she said. "But I'm being . . . watched."

"Gotcha." Sarai winked. "Tell you what." She reached into her giant leather purse and extracted a miniature bottle of gin. "I don't know if you're supposed to give a gift at a funeral, but hey: If you need this sort of thing on any occasion, I figure it'd be this one." She handed it to Tatiana.

Sam, eyes wide, snatched it from Tatiana's hand and tucked it behind her back, then dropped it in her small black cross-body. "Um! We should not . . . have that . . . here. Sorry. Sorry."

Sarai narrowed her eyes at Sam, then smirked at Tatiana. "What's with your friend? She thirsty or something?"

"It's a long story." Tatiana rolled her eyes. "I'll catch you up later. It's . . . been a lot."

"I'll bet." Sarai nodded. "All right, I'm out. You hang in there, sweetie, okay? You and Mads are gonna be okay."

Her daughter looked up at her and asked, "Mommy, is that juice? Can I have some juice?"

Sarai laughed. As she walked away, she said, "Not that kinda juice, honey. I'll get you a smoothie in a few."

I turned my head back toward the crowd and caught B's youngest brother watching Sarai's exit. Hopefully, he hadn't seen the whole interaction.

Small, round tables covered in white cloth dotted the room when we walked back in. Two rectangular tables leaned against the back wall. They held pitchers of water, neat rows of soda, two large charcuterie platters, and four trays of hot food. Because of the arrangements Sam had made, Tatiana didn't have to pay for the service. I wondered who had paid for the reception.

Sam and I sat at a table with the same two aunties I'd met at Tatiana's house. I should have asked, again, for their names, as no formal introductions had been made that day. Instead, I pulled out my phone and pressed and held the power button. I saw Sam do the same beside me.

I excused myself to use the bathroom. On the way back, I lingered by one of the wall-to-wall bookshelves. The books were sectioned by theme and labeled neatly. My scanning stopped when I reached a shelf with a printed label above it: *Mythology*. Just underneath the label was a book called *The Descent of Persephone.* "Oh, Lord." I didn't mean to say that aloud—in a church, no less—but recalled as I did the psychic Tatiana dragged me to in New York, what she said to me just as we were leaving. Though I'd rolled my eyes at the time, when I got home that night, I did a five-minute Google search of the Persephone myth. Then I rolled my eyes again, unclear what the myth, or Greek mythology in general, had to do with me, my life, my people, or, as the psychic had decreed it, my "unwellness." I hadn't thought about it again until now.

"You can take it," a friendly, familiar voice said beside me. I turned. It was the celebrant who'd led the service.

"Oh. Um . . . no, sorry. I couldn't. I was just about to sit down and—"

"That's a really good one." She smiled. "In fact, I just reread it. Needed some reinforcement before I go through this again." She patted her large belly.

I didn't mean to frown, but I did.

She shrugged, her smile lingering. "Yeah, I know it's kinda strange. But hey, motherhood is . . . well." She looked around the room. "Reading about a descent into the underworld really puts things into perspective. I mean, it's a weighty myth, depending on how you read it. I prefer to read it as a story about the power of surrender. Figuring out how to choose what was chosen for you. Something powerful about that." She tapped the spine of the book, then folded her hands together. "Are you a fan of Persephone?"

I shook my head, tucked my hands behind my back. "Mm—not really. I don't . . . It's just something somebody mentioned to me, a long time ago. And I saw the title, so—"

"Well, maybe it's a sign." She raised an eyebrow. I didn't believe in signs, but I offered a polite smile. "Seriously, you can take the book. I won't call the cops on you." She winked. "We have a 'take a book when you need it, leave one when you get the chance' policy around here."

"I'll . . . think about it." I nodded. I wouldn't. "Thank you. Um." I shuffled back to my table with an awkward wave. Safely slid back into my seat, I busied myself with pressing random buttons on my phone and getting up to pile cheese and crackers onto little paper side plates. I drank two cans of Coke, which had always tasted like battery acid to me, and looked down at my phone. There were eight text notifications—all from Zeynep.

Hey! So so sorry I flaked on the phone call.

Things are hectic here with freelance stuff, and my partner keeps having meltdowns and then I keep having meltdowns and then, etc.

(We really need to work on better coordinating our meltdowns.)

Thx for sending the update about the whole funeral situation--r u ok? That all sounds super intense.

BTW I got the photo and YES. YES. THAT IS TOTALLY HIM. THE DAY STUDENT FROM THE INFIRMARY. OH MY GOD.

What are the chances?????? Tell me EVERYTHING.

But also take care, that seems like a really really stressful scary situation

Ok my partner and the doggo are currently having a standoff, gotta go KEEP ME POSTED

"Hey . . . Mercy . . . You want to hold Maddie for a sec?"

I looked up. Sam wasn't in her seat; the aunties waved and smiled at Maddie. B held Maddie out to me, and I could see it wasn't a question. I didn't like doing unfamiliar things in public. The transfer of Maddie from his arms to mine wasn't graceful. For several seconds, my forearms brushed the stiff fabric of his jacket. I thought, *If I were him, I would be sweating.* But he looked like he just came from a business-themed stock photo shoot. His eyes stayed on mine as I pulled Maddie closer. "You're good with her," he said, nodding. His smile then dropped like it had never been there. He said, "I'm going to head out now," and walked away. Across the room, two of his enormous friends gave him dour bro hugs. He indulged them, crossed over to his mother, said something brief, and stalked out of the room.

I blinked at Maddie. She blinked at me. "Hi," I said dumbly. The aunties laughed.

Tatiana crossed from the opposite corner, bounding toward Maddie with her arms stretched wide. "My baby! Come here, little." I repeated the same awkward motion in reverse, standing halfway and reaching forward to transfer Maddie to my friend. Tatiana lifted her all the way up, grinning from ear to ear, then dropped her back down. "Thank you for being here, Mads. Thank you, thank you. Your brother loves you. Your mommy loves you."

"That's very nice." An auntie nodded her approval.

Tatiana patted Maddie on the back. "And your daddy is an asshole, but we don't talk about hiiim," she sang in a whisper.

"Tatiana!" Ms. Bishop clicked her tongue. She rubbed a hand across her short, straightened bob. "Control yourself."

Tatiana shrugged, smiling at Maddie but gazing toward the exit B had just walked out of. "What? I call it like I see it."

Behind us, Uncle Aman slid his phone back in his pocket and strode toward us. "Time to go." He'd picked us up from Dorchester in the morning, so he was our ride back, too. "You girls have everything you need? Where is the other one? The, uh, the white one."

"Oh my God, Uncle, her name is Sam." Tatiana pointed back to the foyer, where Sam was chatting with the rabbi. By all accounts, Uncle Aman was a detail-oriented man. I had to imagine his lapse had more to do with his alleged Black Panther ideologies than his memory.

"Well, we need to go." Uncle Aman stepped in closer and lowered his voice. "I have some errands to run related to the, uh . . . something your mother asked me to do. That her lawyer friend asked her to do. It's already getting on three. I'll drop you off first and make my way across town. I'll give you a moment to say your goodbyes to, uh . . ." He trailed off.

Tatiana rolled her eyes. "Brigitte?" Her uncle shrugged and left the room. Tatiana handed Maddie to Ms. Bishop. I was beginning to feel like we'd all been signed up for a high-stakes game of hot potato. Did this child have a stroller?

Sam frowned and made her way toward us as we approached a cluster of people giving their condolences to Brigitte.

"Everything okay?" Tatiana checked in, and Sam nodded.

"Of course. I was just thanking my friend. You know, for helping get everything together so quickly. This was a very nice service." But as Tatiana and I stepped forward, Sam reached out her hand and placed it on Tatiana's forearm. "Tati?" Sam spoke under her breath, releasing her hand and tugging on a strand of hair. "I spoke with my mom. About the . . . well, everything that's going on. I hope that's still okay? You know she'll be totally discreet. Anyway, so—"

"Just one second, okay? Gotta get this over with." The cluster of people dispersed, leaving only Brigitte. Tatiana cleared her throat. "Brigitte? We're going to head back home. Just wanted to say goodbye." She said it in her work voice.

Brigitte turned and folded her hands in front of her. "Of course." Her smile was tight. "I imagine you're tired. I know I am, though I have to say I found the service quite moving, despite the . . . untraditional setting." Her smile widened into something politely feral. "And what a flavorful selection of refreshments. May I say goodbye to Maddie?"

Tatiana bit down on her bottom lip and cocked her head toward Ms. Bishop, who paused a beat too long before approaching with Maddie. But she refused to let go.

Brigitte blinked twice, laughed a little, and reached out to stroke Maddie's face. "See you soon, little one." She laughed again. "You know, it is so interesting."

"What is?" Tatiana, Sam, and Ms. Bishop asked, nearly in unison. Tatiana snorted; her mother elbowed her in the side.

"Luca was just so fair. His skin was angelic . . . and those beautiful eyes . . . Madeleine looks so much more like your family, Tatiana. But you just never know how these things will work out." Her eyes panned Tatiana's body, starting from her black ballet flats, landing on the exposed roots underneath her box braids.

"Okay, goodbye!" Tatiana stepped back.

Brigitte removed her hand from Maddie's face and laid those long, thin fingers on Tatiana's bare forearm. "Oh, and, dear? Your eulogy was so beautiful. It reminded me that we all want the same thing for Madeleine." Her smile was somehow even wider, wider than faux-WASP protocol demanded, and her eyes gleamed like she'd won the lottery.

"And what is that?" Ms. Bishop raised an eyebrow, half turned away from Brigitte.

"Oh, I just mean we all want the best for her, don't we?" Brigitte winked at Maddie.

Sam, Tatiana, Ms. Bishop, and I exchanged closed glances.

In the middle of rush hour, it took fifty minutes to get back to Dorchester. Tatiana's friends and relatives posed themselves around the lower level; the space somehow seemed bigger than it had when we'd left in the morning. Sam carried her weekend bag upstairs, and Ms. Bishop went to take a shower. Uncle Aman was out running his errands. Tatiana stood in front of the mantelpiece holding Maddie; her eyes, vacant, were fixed on the urn. They'd chosen one in a terra-cotta hue, small and squat.

I slunk into the kitchen and stood by the tea cabinet for the better part of an hour. When mourners passed through, I raised an unsteady palm to greet them. "Oh, are you Tatiana's friend?" they inquired. "I heard you came all the way from California."

"Of course," I said with a forced smile.

I eyed the refrigerator with a longing that startled me. I wanted to open it and pull out whatever was cooled inside and slide it through my parched lips. I wanted a scalding bowl of instant macaroni, or a roast chicken stuffed with cheese, or a cauldron of spicy chili, or anything else I could eat or crawl into.

"I'm so tired." Sam sidestepped past me and flipped on the kettle. She whispered it as though fatigue was some taboo in grieving spaces. Maybe it was.

"Me, too," I said at a normal volume.

"Want some tea?" It wasn't food, but it was something. "Or coffee? I forgot there was a coffee maker."

"Coffee sounds good. I can make it if you want?"

"No, no." She flipped off the kettle and filled the carafe with water. "I got it."

"Thanks." I pressed myself farther into the cabinet.

She frowned. "You're not gonna sit down? I thought you were tired."

"Oh, no, I sit all the time for work, so I don't mind standing." The first part was true, the second part not so much. It would have been prudent, after the second-longest four days of my life, to sit or recline whenever logistically possible.

"Seriously, sit. You've been so helpful to Tatiana this week."

"Right. Uh . . . you, too, I mean." I pulled a folding chair into position. Its metal legs screeched against the Formica. I squeezed into it, too close to the table, and folded my arms across my chest.

Sam prepared the coffee, pressed On, and slid into an open chair across from me. She leaned back with one leg stretched in front of her. "Hey, I was thinking about what happened earlier. About . . ." She leaned in and whispered. "Brigitte. What she said about Maddie's skin."

"Oh?"

"Yeah." Sam screwed up her face. I wondered if she was angry or confused. "I just . . . It's crazy to me that anyone could be so blatantly . . . like . . . like . . . you know."

I kept my face frozen. Any expression I made would have been mean. "Mm-hmm."

"I mean . . . what do you think about it? Like, have you gone through that kind of thing?"

I wanted to say, *What thing? Being impregnated by a possible droid who was raised by possible Klan members?* I cleared my throat. "I guess."

She leaned back again, raking a hand through her hair. "Wow. But not in college, right?"

"Um, yes, in college."

"Oh." Sam frowned. "Can you give me an example?"

"What do you mean?" I frowned back.

"I mean, like, an example of the racism."

It exhausted me, more than most things, this impulse inside of white people to demand proof of the things they did every single day. "I don't know. I'd rather not get into the specifics. It's just like . . . you were always hyper visible when it'd be safer to blend in, you were invisible when it mattered to be seen. Being a Black girl at schools like that—you couldn't, like, relax. Let loose. You always had to be . . . on guard." I attempted a touch of diplomacy. "I'm sure everybody's different, but it seemed like white girls there kinda had free rein."

She darted her eyes from one side of the room to the other. "But Tatiana was so popular. And, like, weren't you in pretty much every single showcase? Like, I don't know if you know this, but everyone called you 'dance girl.' "

I bit my bottom lip and winced. "You know? It's not really important. So. Yeah."

"Oh my God, no!" Coffee dripped behind us, so slowly I wanted to scream. "I really want to understand."

"Mm-hmm." I tilted my head to one side. No crack, unfortunately. "Well, it's not easy to explain. It's just something you know. You don't want it to be like that. You try to convince yourself it isn't. But when it's like that, you can feel it. It's not usually as obvious as it is with Brigitte. Sometimes it's unspoken. Sometimes it is spoken and it's not mean, it's just . . . annoying. Distracting." *Like, say, the conversation we had when we met*, I didn't say. *Or the conversation we're having right now*, I didn't say either.

"Yeah, I guess." She shrugged. "But Elmwood is such a liberal school? And, like, there are so many Jews there. We fought for you guys in the Civil Rights Movement, so . . . it's just hard for me to imagine, I guess."

"Well, anti-Blackness isn't happening to you. I guess that's why you even have to imagine it." My voice was escalating; I pulled it down. "And for sure, Jewish people can be allies. Jewish people can also be white. So."

She pulled her head back. "I find that a little offensive and also not entirely accurate. I mean, I get that you and I don't look the same. But nobody has been through what we have. Some of us may have success, but that isn't the same as privilege, you know?" I bit my tongue, stared down at the table. She continued, shaking her head. "Like, our parents raise us to be hard workers, to push through some seriously shitty circumstances, and then we're demonized, basically for surviving, when people keep literally trying to kill us."

A bead of sweat trickled down into an eye. I winced and pressed on my closed eyelid repeatedly until the sting was bearable. "Right, well. I'm sorry. Those are seriously shitty circumstances." I poked at my eyelid again. "For the record, though, Black parents also raise their children to be hard workers; it's just that—"

"I do get where you're coming from, Dzifa. I really do. I don't know if Tatiana told you, but my parents were not the most attentive growing up, so I was basically raised by a Black woman. She was our housekeeper, technically, but she was basically family."

I may have been jumping to conclusions, but stories that started this way typically ended with some version of the proud declaration, "And that's why I alone am so comfortable around Black people!" I reached up a hand to nudge my head to the side. My neck strained but didn't crack. "Op, the coffee's ready! I'll get it."

"No, it's not. There's still like three minutes."

"Oh, okay, I'll put it back after I grab a cup. Sorry. Just really need caffeine." I tilted the nearly half-full carafe into a small ceramic mug. Brown-black liquid sloshed onto the counter, little drops of it falling to the base of the coffee machine. I didn't like coffee without milk. I kept it black and carried the mug to the table with both hands.

"If this is too hard for you to talk about, I get it. I just thought it was something we had in common. It sounds like we've both faced adversity."

I looked into my mug. "Of course. Yeah, happy to talk about anything. I'm sorry . . . for everything you've had to deal with." And I was. Well, I was sorry she lived under the constant threat of anti-Semitic violence, and slightly less sorry that her parents' neglect had necessitated familial proximity to a Black woman she seemed convinced was a close family friend and not an employee.

"Ladies." Ms. Bishop wore a change of clothes. Same muted color and modest cut as the last set. "We're about to say goodbye to our guests. Family can stay. And you two, of course! Aman's mother is bringing some food, so we'll all eat soon. If I can figure out how to make this table bigger."

We shook hands with mourners as they departed. Tatiana stayed by the mantelpiece, staring at Luca's urn, which was now surrounded by vases of flowers. When all but the aunties had left, we scattered around the living and dining rooms. The dining room contained one small table, a lopsided desk, and piles and piles of papers. Ms. Bishop muttered to herself while she cleared them away.

"Tati, have you thought about maybe getting some of your church friends to come visit? It might be good to have some friends check in on you in the next few weeks. Spirituality is so important in times like these." Sam pulled her legs against her chest. Tatiana finally took a seat on the edge of a threadbare couch, her arms still wrapped tight around Maddie.

"That sounds nice." She shrugged. "I just don't know how practical it is." She threw a glance at her aunties, who had occupied themselves by examining their fingernails and picking at stray pieces of lint on the furniture.

The door creaked open. Uncle Aman entered and spoke in a clipped tone, adjusting his earpiece with one hand while he balanced four rectangular aluminum trays in the other. "My mother gave me the food because she's tied up, but she'll come tomorrow." He extended the trays to Ms. Bishop and returned to his phone. She nodded and carried the trays into the dining room, spreading them out evenly and folding back their tops. The condensation from inside dripped onto the old, white tablecloth, and the scent of cardamom, garlic, and pepper drifted into the living room. As Ms. Bishop removed the lids, I let my eyes drink in the spiced lamb, goat stew, the tightly packed rolls of fresh injera. I sat in a folding chair in the corner of the room and tucked my hands underneath my thighs, eyeing the pitcher of water across from me. Tatiana spun Maddie in the opposite corner; Maddie squealed.

"All right, everybody, let's eat."

I lingered in the kitchen after everyone else went to bed. My limbs felt leaden, and I had a headache, though at least the persistent hunger had finally abated.

I lay my head upon the slightly sticky kitchen table, a lukewarm cup of peppermint tea beside me.

"You all right, hon?" I looked up. Ms. Bishop stood in the doorway, her hands in the pockets of her sweatpants. She'd removed the tasteful makeup she wore at the funeral. She looked younger in her pajamas, more relaxed.

"Oh yes, thank you. I'm fine, just—"

"Overwhelmed?" I shrugged and she smiled a little. "Yeah, I am, too. Although," she added, "Aman really came through with the food today. And that's not nothing. He's a good egg, that one." Ms. Bishop sat across from me. I noticed, for the first time, a narrow, lopsided ledge with a few mismatched photo frames resting on it.

Ms. Bishop followed my gaze and plucked one of the frames off the ledge, setting it in front of me. "That's Aman right there." She pointed to a younger version of Tatiana's uncle, tall and just as stern as he was now, standing with a younger girl who looked related to him—who looked uncannily like Sarai, actually—and Ms. Bishop in what looked to be her early twenties. She was beaming, her hair in a perfectly coiffed Afro. She stood, one hand on her hip, the other holding what looked like a diploma, in a paisley wrap dress. "He and his sisters grew up right down the block. Good family. They weren't Christian, but my parents cared about character as much as they cared about their faith. They trusted his family."

I looked more closely at the photo. In particular, at Uncle Aman and his sister, their striking bone structure. I frowned.

A smile lingering on her lips, Ms. Bishop looked up at me and chuckled. "Before you ask the question I can see you want to ask, I'd like to share another one with you."

I flushed, glad she was focused on retrieving the next frame rather than my embarrassment at having such transparent thoughts. This photo was larger, newer, though it had clearly been handled quite a bit, as the edges were faded and there were spots of discoloration peppered all over it. Still, I could see nine or ten smiling people—eleven, if you counted the slightly older version of Uncle Aman, who was still not smiling but looked, at least, relaxed. They were seated in a park with yellowing grass. Ms. Bishop wasn't in the photo—perhaps she was the one to take it. In the center was a five-year-old Tatiana, beaming from ear to ear, her arms extended wide, her legs crisscrossed beneath her, with a McDonald's Happy Meal bag resting on her lap, a half-eaten french fry dangling from her mouth. Around her, the smiling faces, all different ages, sizes, genders, shades of brown, enraptured with her joy.

"You know, Dzifa," Ms. Bishop explained as I stared at the photo, "I've always felt that the families we make are far more vital to who we are than the ones we're born into. If we're lucky, there's overlap. I was lucky that way. But sometimes we aren't." I swallowed, dropping my eyes to the table as she continued. "Either way, if there was nothing else I wanted to teach my daughter, it was that every single person in her life, who raised her with me, chose to be there. Nobody was there because they *had* to be, or because we were blood related, or because the law said so. We were all there because we chose to be. Tatiana was chosen, wanted, and loved by every single person in that photo."

My eyes filled with tears. I blinked to keep them at bay.

She continued. "I took a lot of flak at my church for the choice I made. But I know I've done right by God, because I know I've done right by my daughter. She's her own person, as you know, but she is loved. *That's* what a child needs. Not the picture-perfect picket fence." She laughed and gestured around the kitchen. "Which . . . as you can probably see, home improvement has never really been one of my priorities, so if I even had a fence, it would've fallen apart by now in any case." I reciprocated her laughter with an awkward, and hopefully not judgmental, half smile. "No," she added. "Children just need to know they've been chosen, and they need to know they're loved. That's it." She reached out and placed her hand on top of mine. "I appreciate you being one of the people who has chosen to love her, to raise her up with the rest of us. I'll never forget that."

I blinked, fast, but the tears escaped my eyes before I could stop them. I wiped them away with my free hand, which was shaking. I wouldn't have asked that question she was alluding to anyway, but now I could see that even if I had, the answer wouldn't have mattered. "It's . . ." I took a breath. "She would have done the same for me, so." I took a sip of my tea.

"Hm." Ms. Bishop dropped her eyes to her tea, then placed the photos back onto the ledge and stood. "You should go on and get some sleep now. You've earned it."

CHAPTER 12

In fifth grade, our dance studio's end-of-year concert was Esther's last-ever high school performance. I loved the moments just before a show, the directed sense of community, the lack of ambiguity. I could handle this kind of small talk: "Can I borrow some of your blush?" or "Oops! That shoe strap is a little crooked. Want me to fix it?" There was a collective affection I struggled to access elsewhere. And we went to a serious enough studio that as soon as class started, the chitchat ended. If you talked in class, you got hit with a stick. Most important, Esther's excellence and popularity legitimized my presence, which made it possible for me to get by with minimal harassment and, even better, minimal masking.

After the show ended and families trailed out of the auditorium, I spotted my sister. She sat, pink tights dangling over the edge of the stage, so close to the wings a long black curtain grazed her shoulder. She smoothed her blood-red tutu over her legs in a rhythmic motion, seemingly oblivious to the noise of excited families packing up from their chairs in the audience or congratulating their loved ones backstage.

I hesitated. I could have already changed out of my last costume, a blue-and-white gingham dress. I'd had over a half hour to do so since Esther's group closed out the show with excerpts from *Paquita*. But I liked the feeling of the ballet tights compressing my round stomach, the costume fitted and secure against me. It made me aware of, secure in, the limits of my body, and I didn't want to change back into my hand-me-down sweatpants and T-shirt; they were too loose.

Copious sweating had smudged and caked the foundation and cream blush against my face. Even after the rigor of her performance, Esther's makeup was still impeccable, the winged eyeliner and shimmery amber eye shadow unsmudged, though her face and arms were covered in a sheen of sweat. I held out a thin bouquet of Ralphs flowers. She ignored them. I sat beside her, letting my ballet shoes dangle over the edge of the stage.

"Mom got you these. She's talking to Mrs. Reisner out front." Probably negotiating my class fees for next year. It was a miracle she'd shown up at all.

"How generous," Esther deadpanned.

I ran my tongue over my teeth, tasting a spot of lipstick on the top row. I winced. "You were really good. I bet everyone here is gonna miss you."

"Thanks." Esther shrugged, staring out into the emptying audience.

I swiveled slightly to face her and laid the flowers on her lap. She shoved them to the other side of her tutu like they were infected. "This is a rental, Dzifa," she scolded, gesturing at her pristine costume.

I sighed. "I'm really sorry things didn't work out. About, um, school, I mean." I declined to say *Barnard* out loud. We thought our plan had worked: Mom told us, before the new year, that Dad would allow it. Esther was elated, even more so when she got in in March. By April, she already had half a suitcase full of Barnard sweats at the ready. Then Mom received a curt email: Dad paid a tuition deposit to Yale instead, citing: There was a fine arts department there, too. Never mind that dance was a performing art, but our dad never took it seriously enough to know what category it belonged to; he'd always laughed when we spoke of the discipline and strength required to dance. "Sure," he'd chuckle. "Tell that to a real athlete sometime."

"You can still take a train to New York from New Haven. And I was reading about it. And Yale actually has some really cool-sounding dance stuff. And you could study abroad in F—"

"Stop, Dzifa." Esther blinked a few times, fast. "It's done." She moved her hand to my shoulder, pressing down firmly. "Stop," she repeated.

I heard her long inhale and kept waiting for her to let it out, but couldn't tell if or when she had.

"Anyway." She shrugged. "I'm not gonna cry because my dad is making me go to *Yale*. Like, it's not something to be upset about."

Frowning, I nudged her hand from my shoulder, shaking off the lingering sensation from the unexpected contact. "It's not about that. It's about his going behind your back, not even bothering to call you or tell you or ask you what you thought and—"

"Dzifa, you're too hard on him."

I scoffed. "Are you kidding me? He avoids us like 360 days out of the year, then just drops these . . ." I grasped for the word. "Edicts . . . out of nowhere, when he doesn't know anything about us. He doesn't know us at all."

"Well?" Esther clicked her tongue. "Can you blame him? Look who he's married to. I'd be gone 365 days out of the year if I could." She began untying one of her pointe shoes, pulling her foot up onto the stage for better access. "Speaking of which"—she kept her eyes trained on the satin ribbons—"you might not see much of me, going forward."

"Well, I know you're going to Accra this summer. But I'll see you just before you leave for Y—um, school. And then Thanksgiving, right?" I crossed my arms and pressed them in close against the thin fabric of my costume.

Esther paused, the ribbons of one shoe unlaced, before slipping it from her foot and wincing at the freshly cracked calluses at the back of her heels and the sides of her toes. "I can't come back here." She began on the other set of laces, tugging harder than she needed to. "I'm not coming back here. Ever."

"But . . ." I trailed off. "Okay." I couldn't argue with her. If I could leave, too, I would. But I couldn't. And I didn't know what else to say. I should have fought harder for her to go to Barnard, but I didn't know what else to do. Maybe if I wasn't so inexplicably tired all the time, I could have done something else. Maybe if I were more the daughter my parents wanted, my opinion would have carried more weight. It was just like my middle sister, Mary, said on the rare occasions she came through the Bay from Accra. She always said it softly, with a combination of wonder and pity: "I think, Dzifa, when you were born, you just weren't fully cooked yet, you know?" Then she'd smile and pat me on the head.

Esther's grip on her laces softened. "Dzifa, I'm sorry you have to be here, with her, by yourself. For some reason, you don't seem to understand how bad she is, which really scares me. You seem to think she's quirky or something, and I am telling you right now there is something very, very wrong with that woman."

I pulled my own feet up and crossed them, squishing my hands underneath my thighs. My mind drifted to our last meal together, the three of us, my mother's sharp brown eyes as she delivered the news about Barnard, without a hint, even, of her typical quick-boiling ire for my father's avoidant communication style. She'd looked up at Esther, said, "You'll appreciate this soon enough. You don't have the disposition to handle New York. With your body type and lack of discipline, it's better to avoid such unregulated environments."

If my mother's disparaging assessment of me hinged on my fundamental brokenness and, occasionally, unseemly fatness—which she reinforced by making me wear clothes four sizes too big and insisting they were too tight—her assessment of Esther hinged on an almost comically unfounded terror of her second-youngest daughter's potential sluttiness.

"You were there. When she said she wasn't sure if she couldn't feel for other people, or if she could and just didn't care." Esther shook her head vigorously as if trying to exorcize this image from her memory. "What she has—what she is—is not curable. It's never going to change." She removed the second shoe, rolled the convertible tights up to her ankle, and began massaging both feet. "You spend too much time alone. You're overly sensitive. She uses you . . . and you don't even see it. You need to do what I did, okay? You just tune her out. Just say, 'Yes, Mom,' but tune out whatever she says. Don't let her convince you she needs your help, your pity, your sympathy. She doesn't need anything from you. And you don't need anything from her."

I stared at her feet, unable to meet her eyes. It wasn't that I thought she was wrong, I just doubted I'd ever be able to achieve such a healthy disdain for our mother. Esther was leaving, not coming back. If I didn't have Mom, who did I have?

"You're smart enough; you can get out earlier than I did. You can go to boarding school, like Mary and the others did." She nodded in reference to our older sisters as if reassuring herself.

"You were smart enough to get out earlier, too," I mumbled.

"Yes, but then who would have taken care of you?" Her words, true and undeniable, hit me in my stomach, where the guilt about this fact already lived and festered, solidifying my feelings of unworthiness by the day. "Anyway, it's fine. Don't worry about me. Maybe I'm going somewhere I don't want to be, but the important thing is I'm not gonna be here."

I chewed my lower lip, smudging the lipstick even more. It tasted sickly sweet, chemical. My stomach roiled. "Okay," I said quietly. Unable to dwell further on Esther's announcements, I changed the subject. "Are we still going to the Cheesecake Factory?"

Esther stood, abandoning the bouquet at the edge of the stage. "I'm going, but if it's okay with you, I really just want to spend some time with my friends. Mom will drive you home."

The churning in my stomach escalated; my eyes filled with tears. I tried to blink them away, but they were too full. Instead, I turned away from Esther and nodded. "Yep, sure. Cool. Have fun. See you later." By the time I turned back, Esther had already disappeared through the wings.

—∾—

Tatiana's childhood bedroom was not a time capsule, the way mine would be if I had one still. There were no over-hugged stuffed animals wedged by the window or teenage music posters peeling from the walls. The small space had a full bed pushed against the right wall and a scuffed wooden desk and cobalt-blue office chair against the left. A worn mauve area rug provided some cushion against the uneven floorboards, and an oversize macramé tapestry hung above the double windows, grazing sheer curtains. Ms. Bishop had offered to stay with Maddie for the night.

Although Sam, Tatiana, and I crowded into the bed at Tatiana's insistence, I lay still and awake at the very edge and slid off onto the floor once the other two were asleep. Around four, I reached across the rug for my phone and booked a flight to San Francisco, dimming the screen light as far down as it would go. There were a few different options, the most cost-effective a couple of days out. I booked a same-day for a higher price. This, along with the flight here, completely depleted my savings and most of my checking, too. But it was time for me to go.

The ambiguity of whatever might come next felt untenable, and it had been jarring enough to wade through the ambiguity of this week. I had no idea how to show up, how to stay, among people who so openly loved one another the way the Bishops did. Loved one another enough that, unlike my family of emotionally peculiar control freaks, they didn't need color-coded spreadsheets for basic task management, 24-7 pristine cupboards, and formal appointments to have casual conversations. Grief was probably supposed to look messy; people were probably supposed to be so distraught they left the dishes undone. I just couldn't quite get myself to surrender to it. Not for this long.

Sam and Tatiana were in and out of sleep but seemed committed to staying where they were, so I slipped through the bedroom door with a change of clothes, though none of them were clean, and took a shower.

Before she stepped out to run some errands that morning, Ms. Bishop paused by the front door. "Tati, can you come here for a second, please?"

Sam and I exchanged a look, silently agreeing to retreat to the kitchen. The house was small enough we could still hear muted voices, but it was impossible to make out what the two were talking about. When the front door opened and closed a few minutes later, Sam and I returned to the living room.

"All good?" Sam asked, the lightness in her tone a little forced.

Tatiana set Maddie down on the ground, holding her little hands up as she walked her around the room, her daughter's legs wobbling. Maddie grinned and squealed, but Tatiana's face was still. "Dzifa, I'm gonna drive you to the airport, okay? If you insist on leaving today, which I still don't super love."

"You really don't need to do that. There'll probably be a bunch of traffic, and it really wasn't a problem to take the T here when I came." I stepped aside as Maddie, still assisted by Tatiana, nearly stumbled into me.

"No, I'm driving you." She nodded as if that was that.

"I'll come with!" Sam added. I congratulated myself on not groaning.

"There you have it," Tatiana concluded. "It'll be a mini girls' trip. Road trip. Something. That's what's happening, so get into it, Dzifa."

"All right." I held my hands up in surrender. "If you feel that strongly about it. Thank you."

"I mean, obviously." She shrugged and lifted Maddie back into her arms. "Want some coffee? I'm gonna make some."

"God, yes." Sam clapped her hands together. "I feel like a zombie today."

"Sounds good," I agreed. "Me, too."

"Really?" Sam cocked her head to the side as Tatiana made her way into the kitchen. "You seem like . . . the same as always. But then, I guess it's different when you normally aren't, like, high energy. Like I pretty much came out of the womb just ready and raring to go, you know?"

"I bet." I flashed a grin and stepped past her to enter the kitchen. Tatiana was sitting at the kitchen table, gazing solemnly at Maddie. "You want me to make the coffee?"

"Oh." Tatiana blinked. "Yes, please."

"No problem. I'll just make a full—"

"Oh, I can make it, Dzifa," Sam interjected, suddenly beside me. Before I could object further, she pulled out a filter and began pouring from the half-empty tub of Folgers. "I have a special trick to make it, like, Starbucks-level good."

I considered protesting. Was that a level of good we really needed to aspire to? I shrugged and stepped back until I was leaning against the tea cabinet, my arms folded across my chest. Only a little while longer. "Hm," I heard from the corner. It sounded almost involuntary. I watched Tatiana, waiting for her to say more.

"You okay?" I asked. Stupid question, but it was too late to take it back.

She raised her eyes to meet mine, then resumed her somber staring match with Maddie. "Oh, sure. Mommy got a call from her lawyer friend Shannon this morning. There's been some . . . activity from the Adams. And the detective. She's gonna stop by her office to find out the details. I told her I'd come with, but she said she wanted me to concentrate on Maddie right now, that she'll fill me in later. Plus, Shannon is doing her a favor seeing her on a Saturday, and Mommy doesn't want to take up too much of her time."

"Shit. Oh, Tatiana." Sam covered the top of the coffee maker, hastily pressing the On button. She turned around and swooped down to give both Tatiana and Maddie a hug. "I'm so, so sorry, sweetie. Can—do you want to talk about it? Do you want me to call my mom? I could get her on speaker, if you want, or maybe I could even ask her to—"

"We should leave now." Tatiana stood abruptly, the chair screeching behind her. Maddie whined at the noise. "Traffic is gonna be hell, so we might as well get ahead of it." She left the room.

"Okay." Sam turned toward the coffee maker, back toward me, then got stuck somewhere in the middle. "I guess I'll just . . ." Frowning, she pressed a few buttons on the coffee maker. It continued sputtering, little drops making their way down into the glass carafe. "Well." Sam shrugged, unplugged the coffee maker, and shrugged again, walking past me and out of the kitchen.

"Sam, do you mind watching Maddie while I walk Dzifa to the terminal? She's about to fall asleep again, but if she doesn't, just give her more of the bottle. Here, I'll leave you the keys." She stretched her hands across the console, jingling the keys.

"Sure, of course." Sam accepted the keys, and Tatiana stepped around to the trunk to pull out my bag.

We stood just to the left of the sliding doors at Logan's entrance. "Okay, Queen Quartey, this is where I leave you. Or rather, you are leaving me. Rude. But you'd better fucking come back, okay?" Tatiana reached her arms out. I stepped into them. "I know you don't like hugs, and I don't care. Thank you so much. So much. For being here. I'm sorry it's been such a shit show."

"Don't be sorry." I laughed incredulously. "Of course I came. And I didn't even do anything. Except drink all your tea."

"You did plenty." She didn't laugh back, just held on to my forearms tightly. "I'm serious. I couldn't have gotten through this without you. And . . . if I'm being honest, I don't think I'm gonna get through this . . . other situation, whatever it is, without you. You know that, right?"

"I'm not going anywhere. I mean, I have to go back to work, but I'm not going anywhere." I squeezed her arms, then gently pulled mine back to my sides, lifting a shoulder to slide my bag more securely onto it.

"I know that. I just . . . I wouldn't blame you if after this week you wanted to . . . I don't know. Not be in the middle of all this. So I totally get it if you can't, but I'm just telling you, without you, I'm kind of on my own. As much as I love Sam, she doesn't get it get it, you know? You get it."

I shouldn't have felt so much pride, or relief, as I did. "I don't know about all that. But I consider you my sister, Tatiana. Sisters don't abandon each other. No matter what." I gave her another hug.

"Call me when you get to Oakland, 'kay?" She looked so small. She was just as tiny as Sam, but I forgot all the time.

As I walked into the terminal, it occurred to me that I'd already abandoned her when I left New York. Here I was again, leaving. This time, at least, I had every intention of keeping my word.

CHAPTER 13

Naya was out when I got back to the apartment; I'd forgotten she was spending this weekend on a road trip with her sister. Relieved I'd have a day and a half to myself, I dropped my bag in my room, stripped off my travel clothes, and stepped into the shower. I turned the water up to its hottest setting and stood there for thirty minutes, until it was cold again. After the first five minutes, my recently reawakened eco-conscious-Californian voice nagged at me to be more mindful; we were in a drought. But then other thoughts entered: the sad, lost look on Tatiana's face as I walked into Logan Airport, Ms. Bishop's unbearably kind words, the fact that, even after Zeynep confirmed my suspicions, I'd forgotten to tell Tatiana I had, in fact, met B before. And so I kept standing, one hand braced against the tiled shower wall, letting the water run over me.

When I got out, I dried off but didn't bother to dress, instead taking the few carpeted steps from the bathroom to my bed and collapsing.

The vibration of my phone woke me. I scrolled through the notifications; there were a few from Tatiana, a missed call from Zeynep, and four missed calls from Esther. It wasn't like her to call repeatedly like that. I checked my messages:

> DZIFA. Pick up your phone. Nobody is dead but you need to pick up the phone. See you here tomorrow.

I frowned. "Nobody is dead?" I read out loud. I checked the time at the top of the screen. 2:17 A.M. Her last call was at 11:58. I considered what would be worse: her irritation that I woke her up in the middle of the night, or her wrath if I didn't respond until the morning. Groaning, I hit Call and held my breath as the phone rang.

Esther picked up on the last ring. Her voice was alert. She must've been awake, still. Not a good sign; Esther went to sleep at ten o'clock on the dot, every single day. "Dzifa, Jesus! Why didn't you answer?"

"I was sleeping," I grumbled. "I'm exhausted. Can this not wait until tomorrow?"

"No," she countered. "I'll get to the point: Mom is back."

PART 3

CHAPTER 14

Senior year of high school, my mother put our house up for sale. It was a relief, an overdue one, after the third or fourth foreclosure threat, the years of clandestine selling of valued possessions and shuffling around of apparently valueless assets. To my surprise, she promised to divert as much of the proceeds as she could toward my college tuition. The rest, my father would use on whatever he had going on elsewhere.

I wasn't as smart as Esther, but I still wasn't dumb enough to trigger a repeat of the Barnard fiasco. So despite having achieved proficiency in the language and more practice, though not perfection, in the art form, I kept my fantasies of Italian dance programs to myself. Elmwood wasn't my dream, but I could settle for it being the start of my freedom. All that mattered, I told myself, was that I was finally, legally, an adult. I chanced one last visit home.

The house was nearly empty by then, my mother having sold most of the furniture, paintings, artifacts from my father's people, well-preserved memorabilia from hers. The scale of the sprawling, two-story structure was even more jarring now than it had been then. As I walked through, scanning the high ceilings and long hallways, I considered the cost of it all. Whether the exchange had been warranted: all this lofty, white space, for the lack of anything substantive inside of it. Only my mother's bedroom was still fully furnished, though there was now a medley of mismatched cushions displaced from other areas of the house, artfully perched in the expansive living room.

In those ways, it had changed, but as I walked back into the white stucco halls and felt my breath constrict, I knew it hadn't changed in the one way I always wished it could. All these years later, the beautiful, barren structure still bore the slow-creeping heaviness I considered its signature. The house, in spite of all its floor-to-ceiling windows and bright, pristine surfaces, had a way of weighing a person down from the inside out. I knew I wasn't alone in feeling it. One time years ago, Esther and I discussed it. "Why do I always feel so sleepy here?" I'd complained, struggling to pull myself off the couch.

"It's not sleepiness," Esther had countered, rubbing a hand over her own eyes. "I'm pretty sure we've been getting a slow drip of carbon monoxide poisoning this whole time."

Back in this house after three and a half years, I swore I could feel the consciousness drifting away from my body, settling into some far-off container where it could not be compressed beyond repair, the way the rest of me felt most of the time. It was a place in which, for its size and white-walled-ness and suburban placement, one felt one *should* feel well. Jubilant, even. Grateful, certainly. It was a place in which none of those appropriate reactions were willing to manifest in me. Instead, there was only, and had only ever been, the inappropriate impulse to run.

My mother seldom cooked and she compulsively cleaned, so the granite countertop was gleaming like new when I met her in the kitchen that night. To my surprise, she didn't chastise me for sitting on the counter. Not something I'd have chanced usually—military-grade manners were her religion—but there were no longer any chairs in the kitchen. She followed suit, laying out the Mexican takeout we picked up on the way back from the airport.

"Do you know where you'll go yet?" I asked through a bite of quesadilla. "When the sale goes through, I mean? Will you go back to Accra?"

She was still, one leg crossed over the other. I eyed her shoes; cool-blue mules. The same color as the Mercedes she'd bought when we were kids, that she sold once we were gone. Once it was a choice between the car or the house. "Your father is in Accra." She frowned.

My brows drawing together, I shrugged. "Yes, but he doesn't *own* Accra. You've spent plenty of time there. I mean, you used to. You speak some Ga. Do you still have any contacts there? Or wouldn't Mary be able to host you for a while? Her house is pretty big, right?" I'd never been but had seen it in photos.

Knife and fork in hand—the European way, as she'd taught me—Mom cut a neat piece off a sliver of grilled steak and brought it to her mouth. She chewed slowly, swallowed, shook her head. "No. I would like my own place. Something of mine that is not also his."

I took a breath, then another bite. "All right. Is that . . . with . . . Financially, is that feasible?"

She laid down her utensils and wiped the corners of her mouth with a napkin. "My finances are not your concern, young lady."

I begged to differ, for a million reasons, one of which—college—I thought she and I had already agreed to. I took another bite, wincing at its sluggish, choppy trajectory down and into my stomach. "Yes, Mom," I said quietly. "Then . . . where will you go?"

She looked up, reached over, and squeezed the top of my hand. "I'll go to Massachusetts, of course. To be near you."

It would have been best to say nothing. If I couldn't help but say something, it should have been something daughterly and polite. But my guard was lowered by years of distance, my belly unaccustomed to being so full in this empty house. Sideswiped by the escalation of my heart rate, the seizing-up of my stomach, I told the truth. "Please don't," I said. I dropped the rest of the quesadilla on top of its brown paper bag, held one greasy hand up in supplication.

My mother's head snapped back. Her hand tightened, viselike, on mine, then retreated. My fingers free but shaking, I curled them into a fist, pressed it down into the granite. Her lips tilted upward slightly, her eyes sharp, opaque. "Excuse me?"

I swallowed. Her eyes used to switch like that all the time. In an instant, they'd change, taking things in with open, electric curiosity one moment, in the next, switching to the eyes of a vulture—scanning the ground below it for weakened, sluggish beings. It had always been hard to say, hard to know, what triggered the switch. Sometimes she was set off by our independence, or the threat of it. Other times, it was the obligation to raise us that sparked her fury.

Either way, the switch was how Esther and I knew it was time for the hiding game. "Here are the rules," Esther used to whisper, in the backyard, in a seldom-visited closet, behind a neighbor's house, or, in a pinch, under a large pile of laundry. "Whichever one of us can hide from her the longest, wins." *I'm only here for a few more days*, I thought. *And then never again.* "I just—please, I really would appreciate some space."

"Space?" My mother tested the word like its shape was foreign to her, needed to be practiced, verified. "Space?" she repeated, sliding off the counter, and stepping into mine. "What space is it that you think you need from your mother? Have you not already had *four years* of space?"

I slid back, the curved rim of the counter bruising against the inside of my knees. She stepped toward me again. "I just meant, it feels like I'm really close to—" I braced my hands against the counter, tried to steady my breath. I stood as straight as I could manage and tried again. "What I mean is: I am doing my best to move forward, and with Elmwood—"

She laughed, the wideness of her smile as sharp as the acid in her gaze. "What exactly is it you feel the need to move forward from? This beautiful house we built for you? The phenomenal schools we sent you to?"

I stepped back; she followed, again. Turning my head, searching for anything but her to anchor my eyes on, I settled on a fly buzzing its way up the ledge of the nearest window. "It's not—I am just—" I tried a different approach, the wrong one. I knew it, but couldn't think straight. "My counselor at school, she said there's some stuff that I . . . some trauma that I might be—"

"Oh my Lord." She rolled her eyes, her smile wide, rigid, feral. "Trauma? My dear, I have survived challenges you could not even fathom, and yet—trauma? Not a pinch. It's called *resilience.* A trait which somehow seems to have skipped you entirely. Your counselor, like all so-called psychologists, is a charlatan."

I tried, failed, to quell the burst of anger that rose up through that tight spot in my chest. It expanded for a moment, swelled as I opened my mouth to speak, for a second time, my ill-advised truth. "Maybe I wouldn't need to see one if you had."

My mother outpaced my retreat. At the very edge of the counter, she stepped in front of me. One at a time, she braced her arms on either side of my thighs. "I don't need any help. Not from some overpaid pseudoscientist, not from any of the miscellaneous white people you feel so stupidly comfortable spilling private family matters to, not from anyone. Nor should you." She placed her index finger against my hairline and pressed hard.

I tried to steady my breathing, to find some way to duck underneath her arms. I didn't dare push her. I'd once followed this impulse, when I was thirteen—I was almost her height by then—and it did not end well. The problem, I learned, was never that she was bigger than I was. It was that she had no qualms about causing harm, whereas my entire existence was an immobilizing, self-flagellating battle with such qualms. Even then, I did not believe that she sought to cause harm; it seemed, more so, that its effects registered as inconveniences rather than moral errors, so she did not take great pains to avoid it. Perhaps, I was now realizing, that had been too generous an assessment.

"What do you mean?" Instead of leaving the cage she'd created, I stared down at her unscuffed shoes. "I'm already eighteen. I'm my own person—" I yelped, flinched, when one of her elegant hands, which I'd forgotten were so much stronger than they looked, grabbed me by the forearm and held on tight.

"You will never be your own person." I bit down on my tongue and pulled my arm away from her. She grabbed it again. "You will always be the person I made."

With one side free, I slipped away from her grasp. She held on, moving with me, past the counter, toward the window, where the fly was now buzzing in the night-shadowed center of the windowpane. "I—" I bit my tongue. Tried again. *Just another week until I'm away from her again. Just another few months, and I'll be free of her completely,* I reminded myself. "Okay. Okay. I'm really tired, Mom. I'm just going to go to sleep, okay?"

Her hand tightened on my arm. She surveyed my face, relaxed her grip. "Very well. Don't forget to clean up your trash." She pulled her hand away and waved it at the leftover takeout still sitting on the counter.

"Yes, Mom." I nodded, stepped away.

Upstairs, surrounded by the pale yellow walls of my childhood bedroom, I released a long, choppy breath. Close call, but I'd be out of here soon. Wouldn't have to deal with this anymore, ever again if I didn't want to—and I didn't want to—soon. I spotted my old CD player; oblong, accented with a white stripe, it sat on a ledge beneath the window. I'd spent so much time staring out that window. My father, back when he still pretended to have any intention of living here, promised Esther once he'd plant her an orange tree in the backyard. If it existed, we'd both be able to see it from our rooms. I found myself looking for it, sometimes, as if somehow my father had planted the seed when he'd made the promise, and the tree just needed enough attention to finally grow. It never did, of course, because he never did plant it. Nobody did. I dusted off the loose CDs that lay beside the player, popped in the CD on the top of the pile.

Even with *Paquita*'s familiar string arrangements diluting the sharpness of my thoughts, it was hard to fall asleep. My mother's words kept creeping in, wedging their talons underneath the tender skin of my burgeoning hopefulness. *You will always be the person I made.* I resorted to counting sheep, shadows, then my own breaths; eventually, I drifted off.

Hours later, the room still dark, the CD player stalled, I awoke to a chorus of rustling clothes, thumping and shouting on the stairs. The lights flashed on, fluorescent and blinding. There were voices, but in my confusion, I could not make out what they were saying. Even as my vision cleared, I could not accept what I was seeing, so I hardly saw at all. My eyes recorded only the highlights: pale hands, male, efficient, grabbing my arms with the casual roughness reserved, I already knew well, for melanated women; the shining glint of deadly metal peeking out of navy pockets, affixed to cold black belts; pale hands, resting, sweet and cozy, on the metal, when they weren't taut and tenderless, hauling me. Up and out of the bed, down the stairs, out the door, into the night, into another set of open doors.

When I remembered it later, I liked to rewrite it. To rewrite it so that when they grabbed me, I screamed. Protested. Explained that they were making a mistake; made the case to stay where I was. Even though, if I would've done so, they might've killed me. Not out of malice, just out of habit. But I liked to rewrite it anyway, to rewrite myself brave.

As it happened, I said nothing. Made no sounds. Didn't fight. Didn't know the limits of my own form anymore, baffled as I was by how one moment, the surface of my skin felt only the fabric of my pajamas, the comforter, the still air of my childhood bedroom, how the next, my skin was flush with other skin, foreign skin, violent skin, skin on duty, doing its lauded, compassionless works.

When my body, me somewhere near but not in it, met the night, my eyes adjusted again, my sight let in one full vision: my mother ambling closer, slow and serene, wrapped in her favorite silk nightgown, the one patterned with loosely sketched cherry blossoms. I looked up at her from the gurney I'd been strapped into. There they were again: Those penetrating eyes. That shining, sharp, and gleeful sparkle, just for me, just as the doors shut. "Thank you, gentlemen," I heard—calm, motherly—on the other side of the doors. "I just hope she gets the help she so desperately needs."

My mother came on day five, the day before Christmas. I begged the nurses not to let her in. She wore new-looking Prada pumps, a formfitting green silk dress that came down to just above her knees, and her concerned mother persona. "Well, Dzifa," she said calmly, across from me on a rough-fabric, rust-orange couch. "Anything you wish to share with me?"

I sat there in my oversize, hospital-issued blue scrubs and bit my tongue, dug my fingernails into my palms. I couldn't begin to understand what she was getting out of this. I couldn't begin to think of an answer besides the truth, which she clearly wasn't interested in. Which had gotten me here, I supposed. "It should be you here. It should always have been you here."

My mother smiled. "Evidently not." She stood, brushed the creases from her dress. "It seems like maybe you need more time to reflect on your actions."

She pushed for me to stay another week; I got out two days later. I did so by becoming an expert practitioner of the hiding game, by compressing myself just right, by being a very good girl, by imagining how Esther would get through it, by letting my mind leave my body, by promising myself that when I got out of here, I would never come back, that I would sooner die than come back. I clung to this promise even and especially when the facility director who signed my discharge papers threatened, "You'll be back here. Everyone who comes here ends up back here."

My mother picked me up, hugged me until I gagged, and drove me to a Berkeley tea shop to get scones and oolong. She sipped on her tea. I stared at my scone. It looked stale, the scattered raisins dry and flaky. "So. How was that for you?" she asked, her smile easy, sweet. When I didn't respond, her smile dropped. She leaned back in her chair and sighed. "You may not understand yet. But this is how it is, my love. In this world. You need to learn how to keep it together. Tidy." She adjusted the fabric at her collarbone. "You don't spill all your business to strangers or burden other people with your supposed traumas. If you really need to fall apart, you do it when no one else is looking, you pull yourself back together before they see. That's how you survive. Not by being loose, with your insides, with your trust."

I was looking, I didn't say, my mind's eye dredging up the years she retreated, slipping in and out of the doorway of her master bedroom, clutching that same silk robe, unavailable to me or to Esther. She made herself scarce, but we saw her. The lack of her. Felt her gone. Around me, I registered the voices of other customers, the barista, but muted, like they were miles away or in some other dimension.

"I did you a favor," she continued.

I could have died, I didn't say.

"Better you understand now. Out in the world, there is no safety for women like us. No softness. No mercy."

Then why did you name me that? I didn't ask. Unsure if I wouldn't or couldn't. My eyes stayed glued to the scone.

She huffed, adjusted the brass barrette holding her chignon in place. "Well. You'll see. You are lucky to have a mother who loves you. I didn't. My mother didn't like me, didn't love me, barely registered my existence. Really." She raised her eyebrows as if this had just occurred to her for the first time. "She was a very respectable lady. And a very mean lady, though she'd never say it. If you asked her how she was, it was always, 'Fine, thank you,' but you could just *feel* she'd throw me into the nearest ditch if she could get away with it." I felt the heat of her eyes on my face.

What if they'd shot me? I didn't interject.

"She never loved me enough to really meet me. To get in the dirt and teach me what I really needed to know. I had to learn, all by myself. That we can create safe spaces for ourselves, for each other, at home—that when we need to be messy, we can do it there. Never outside, Dzifa. But you have no idea how lucky you are to have had *any* place to be yourself. I didn't."

I exhaled, registering my hands clenching into fists beside my thighs, my sweat sticking the skin to the plastic seat.

"This is what love is," my mother continued. "Sometimes we have to make difficult choices to protect our children. Especially our daughters. You'll see, one day."

I already see, I didn't scream. *I am drowning in the sight of it*, I wanted to scream. To open my mouth, my arms, extend my fingers, release them, sharpen my nails, feel them scratch against the nearest walls. I wanted to roar, unholy and feral, to chastise her for so brazenly, conveniently rewriting the history she'd just conscripted me to. Wanted to punish her for ascribing measuredness, let alone affection, to actions I was fairly sure had been, in the moment she set them into motion, driven by vindictiveness, not by anything remotely resembling love or reason. But I felt tongueless, toothless, like I'd never had a voice to say anything, like it was no longer worth having anything to say even if I could recover the mechanisms to say it.

She folded her arms across her chest, took a deep breath, exercised unprecedented patience as she waited for me to digest her love, her venom.

"Yes, Mom," I said. I unclenched my fists, lifted the scone, took a big, dry bite.

CHAPTER 15

"Dzifa, need I remind you this very same woman was the *reason* you came to Elmwood two years late?" Tatiana paced as she spoke, the phone unsteady in her hands so all I caught of her house were blurred glimpses of the floorboards and the mantelpiece.

I rested my phone on the dashboard so she could see me better. "Yeah, well, most people don't have college savings, so. It's really not that unique a situation. Wasn't ideal, but I'm gonna have to forget it tonight if I want to get through this dinner."

Tatiana groaned. She plopped down onto a carpeted floor—dropping the phone, retrieving it, and steadying it with both hands. "It is a *very* unique situation! Your mom was literally like, 'Oh, don't worry, Dzifa, yes, you can totally go to college next year—Just kidding—I used all the money to buy twenty pairs of shoes and a house nobody needs.'"

I laughed. I had to laugh; otherwise . . . and anyway, my delayed entrance to Elmwood was hardly the worst part of it. My mother wasn't even the worst of it; it could be argued she was simply being herself. The worst part was that absolutely no one else in my family, not even Esther, tried to intervene in the aftermath of her creative, state-sponsored admonishment of me. I couldn't tell if they didn't believe me or if they just didn't care. I couldn't tell which was worse. "To be fair, she didn't use all the money. My dad took most of it. And as long as she didn't come near me, I never really cared. And," I added, feeling the need to strengthen my case—grasping for straws, really—"at least she's finally divorcing him. Apparently, that's why she's back. I don't know. Maybe she'll be . . . different now." We both knew this was unlikely, but I didn't bother to backtrack.

Tatiana shook her phone—the best alternative, I supposed, to shaking my shoulders. "Girl, you know I love me a bit of optimism, but now is not the time to be delusional! Do not go into that house, Dzifa. I am telling you."

I shook my head, sighing. "Look—I don't disagree with you. It is not an accident I haven't seen her in over a decade. But this is an extenuating circumstance because—"

"All right," she interrupted. "Here's what I'm gonna do. I'm gonna figure out how to get a flight there. Just let me—"

"Please don't do that. I mean, you can't do that. It's fine," I persisted when she tried to interject. "I'll be fine. It's just one dinner. And Esther'll be there; it's not like I'm on my own. One or two hours of my life isn't that big a deal."

It was the biggest of deals. I didn't know why I was downplaying it or why Tatiana was as upset as I probably should have been. Before this call, I'd spent the past twelve hours in a full-blown panic. Tatiana was right. But I owed this to Esther. And if I weighed what I'd been through against what Tatiana had just been through . . . I should be able to handle this. I should be fine.

Five minutes later, as much air as I could muster stored up in my lungs, I walked up the steps to Esther's front door, raised my hand, dropped it. I cleared my throat, shook my shoulders out, and knocked.

As soon as we'd cleared the dishes, Esther's husband escorted their three restless sons upstairs. Esther asked, her voice flat, "Mom, what's your plan?" She leaned forward, forearms on the table as we'd been taught never to do, and narrowed her eyes. "It sounds like there's another foreclosure looming in Maryland, and frankly, I don't have the capacity to get involved in the fallout of that. I would appreciate your doing something sensible about it, before things get bad again."

Mom took a sip of wine. "Well, I'll stay out here for a while. There's more work here than there is in Accra anyway. I'll find something. Maybe get a studio or a one-bedroom. While I save up a little, for the mortgage payments. If I could live in the Maryland house, I would, but it's just not equipped for daily life at present. I'd like to live in Pacific Heights; there are some gorgeous townhomes there."

I raised an eyebrow; Esther stifled a laugh. "Yes, we'd all like to live in Pacific Heights," she retorted. She took a breath, regrouped. "And yet we don't all have Pacific Heights money. What is your actual plan?"

"It baffles me, Amatso." Mom shook her head. I flinched at her use of Esther's Ga name. "You never miss an opportunity to weave tales of my supposed meanness, and yet every word out of your mouth is an insult. That is my plan." She lifted a shoulder, tapped a sable-painted nail on the base of her glass. "Pacific Heights is optional. Do forgive me for having aspirations; I know you're too righteous for anything resembling pleasure."

Esther leaned her head into her hands. I was glad the kids had gone to bed. I knew how hard she tried not to let her sons see how much the pressure depleted her—the pressure inflicted by others and that which she inflicted, as if insufficiently burdened, upon herself. But I could see it in the bags underneath her eyes, in the low hum of anxious energy that betrayed her hard-won performance of stillness, and most especially in the blanketed fury in her gaze, now directed at the tabletop. I wondered if, when, her fury would finally boil over. It had to go somewhere, and I hoped she'd take my life thus far as a case study in why trying to swallow it was not an effective long-term solution.

"Mom." Esther lifted her gaze from the table. "Do you ever feel any remorse? Whatsoever? I mean . . ." She blinked, her eyebrows scrunched together. "Do you?"

"You know, Amatso . . ." Mom shook her head, a smile stretching across her face. "You have a little too much of my mother in you. Her favorite admonishment of me was always: '*Soften*, dear.' If I raised my voice above the flutter of a butterfly's wing, if I moved too freely, dreamed too big, felt too expressively: 'Oh, soften, dear, wouldn't you?' She'd say it in a whisper as sharp as a blade." Her gaze hardened even as her smile stayed wide. " 'I would love to,' I always wanted to say. 'If you would just give me somewhere soft to land.' Of course, we didn't dare talk back, in my day. Still, it confounded me, how she could mistake her violence for softness, just because it wasn't loud.

"And it confounds me," she leveled a taut index finger in Esther's direction, "how a woman raised *by me* could be so attached to these absolutely ancient expectations: these regressive performances of contrition. As if the sacrifices I made for you were not enough." She crossed one leg over the other. "Do you think there weren't other things I'd rather have done with my time than shuttle you back and forth to ballet, or music, or whatever expensive activity required me to sit on the sidelines and have inane conversations with the most insipid women imaginable?" Mom sat back in her chair, crossed her arms across her chest, raised an eyebrow.

I cleared my throat. Should've said nothing, couldn't help it. Couldn't withstand Esther's silence, every unsaid thing I wanted her to say on her own behalf, knew she was too much the good daughter to speak aloud. "We know there were things you'd rather have been doing," I chimed in, unwisely. "You told us. Repeatedly."

"Would you rather I lied?" Mom laughed, patted the bun twisted at the base of her neck. "You have no idea how lucky you are to have a mother who was honest with you. That's what motherhood is, my loves. It's an ending of the life that you knew. That doesn't mean there wasn't anything good after that end." She paused, darted her eyes toward the staircase. Was it a struggle for her to find a concrete example of anything good? She turned her eyes back to Esther, then to me. "I love all of you. Obviously. But it's like I always told you: I was just eager for you to finally grow up. To become interesting. Which—not that I've ever been thanked, but you're welcome." Our mother pursed her lips. "To suggest, however, that the daily, soul-sucking, mind-numbing routine of raising dependents, 24-7, is somehow a pleasure? Mm." She shook her head. "Any intelligent woman, anyone with half an active mind, half a working dream, who tells you that is lying to herself and to you."

"That's not true," Esther bit back, her eyes boring into our mother's. She looked away and lowered her voice. "I love being a mother. It's the best thing I've done. By far."

Mom regarded her with a faint smile. Tapped a gentle rhythm against the wineglass. "Whatever you need to tell yourself, Amatso. If you need a villain, I'll be the villain. In your story. But I'm still the heroine of mine. And I don't regret a thing."

We sat in silence. Esther, her head resting in her open palm, her eyes glossy. Me, frozen, empty, miles away from myself. I ran my tongue against the back of my teeth, pulled numb hands out from underneath my thighs, and stood. My chair screeched against the tile. I winced and looked at Esther. "Right, well, this was . . . a whole lot. Esther, thanks for dinner. Mom—" I threw my hands up, searching for words. Any words. "Glad you had a safe flight."

I stood, collected my bag from the entryway. Esther remained seated. "Yeah." Her voice was quiet. Maybe she was miles away, too. "See you next Sunday?" she asked.

I shrugged. "We'll see."

Mom stood, pushed in her chair without a sound, picked up the wineglass. There were only a few sips left. A merlot. She'd brought it; Esther didn't drink. "Are you going to give me a hug?" she asked.

I tipped my head to the side, exhaled through my nose. "No thank you."

"You know . . ." She turned so she had both Esther and me in her line of sight. I stepped closer to the door. "I could hear you two. In the Walnut Creek house. Talking about how I supposedly just threw Dzifa's drawings away. But I still have them. Organized by month and year. In manila folders. Every single one of your performances, too, Esther. It's all in the basement of the Maryland house. If either of you would finally come and see it, you'd see."

Esther said nothing. I didn't know what to say. Her words floated around in the still, temperature-controlled air of the spacious, spotless living room. They failed to sink in, were incompatible with my remembering of that time, my concept of who my mother was then. Who she still was.

My hand on the doorknob, I turned back to face her. "Why do you keep doing this?" I asked, my arms folded across my chest, back against the front door to Esther's house. I'd learned my lesson from last time; always be near an exit to begin with. "Why do you insist on . . . inserting yourself . . . just as soon as I'm about to get my life back? Is it like—do you set a timer, or something?"

Afraid as I was to do so, I scanned my mother's eyes for the dreaded shift. Her gaze was steady. I couldn't detect any vulturelike scrutiny. She was impeccably dressed as ever, but her charge was quieter, less electric, than when I'd seen her last. Maybe it was the divorce. Though, why this release from the expensive ruse of being my father's partner would dim her light, rather than ignite it, I didn't know.

"Dzifa," she said, her voice absent the taunting I was scared it'd be laced with. What remained was worse: a soft depletion that incited my sympathy. She looked away, beyond my shoulder, even though it was too dark to see anything through the door's designer glass cutouts. When she met my eyes again, she said, quiet like she didn't want it heard—by me, by Esther, or by herself, I didn't know—"Truthfully, you're the only thing I have that isn't also his. And I need that."

I hated, wanted to annihilate, the part of me that wanted to engage. To comfort her. The remnants of my child self that ached to propel my feet forward, my arms open, to hug her and say, *That's not true.* To demand, *What do you mean?* To reassure her, *You had so much else before him.* To give her a pep talk until she felt better, the way I used to draw her all those pictures she claimed to have kept. *In what way am I not his?* I wanted to ask. But it didn't matter in what way. We both knew it was true in any way that mattered. I pressed my arms firm against my rib cage. "I am not a thing," I said. "And if I were, I'd belong to myself." I uncrossed my arms, reached one behind my back to turn the door handle, and made my way out.

I called out from work the next day. The next, I didn't bother to. I wasn't bedridden; I was floor-ridden. Not heavy, but empty. It was New York all over again; worse, maybe, because I'd already lived this, already been here, shouldn't have found myself here again. I stared up at the ceiling for hours, from the time the sun came up to the time it fell, then I pulled the blankets over me and drifted into motion-capture nightmares. My manager politely waited a full five days before firing me. Aside from a couple of cursory texts to reassure Esther, Tatiana, and Zeynep, that I was, in fact, still alive, it took me until the following Monday to speak to anyone again. I neglected to tell Esther I'd been fired. Zeynep was nonplussed; she, like me, had started and stopped dozens of jobs in her time. Tatiana left several missed calls, and after the third or fourth, I finally picked up, chastising myself for letting her calls go to voicemail after everything that had happened.

She was the only person to whom I felt I owed the full story, but I only had it in me to tell about half of it. When I got through the bare essentials, there was a long pause on the other end of the line. I waited—for Tatiana to make a joke or to stealth-shame my most recent doom spiral. Instead, I heard her deep sigh, then a sharp intake of breath. "Dzifa. I'm really sorry you've been dealing with all of this. I actually . . . I was trying to reach you because there's been an update with the whole B and Brigitte situation. You know, with the lawyers? And I can't text about it or leave a voicemail or anything."

A hand pressing into my chest, I adjusted my position on the carpeted floor where I lay. "Oh? What happened? Were you able to . . . figure things out?"

She let out a short, incredulous laugh. "No. Definitely not. He's suing for full custody."

I closed my eyes. "What? I mean . . . I get that they were following up on . . . on Luca, and you guys were trying to work out your schedule now that you're not living together, but—"

"It's not like a criminal case or anything," Tatiana said, her voice wavering. "It's not really about Luca. I mean, it is and it isn't. It's a custody suit. They don't think I can take care of her. At all."

My mind stuck on our grief ritual, the night we brought Tatiana home from the concert. I tried to stop the memories from spinning, but they had their own will. I saw Tatiana, arms reaching out for Maddie to crawl toward her; B, kissing his daughter goodbye before we left for the Bishops' house; Tatiana, reading her eulogy with steady voice and steady tears; B, reading his, voice quiet, eyes vacant. Luca, laughing up at his mother through the phone screen, the last time I saw him. "Oh my God," was all I could say.

"Yeah," she said. "Anyway. Um. It's all kind of chaotic now. Well, I guess it was when you left, to be honest." Since I left, it did sound like the chaos persisted, but it also seemed it was settling into a new, if uncomfortable, normal. The last time we'd spoken, B hadn't been to see Maddie since the funeral. It was disconcerting, but everyone was waiting to see how things played out through the lawyers.

"As of this week," Tatiana continued, "I can have Maddie Monday to Thursday; he has her weekends." She takes a breath. "We have to write down all the details of our parenting time apart. Some custody rep is gonna stop by to check in on each of us, like how our homes are set up, how we are with Maddie. And we have to be supervised every time one of us drops Maddie off to the other's care. So Mommy's gonna come along. And unfortunately, so will Brigitte."

At a loss for words once again, I stayed quiet. Tatiana laughed, humorlessly. "As if that wasn't enough, Mommy's lawyer friend? Shannon? She suggested I upgrade my living situation to be more 'child-friendly,' which—I cannot afford to do. But she's right; Mommy's house is hard to childproof properly. So Uncle Aman offered to take us in, at his place in Milton. We were thinking about it before this all happened anyway. I just didn't think we'd have to move *now*. But you know, it's bigger and cleaner and . . . zip code reads better to the court."

"I'm so sorry," I said, hating the inadequacy of these words. Wasn't Brigitte's whole angle that she didn't want B involved with Tatiana's family at all? That she hadn't wanted him to have kids with her? Why, if she was behind this, was she suddenly angling for grandmother of the year in the worst possible way?

"Yeah, well—" Tatiana sighed. "'Tis what it 'tis. And . . . I have a favor to ask you."

"Okay?" I pulled myself up to sit against the nearest wall, my back stiff. It felt like I hadn't been upright in years. My head hurt; everything hurt.

"Did you really mean it?" The uncertainty in her voice unnerved me. "When you said you had my back, no matter what? Like . . . when I got pregnant with Maddie, I mean."

I pulled my knees up, wrapped my arms around them to steady myself. I hated that she even had to ask. But the question was called for; when she was pregnant with Maddie, I didn't act like I meant what I said. "Of course."

"So . . ." She cleared her throat. "It looks like we're gonna need statements. From witnesses, who were there when . . . well, who were there. In the days after. To corroborate our side of the story."

She hadn't even asked the question, but I knew the answer right away: the one I should give, must give, would give, even as I recognized the counterargument of a wound so many layers deep I hadn't gotten around to feeling it. It spoke in pain rather than in words, but I sensed its meaning nonetheless.

"Sam already agreed," Tatiana said, and I wanted to cling to my flare of irritation. I wanted to use that irritation as a wedge, to carve out and discard the answer that was so habitual, so deeply encoded, and so painfully unwanted. "All you'd have to do is tell the truth, Dzifa. But yeah . . . totally your call."

I pushed away from the wall, let my body drop against the carpet, resumed the position I'd been in all week. Prone, spent, playing dead. "Of course," I heard myself say. "No problem."

"Great! Thank you so much." Tatiana's relieved sigh seemed to drain any lingering uncertainty from her voice. When she next spoke, she sounded as sure and steady as ever. "Now that I got that out of the way, let's *please* talk about something less depressing."

"Um." I couldn't find a more solid surface than the ground, but I felt dizzy anyway. I tried to catch hold of myself, of the headache, the stiff back, anything that made me feel like I was a person, not a concept. I focused on the headache and sifted through the week's events for something positive. So did she. We waited a few seconds. Came up with nothing. She laughed. We promised to check in with each other more regularly.

Later that night, she sent me a screenshot of upcoming flights to Boston and a text.

Pick one. It's on us. We got you, Dzifa.

—∾—

My car was the first thing to go after I lost my job. Having spent most of my savings getting to and from Boston, I had just enough with my final, partial paycheck to pay one more month of rent. I'd have to move out by October 15. Naya put up an ad for a new roommate as soon as I was fired; I didn't blame her.

I went to five interviews; none went anywhere. I couldn't sleep anymore, and it showed. My body language, the bags under my eyes, my wrinkled clothes, my entire energy field said, "I wouldn't hire me either."

I was frozen: too frozen to go to the movement circle or accept Zeynep's invitation to make virgin piña coladas and watch a *Powerpuff Girls* marathon at her place, or to make either one of the two choices I realistically had at this point: come crawling back to Esther's house, or take Tatiana up on her offer. Neither choice seemed like a step forward; I felt I was deciding, really, between becoming either one person's burden or another's. To go to Esther's would put me squarely back in my mother's orbit; dodging her calls and attempts to visit in the month since dinner had been hard enough. With everything Tatiana had been through, was going through, I could not bring myself to become another problem she had to deal with. I couldn't decide, had fifteen days left in this apartment. Had to decide.

I stood at the edge of the bus shelter and watched young Black, brown, and Asian families pass through the public hospital I'd just left. I wondered, not for the first time, if it was strange that I always went to the doctor alone.

I pulled the paper the doctor gave me out of my bag and scanned the two notes he'd scrawled with a dull pencil. The first was a book I'd heard of many times, and read a few excerpts of, about the physiological impact of trauma. I wasn't in the mood. The next note was a URL, with the words *Directory of therapists: Medicaid, East Bay*. I folded the paper in two, halved it again, huffed a sigh. I opened it again, scanned the words again, chewed on my tongue for a good thirty seconds. An overfilled trash can sat on the other side of the bus shelter. I crossed to it, crumpled the paper, and threw it in. My phone rang; I ignored it, assuming it was Esther, calling to scold me for my absence at the last few Sunday dinners. When it rang again, I snatched it up, prepared to turn it off.

I withdrew my thumb; it was Zeynep. "Heeey! I hadn't heard from you in a bit so thought I'd give this a shot. Is this a good time?"

I looked out at the still-empty road. I hadn't checked when the next bus was coming. "Um . . . yeah, this is okay. What's up?"

"Oh, nothing; my parents are gonna be in town soon, so I've been hiding in my bed, avoiding reality and all my memories." Her tone was so upbeat, it took me a minute to register her words.

"Yikes." I grimaced. "Are you okay?"

"Meh." She soldiered on, "I mean, at least they gave me a heads-up. I still feel so bad your mom popped up out of nowhere, just like, BOOM! You are amazing for keeping it together." If she could see my current situation, I wasn't so sure she would classify my behavior as "amazing" or "keeping it together," but the vote of confidence felt nice anyway. "Remember that one time at Council, when you came back from class and she was just, like, there? In your room?"

"I'd blocked that out, but thanks for the reminder." I bent my knees a few times to get the blood flowing in my legs.

"Whoops, sorry." Zeynep laughed nervously. "But on to happier subjects: I was wondering if that movement circle was still meeting?"

I hadn't been since Boston, so I wasn't sure. "It might be. I can check, if you want to go."

"Well, actually, I was thinking I could host it one time, if, like, they needed someone to host? But only if you come, of course."

"Um." My bag slipped off my shoulder. I zipped it closed and wedged it between my feet. "So . . . I'm actually. I don't know if I can. Things are kind of . . . challenging, right now."

"Oh no!" I heard barking on Zeynep's end, then someone else shushing the dog. "Is it your mom again?"

"Not . . . exactly." I considered how much I should say. I trusted her; I was just embarrassed. It felt like ten years ago all over again. "I lost my job—it's my fault—and then things have been kind of shitty with my health. I actually just had a doctor's appointment."

Zeynep gasped. "Oh my God, are you okay? You need me to come pick you up? I mean, I don't know how that would be helpful since I can't drive, but—oh wait, no, I could Uber to you and then we Uber back?"

"You're good." I smiled a little. "Thanks, though. No, it's nothing serious. He was just kind of getting on me for not going to therapy anymore. He was convinced that would help with all the fatigue, which . . . I don't know. Like, when we were at school, therapy was . . . fine? But it's like . . . it didn't really *do* anything."

"I get that," Zeynep said. Though I couldn't see her, I could envision her enthusiastic nodding. "Same for me, pretty much. But hey! I got lucky last year and finally found someone I didn't have to spend, like, forty-five sessions explaining my cultural norms to. She's not even first-gen or Muslim herself, she's just like . . . emotionally intelligent and good at her job. So that's been good. And actually? She's helped a lot. I mean, there were a good few years there where I did not leave the house, *ever*."

An elderly couple crossed the street, arms linked. "I'm glad you found her, then. That must have been hard, and . . . yeah, I'm really glad you found someone who's a good fit." I hoped my sincerity came across but was afraid there was too much sadness seeping into it.

"I wish I could offer for you to stay here again, but it's complicated with my partner living here part-time, though obviously, if you need for a few days here and there, you can—"

My cheeks flushing, I shook my head, even though she couldn't see it. I was mortified that she'd think I was telling her my situation to stealth-beg for a place to stay. "No, no, no. I would never ask that again. Don't even—"

"Hold up," Zeynep gasped. "Circling back to the therapy thing, I would've already recommended mine, except she doesn't take Medi-cal. Not to assume, I just thought, but if you're not—"

"Yeah, I'm on Medi-cal." I laughed, putting her out of her misery. "It's fine."

"Okay, I am cooking up an idea. I am *concocting a plan*!" she bellowed, and the dog started barking again. "Oops. Okay. I can't guarantee anything, *but* I know she does sliding scale, and she's super-duper social justice oriented, so . . . yeah, I can't guarantee anything, *but*. Would it be okay slash helpful if I reached out to her and told her just like, bare bones, what you were looking for and then see if she can help?"

I didn't allow myself to feel hopeful, but I was grateful for Zeynep's attempt. Taking a deep breath, I forced myself to accept the help. "Um . . . yes, actually . . . I would appreciate it. No pressure, though. Just, like, if you can. Thank you so much."

"*Done.*" Zeynep clapped. "Well . . . let's be honest, I'm probably gonna forget in, like, two minutes, but if you remind me right before my session tomorrow night, I will totally do it."

I could live with that. "Okay, no problem. Thanks again. And, uh . . . I'll reach out to Henrietta and Sarah and ask them to add you to their circle LISTSERV."

Zeynep whooped. "Thanks a bunch! And if I get to host, you'll come, right?"

I hesitated. "If I can. Of course."

There was a pause, then a slow inhale. "You'll be okay, Dzif. You know how I know?"

Finally, I leaned against the cracked wall of the bus shelter; germs be damned. There was a bullet hole in the top corner. I let my body relax against the glass. From the corner of my eye, I watched the bus sputter into the entrance of the hospital complex.

It pulled to a stop in front of me. I hauled myself up and dragged my feet forward, one at a time, onto the bus. "Because," I could hear her easy smile through the phone, "you always are. Like, even when it seems impossible. You just always are."

"Thanks, Zeynep. I appreciate you," I said quietly as I found a seat toward the back. "I'm on the bus now, so I should probably—"

"Yeah, totally, get home safe. Text me if you need anything."

On the bus, I remembered the blue envelope I'd found in our mailbox that morning. I slid a fingernail under the adhesive that held it closed. I pulled out a single sheet of standard printer paper, folded neatly into quadrants. Typed in the corner: *Myra Jameson*, and an address in Boston. In the middle was a notice of a deposition: November 10. My birthday.

Tatiana had stuck a blue Post-it to the bottom-right corner of it:

> *Here's the notice I mentioned over the phone; they've set the date. You can do your part over the phone but if you're already here, we'll take you out to celebrate your b-day after! Thank you x a million.*

In the corner of the Post-it, she'd drawn a heart.

CHAPTER 16

October 10, Tatiana picked me up from the airport just before nightfall. Small talk wasn't usually our style, but asking the situationally pertinent questions ("Hey, how you holding up since an unbearable cascade of tragedies befell you?" or "Hey, how you holding up since your mother's untimely return tipped you into yet another Abyss?") seemed an odder choice. We stayed silent as regional pop rock played on the car radio.

Fall was making its way, trees across the city buttressed by growing piles of sunset-hued leaves, just as they'd been when we met at Elmwood. I zoned in and out on the drive to Uncle Aman's house, catching glimpses of skyscrapers shining through the dimming light, stouter brownstones crowded together like ancient LEGOs, signs marking turnoffs toward suburban outlet malls and historical sites. Even in high school, I'd never cared about Boston's perceived historic-ness. But as Tatiana drove, I had to admit: Within the invented confines of this collectively hallucinated nation, the illusion of more time passed gave me the illusion that the ground underneath me here was more solid than it was in Oakland. That would do, for now.

Half an hour into the drive, Tatiana switched the music to an audiobook. *The Birthright of the Divine Feminine* was the brainchild of one of the more enterprising members of her church. The narrator spoke slowly, her lilting voice sure, hypnotic. I wondered if I'd seen her at the funeral, but I could only envision the person who matched this voice in a jewel-toned gown, lounging in a velvet armchair with an altar of gold-bolstered candles glowing about her, and I had seen no such person or altar at the funeral. If I had the energy to raise my eyebrows at the content she espoused, I might have. I didn't, so I let it wash over me as we drove.

Sensing my reaction without my having expressed it facially or vocally, Tatiana finally spoke. "You seriously have to download this book. Or you could check out her YouTube channel. I know, I know," she interjected before I could remind her that I identified as being *too old to follow anybody on YouTube*, "you're thinking you won't be into it. But I'm telling you. Carlotta is a Black woman, okay? Well, she's kinda swirly, but potato, potahto. And she is all about helping other Black women access the kinds of high-value lives and relationships that women of other races have access to, so we can secure our wealth and position in society. Which we are *way* past due for, am I right?" When I asked what a "high-value life and relationship" entailed, Tatiana laughed. "It's how you're gonna raise your self-esteem by like 5,000 percent, *and* it's how you're gonna stop dating people who are somehow even broker than you."

Since I couldn't disagree with those foundational assessments, I shrugged. "Okay, well, I don't know if I'm after wealth and position; I'm more so trying to figure out how to make life . . . manageable."

Tatiana grimaced. "Ew. Manageable is not hot. No, no, no. I need you to aim way, way higher, my friend. But don't worry. Now that you're here, we can figure it out together."

We stopped at a shopping center a few miles out from Uncle Aman's house, on the outskirts of Milton. "We need to be quick, 'cause my uncle is watching Maddie and he has to go back out to work in a bit."

We had to circle the parking lot twice before we found a spot. "He works at night?"

Tatiana stepped out of the car. I followed suit and walked with her toward the grocery store. We stepped through the automatic doors, the air-conditioning hitting us in a cool waft. "He works all the time." She rolled her eyes. "I don't even know if he has any friends, or dates or anything. Like, as long as I've known him, he pretty much works, helps out his mom and Sarai—his sister was Sarai's mom, and he's kinda pitched in since she passed away. Or he helps out my mom and her sisters. Every now and then, he goes to official stuff like weddings." She ducked into the cereal aisle and paused to peruse the options.

"Is that . . . um—" I paused. I hadn't realized the connection between Sarai and Uncle Aman. I hadn't asked. I remembered the photo Ms. Bishop showed me in her kitchen, of the two of them and another young woman. I wondered if that was Uncle Aman's sister. "Is that . . . bad?" I ventured.

Tatiana tipped her head to one side, then the other. "What kind of cereal do you want? My uncle doesn't really eat breakfast, but he has some, like, Roman Meal bread and butter and stuff. Bleh, not for me."

When I shrugged—it didn't feel appropriate to be making menu selections for a house I was a guest in—she pulled down a box of Frosted Mini Wheats. "Oh," she continued. "And no, it's not bad, it's just like . . . weird. I mean, I like having my space and time to myself. People always think I'm an extrovert, but I'm secretly an introvert, you know?" I didn't, and doubted it. "But," she continued, "I don't get how he spends so much time by himself. He seems okay, but I always wondered if he was depressed or something. No offense." She cut her eyes toward me.

I shook my head. "It's fine." I started down the aisle again, assuming we were done here. "Maybe he likes being alone."

"Nobody *really* likes being alone," Tatiana said once she caught up with me. She picked up diapers for Maddie next, then made way for the refrigerated aisles. "I mean, people say that, but it's always people that, like—don't have any social skills. No offense."

"None taken."

"Or, like, they just say that because nobody wants to hang out with them and they're pretending that's their choice. Which, Uncle Aman is really nice, and he's really talented and actually has had a super interesting life, like, epic, if you can ever get him to talk about himself, which, by the way, good luck, 'cause if I couldn't get him to talk in all these years, then—" She held out her hands, palms up. "So I bet he could get himself a nice little crew if he'd just put himself out there a little."

I stepped back to allow an elderly white woman to push her cart past us. Tatiana pulled out a quart of skim milk. "This good?" She held it up for my approval. I nodded. I felt that milk should either be whole or skipped entirely, but again—not my house.

"Well, you know him better than I do." We proceeded to the checkout aisle with the shortest line.

"And anyway"—Tatiana raised an eyebrow—"if he would rather be alone, that's too bad. 'Cause he's about to have a full house. As it is, I wouldn't be surprised if he's taken on even more work since me and Maddie moved in."

I bit the inside of my cheek. We moved up one in line. Maybe I hadn't thought this move through enough. It was only supposed to be temporary anyway. Just a few weeks, maybe, to figure out my next steps. To find a job, either here or . . . I didn't know where. All my energy had been directed toward packing up my life and making it through the flight here. I was about to further disrupt the routines of a person who had probably built his life precisely to avoid such disruptions. Taking in Tatiana and Maddie was one thing; they were family. I wasn't.

When we reached the register, I held out my EBT card. Tatiana batted my hand away. "Save your pennies," she chastised. "This one's on me."

I swallowed, closing my eyes against the unexpected tears welling up. "I—" I swallowed again. If there was anywhere I could stop pretending I had anything under control, it was here. "Thank you so much."

"Dzifa." Tatiana rolled her eyes as she paid. I grabbed the milk and diapers; she took the cereal. "It's, like, five dollars. Calm down."

I waited till we were in the car again to say, "No, it's not. You got me a flight here. You helped me get through the last few weeks. I don't even know what I would've done."

She started the engine. "Girl. That is literally the point of having friends. I mean, it's fun having fun times when the going's good. But let's face it. Life"—she put on her seatbelt—"as I have recently been reminded, can be a real shit show." Her finger hovered above the On button for the sound system. "That's when you call your sisters."

Where Esther was concerned, it was when I left mine. But maybe chosen family really could, and did, count for something. "Still, I want you to know I really, really appreciate this. And I'll be out of your hair as soon as I can."

"Shush." She turned the sound back on, resuming Module 3. "Oops, by the way." She turned the volume to zero. "You and Sam are gonna do your depositions on the same day. If you're still up for it, that is."

"Of course." I nodded. My stomach churned; I ignored it. "Do I need to prepare anything?"

Tatiana shrugged. "Don't stress about it too much. They're probably not gonna grill you. Not like they're likely to do with me anyway, if yesterday's home visit was any indication."

I glanced at her. Her expression was neutral. She backed out of the spot. "Did . . ." I cleared my throat, started again. "Do you want to talk about it?"

Tatiana kept her eyes on the rearview mirror, paused as an elderly woman inched past, using the shopping cart for support. "No," she said.

I waited for her to elaborate. "Okay, sorry."

"Yeah, well." She shrugged. "At least I can confirm Brigitte definitely knows how to astral project, 'cause if that wasn't her soul sending out demonic bat signals through that social worker's body, I don't know *what* was happening."

"Oh. Oh no. So, did—"

"I said I don't want to talk about it," Tatiana clipped. I closed my mouth, turned my head to face the window. "Anyway," she continued, her voice less trained, "about the deposition: All you have to do is tell the truth, 'cause that's what Brigitte and co are trying to distort. I don't know exactly what they'll ask, but I'm sure you'll have the chance to hit all the main points: I'm a good mom, I don't have a drinking problem, B's family is a white supremacist nightmare, blah, blah, et cetera. You know, nothing crazy."

"Yeah." I nodded again. The churning didn't let up. I rubbed at my stomach. "Sorry, I guess I need to eat soon. Um. Yeah, that's fine. Just, I guess keep me posted if there's anything else I need to prepare."

"Prepare?" Tatiana turned up the volume again. "Dzifa, you worry too much. Like I said; just tell it like it is. Okay." She gestured toward my seatbelt. "Buckle up. We about to go deep"—she paused, took a dramatically labored breath—"into suburbia."

CHAPTER 17

Day one at Uncle Aman's, Tatiana took me on a tour after breakfast. She sat Maddie in her playpen with a cup of Goldfish crackers and a fresh bottle and led me out the front door.

"Okay," she said, setting her hands on her hips. "So this is obviously where we came in last night. But just so's you know, there's a code to get in." She demonstrated, then had me repeat it.

"Got it." I nodded, tugging my sweater around my shoulders.

"Cool. Let's . . ." She dragged out the word, then clicked her tongue. "'Kay, let's do the basement, 'cause I hate it, so we'll get it out of the way, then the rest." Tatiana pushed open the old door. I squinted, trying to determine if it was red, brown, or something in between. I followed her in. "The kitchen, you've seen, living room, what there is of it, you've seen."

The kitchen was small, with a U-shaped countertop and a compact fridge-freezer unit. The living room was large, segmented in two by ceiling-height moss-green curtains. On one side, three couches of varying sizes and varying beiges faced a TV; on the other, a midsize, dark wood dining table faced the large windows overlooking the street. There was no decor in any of the three rooms, save two photos—one of Uncle Aman's family and one of him, Ms. Bishop, and Tatiana at Tatiana's high school graduation—and Luca's urn. My breath caught when I passed it on our way to the basement. Tatiana pointed it out when we got in last night; she'd stopped to replace the fresh flowers she always kept on the mantelpiece, right beside him.

"Are you coming or what? You are, like, extra spacey these days, I swear." Tatiana shook her head and opened the basement door. She was halfway down the steps by the time I reached the door.

"Sorry about that," I said. "I know. Just . . . I don't know. Jet lag or something."

"S'fine. So here's the basement. Like I said, not a fan. Not my vibe. Spiderweb city."

I didn't look up, or too close to the walls, to verify. She kept to our corner by the stairs and pointed to the far side of the big room. There was a half-window at the very top of the walls, so I could see enough to see the washing machine and dryer there.

"Here's the laundry stuff and, like, a bunch of storage." She gestured toward the rest of the room. There had to be at least twenty, twenty-five boxes, closed and neatly stacked, pushed against the far wall.

"Wow. Is this—is that your uncle's stuff?"

"I don't know, girl." She shrugged. "It's not mine. I asked him about it once, and he said he'd meant to clear it out ages ago but didn't have the time."

I frowned, nodded. "Okay. Um—well, thanks."

"Yeah," she sighed. "Let's go back upstairs. I don't know what it is about this room; it feels haunted to me or something. You believe in ghosts? Have we talked about this before?"

I cleared my throat as we trekked out of the basement. "Probably at some point. I don't know—my answer's always been the same. If they exist, I don't wanna know about it."

"One hundred percent." Tatiana nodded, closed the door behind her.

"Like, sometimes I think it would be convenient if they existed, because . . ." She cut her eyes to the living room. "Well, because then it's like, it's not all over. On the other hand, some of the women in my church are *super* tapped into that kind of thing. And it's not like you can pick and choose which ghosts you see, if you can see them. That doesn't really work for me, you know?"

"I hear you." I grimaced. "Doesn't work for me either."

"Also . . ." She paused on the first step leading up to the second floor of the house. "It's kind of sad, I think. I mean . . . I was talking about it with my therapist the other day, and like . . . I don't know if that's what I'd want for Luca. For him to be, like, hanging around here . . . especially not now." She closed her eyes for a moment. "If he can't be here, like *really* here, then I'd just want him to be free."

I didn't know what to say. Wanted to say, *I'm sure he is.* Couldn't guarantee any such thing. "We can do the tour another time," I said instead. "Or . . . I can just find my way. I'll probably just sleep mostly today anyway."

Tatiana opened her eyes, shook her head. "Nah, it's fine."

"Mama, mama, cackah, cackah," Maddie chanted from the living room.

Tatiana sighed. "Just kidding," she said. "I'll do the rest in a few, okay? This kid and her Goldfish, I swear to God." I stepped back to let her pass. She went to Maddie.

I started up the stairs, called out, "I'm gonna finish unpacking, okay? Let me know if you need me."

"That's fine. We're good here," she called back.

I stepped into the guest room, surveyed it in the daylight: double bed, patchwork quilt draped over it, a slightly lopsided wooden wardrobe in one corner, my open suitcase in the other. Window facing the little alleyway between this house and the neighbor's.

I crossed to the suitcase, which I'd already unpacked last night. I felt guilty, presumptuous as I did, but it was a habit: I always unpacked right away, no matter how many times I'd moved, no matter how little time I stayed in any one place. I zipped the suitcase closed and wedged it under the bed. I kicked off my jeans and sweater, slipped under the covers, and tucked them tight on each side of me. I lay there, trying to land where I was, trying to remember how I got here, trying to sleep, and when I couldn't, trying to reassure myself—this was fine. This was for the best.

—~—

Week three in Milton, I'd found my routine. I woke around eight, sat at the edge of the bed, the worn quilt wrapped around my shoulders, and ruminated. When I'd gone through my four primary thought cycles a sufficient number of times—(1) unwanted-houseguest guilt trip, (2) deposition-that-could-make-or-break-my-best-friend's-life anxiety onslaught, (3) given-what-my-mother-said-is-my-whole-life-a-sham shame coaster, and (4) going-to-die-alone-and-unremarkable doom spiral—I tiptoed down the wooden steps to the kitchen, congratulating myself on my efficiency. Sure, maybe I was trapped in the hellscape of my own mind, but not everyone, I imagined, managed to cycle through four toxic thought loops multiple times in under an hour. I was not without my gifts.

Tatiana used a single-serving French press in the mornings; I preferred the ten-cup drip coffee machine wedged in the far corner of the kitchen. She'd received no less than eight condolence gift baskets—*I'm so sorry for your loss, here are six teensy pots of jam and a brand of multigrain cheese crisps you've never heard of*—and assured me it was all right to use any of the flavored coffee grounds in it. While a coffee titled, and somehow, convincingly flavored "Autumn Aspirations" filtered down into the glass carafe, I washed the tall pile of dirty dishes left over in the sink.

At ten, I registered Tatiana's sleepy "Good morning" from upstairs. She slept in her double bed with Maddie, who I had to imagine woke up much earlier. Maddie had a good-size nursery here, but it was only ever used as a playroom. Tatiana turned on the shower to preheat it, then hit Play on the day's Marriage-Minded Abundance Activation lesson: Module 6 in the *Birthright of the Divine Feminine* course. For the next two hours, I knew I'd hear her footsteps, back and forth between her room and the bathroom, as the ever-confident Carlotta McNeal blasted her wisdom at full volume. Although today, between the blow-dryer, Maddie's cries, and my now-automatic instinct to tune out Tatiana's phone, all I overheard was "high-value men are attracted to high-value women" and "condos in South Florida."

When I finished wiping down the kitchen, I opened the refrigerator and took out one of the six presliced loaves of Roman Meal bread Uncle Aman kept stocked in the bottom drawer, wedged on top of a couple of bottles of wine. According to Tatiana, her uncle didn't drink, and she'd stopped the week after everything happened. I assumed she brought the wine with her when she moved in and forgot about it. I extracted a bucket of I Can't Believe It's Not Butter! and searched a low cabinet for the store-brand strawberry jelly I used every morning. Tatiana bought cereal every now and again, but I was the only one who ate breakfast in this house.

In a round, crimson Harvard mug, I poured an inch of whole milk and the steaming drip coffee over it. I sat at the dining table and opened my laptop. First, I checked my personal email. Most of it was spam, though today, my thirty-nine-year-old sister, Faith, a defense attorney who, like Mary and Charity, had long since moved back to Ghana, sent an email with the subject line Have you ever thought about being a paralegal? I wrote back "thanks" without reading the rest and deleted the email. Next, I checked my work email. Work was a "part-time" remote data entry job that, due to my lethargy, took up forty hours a week and, between that and my EBT card, paid just enough for me to buy a small round of groceries each week. Since we were so far outside of the town center, I had to walk quite a ways to the store, unless I could convince Tatiana to stop there on one of her occasional Starbucks runs. She usually didn't want to go. My second week here, I assumed that at some point she'd have to go back to the store to stock up on baby food, or diapers, or something, but then I realized that Ms. Bishop stopped by occasionally to restock the diaper supply and that Maddie's diet consisted almost exclusively of formula and Goldfish crackers.

I could have asked Tatiana about it, but wondered if my asking was judgmental. If it was a projection, based on my assumption that parenting necessarily involved fixed nap times, bedtimes, snack times, and an ever-growing list of boring but science-tested tasks engineered to help infants reach developmental milestones. I'd picked up this assumption from my time as a nanny on the Upper East Side and my time as an auntie to children whose parents had clinical-grade anxiety. But those were all two-parent families with a lot of resources and a lot of attitude about making sure everyone in their social circles knew that their children were Ahead of the Curve. Tatiana read to Maddie, it just wasn't on any kind of schedule I could discern. She fed her regularly, it just wasn't with the nutritional vigilance with which Esther fed her young children. Most days, we all spent the day shuffling without any urgency from the dining room table to our rooms and back again. Bedtime for Tatiana, and thus for—or perhaps due to—Maddie, was late. I retreated to bed whenever I got too sad or bored to remain conscious. Usually before ten.

I felt off-balance, most days, unmoored by a disjointedness I couldn't quite pinpoint, much less correct. There was nothing wrong, per se, besides everything wrong with the world, and with those who kept Tatiana under the looming pressure of the custody decision. After day three of my stay, I stopped asking how the home visit had gone. Even when Ms. Bishop brought the case up on her supply drop-offs every few days, Tatiana responded with stone-faced silence, followed by a retreat to her room and a phone call to Sam or her cousin Sarai. If pressed enough to elaborate about the visit, Tatiana would answer, only, "Whatever. It's over."

But was it? It was peculiar, to be bracing for something, without the usual adrenaline surge, the tightening up in preparation to spring forward or close in, that bracing entailed. I tried to dismiss this uncanny unevenness, to avoid adding it to my daily wheel of thought loops. After all, Tatiana's affection for Maddie was undeniable, unfailing. Maybe, I told myself in moments when I wondered if my friend was functioning okay, if it was reasonable, expecting someone to function at all under the circumstances. Maybe unfailing affection was all that really mattered, as far as consistency went.

I looked closer at my emails; there were two new data entry assignments from the job Naya gave me a heads-up about before I left Oakland. Two new assignments meant thirty dollars, paid out sometime next week. I opened both of them in separate windows, then x-ed out the tabs already on the screen: the three grad schools I'd been contemplating.

I shook my head, shut the laptop, trudged back upstairs. I surveyed the room for distractions—there was nothing—then kicked off my jeans and wrapped myself in the comforter, settling in for another hour of ruminations. When I heard footsteps descending the stairs, I sat up and waited five minutes before going back down.

Tatiana faced the kitchen counter, waiting for her kettle to finish boiling. She waved a hand behind her. Maddie sat in a collapsible playpen at the edge of the dining room. "Oops." She turned to her right, stood on her tiptoes, and struggled to open the top cabinet. "Can you open that for me?" I did. "Can you just get that big plastic—yeah, thanks." I heaved a massive, clear plastic container of Goldfish and set them gently on the counter.

"Why do you keep them up so high?" I asked.

"'Cause that's the only cabinet where they fit." She turned off the stove. "I'm just gonna—" She gestured to a lower cabinet. I stepped back toward the refrigerator. "If you don't want to get them every time, that's fine. I can just leave them on the counter." She pulled out an earthenware mug and poured her coffee, then a couple of drops of skim milk.

"No, it's fine." I shrugged.

Tatiana set her coffee on the table, pressed a kiss to Luca's urn with her fingertips, and returned for the Goldfish. She popped open the red plastic top and poured generously into a rubber-looking bowl at the edge of Maddie's playpen. "Here you go, sweets." I peered farther into the dining room; Maddie already had a full bottle of formula.

I couldn't stop myself from saying, "Wow, she sure loves Goldfish."

Tatiana snorted. "You have no idea. She refuses to eat anything else. Just like her mama, this one. Picky, picky. Knows exactly what she wants." She pinched Maddie's cheek playfully, then bent down to give her a kiss. "And unlike her dada," she stage-whispered into her daughter's ear, "she doesn't ruin everybody's life to get it."

I slipped my headphones on and plugged them into my computer.

"Okay." Tatiana sat and opened her computer. "I have therapy soon, so I'm gonna leave in like half an hour. Are you coming again, or . . . I mean, I know there's not a lot to do around there, but it's probably more exciting than staying here."

I glanced at the back door. The two tall windows on either side of it, their blinds drawn, as always. "Um. Actually? I think I am gonna stay, if that's all right." I sat down and pulled up my work assignments. "I really need to get more of these entries done. I am not making anywhere near a living wage."

"Well, girl"—Tatiana shrugged—"that's on you, 'cause you *know* I've offered like ten times to give you the log-in for my Abundance program. Getting paid by the hour is a scam, and you know it."

I forced a smile. "Yes, well—it's the best I can do right now. And I appreciate the log-in, I just—"

"I know, I know." She rolled her eyes. "Not your vibe. Whatever. Your loss. I'll still invite you to my mansion once I move in, 'kay?"

"Yep. Thanks. I'm gonna—" I nodded at my screen, turned on my music, got to work.

Today, I wouldn't have to rush. I opened the blinds, then the door, and stepped out into the backyard. It was a modest-size square, closed off with a high wooden fence. The grass, even at the start of November, was healthy, well kept. It looked neat, but natural—not sharply manicured by industrial equipment. It was tall enough to graze my ankles. It could not be possible, I thought, in this climate, that this lawn magically cared for itself. Did Uncle Aman hire someone to take care of it, or did he do so himself—which, logistically, he'd have to do in the dead of the night? True to Tatiana's word, he was gone by the time either of us woke in the morning and usually came back long after we'd gone to sleep.

The middle of the square plot was bare; on the far side of the fence was a mural, painted right onto the wood. It was abstract—composed of little dots and flowers of varying sizes and colors, but unmistakably the form of a woman. The only other objects in the backyard were the maple tree, at the far-right corner—half its leaves having shed in a warm-hued pile by the time I'd arrived, and a low bench—metal, painted bright blue, with a tall back, perched just beneath the tree's great branches.

Usually, I stood or sat, just long enough to finish a cup of coffee or hum a song to myself. Today, I lay on the grass nearest the door and stayed for a full hour. Out here, the thought cycles looped, but not as loud. It felt like they had more space, somehow, that they were not confined to my body. As I lay, I wondered if I should feel guilty, sharing my thought loops with the air, with that great, beloved tree, with the grass pillowing my form. But I did it anyway; I needed the reprieve.

I didn't see the backyard until a week into my stay. I didn't even notice it at first; the blinds were usually drawn on the two windows on either side of the back door, and I didn't think it my place to open them. So I waited until, on an unseasonably warm day, Tatiana opened the blinds and cracked open the door. I asked her, during that first foray outside, about the mural on the fence. "Oh." She frowned. "Yeah—that's Uncle Aman's sister. He painted it himself. Five years ago, or something like that. And the tree . . . well, that *is* his sister."

"I . . . Sorry, what do you mean?" I took a step back, scanned the tree from top to bottom.

"Yeah, remember I told you how I thought the basement was haunted?" She gestured toward the tree. "His sister's remains are, like, planted with the tree. And even though he won't confirm, I'm pretty sure those boxes are all her old stuff. At some point, I'm gonna ask Sarai."

"Oh . . ." I stepped backward, prepared to retreat into the house. "Is it . . . Should we not be out here? Is this, like . . . is that why the blinds are always closed?"

"No." Tatiana shrugged. "I don't think so. That's more of a heating decision. My uncle's pretty frugal. Also, whenever me and the kids—" Tatiana paused, pursed her lips, cleared her throat. "Whenever we used to visit, he was always happy for us to come out here. He said it was nice that someone was able to enjoy it, since he's hardly ever here."

"Okay." I let out the breath I'd been holding. "I feel slightly less terrible that I just sorta barged out here. I mean, I still feel kind of bad that—"

"Although," she continued, tapping her temple, "I keep pitching him ideas to jazz this place up a little bit. Like, inside the house *obviously* needs a makeover, but also—he could totally fit a water feature out here. Maybe some stones? Fairy lights? It could be really cute. Maybe that'll be my side project, while we're here."

I looked sideways at her. "Are you sure that's okay? I mean, it seems like this is kind of a . . . I don't know, a sacred place or something."

Tatiana play-swatted the back of my head. "Girl. My family may be a *little* unconventional, but we're still Black. I would never disrespect my uncle like that. This is his house. I'm not gonna, like, stealth-redesign his backyard. I just meant I have some ideas, if he's ever open to them."

"Cool." I nodded, even though I wasn't sure it was cool. Yes, there was unclaimed space out here. But I sensed that was kind of the point.

Tatiana texted she was on her way back. I came inside, locked the back door, lowered the blinds. I poured another cup of drip coffee and sat in the living room, took out my phone, and made the call I'd been avoiding for weeks.

"Hi," I greeted when I reached her voicemail. "My name is Dzifa Quartey? Um, my friend Zeynep is one of your clients, I think. And she said you might be able to help me. Or, I guess, help me find someone I can talk to. Anyway, I'm on the East Coast at the moment, but please give me a call back when you have the chance." I left my number, hit End.

I sat back on the couch, stretching my upper spine against it. I reached for my coffee and took too big a sip, oddly thankful for the distraction of the resulting coughing fit. I appreciated Zeynep connecting me with someone who could, maybe, help me cope. But after three weeks in Boston, it wasn't clear if I wanted help coping with this situation or if I wanted out of it entirely.

I took another big sip, coughed it down again. Clearly, I couldn't sit with these feelings, as the only respectable thing to feel was gratitude for the refuge Tatiana's family provided. For Esther, taking on the aftermath of our mother's return without my help. For Zeynep, connecting me with her therapist. What was I offering, in return, to any of these people, besides my persistent excellence at relentless lethargy? When I let myself care about my impending birthday—and I tried not to, because it was also the deposition day—I imagined I'd been lingering in a sort of winter for the decades thus far. And I wondered if winter was just where I lived, or if there were different seasons available to me.

For the next twenty minutes, I perused the site for the Milan program. I scanned through the page for what must have been the twentieth time, then x-ed it out with unnecessary vigor. *I should do something more practical,* I reminded myself, like either of the U.S.-based teacher-training programs I'd been eyeing dispassionately—one in Boston, one in Oakland.

Tatiana shuffled through the front door holding Maddie, her purse, two Dunkin' cups in a cardboard holder, and a large shopping bag. I rushed to relieve her of the cups and bag, setting them on the kitchen counter.

"How did it go?" I wasn't sure this was an appropriate question, but I was running out of small talk.

"Oh, it was awesome, as usual. I think I already told you, but my therapist basically told me months ago that I'm the sanest patient she's ever had. I was like, 'Are you sure? I'm kinda stressed.' And she told me I really don't have any problems, mentally, but that I could keep coming back if I wanted a li'l extra support. Honestly, we're friends at this point. I mean, she loves me and I kinda love her, so what the hell. Plus, Mommy's paying for it."

"Cool," I said. "That's . . . great." Was it? I wondered. Since I'd been back, it was as if Tatiana found some hidden compartment for her grief. Tucked it away, maybe for Maddie's sake. Like the tightly wound fury I'd occasionally glimpse Esther trying to hide, Tatiana's grief had to go somewhere, at some point. I hoped the therapist was preparing her, at least, for when it burst through.

"What did you end up doing?" Tatiana asked. She set Maddie down in her high chair, then washed her hands.

I thought of the call to Zeynep's therapist, the grad school research.

My time outside. "Not much." I shrugged. "Just had more coffee and did some work." I wasn't sure why I declined to tell Tatiana about what I was up to, but there was a growing list of things I hesitated to tell her. Any action related to my own forward motion felt private and fragile, like I had to keep it close to the vest and guard it carefully, or it would, in its tenuous infancy, disintegrate.

"Boring, but okay." She shrugged back. "So what did you used to talk about when you went to therapy back in high school? You went to, like, an old white woman for a while, right? I feel so lucky I found a Black woman to therapize me. And she's only in her thirties, which is, like, old but not *old* old."

"Lovely." I rolled my eyes.

"Oh, shut up, you're technically still twenty-nine! And you don't look a day over twenty-seven. You good." She winked.

"Thanks?" My stomach grumbled. "She was all right. The least bad of the ones I saw. We usually talked about my family or just day-to-day stuff. I think I'm gonna make some lunch. You hungry?"

"Meh, I got a snack at Dunkin'." The edges of Tatiana's mouth tipped down. "So, what'd she diagnose you with? Don't be cagey; I won't judge."

I opened the fridge, eyed the stacks of kosher hot dog multipacks in the bottom-right drawer. I pulled out a fresh pack and a dwindling bag of Roman Meal bread. "I mean, besides the depression and trauma stuff every therapist brought up? Nothing. She was a clinical social worker, not a psychiatrist."

"What's the difference?"

"Um. Clinical social workers are more . . . human. In my experience. Every psychiatrist I've seen has been like an eleven out of ten on the psychopathy scale. I think some people have a fetish for that kind of power dynamic. It is *not* a coincidence white men made that shit up."

"Awkward." Tatiana laughed. "Hey—don't forget your coffee. I made sure they put all the cream and sugar in it."

I offered her a quick salute. "Thanks. I'll pay you back." She waved me off. I looked back in the fridge, frowned. "Actually, I know you just went out, but—do you think we could stop by the store tomorrow? I could use a vegetable or two. Feeling a little scurvy-adjacent these days."

"Yeah, sure. We could probably actually go tonight. I'm a little stir-crazy today. I need to get out of here more often. Maybe we could even go to the mall in the city or something."

I eyed the shopping bag—I didn't see a label on the outside, but there looked to be two shoe boxes inside—then popped two hot dogs in the microwave and two slices of bread in the toaster. "Oh . . . but don't you have the drop-off tomorrow morning? Won't that be stressful? All the driving back and forth?"

Tatiana's hands tensed around her coffee cup. She set it down, started making a fresh bottle for Maddie. "I can manage my own schedule, Dzifa."

I leaned back against the counter, my own hands tense around the rounded edge of it. "Oh—that's not what I meant. I just didn't want you to have to dri—"

"I'm gonna take this upstairs." She picked up the shopping bag. "You mind finishing up Maddie's bottle? I'll be right back."

"Um." She'd already mixed the formula. I just needed to put it in the bottle warmer. "Sure, no problem."

"Great," she said, already headed toward the stairs.

After lunch, I brought my laptop to the living room and looked, in vain, for Boston-based jobs. I wasn't sure, but it had occurred to me that I wasn't finding work either because of the clear lack of enthusiasm I displayed in cover letters or because I'd had a dozen jobs in half as many years. Probably both.

Despite my lethargy and possible psychosocial incapacity to be in an office forty-plus hours a week, I wanted a full-time job. Or at least, I wanted the money and affirmation that came with a full-time job, that I was a Real Person, Worthy of Taking Up Space. Having one would make me feel less guilty about staying with the Bishops, and how I had no idea when I'd be able to leave. At night, I tiptoed downstairs and searched my browser history for the school applications I'd unceremoniously closed but had yet to fill out. Aside from the reservations I had about the Italy program, it was the recommendations section that drew me to close the browser windows every single time. Who would recommend me for anything at this point?

Most days, Tatiana alternated between talking at Maddie, avoiding any conversation about Luca or the upcoming deposition, listening to her Abundance Activation modules, and researching various scams online. I wasn't sure they were scams, but she'd charged $10,000 to her Amex for a finance-focused personal development scheme that "guaranteed" that a year from now, she'd be making millions. I could judge all I wanted, but for all I knew, her brand of forward motion could turn out to be leagues more realistic than mine.

She claimed she was waiting for the right time to get back into the workforce. Membership in the Divinely Feminine Abundance sisterhood, which Tatiana explained was a long-term lifestyle shift rather than an immediate career solution, demanded an ongoing set of tasks. It involved high-priced group coaching calls with other aspiring "Muses," as Carlotta deemed their future station in proximity to the wealthy men they'd attract, and course materials Tatiana had to print herself. She frequently lamented how broke she was; I wasn't sure where she was getting the money she used for these programs or whatever she'd bought after her therapy appointment, but I assumed it came from a combination of her credit cards, her mother, Uncle Aman, and B. Anything she'd saved from her tech job in New York had to be long gone by now. Or maybe she'd always had more than she let on; I learned pretty quickly at Council that people who'd grown up with generations-deep safety nets used the word *broke* a little more liberally than people who hadn't. Broke, to me, meant zero, or less.

Tatiana returned ten minutes later, in marginally better spirits. She hit Play on a very long, very loud YouTube series about the Federal Reserve. Understanding the system, she explained to me, was essential to hacking the system. And, I gathered, since this was the end goal of all her current endeavors, becoming a multimillionaire in five years or less. Every ten minutes, she laughed and waved a hand at my glazed-over face. "Are you hearing this?" When I inevitably took too long to respond, she rewound and played it again, interspersing the video with custom commentary and casual threats to ensure I was engaged. At four, I excused myself to do some laundry and asked if she had any I could add to the pile. She gestured at a pile in the corner of the living room. "Wash the colors separately, please," she said, her eyes still on the video.

I stumbled on the last step of the basement and tried to right myself without touching anything. The washing machine was sticky with previous layers of spilled detergent; I added another layer and set it to permanent press.

Back in the kitchen, I made another two pieces of toast. I offered Tatiana one, and surprisingly, she said yes. "No butter," she instructed.

When the washing machine rattled and dinged, I went downstairs and put the first round of clothes into the dryer. I inserted the next and walked back upstairs, trying not to fixate on those stacks of closed boxes.

By six, Tatiana had made no mention of heading out to the store or the mall, so I made penne with diced chicken and grated mozzarella for dinner. "Do you want any?" I asked.

"Meh." She continued typing. "I'm in the mood for some mozza sticks or something like that. I'm gonna ask my uncle if he can pick some up. Wanna go halfsies?"

I really didn't. I'd spent forty dollars getting last week's groceries, not to mention the hours it took to walk to the store and back. I'd be willing to spend a little more on something with any discernible nutrients, but not on mozzarella sticks. "Mm . . . I don't know. I already made this, so—"

"Put it in a Tupperware!" She laughed at something on her screen.

I sighed. "Are you sure you don't want to just eat this, and maybe tomorrow after the drop-off we can get—"

"No," she snapped, closing her laptop. She took a breath and approached the kitchen. "I'm tired of eating here."

I tapped my fingers on the lid of the pot I'd used to cook the pasta in. "Fine."

"Cool, I kinda want to ask him to pick up some wine, too, but he's too pious to drink, so maybe not." She laughed. "Oh, wait, I have some already." She walked past me and opened the refrigerator, opening the bottom drawer and digging past the sepia bags of bread. "Want a glass? I also have a pinot somewhere in my room."

"Uh . . ." I leaned back on the counter.

"The pinot was a present, from Sarai," she explained. "Here, have some wine. You seem stressed."

I waited for her to pour both glasses, then asked, "I thought you weren't drinking right now?"

Tatiana rolled her eyes. "It's a glass of wine, Dzifa. What are you, the Prohibition Police?"

"No." I shook my head. "I was just . . . 'cause you asked me to remind you that you weren't drinking."

"Oh, come on." She pushed the glass toward me. "One glass isn't gonna kill either of us. What's the point of being in your twenties if you can't have a little fun? And you've only got a couple of weeks left till you're not even in your twenties anymore, so, better live it up!"

I slid my hand off the lid and picked up the glass. Maybe I was being unreasonable. It wasn't as if she was bingeing. If anything, I was the weird one for not indulging in a glass of wine with dinner. "All right. Thanks. I'm gonna eat. I'll just cover the pot in case you want any later." The first sip of wine slid down my throat, dry and bitter. I grimaced. When Tatiana went upstairs, I poured the rest down the drain and turned on the faucet to wash away the evidence.

At seven, I was still at the dining table, staring at the work assignment I should have been able to finish hours ago. Tatiana reentered the dining room, Maddie in her arms. She wore a fresh face of makeup and a cream sweaterdress over tights. "I think I'm gonna go out. Do you mind watching Maddie until my uncle gets back?" She didn't wait for a response. "Thanks. He's gonna be home in like fifteen minutes, so honestly, you just have to make sure she doesn't leave the house. He'll put her to bed, and I'll be back before you know it. Oh, and sorry, I decided I'm gonna eat when I'm out, so I told him not to do the mozza sticks." She regarded my flannel pajamas with unmasked disdain. "I'd invite you, but . . . I'm gonna meet Sarai at her place first, and I've been promising her we could catch up for ages, just one-on-one. Do you mind?"

Did it matter if I did? "Oh, no worries. I was just gonna find a movie and stuff my face some more. I'll watch Maddie."

"Okay, girl." She raised an eyebrow. Her eyes were slightly red. "See ya later. I'll be back at like ten. We're just going out for a couple of drinks."

"Oh, okay. Have fun!"

When she was halfway to the front door, coat on and sliding into over-the-knee suede boots I'd never seen before, I glanced at Maddie, then at Tatiana. "So, you guys are going to a bar?"

"Oh my God, Dzifa." Tatiana adjusted the top edge of her boots. "I'm not actually an alcoholic; I just said I'd take a break from it so I could get my energy levels up. I've been feeling kinda, I don't know, like, lethargic since I moved here. I love my uncle, but vibes-wise, this place feels like a tomb sometimes. I'm just gonna have like two drinks, and then I'll be back on my usual health kick. Also, I deserve to have some fun once in a while. It's not like Fuckface and his 'special friend' who looks like her family for sure owned slaves aren't living it up the entire week I have Maddie."

By "special friend," I assumed Tatiana was referring to the white woman we both learned, two weeks ago, B had moved into his Back Bay apartment. Or at least that he was now admitting lived in his Back Bay apartment. According to Tatiana, this "special friend," a colleague of B's, had been lurking long before the funeral, though B always claimed they were strictly platonic. "Like I always say," Tatiana quipped the last time this woman came up, "men like B would date a literal vanilla ice-cream cone just to distract themselves from their own Blackness. Like, could you at least find one with an active pulse? Somebody who has ever encountered a spice? Jesus." Even though I'd never met this woman, I couldn't bring myself to disagree with Tatiana's assessment because, generally speaking, I didn't.

I poked a finger against my temple, which had begun to throb. "Sorry, yeah—I didn't mean, like, you had a problem. I was just . . . because of the custody, um, thing, and tomorrow's drop-off—" I clocked her glare and shook my head. "Never mind. Sorry. Have a good night!"

"Niiight," she called as she walked out the door. It did not escape me that she said it with the same amount of sarcasm that she used to tell Brigitte, "Okay, byeee," at pickups and drop-offs.

Maddie waddled back and forth in her playpen, munching on one of the several animal crackers she gripped in her fists. "Okay," I resolved, picking her up and holding her at my side, "you're gonna have to eat something besides crackers, sweetie."

With my free hand, I diced a bare piece of precooked chicken into little pieces. I'd seen Ms. Bishop give Maddie meat before, so I knew she had enough teeth to manage it. I diced them smaller, just to be safe.

I gently extracted the remaining crackers from Maddie's fists and set them down on the counter. Replacing them with a piece of chicken, I smiled and said, "What do you think?"

Maddie chewed for a few seconds, then stopped. She smiled and held out her little hand. "Cackah?"

"Chi-cken," I corrected. "Chi-cken." She waved her fists merrily while she chewed the next piece.

It was only after the fourth piece that I realized that she wasn't swallowing. "Shit!" I set her down on the floor and crouched. "Shoot, sorry, Maddie. Maddie, can you open? I just want to make sure you don't have a bunch of chicken in your mouth." Maddie laughed around what I now saw was a sizable mouthful, pushing into the corner of one of her cheeks. I thought of little Luca, breathing until he didn't anymore, while Tatiana slept. I was not qualified to be an auntie; I was not qualified to be here at all. Here I'd been, side-eyeing Tatiana's lax parenting style, and I couldn't even feed a child properly. "Maddie," I said more sternly than I intended. "I need to make sure you're not gonna choke. Okay? Can you please open your mouth so I can check?"

Maddie giggled, continued her side-to-side, waddling dance. "Oh my God." I floundered, flapping my hands about. Should I call Tatiana? I sent her a text:

> Hey, I gave Maddie some chicken, cut up, but I think she didn't swallow it. What do I do?

There was no response. How could I be so stupid? This was why people pureed baby food. Just because I saw my little nephews eating pieces of chicken didn't mean I knew how to prepare them correctly.

"Maddie," I pleaded. "Can you hold still for a second?" I tried to hold her arms in place, and she whimpered, stepped away from me with panic on her face. "I'm sorry. I'm so sorry, sweetie. I'm just trying to—" I reached out again and she toddled toward the living room, beginning to cry. I began to cry, too.

The front door creaked open. I blanched and retrieved Maddie with sweaty hands. I stood up, watching her face and her breathing. Uncle Aman walked in unevenly, battling several plastic grocery bags. I hadn't seen him in over a week, had no idea he ever came back this early.

"Hey, Maddie, Maddie," he said.

"Hi." I stepped toward him. "I'm so, so sorry. I gave Maddie some chicken because . . . well, I cut it up, but . . . I don't know what to do . . . I—"

He stepped toward us, squinting his downturned eyes at Maddie. "Oh. One sec." He walked to the kitchen sink, washed his hands, then dried them on the tea towel hanging from the cabinet underneath the sink. His movements were efficient, but unrushed. He walked back over to me and Maddie, withdrew a shapeless ball of chewed-up chicken from her mouth. "Yeah, she likes to do that," he said without a trace of panic or anger in his voice. "I don't know if she's saving it for later or what."

"I'm so, so sorry." I ran a hand over my face. "I didn't mean to do that. I was just trying to feed her and—"

"It's fine." He took Maddie and gave me a small, reassuring smile. "Is Tatiana upstairs? I got some fried foods she asked for; she said you girls were hungry." He gestured toward the biggest bag.

"Oh. Um." I glanced toward the stairs uselessly. "I thought Tatiana called you. She went out? With Sarai? Sorry." I didn't know why I was apologizing, exactly.

He stared at me for a moment, then looked at the kitchen counter. "All right. Well, it's Maddie's bedtime. I'm going to put her down. You help yourself—I ate at work."

"Thank you so much. What do I owe you? I don't have cash on me, but I can walk to the ATM at Stop & Shop tomorrow. Or I could maybe find one after the drop-off, while we're out."

Tatiana's uncle waved a hand dismissively on the way up to his bedroom. "You don't owe me anything."

That was categorically untrue. I gave the kitchen another thorough cleaning, then ate a few mozzarella sticks. When I finished, I wiped down the kitchen again, brought my computer and various charging cords up to my room. It was barely eight, but I took a quick, lukewarm shower, put on a fresh pair of pajamas, and slid into bed. I remembered then that there was another load of laundry I needed to dry. I decided to leave it until the morning and commenced my nightly ruminations. I got through all four, fell asleep by ten.

CHAPTER 18

A series of loud knocks jostled the flimsy wooden bedroom door in its hinges. I jolted awake and clambered to the door. I swung it open. Tatiana's uncle stood on the other side; I released the breath I hadn't realized I'd been holding. I'd thought maybe the social worker was back for an unannounced second visit. I'd closed the curtains but could see early daylight streaming through a dusty window on the other side of the hallway, just over the stack of boxes that partially obscured it. I tugged at the hem of my sweatshirt self-consciously. "Is everything okay?"

"Have you heard from Tatiana?" He held up a large smartphone.

"Um, no. I don't think so. Let me check; I might have turned my phone off." I hadn't. I brought it to the doorway and held up the messaging app. "She didn't send me anything. What's wrong?"

He gestured at the hallway window. "It's seven already, and she's not back. I did get a message last night, where she said she would be back by ten last night. Are you sure she didn't call you? The drop-off is today, and I need to get to work."

"Oh my God. Gosh, sorry," I amended. "Should we . . . call the police or something?" I shook my head; that was rarely the solution. "Or do you have Sarai's number?"

"I tried that already. No answer. And no, no police." His eyes, normally cool and kind, were narrowed in frustration.

"Right. Okay. Um . . . that's not good." I looked around my room as if there was some answer hidden there. "Look, I'll watch Maddie. Doesn't Ms. Bishop usually come at like eight? For the drop-off?"

"Yes." He nodded. "That will be fine. I'll let you—" He gestured at my pajamas, averting his eyes even though I was covered from head to toe. "I'll wait downstairs."

I brushed my teeth for half a minute, changed into a pair of jeans and left on the sweatshirt I'd slept in. Tatiana's uncle had stationed Maddie in her playpen with a small, fuzzy blanket. She was curled up in a ball, in and out of sleep. "Kalisa is on her way. Traffic wasn't great this morning, but she'll be here within the next half hour."

"Okay, thank you. I'll let you know if I hear from Tatiana."

"Sounds good." He stood from the dining chair he'd pulled out. He turned it the right way and pushed it in. "I've been meaning to ask you . . ."

I tensed as I imagined how the sentence would end:

What is wrong with you? And could you please get out of my house?

Or, *Could you please get out of my house? You should have a real job by now.*

Or, *Could you please get out of my house—*

"Tatiana mentioned, a little while back, that you might be going back to school. Is that right?"

I frowned. I hadn't told her about my grad school research. I shook my head; probably I'd mentioned the idea offhand a few times since I moved back to California. But I wasn't serious about it then. I was surprised she'd remembered. "Um. I'm thinking about it, but I haven't decided."

"Oh, okay." He nodded solemnly. "Well, there are a lot of good schools in Boston. It's no pressure, but if you wanted . . . I think it's good for Tatiana to be around somebody, ah . . ." He shuffled his feet on the carpet. "Well, if you wanted to go to school in Boston, you're welcome to keep living here. Free of charge, of course." He stuck his hands in his coat pocket.

I had to force my mouth closed. "Wow. Um. That's extremely nice of you. You've already been so kind to me. I . . . will definitely think about it. Thank you."

"I'm just thinking." He ran a hand over his close-cropped curls. "Maybe you could help Tatiana stay focused. Her mother has been wanting her to go back to school, as well." He shrugged. "You seem like a good girl."

I stayed perfectly still. "Oh, I'm not, I'm just clinically depressed," I said reflexively. "Sorry," I added.

"Okay." He opened the door. "Well. Think about it." This was the longest conversation we'd ever had.

When he shut the door behind him, I sat heavily on the same chair he'd just pushed in, staring at Maddie's playpen. This wasn't the first time a friend's or classmate's parents had not-so-subtly asked me to keep an eye on their daughter. It had even happened with Zeynep, once, when her parents visited Council to berate her about her GPA. I could not possibly be a less inspiring influence, but any parent I wasn't related to seemed oblivious to this fact. All the things that gave me the veneer of a good girl were accidental—the only reason I'd never done drugs was because I wasn't cool enough to be offered any. I was a late bloomer not because of any particular morals but because until well after college, I was too tired and withdrawn to bother trying to garner anyone's attention—and they certainly weren't going to offer it freely. Since then, largely with Tatiana's motivating support, I'd attempted to play catch-up on the previously inaccessible concept of "fun." I'd had more sex than anyone probably suspected; I just didn't usually talk about it, because (a) it was a neutral activity to me, like table tennis, or Monopoly—something one did when one was looking for something to do, and, as long as it was neither notably good nor bad, and it was almost always neither, did not particularly reflect on afterward—and (b) it was irrelevant to my overall sense of self.

I didn't know if this erroneous depiction of me, on the part of the Bishops and others before them, was because it was impossible to be raised as an African girl without at least learning to disguise oneself as conventionally respectable.

In New York, I once went out with Tatiana and Drea, a friendly-enough former high school classmate who moved to the city around the same time. We went for a drink in the lobby of a Midtown hotel; Tatiana mandated we dress formally that evening. The bartender, a Lithuanian man in his forties, looked Tatiana up and down after she removed her coat. "Wow, wow, wow. You look like a goddess." She beamed and said, "I know." He turned to Drea. "And you, you look like a movie star from the thirties. Gorgeous." When he looked at me, he blinked, frowned, and said, "You look like a kindergarten teacher."

Ms. Bishop arrived an hour later. She rushed in and hung her coat on the door. "Hi, Dzifa. I'm so sorry we left you stranded like this. Traffic was horrible; my goodness." Maddie woke when she heard her grandmother's voice. Ms. Bishop reached into the playpen and picked her up, keeping the blanket securely in place.

"Oh, no worries." I had been worried, but fortunately this time, I decided to let other people handle Maddie's meals. I stood and pushed the chair back in. "Is it time to go? Have you heard from Tatiana?"

"Yes, we should go. It's a little early, but it can't hurt." She managed to get her coat back on while holding Maddie. "And yes. Tatiana sent me a text message. She'll meet us there. I hope she's on time, because it is not going to be good if she's late."

She opened the door and held it with her foot. I opened it wider and waited for her to step through. My key was in my jacket pocket. I locked the door, shivering while I shrugged the jacket on.

"Careful on your way in," Ms. Bishop warned as I stepped over a fresh and probably deeper-than-it-looked puddle. I climbed into the passenger's seat while she set Maddie up in the back of her old Buick. Her car seat was in the middle.

"Gama, cackah!" Maddie began her food-conjuring ritual.

"I don't have cackah, my love," Ms. Bishop said. "Here's something else for ya." She handed Maddie some sort of plastic tube, with the top ripped open. There was an apple and a pear illustration on the front.

Ms. Bishop sighed deeply when she settled into her seat. "All right. Let's get going." She put the car into drive; it was a stick shift, which I hadn't seen in a long time. "Traffic isn't so bad out here, thankfully, so it won't be long."

"No worries." I wished I hadn't put my coat on. The heat in the car was on full blast, and my armpits prickled with sweat. "Did Tatiana tell you where she's coming in from?"

"She said she stayed over with Sarai. Have you met her yet? She's the daughter of Aman's late sister. She lives over in Worcester. At least she did the last time I caught up with her; she moves fairly often. Maddie, please don't play with the snacky. Thank you, lovely."

"Oh, okay. That's good."

Ms. Bishop raised an eyebrow. "I don't know about good, but considering my daughter veered from her originally stated plans last night, I'm relieved she was at least with family. Even if Sarai is a little . . ." She lifted a hand from the steering wheel and wiggled her fingers. "You know."

I really didn't.

Ms. Bishop turned into the Dunkin' parking lot. "This is it. Better look for Tati—oh, there's her car. Thank goodness. Why don't you two catch up; I need to make sure Maddie's things are together. I got what I could from home."

As I reached for the handle, Ms. Bishop laid her hand over mine and squeezed, gently. "Dzifa?"

"Mm-hmm?" I turned to face her.

She smiled, but her eyes were serious, penetrating. "I'm not sure what"—she took a deep breath—"condition Tatiana is going to be in this morning. But it's especially important today to bear in mind what I told you at the last drop-off. You remember?"

"Yes." I nodded. "Keep it light, keep it polite."

"Exactly." Her smile faltered. "No matter what," she added, then released my hand and nodded for me to exit the car.

I waved at Tatiana when she walked around her car. I couldn't quite tell, because her peacoat was covering her outfit, but she seemed to be wearing the same clothes, and makeup, from last night. One of her new boots bore a scratch along the edge. Her eyeliner was a little smudged.

"Hey." She nodded. "I'm gonna go use the bathroom." She stalked off into the restaurant.

I caught Ms. Bishop's eye through the open driver's-side window and gestured after Tatiana. "I'll just . . . yeah."

I opened the door and located an empty table with three brown metal chairs. We didn't necessarily need to linger here, but Tatiana liked to look relaxed, and she liked to be first, as if she owned Dunkin' and sat there casually all the time. Her theory was that this production would make B feel unprepared and uneasy, but for the last two drop-offs I'd been party to, he wore the same closed, slightly frowning expression every time.

The same as today, I noticed, as he walked in ten minutes early with Brigitte and a tall, brown-haired white woman, gliding in behind him. The woman wore two-toned duck boots and a pristine, light down jacket whose hood was lined with probably real fur. She looked familiar, but I'd never met her. I assumed, based on her inclusion in this legally charged drop-off ritual, that she was the "special friend" Tatiana had also been referring to, interchangeably, as "Whatsherface" and "L.L.Bean Bitch."

I threw a panicked look out the window and waved toward Tatiana's car, hoping Ms. Bishop would see me and bring Maddie in. I couldn't really see through the car windows from here.

"Oh, don't worry, sweetie. We're early—there's no rush." Brigitte's smile opened up, those Disney princess eyes scanning my ill-fitting attire. I'd hoped to look employed today, but given the time constraints and limited costume budget, I doubted I pulled it off.

I faced forward in my chair. "Um, thanks. Hi." I considered smiling, in case not smiling would be recorded as a mark against Tatiana, but I couldn't muster up the energy.

"Hi, dear. You know, your name is on the tip of my tongue, but I just can never quite remember." I forced my eyes to remain still in their sockets. This was the third time she'd seen me in as many weeks. "It's so tough these days, with all these exotic names, you know?"

"It's Dzifa," B said levelly. "Nice to see you." He nodded. "I didn't realize you'd still be in town. This is Avery, by the way. A colleague and friend of the family. I don't think the two of you have met."

I bit the inside of my cheek and forced my lips to curve somewhat upward. I glanced at the now-identified woman beside Brigitte. She looked like most of the girls I went to high school with. Those girls, with those very same duck boots, showed up ready from day one, preened and poised to be matched with the right kind of boy. I wondered what her family, whom I knew nothing about but felt I already knew, thought of her spending so much time with her "colleague." Half-Black and new money? Couldn't be their favorite. "Nice to meet you, Avery."

She extended a French-manicured hand and copied Brigitte's perusal of my appearance. "So nice to meet you, Deena."

"It's actually—" B started, and I held up a hand.

"No worries. Yes. Well. Happy to be here." I grimaced, unsure why I'd expressed this sentiment when not one of us was happy to be here.

He nodded again. "Good you're still in town. It must be nice for Tatiana to have a friend around."

"What's nice for me?" Tatiana said, closing the door of the bathroom behind her. She'd put on fresh eyeliner and lipstick, but she still looked tired. When she saw B, his mother, and Avery, she frowned. "You're early."

"Yes, well." He looked at the ceiling. "You did comment last time that I was two minutes late, and then you noted it in the log, so . . . didn't want to inconvenience you."

"Absolutely, dear." Brigitte smiled at Tatiana. "We know you must have so much on your plate. It looks like you've had a busy evening." Her eyes paused at the scratch on Tatiana's boot. "Speaking of which, these two need to get back to work. Would it be all right if we went ahead and got going?"

After a tense few seconds, in which Tatiana took one step closer to Avery and offered her a tight smile, Ms. Bishop scrambled into the restaurant with Maddie in her arms. "Sorry about that—I didn't see you three come in at first." She handed B a large diaper bag, then Maddie. "Here are her things."

"Thanks, Mommy." Tatiana stepped forward to kiss Maddie. "Bye, munchkin. Be good, okay?" She stepped back. I wanted to high-five her for her restraint. I wasn't sure I'd have done as well.

"Great, we'll just get going, then. Bye, Kalisa. Dzifa." B opened the door, and Brigitte stepped through with a flimsy, backward wave.

"Wait just one second. I need you to—" Tatiana stopped when Ms. Bishop cut her a warning look. She took a deep breath. "Can you please, as noted in the parenting agreement, remember to return Madeleine in the clothes that I send with her? I would prefer not to receive her in . . . somebody else's clothing." She cut her eyes toward Avery.

At this, Brigitte leaned back through the door B was holding open. "Oh, we're terribly sorry about that, dear. Avery brought home some gorgeous little outfits for her. One of her clients is a major fashion house—I'm not sure if you knew that. We really just thought that while you're figuring out your next steps, you might appreciate your daughter continuing to enjoy the standard of living to which she's become accustomed at her father's house. And"—she furrowed her eyebrows in feigned concern—"I did notice an odor on one of Maddie's jumpers last time. Maybe you spilled a refreshment on it? I asked B to make note of it in the log, just in case. You know, since we're all so committed to being detail-oriented when it comes to Madeleine's care."

Tatiana's head cocked to the side. "Excuse me? I really hope you are not—"

Ms. Bishop squeezed Maddie's cheeks. "It's so great to see you all—have fun, Maddie!"

I steered Tatiana toward the doughnut display and exhaled when I heard the door creak shut.

"Sweetie, I need to get going," Ms. Bishop said, standing a few paces away from us. "We'll talk later." It definitely wasn't a question.

"Okay, bye, Mom. Thank you." Tatiana was impassive, her eyes focused on the menu she'd already seen a million times.

While she decided, I ordered two glazed doughnuts and an extra-large coffee with cream and sugar. Basically cocaine, but I needed it.

Tatiana finally ordered a coffee with almond milk and a bacon breakfast sandwich meal.

"You okay?" I asked, trying to seem nonchalant by staring at the lid of my coffee cup.

"Yep." She popped two hash browns in her mouth.

"Your uncle was pretty worried about you."

Tatiana's eyes widened, her face otherwise still. "Okay."

I took a sip. "I was kinda worried, too, if I'm being honest. 'Cause you said you'd be back at ten."

"What're you, my mom? I was with Sarai the whole time. It just got late, so I wanted to get some sleep, and it didn't make sense to drive all the way back."

When I looked up and saw the red in her eyes, the bags under it, I wondered if she was hungover. "Oh. Okay. Your uncle got mozzarella sticks, after all."

"Cool. Can we go? I'll drive," she said, as though I ever did.

I hurried after her, trying not to spill my coffee while I stuffed the second doughnut in my mouth. It was already stale, so I choked a little bit. "Sure. Um. Lemme just—"

Tatiana unlocked the car and climbed in. I half jogged to catch up. She started the engine. "We're going to my mom's, by the way. We'll stay there this weekend."

"What?" I put my seatbelt on. "I didn't pack anything. I thought we were going back to your uncle's."

"Well, we're not. Milton is boring. You can wear some of my clothes or my mom's." She began pulling out of the spot, then pulled back in and put the car in park, engine still on. "These shoes are so *fucking* uncomfortable." She pulled her new boots off with a huff and threw them in the back seat, narrowly missing my head on the way.

"Careful!" I held up a hand to block a boot as it soared past me. "If they're so uncomfortable, why did you get them?"

"Ugh." Tatiana put the car back in reverse. "Sarai was right."

I tugged at the seatbelt, trying to loosen it against my chest. It wouldn't budge. I relented, sank back into the seat. "What are you talking about?"

"Never mind," Tatiana mumbled. "Let's just go."

I stayed quiet the rest of the drive back to Dorchester. Tatiana played Sisterhood of the Divinely Abundant Herteps, Module 7, through the Bluetooth in the car. As we pulled into the street of her mother's house, she said, "I have a confession to make."

"I'm not a priest, but sure." I snorted while she parked.

"So, you know how I said I was out with Sarai last night?"

For a moment, all the blood in my veins seemed to go in the wrong direction. "Yes?"

"I was." She paused. "At first. But . . . she actually introduced me to this guy she knows."

"Okay." I tried to remain calm, even-keeled, even as flashbacks of the night she told me about B tried to knock me off-center. "So . . . what happened?"

"Nothing." She shrugged. "He wasn't cute. I mean, yeah, basically, I've been talking to Sarai about my Abundance Activation training? And I think she, like, kind of misinterpreted what it's about."

"Oh?" I bit down on my tongue.

"Yeah . . ." She adjusted the heat in the car. "I guess she thought I was looking for a sugar daddy?" Tatiana laughed, but the smile didn't reach her eyes. "Which, I would obviously never do." She darted her eyes toward me.

"Obviously," I echoed.

"Right. So anyway, little misunderstanding. *I* thought she was introducing me to someone she legit thought I should date. And he wasn't at *all* my type. Way older, I mean bonus points for international, but, like, no. But"—she sighed—"I felt like, hey. It doesn't hurt to go on a date. Like, clearly B has already moved on. Maybe it's time for me to put myself back out there. Just a little."

I swallowed the responses that came to mind first and scanned for a feasibly diplomatic one. "What does that really mean, though? Moving on?"

Tatiana didn't answer.

I dabbed at a spot of condensation on the window. "Never mind," I said. "Continue."

"I don't know, Dzifa. I . . . I feel tired. Like, no matter how much sleep I get. I don't *feel like* dating, no. But I refuse to be this, like, sad, broken person who can't get it together."

I winced. "Don't you think you're being a little hard on yourself? I mean, nobody would blame you for needing some time to . . . I don't know. Just some time."

"I don't want more time feeling like this," Tatiana said. "I want to be better. Over it. I don't wanna date right now, but I want to *have* dated. I want to *have* found someone. I want to *have* made my millions, secured that mansion for me and my mom. I seem to have no energy to make any of it happen right now. But I just want to *be* there already." She reached up, pulled her braids out of their ponytail, massaged her temples. "So for a hot second, last night—this guy, he wasn't, like, a monster—he just wasn't cute. And I thought, why *not*? Why not let someone else take on some of the work? What am I trying to prove, doing it all myself? That I'm a strong Black woman? That doesn't matter to me. I mean, where does that even get us?" She shook her head. "I don't wanna be strong. I want to be happy. I want to be safe. I want to be loved. That's it. You know?"

"Yeah," I said. I wasn't sure what was harder to realize: that I had the same wishes, or that when I heard them spoken, my first thought was: *Impossible.* "So, just to clarify: Did you . . . I mean, did you go back to Sarai's, or—"

"*Jesus,*" she snapped. I jolted in my seat. "Are you kidding me, Dzifa? I told you: He was not my type, *and* I'm not looking for a sugar daddy. Nothing happened. I just . . . I thought about it. And I told him I just wanted to get home. He offered to give me a ride home, and that was it."

"Got it. Okay." I nodded. "Wait—*he* drove you?"

"I should never have told you this. I *knew* you'd overreact. Sarai knows him; it's not like he was a total stranger or something. And like I said, nothing happened."

"Sorry." I shrugged, not sorry. "I was just worried. I mean . . . I'm glad you were able to get back to Sarai's, then."

"I know." She cleared her throat. "And at least now, Sarai knows: The next time she sets me up with someone, it should be—like, *not* that kind of thing."

Any chill I'd tried to hold on to evaporated. I finally managed to loosen my seatbelt; I swiveled to face her. "You aren't seriously thinking about doing that 'kind of thing' again, are you? I mean, I kind of cannot believe Sarai would just leave you there with someone you'd never met before."

She turned her head away from me, tapping her cheek with a blue-painted fingernail. "Nothing happened, Dzifa. You are so dramatic. Just because you're, like, afraid of everything, doesn't mean everybody else has to be. And"—she paused, turned back to level me with a death glare—"since you seem so interested in the goings-on of my uterus, I'm planning to get an IUD soon."

"That is *not* what I'm worried about." I ran a hand over my face. "Just." I cracked open the door and snuck a foot out of the car. "Just, if you're going to do that again . . . like, hang out with someone you don't know, please, please let me know. Or let your mom know. Or—well, frankly, I'm not sure Sarai is helpful here, but, like . . . could you text Sam or something?" She didn't respond. "I'm just—" I softened my tone. "I'm not judging you. I'm glad you're okay, and obviously, you can do whatever you want. I know it sucks for everyone to be watching you all the time, but the situation right now is like—"

"Oh, you're not judging, huh?" She swallowed loudly. "Well, that's new. As if you haven't done shady things to survive."

"I never said I didn't." Given the frequency with which I'd been on the precipice of homelessness, particularly the year I graduated high school, I'd had to follow through with more than a few quests for what I liked to think of as "alternative income streams." But much to the detriment of my overall financial security, I never had the social skills, wardrobe, or entrepreneurial aggression to turn a halfway decent profit. Still, I knew enough to know that even sex-adjacent work had the word *work* in it for a reason. I reached a hand out to pat her awkwardly on the shoulder. "That's exactly why I'm saying this. If you have other options, take them. And if you don't, then just make sure somebody is watching your back, okay?"

"Whatever." She shrugged my hand off. "Let's just go inside."

Ms. Bishop was knitting in the living room when we came in. "Hi, lovely. How was your surprise sleepover?" She raised an eyebrow at Tatiana. "You know you can't just do that, right?"

"Not right now, Mommy." Tatiana plonked down on the couch beside her mother. I took an armchair in the corner.

"This is not all about you, my dear," Ms. Bishop countered. "A lot of people have been working hard to make sure Maddie is where she should be. Please don't take that for granted. It isn't easy for any of us."

"I said, not right now." She lifted an arm to cover her face and blew out an exasperated breath.

We avoided each other for the rest of the night. I rooted around in the fridge for leftovers; Tatiana, as usual, seemed impervious to the need for sustenance and trudged up to her room. I arranged the pillow, sheet, and knitted blanket Ms. Bishop left for me on the couch.

I couldn't sleep. I let my mind drift to thought cycle #2: the deposition-that-could-make-or-break-my-best-friend's-life anxiety onslaught. *Just tell the truth.* I let Tatiana's favorite refrain reverberate in my mind. For the first time in that thought cycle, I let myself acknowledge: This refrain did not offer the comfort I wanted it to. I had no idea what truths the attorney who questioned me would demand. And I wasn't so sure of my ability to respond with the streamlined certainty I felt I should.

It wasn't her capacity for motherhood I doubted. I figured that mothering, even for women like Esther, who were praised for being naturals at it, was something that had to be grown into. A growing parallel to, even as it was responsible for, the growth of the child. It was Tatiana's will that I wondered about on days like today. I couldn't always tell—couldn't really know with a level of certainty I could bank on under threat of perjury—what distinguished a woman committed to growing into a mother, from one who, like my own, was prone to resisting, at her children's expense, any such transformation.

CHAPTER 19

Monday morning, Maddie was scheduled to arrive at 10:00 A.M. Tatiana slept in; Ms. Bishop was out at the dry cleaner. Saddled with the same unease I'd been feeling all weekend, I only managed a couple of hours of sleep. I checked the time on a lopsided clock clinging to the kitchen wall. There was still an hour and a half until the pickup.

I shut the front door behind me as softly as I could and started walking. If I was quick about it, I might have time for a coffee, but mainly, I just needed to move my limbs and get out of my head. I hadn't really taken the time, before now, to look at the street Tatiana grew up on. I thought of Uncle Aman as I passed the house he and his sisters grew up in, a narrow, two-story brick house with fresh yellow paint. It now housed a young white family. The parents sometimes waved through the window of the Bishop house as they pushed their high-end stroller around the cul-de-sac. Ms. Bishop made a point to smile and wave back, though her smile dropped as soon as they crossed out of her line of sight.

My mother once told me she felt claustrophobic in neighborhoods like this, where the houses were so close together, that she'd felt claustrophobic when she moved to Harlem as a teenager, and it felt like everyone was on top of each other all the time. According to her, that was why she'd put so much stock in living in big houses with big backyards, far away from any unplanned social contact. But as much as I shared my mother's avoidance of small talk, I liked Dorchester. I liked how many different people there were, how many different shades of brown, how many different languages spoken.

I crossed through a small park on my way to the nearest Dunkin'. Just as I was leaving the paved pathway to cross the street, I heard my name. I turned in a circle, looking for the source of the voice.

B stood beside a low bench, his hands in the pockets of his black fleece pullover. "Hey, Dzifa—can I talk to you for a minute?" I scanned the park with my eyes; there were only a few dog walkers out.

"What are you doing here? And where is Maddie? The pickup is in like an hour."

"She's fine, she's with Avery. Look—"

"You should not be here." I shook my head. "This is not good. You're not even supposed to talk to Tatiana without supervision. What do you think you're doing, lurking like this? Were you *following* me?"

He sighed. "We just came early; that's all. We didn't want to wait outside the house, so Avery took Maddie to get a snack, and I saw you down the block. I've been meaning to talk to you, and I wasn't sure when else I'd get the chance."

I tugged at the edges of my hat. It was getting too cold to just stand around like this. "You and I don't have anything to talk about." I turned to cross the street, then wondered if Avery had brought Maddie to get a snack at the same place I was headed. I turned back around, stalking past B.

He reached out an arm to stop me; I flinched, and he stepped back. "Sorry—I wasn't. Just, please, just two minutes. I will not bother you again, I promise."

"No, you won't bother me now." I shook my head. "Anything you think you need to say to me, you actually need to say to Tatiana, or her lawyer, or your lawyer. Probably all three."

He sat on the bench, rubbing his hands up and down on the legs of his pressed chinos. "Please," he said. "This is important. I really will leave you alone after this. Two minutes."

I looked around the park, then sat stiffly, at the very edge of the opposite side of the bench. "It's a minute and fifty now."

"This has not been easy for me, you know."

I stood up. "Yeah, I'm gonna go."

"Wait! Sorry. Please, sit."

Reluctantly, I took a deep breath and resumed my uncomfortable position.

"I just mean, I know you don't believe me, but I actually love Maddie. That is why this has all been . . . I'm just trying to protect her. And I know you used to be close with Tatiana, but you didn't see her day after day like I did, not when Maddie was born, and then . . . you didn't see what she was like."

"I'm not talking about this." I folded my arms across my chest. "You must be out of your mind to think this is appropriate."

"Your deposition is coming up. I'm just asking you to tell the truth," he pleaded. "I know she's not . . . evil or something. I guess. But she's not very responsible."

"Are you really in a position to be asking that of me," I bit back, "when you and your mother have been peddling lies, making life even worse? Not just for Tatiana but for your own daughter? Don't think I haven't heard about your mother's behavior, before everything happened."

What little color B had seemed to drain from his face. He opened and closed his mouth a few times. "My mother didn't do anything wrong. When she . . . When Luca . . . It wasn't her fault. She didn't do anything wrong."

"Wait, what are *you* talking about?" My head jerked back. "I was talking about how she treated Tatiana, with all the adoption talk and the formula shaming. What exactly did your mother do?"

B shook his head, ran his hands over his face, dropped them into his lap. "It doesn't matter now."

"Yes, it does. If you know something . . . if your mother has some fault in this, you can stop all of this from happening."

"No." His head snapped toward me. For once, I considered that his signature vacant expression was not, in fact, a lack of feeling but a form of disengagement with which I was all too familiar. His brown eyes were full now, unshed tears creating a liquid veil over his grief. "I mean, it's too late to . . . This is already fucked up. Maddie is gonna be so fucked up because of this. It's better just to let things play out. With or without your help. I can't—"

I bit my tongue to avoid the most obvious, least diplomatic truths from escaping it. For starters, that he shouldn't have started and been so complicit in something that was in danger of "playing out" at all. Instead, I said, "It is not too late." I took a breath. "What you've already done is part of Maddie's story now. You can't change that part. But if you could remove your head from your own ass, or Satan's ass, or wherever it is, you can give her a different kind of story. One where her parents were not perfect, but they cared enough about her to figure out how to do better." He stayed silent. I didn't even know why I was bothering to give him the time of day, but while I was here . . . "Maddie will remember that effort. It will count. If you don't, if you put your, forgive me, but *god*awful mother ahead of an innocent person you chose to bring into the world—"

"I didn't choose—"

"You did. You did make that choice. And now she's here. Whatever happened with Luca, Maddie is still alive. So if you're not happy with how you've been doing, and it would really be a rare sign of self-awareness if you weren't, then try something different."

His eyes scanned the gravel path in front of us. "Would it make a difference to you if you were in her shoes?"

"I don't know." I shrugged. "I'm not. Maybe it's a more productive exercise for you to ask yourself that question. Would it have made a difference to you if your mother had course-corrected earlier in your childhood?" I thought of Brigitte's vague allusion to having been less than prepared when she had B.

"Course-corrected?" B tapped agitated fingers on the arm of the bench. "You don't know anything about my childhood. My mother did the best she could."

I raised an eyebrow. "If you say so." *You're the only thing I have that isn't also his.* I batted away the memory of my mother's face, the childlike sadness in her voice. "But you might want to consider there's a difference between the best we can do now and the best we are willing to do going forward."

He frowned, his hand stilling. He opened his mouth to respond, closed it again. I waited a few seconds, then shrugged again. "For example—and in spite of the fact that you *and* your mother are at this point champions of overstepping, I'll try not to overstep by making assumptions about your childhood or whatever necessitated you visiting our school's infirmary as often as you did. I'll speak for myself, okay?"

I looked behind and beside us to verify we were still free of an audience. "I could completely buy that my mother did the best she knew how to do at the time. That she had no guidebook, didn't have the support she needed. But"—I steeled myself, pausing to graze a closed fist down the center of my chest—"once time passed, once she was able to see—or me and my sister were able to tell her—that how she showed up was hurting us, I really wished she'd cared enough to try literally *any* other way of showing up. I don't know about Esther—my sister, I mean—but for me, I never expected my mother to be perfect or without fault. I could easily forgive her for anything she'd done, even the worst of it. I hate that about myself, because it is fucking incapacitating, but it's true." The wind swept a few leaves across our path. I picked one up and absently broke it into pieces, soothed by the soft crunch. "I didn't need her to erase the past or feel guilty for it or even atone. I just wanted her to acknowledge, 'Whoops, that didn't work. Can you bear with me while I try something else?' Or, like, if she had no idea what to do, to ask someone for help. And if that didn't work either, I'd have understood. Because she was putting the value of that effort over the value of projecting this . . . image . . . that things were perfect when they were so profoundly broken. I'd have taken 'broken and working on it' over . . . 'broken, but don't tell anybody; just shut up and drown in it' any day of the week."

Clearing my throat, I nudged the rest of the leaves under the bench with my feet. "Anyway. Your story is whatever it is, and I'm not telling you how to feel about it." I wanted to. I wanted to tell him that I could see, could imagine, how painful it must be, to see his brothers receiving more care, resources, steadiness than he probably ever did. I didn't have to imagine it; in my family, the order of which child warranted mother's actual best worked in reverse, but it stung the same. "But I do strongly suggest that you *not* take your hands off the wheel when you still have a chance to make this right." There was nothing left of the leaf save its spine; I brushed the pieces off my jeans and onto the gravel below. B remained silent. I darted my eyes toward him. He'd moved his hands to the edge of the bench, his knuckles taut and pale. "Though if you are going to course-correct, might I recommend doing so sooner rather than later. Say, before we all have to put on ugly suits and go to a courthouse."

"Hm," he mumbled. "So you do remember Council." He glanced at me; I kept my eyes straight ahead of me until he looked away. B sighed, said, "That's the most I've ever heard you talk."

"Don't get used to it." I sighed. "I'm exhausted. And . . . pot calling the kettle, et cetera."

B crossed his arms over his chest. "I . . . appreciate what you're saying. But it's not that simple. It's not like Tatiana is without fault. Just this weekend, Laurent was reminding me of some of the things she did. Even the way she acted the night after Luca—" He clicked his tongue. "And I can't just—"

"*Who* is Laurent?" I shook my head.

B frowned. "My . . . brother? The youngest one. You've met him a few times now."

I looked away, only marginally shamed; this was probably the same brother I'd taken to referring to as "Tad" since I met him the week of the funeral. I stood, brushed park bench debris from my jeans. "All right, dude, this has been . . . unsettling, but I've gotta go. I don't want to be involved, *at all*, to be honest with you. So unless you're going to share whatever it is you're holding back with Tatiana, then please, please . . . for your daughter, withdraw your claim. You don't have to explain why now, but hitting Pause on this before it gets worse is the least you can do."

I stepped back onto the path. "Why haven't you told her?" he called after me.

"What?" I swiveled around, crossed my arms across my chest.

"That we know each other." He blinked.

I rolled my eyes. "Just because we've crossed paths does not mean we know each other, Brett. And we won't, because you will not talk to me again, thanks." I resumed my path down the walkway, shaking off the guilt his lingering question started to kick up.

On the way back to Milton, Tatiana played the end of Module 8 at full volume; in the back seat, Maddie made quick work of a fruit pouch. Ms. Bishop had sent us home with another week's supply of diapers and formula, plus some more assorted food options for Maddie.

"Now," Carlotta explained through the car speakers, "if you are not yet connecting with high-value men, the first thing to check is your energy. We've been working on some of the mantras the last few lessons, but it's time to kick it up a notch. Remember that as Black women, we need to be mindful of our tone, our disposition, the ways in which we are perceived. So repeat after me: My feminine energy is sacred. My feminine energy is powerful. My feminine energy is soft. My feminine energy is—" I hit Pause on the dashboard.

"Hey!" Tatiana protested. "I was listening to that!"

"I know, sorry. But I need to tell you something." I took a deep breath.

"Ugh." She changed lanes, speeding ahead to pass two cars that were on the slower side. "Fine. What is it?"

"B kind of . . . accosted me in the park. When I was out for a walk, earlier." I braced for impact.

"What?!" Tatiana changed lanes again, driving toward the nearest exit. "Nope, nope, nope, we are going to the Back Bay. I am gonna—"

"Wait, wait, no! Just let me finish first."

Tatiana glanced at me, frowning, then returned her eyes to the road. "I do not like this. I hate this already."

"I know." I took another breath. "So first—um, do you remember how, like, I guess it's already like two and a half years ago now? When you found out you were pregnant with Maddie? Remember how you showed me a photo of B and asked if I knew him while I was at Council?"

Tatiana's pause was so long, I worried she'd tuned me out. "Yes?" she finally prompted, the word quiet, crisp.

I forged ahead, with much higher blood pressure. "And I said I'd never met him?" Her breathing had become loud, almost dragon-like as I struggled to get the words out. "Well . . . um, I was telling the truth. I mean, I didn't remember meeting him. But I realized, um . . . the week of the funeral? When I saw him in person, he looked really familiar. And then I asked this friend I went to high school with, and yeah. I actually did run into him before, in high school. At the health center. A few times. But we never, ever spoke."

I opened my mouth to continue, but didn't actually know what else to say. I decided to wait for her to respond. She sped up a little, passing another slow-moving car. "And . . . *why* have you been lying to me this entire time?"

I shook my head. The guilt felt big enough to drown me; even as I tried to stay afloat, I did wonder if she'd ever confront him for not telling her. I didn't realize until today that he recognized me, too.

"I didn't—I mean, I wasn't lying on purpose. It took me a while to confirm it was him I saw in the health center. And then, there was so much happening that week, I forgot. And then it just seemed like—does it even matter? I still didn't really know him. We never even spoke. So—"

Tatiana snapped her head toward me. "I don't give a shit if you *knew* him or not. I wouldn't even care if you'd *fucked* him. I care that you didn't. Tell me." She punctuated the last three words with sharp vitriol.

"Oh my God!" I brought a hand up to my chest. "*No.* Why would you even say that? I would never do that. I am really, really sorry it took me so long to tell you, but please don't even—I have never been attracted to him. No offense."

Tatiana was quiet for several minutes, her forehead scrunched up, her lips pursed. Maddie played the drums on the sides of her car seat in the meantime. I held my breath.

"Hm," Tatiana finally said. "You know what? Neither was I."

"Sorry?" I turned to face her.

"I mean," she clarified, seeming caught off guard by her own smile, "that I have never really been attracted to him either."

I tried to suppress it, but couldn't help the shocked gasp of laughter that escaped me. As soon as she heard it, Tatiana laughed, too—first, a short burst of air, then a loud guffaw. Soon, we were gasping for breath, tears streaming down our faces, completely undone by the absurdity of her statement. Maddie's drumming kicked up in concert with our laughter, evolving into a jubilant chorus of squeals, backed up by a joyfully uneven beat.

"Oh my God," Tatiana choked out between hiccupping laughs. "Nonsense. Nonsense!" She wiped tears away from the corners of her eyes. "Okay. I have to stop by the grocery store. Hold on. Oh my God, I can't." She took the next exit and maneuvered toward a Stop & Shop.

I finally regained enough composure to speak. "Can I ask . . . if you were never that into him, then why did you—"

"Oh." She rolled her eyes. "I don't mean I didn't like him at *all*. Obviously, there was some attraction there. But I just mean, if I look back on that first night we were together, I mostly thought . . . I could do worse, you know? I don't know; it was the holidays. I was bored."

I nodded. "Yeah, I've been there."

She parked the car in the lot; it was mostly empty at this time of day. Once she'd taken off her seatbelt, she turned toward me and said, "I know you have."

"I really am sorry," I repeated. "And I'll tell you everything he said to me in the park. I mean, it was very brief, and I was mostly trying to get away from him, but I'll tell you everything."

"Yeah, you will. I'm gonna need *all* the details," Tatiana admonished. She popped open the door of the car. "Okay, come on. Let's get some veggies—since my mother spent twenty minutes *lecturing* me about them—and you are going to tell me all about B the butthead and whatever he said when he accosted you. Fucking stalker."

CHAPTER 20

"Have you had any reflections on what we spoke about, our first session together?"

With the phone wedged between my shoulder and my ear, I ripped open the brown packet of turbinado sugar and tipped it into my third free coffee refill, not bothering to stir it properly. I took a sip. IHOP was not *specifically* designed for phone therapy, but I couldn't take the call in the house; the walls were too thin. So I made the extremely long walk here, filling up on all-you-can-drink decaf while I waited for the appointment to start. Decaf didn't taste the same, didn't quite hit the spot, but I was getting too old to keep pretending caffeine made my thought loops any less loopy. "Reflections on . . . sorry. What do you mean?"

"No sorries needed," Carmen reassured me. "Thank you for asking for clarification. Could be reflections about the session, or reflections about what we talked about our first session—like the challenges that have come up for you while staying with your friend . . . Tatiana?"

"Yes. Um . . . about the session, it was helpful not to have to rehash my entire life story just yet. I just don't have the energy right now. And about my situation here in Boston, I've mostly been thinking about the deposition I told you about. It's tomorrow, and I am . . . not feeling good about it."

"Hm," Carmen affirmed. "That's understandable. Can you tell me more about what feels not good about it?"

"Um, everything." I placed my teaspoon on a napkin, watched the coffee residue soak it. "I do not like courts, I do not like anything having to do with the law or governments or official governing bodies. I do not like sitting in hard chairs and being asked questions by someone who was captain of their debate team, whereas the one debate I had to do in school made me have an epic panic attack. Let's see, what else . . . I have slight prison abolitionist tendencies, which make any engagement with the alleged justice system feel like being complicit in something I find morally repugnant . . . so those are a few reasons, for starters."

"Hm." She paused. When I didn't follow up, she added, "Those sound like very reasonable reasons to me. What else is coming up for you, around tomorrow?"

"I think"—I hesitated, took a breath, tried again—"that I've been carrying this fear, since . . . a thing that happened with my mother. I don't really want to get into it right now. But to sum it up, I had the rug pulled out from underneath me in a way that I didn't even know could happen, but was somehow perfectly legal. You could argue she did it out of concern, but . . ."

"Do you feel she did it out of concern, Dzifa?" I was relieved she didn't ask me to elaborate on the specifics; I was appreciating this about Carmen so far.

"No," I said. "I think she did it to remind me of my place. To remind me of her power. And it worked. Since then, I've felt like I need to stay under the radar, out of sight, not do anything too big or noticeable, in case I accidentally get too visible and let my guard down again and then just . . . lose everything, abruptly."

Carmen's exhale on the other end of the line was long and helped me find my own breath. "That's a lot to carry. And if you're open to it, we can work together on how to let go of some of that pressure, let yourself take up more space. But I'm wondering, Dzifa, if it would feel supportive for you to focus this session on how to approach this deposition from an emotional and physical standpoint so that we are minimizing, as much as possible, the stress in what is truly an intense and potentially activating event."

I topped up the cream in my coffee and took another sip. A young waiter walked by with the carafe; I shook my head, and he continued on. "What do you mean by an emotional and physical standpoint?" Was this lady about to have me doing yoga in the middle of a deposition?

"What I'm inviting you to do is to find where you *do* have control in this situation. The opposing lawyer will have their own plan, the setting—an attorney's office, right?" I hmm'd my assent. "Is going to be what it is. The questions will be what they are. Is there a way that you can envision yourself, while you are there, in a setting that feels more supportive?"

I frowned. "But—okay, so I would love to eventually let my guard down in, like, the grocery store, but I'm not sure *this* is the best setting for me to start practicing. If I say the wrong thing, I could cause serious damage."

"I understand," Carmen acknowledged. "You don't need to let down your guard, but I want you, tonight, to do an exercise for me. Think about, and if possible, even visualize, or draw, a setting where you feel totally safe. Something that feels like your place, where you can be yourself, where nobody can pull the rug out from under you. Then notice how you feel when you visualize the deposition in that place, just you and the person who's asking the questions."

"Aren't you supposed to be encouraging me *not* to dissociate?" I asked.

Carmen laughed. "Well, dissociating—or, spacing out, as I've heard you call it—is a coping mechanism. It isn't something to suppress or be ashamed of. I hope to support you so that you can be more present, when it serves you, over time. But there can still be times when spacing out is a valuable resource for you."

I turned to look out the window. The parking lot was mostly empty this late on a Thursday morning. The sky was gray, the pavement caked with frost. "Okay. I . . . don't know if I can do that. The whole visualization thing." And though I was not about to tell her this, I found the suggestion infantilizing. How was giving myself an hour of arts and crafts time going to prepare me for a custody deposition? I watched an old Explorer, not dissimilar to the one Esther used to drive, weaving its way out of the parking lot and back onto the main road. "But"—I turned my eyes back to the empty booth in front of me—"I'll try."

The next morning, I tugged the lapels of my borrowed blazer, aware the arms were too short but glad to have the additional layer today. Ms. Bishop had left it in front of the living room couch in Dorchester before she left for work with a note: *Just don't wear jeans, and you'll be fine :) Good luck, and thank you, Dzifa.* There was also a small box of chocolates with a birthday card resting on top of it. I'd never really liked candy, but I'd eat a few out of gratitude and offer the rest to Tatiana.

Sam drove us to the lawyer's office; as we entered the parking lot, Tatiana drew her head up from where it rested against the window of the front seat. "Welp, this is it," she announced, her tone solemn and a little snide. "No going back now." She perked up suddenly and turned around to peer at me in the back seat. "You feel ready, Dzifa?"

Not at all. I swallowed. "Mm-hmm. Yep."

Tatiana narrowed her eyes. "You look like you're gonna pee your pants. Don't be nervous. Just tell the truth, remember? Just, if you tell them that—"

"I know," I interjected. "I know the spiel."

She hesitated, then nodded. "The spiel?" she frowned, turned toward Sam. "What about you, Sam? You good?"

Sam nodded, a few too many times. "Totally. My mom is a lawyer, remember? I am very much accustomed to these types of settings."

You're accustomed to depositions for your best friend's morbidly timed custody dispute? I wanted to ask but didn't bother. I just wanted to get this over with.

"And then when it's all over, it's time to celebraaate!" Tatiana whooped.

"You are officially in your dirty thirties! Dinner is gonna be lit. And I finally get to meet this Zeynep person."

"Oh, you have a friend coming in, Dzifa?" Sam asked, her curiosity piqued. "I didn't realize you were so popular." She laughed. I didn't.

"Yes," I said. "Zeynep is a friend from high school. She lives in Oakland, but her parents live in Philadelphia. She's been out here for a family thing this week, so the timing worked out."

"Aw, that's so sweet!" Sam crooned. "Oh my God, it's so hard to imagine you in high school!"

"Then don't," I countered with a saccharine smile. I wanted my birthday dinner to be simple, low-key, and passive aggression–free, but Tatiana said it would have been awkward not to invite Sam, since she drove all the way out here.

Tatiana looked as if she might start playing referee, but Sam pulled into a spot and cut off the engine. I heaved a labored breath and exited the car, smoothing down my wrinkled A-line skirt and straightening my coat.

We entered a conference room at the very end of the office, with a long, oval wooden table in the center. The wood was smooth, lacquered, and dark. The wide windows offered a view overlooking the city. Shannon, Ms. Bishop's lawyer friend, sat next to me, the court reporter, a fatigued-looking white woman with graying red hair, at the head of the table, and a videographer in the far corner. I sighed. I hated people taking photos of me, let alone a video of one of the most stressful moments of my life.

On the other side was B's attorney, Ms. Jameson, a young woman with shoulder-length, straight black hair. She might have been mixed or Dominican; it was hard to tell. Maybe it didn't matter. Probably everything mattered in situations like these.

I remembered what Carmen asked, yesterday, when there were only two minutes left in our session: "Dzifa, do you feel this situation in Boston is a supportive environment for you? It sounds very stressful, very activating." Our time ran out before I could come up with an answer I was willing to voice aloud.

"Ms. Quartey," the court representative continued the proceedings. "Do you swear to tell the truth, the whole truth, and nothing but the truth, under penalty of perjury?"

I cleared my throat. "Yes, Your Honor."

Shannon leaned over to whisper in my ear, "She's not a judge; you don't need to say *Your Honor*."

I closed my eyes for as long as I thought I could get away with, took three deep breaths, and tried to place myself, as best I could, in the safest place I could imagine.

"Ms. Quartey," B's lawyer began, "can you tell me how you know Ms. Bishop?"

I kept my eyes on the corner of the studio I imagined myself in: warm, the black, taped-down floor worn in but clean, and empty, except for me and the attorney. In the corner, just as there had been at Elmwood, there was a tall, occasionally teetering sound system right next to a small, high-ceilinged dressing room. I tried to relax against my chair—which was, yes, hard—and pretend I was lying down on that floor instead, that the lights were off and the sun hadn't come up yet. From this place, I recalled what Tatiana, Ms. Bishop, and Shannon had coached me on: Don't say too much. Just answer the question.

"Yes. Tatiana and I met in college. I was a transfer student, so I came in as a sophomore, and she'd already been there a year. I think we met in church." I let my brain play a sort of compilation CD of all the songs I used to dance to, alone, in Elmwood's studio.

"Okay." She scribbled some notes. "Can you tell me a bit about your time in college, any memorable experiences you had with Ms. Bishop?"

"Um." I tried to remember, tried to keep myself on the studio floor in spite of the chair's wooden arms digging into my forearms. "Memorable experiences? Um." I swallowed, shook my head. "I don't know . . . we took some classes together. Like dance classes, Italian, French, um . . . we were in a praise dance group together, at the church, for a while."

"I see." Another note. "And when did you next see Ms. Bishop, after college?"

"In New York. We were in the city at the same time. Not living together, but, um, yeah . . . we were pretty close."

"Okay." Another note. I shifted in my seat. My back was getting stiff, too. I stopped resisting it, let myself slouch against the wood. "And Ms. Bishop left New York? My understanding is that she moved in with her family in Boston shortly before she gave birth. Were you still close with her at that time?"

I paused. "Well, sort of. I mean, yes. I actually left New York about a month after I found out she was pregnant. I can't remember the exact timing."

"Okay. Why did you leave New York at that time?"

"Uh." I cleared my throat, for a moment drawn back into the room, the blinking light from the camera. I turned away from it and moved into the dressing room. "I was going through a lot at that time. I wasn't feeling very well."

"I see." She nodded. "And could you elaborate on what you mean by 'going through a lot'?"

Shannon interjected. I jolted a little in my seat. I hadn't placed her in the studio with us. Should I? I shook my head, then glanced self-consciously at the camera, back at the table again. I looked just above the attorney's eyes, hoping it would seem I was fully here. "Ms. Jameson, may I ask how that is relevant to the custody dispute at hand?"

She didn't look up from her paper. "I am attempting to determine the reliability of this witness."

"This witness is not on trial. I would appreciate if we could stick to the dispute, which involves the two parties noted in the filing."

"Very well," Ms. Jameson continued, an eyebrow raised. "Let's move on. Did you keep in touch with Ms. Bishop throughout her pregnancy?"

"Not all the time." I shrugged. "Well, not with Maddie. With Luca, yes. We talked on the phone a lot. Texted back and forth. Every now and then, we'd do a video call."

"When did you meet Ms. Bishop's children in person?"

I looked down at my lap. My palms were sweating. I found a hand towel on the low bench at the edge of the dressing room, wiped my hands, and sat on the floor, on my heels. "Um. I actually didn't meet them . . . Well, I never got to meet Luca, unfortunately. Not in person. I met Maddie the week of the funeral. I'd been hoping to come to Boston as soon as I could, of course." I scanned the closed, mismatched boxes of overworn costumes stacked on one side. "But I didn't know . . . I thought I had more time."

"Of course." She cleared her throat. "All right. Could you tell me about your relationship with Mr. Adams? Had you met him before the week of the funeral?"

"No," I shook my head. "Um—sorry. Scratch that." She raised an eyebrow; Shannon sighed. I picked up a box in the corner of the dressing room and opened it. "Yes. I did see him before, but I didn't really meet him. We technically went to the same high school, but we never spoke then, and I didn't realize that was who Tatiana was with until the week of the funeral. So, I don't know him well, except through what Tatiana has told me about him."

"I see. And what has she told you about him?"

I didn't know what to say or not say here. Inside the box was an electric-blue, Lycra jazz dress, the hem short around the thighs. There was one long sleeve; the other shoulder open, and a slash of a meshed cutout just above the chest. "Uh. Well, I think she was hopeful they might be able to co-parent. When he asked her to move in. But it sounded like that didn't work out."

"What didn't work out?"

"Well. It sounded, from what she told me over those months, like they weren't getting along."

She looked between me and Shannon, her eyes finally settling back on her notepad. "Did she tell you about the nature of their not getting along?"

I began undressing, replacing my warm-ups with the costume. "It sounded like he was not the most emotionally supportive. He criticized her a lot, from what she told me. And . . . yeah, he, um . . . It just sounded like he was pretty critical. His mother, too. Maybe even more."

"Okay. Ms. Quartey, how much concern did you have about this 'critical behavior' she spoke of? Were you concerned that she might be in physical danger?"

I sighed, then sighed again, letting my forehead drop onto the uneven wooden floor of the dressing room. "I don't know. I mean, I wasn't sure.

I did ask, at one point, whether she'd consider moving back in with her mom. But she felt like it was best for the kids if she stayed with B. I think."

"Ms. Quartey, I'll ask again—and if you don't know the answer, it's perfectly okay to say so. Do you believe that Ms. Bishop was experiencing abuse of any kind?"

I swallowed and picked my head back up, sliding my way back onto the floor of the studio. "It's not for me to say. I wasn't there with them."

"Okay, then—"

"But," I interjected, making my way back to the center of the studio in slow, winding movements across the floor, my body never losing contact with it for more than a moment, "I don't think there always has to be, like, obvious physical threat for a situation to feel unsafe. I would probably feel unsafe if I was trying to raise my children and there was someone living in my house, ignoring my parenting preferences, shaming me, telling me I should've put the kids up for adoption. Especially if it was someone whose . . . um." I thought of Brigitte's comments about Luca as we left the funeral. "Whose worldview could hurt the way my kids saw themselves, felt about themselves. I'd feel unsafe." I reached for the glass of water in front of me and took a sip, spilling a few drops on the table as I set it back down a little too hard. I went back to the studio, imagined some unseen hand pouring, very gently, very slowly, a pitcher of water over my head, when I'd danced, and was overheated, sweaty.

"Thank you, Ms. Quartey. I don't have too many questions left; thank you for bearing with me."

"No problem." It was *such* a problem, but there was nothing I could do about it. I lay back on the floor, my head now propped up by a pillow—soft, enveloping.

"Can you please tell me about the conversations you had with Ms. Bishop in the immediate aftermath of her son's death?"

I jolted back to the conference room, the bright lights jarring, Ms. Jameson's eyes cold, evaluative. I crossed one ankle over the other; my knees scraped against the underside of the conference table; I uncrossed them. "Conversations?"

"Yes, did you have contact with Ms. Bishop in the immediate aftermath of her son's death? I understand you flew all the way from California the next day. That's a long flight."

My eyebrows drew together. "Um, yes. She reached out. Right after . . . well, I don't know the timing. It was the middle of the night."

"And?" she prompted. She tapped on the table twice with the end of her pen.

"I . . . told her I'd get a flight as soon as I could. I went to work. I think we texted back and forth a few times. Just . . . logistics." My heart rate escalated. I began to feel a familiar, pulsing pain in my limbs, one I was now realizing was, and had always been, triggered by stress. I tried to put myself back in the studio but was struggling to even recall what it looked like.

"How would you describe her mental state in those correspondences?"

"Her mental state?" Was this a trick question? They were all trick questions, I reminded myself. "Her son had just died. So, I don't know . . ."

"I understand it's a sensitive question." I wondered how long it had taken her to perfect that tone of patient concern. Weeks? Years? Did it come to her naturally, or were there workshops involved? Were they open to the public? "I'm asking, in your opinion, was there anything unusual about her mental state at that time?"

A burst of air escaped through my throat. "With all due respect, I don't think there's a . . . usual way to react to somebody you gave birth to dying? If there is, I wouldn't know. I think I'd be completely devastated. I think she was completely devastated."

A pause. "Thank you." More scribbling. "Just one more question. Excuse me, two more."

"Sure." I wanted to let my head drop onto the table and sleep.

"How would you describe Ms. Bishop's relationship with substances?"

I sat up straighter. "Substances?"

"Yes, alcohol, marijuana, and drugs such as cocaine—"

"No," I blurted.

"No, you've never known her to consume any substances?"

I rested my hands on my knees. Try as I might, the studio was gone. Not even a memory now. I tried to make it okay, then, to be in this place, which was definitively unsafe. I lowered my eyes to the table. Maybe if I just stared at the lacquered wood, I'd forget where I was again.

I considered her question. How to answer it. What I was allowed. What I was willing to say. Though I'd been out with Tatiana many times, this was the first time I'd actually lived with her. I couldn't prove she never did drugs, but I knew she did not perceive them as the slightest bit glamorous. I'd be shocked to discover otherwise. I didn't think weed was worth mentioning, since it seemed she'd only tried it a couple of times and, like me, was unimpressed. I wasn't sure of her reasoning; mine was that my natural, sober personality routinely caused people who just met me to ask if I was stoned. "Sorry, no, I meant—she doesn't do any drugs. And with alcohol—it's not . . . she drank a normal amount. In college. I mean, in general."

"I see. And what do you consider a normal amount?"

A spot at the middle of my rib cage stung. I found it, laid a finger there, and pressed hard, not allowing my eyes to drift toward the camera or toward the lawyer. Not even to glance sideways at Shannon. "Ah—I'm not sure." I thought of how much I usually saw her drinking and subtracted, like everyone does at their annual physical. "A couple of drinks?" *A couple* could be flexible, right? Like *a few*.

"How many drinks, specifically, Ms. Quartey?" Ms. Jameson tapped her pen on the table.

"One or two, I guess."

"I see." She glanced at her notes. "How often?"

I pressed my eyes closed, took a breath. Opened them and shrugged. "Um, well, we both were working full-time. So just at the weekend. Once a week, twice at most." That last part was fully true, if we were only counting times that she drank with me and not the number of drinks.

"Thank you. And has Ms. Bishop ever expressed to you any concerns about her use of alcohol or any other substances?"

I didn't mean to pause. We'd all been expecting this question. Preparing for it. *Just tell the truth*, just like Tatiana said. But in the moment, eyes on the table, hands folded, gripping each other viselike, it wasn't so easy to discern what the truth was. All I knew was that this lawyer had no interest in the truth. Her job was to use whatever I said to defend her client. And who won the case—even though, I was convinced, everyone lost by engaging in it to begin with—had nothing to do with the facts. It had everything to do with whoever told the more convincing story, garnered the most sympathy, beat their opponent to the punch.

My stomach churning, I raised my eyes from the table, picked a spot just below the lawyer's eyeline, reminded myself to breathe. Tatiana wasn't perfect, no. But she shouldn't have to be—how many mothers, if someone barged in on their homes, at the worst moment of their lives, would be assessed as perfect? I had no doubt that, out of the two available options, she was the better parent. Or at least—she had the better family, which, I convinced myself, was basically the same.

Ms. Bishop was one of the most devoted mothers I'd ever met—she wasn't cloying, over-attached. But she was effectively devoted. I saw in her what it was to love someone not in spite of their flaws but in full awareness of all that they were, in full belief in their worthiness of love, even when they're at less than their full capacity. From what I'd seen so far, Uncle Aman offered gentleness and an on-demand, quiet, but functional commitment to his childhood friend and her daughter. He'd provided a space, scaffolding, to hold her and Maddie when they needed it. Tatiana was still a young parent, a new parent. It would take her time to find her own way. But the one truth I knew with certainty was that she was better held than most on the journey. I cleared my throat. That was the truth, I realized, that my answer should serve.

"No." I flexed my back against the wall. "No, she's never expressed any such concern. There is no such concern. I would say something if there was." I added without meaning to, "I was raised by unreliable guardians." Flashes of Tatiana's more puzzling moments sprouted up, threatening to break my resolve: the shopping bag of new shoes, the last-minute overnight with Sarai, the concert on the night I got to Boston. *What if I'm wrong?* the most fearful part of me asked. I shook my head. "She's a good mother."

"I see." She seemed, if not disappointed, then slightly disengaged. I wondered what she'd asked Sam, who went before I did, if she'd already gotten what she needed from that. If I'd proved myself an unreliable witness already, and now she was just asking questions as a formality. "Thank you." She took thirty seconds to continue writing. "I understand you've been staying with Ms. Bishop at her uncle's residence, is that correct?"

"Yes." I nodded.

"And you have observed her parenting practices while at her uncle's residence?"

"Yes."

"You say she is a 'good mother.' But could you share whether you've ever had any concerns based on your observations about the manner in which Ms. Bishop is raising her daughter?"

I thought about the Goldfish crackers, the late bedtimes, the lack of any discernible parenting strategy. Not ideal, but not the worst I'd ever seen. Brigitte's scrutinizing eyes, smug smile, came to mind.

And not the worst I could imagine. "Not at all," I said.

"On October 26, I understand you were present at the custody exchange, where Ms. Bishop was late, and, according to the parenting log, appeared to be hungover. Is that correct?"

"Yes. I mean, no. I mean—" I adjusted the blazer around my shoulders. "Yes, I was there. No, Tatiana was not hungover."

"Are you certain?" Ms. Jameson asked.

"I—no, I suppose not." I frowned. "But she did not appear hungover to me. Just tired."

Shannon placed a hand on my shoulder. "I'll remind you, Ms. Quartey, if you are unsure of an answer, it's better not to answer."

"Okay." I shrugged. "I'm just saying—she did not look hungover to me. But no, of course I can't be a hundred percent sure."

"I see." Ms. Jameson nodded and made a note. "Prior to that drop-off, it would have been Ms. Bishop's responsibility that week to look after Maddie. Who was looking after Maddie while Ms. Bishop was absent?"

I thought back to that night. "Well, mainly, her uncle. I watched her for maybe twenty minutes or so, while he was on his way home from work."

"Does that happen often?" Ms. Jameson asked.

"Sorry?" I scratched at a patch of dry skin behind my ear.

"Does Ms. Bishop leave her daughter in the care of others frequently?"

"No." I shook my head. "No, that's the only time she asked me to babysit. And no, when she has Maddie, every other time, she's been with her. She brings her everywhere."

"Thank you." Ms. Jameson nodded curtly. "You've answered my final question. Is there anything else you think may be relevant to share with me today, Ms. Quartey?"

My head felt heavier than it had in weeks. I stared at the table again, at the little divots in the wood. "No." I was scared that my answer about the night she'd been out with Sarai could have impacted the case. So I opened my mouth again. "Well, actually, um . . . I just. I don't know Mr. Adams well, like I said. But I've been thinking about . . . I guess all of this is supposed to be about Tatiana's character, right? Because he started all of this. You asked if I thought Tatiana's behavior was unusual after Luca died. And I just want to say, the way the Adams have acted with all of this? I think *that's* unusual behavior. That's . . . that's all, I guess."

A desperate part of me—the ride-or-die I wished I were—wanted to tell her more, to tell her everything. To explain about Brigitte, to explain about how B had found me in the park and seemed on the verge of confessing something. I should have said more, earlier. But I couldn't seem to open my mouth again, to speak further. I'd recounted everything B said to me in the park to Tatiana, so if there was something to be done about it, she'd have to do it. I'd done as much as I was capable of. It wasn't enough, probably, but it was all I had left to give.

I couldn't decipher the sound Ms. Jameson made. It seemed more displeased than neutral. "Very well. Thank you, Ms. Quartey. I appreciate you taking the time to record your statement today."

"Thank you," I parroted back, hoping she could sense that what I really meant was *Fuck you.* Ms. Jameson motioned for the court reporter to conclude the proceedings. I closed my eyes, found the dance studio again, let myself collapse against the cool, solid ground.

CHAPTER 21

I'd told Tatiana I wanted to go somewhere cheap and easy, like Chevy's, for dinner, but she insisted on picking the restaurant and said not to worry about it, that she'd pay since it was my birthday. I relented, more out of fatigue than acquiescence. I'd given Sam and Tatiana a heads-up that Zeynep would most likely be late. She was already in town, but she was always late, to everything, and I'd learned to anticipate it.

What I didn't anticipate, when we arrived to the restaurant, was that Tatiana would choose an upscale Italian bistro in the Back Bay, so close to where B lived. But she said that's how she knew it was good, because he'd taken her there that first weekend they were together and a few subsequent nights when she was pregnant. I also did not anticipate, upon entering and being ushered to our corner table with a view of the street, that Sarai would be waiting. She sat in the corner seat, a glass of red wine in front of her, already nearly empty. I looked at Tatiana, perplexed. "You didn't mention you were inviting more people?" I whispered.

She shrugged, playfully sticking her tongue out. "I figured, the more the merrier, right?" I turned away from her so she wouldn't see my grimace. *The more the merrier* was a phrase I would never say, had never said, and had in fact said the opposite of in reference to this birthday dinner. Tatiana sat across from Sarai; Sam slid in next to her.

"Sooo." Sarai winked. "Thirty, huh? Don't worry, girl, you've still got time."

I looked around as if the logic of that statement would be found floating around inside of an errant dust particle. "Time for what?"

"Oh, you know." She smirked. "Find a man, have kids—have you found a job yet? Tatiana told me you've been looking."

"Oh!" Sam said. "Dzifa's gonna get a teaching degree; Tatiana told me she's applying to a couple of schools out here, and I told her about a fantastic program at UMass—oh! By the way, Dzifa, I gave your contact info to one of my old grad school classmates who does admin there. I hope you don't mind; I'm so excited for you! It's so nice that you're gonna do something that really helps people."

Did I even need to be here? A waiter approached and asked us for our drink orders. "We're expecting one more," I informed him. "But, um . . . I'll have a Shirley Temple."

"Girl, what?!" Tatiana laughed. "You cannot have a Shirley Temple on your thirtieth birthday. She'll have a G&T. Actually, G&Ts all around." The waiter nodded and walked away. Tatiana leaned to nudge me with her shoulder and raised her eyebrows. "The drinks are *amazing* here. You will not regret it, I promise. Remember, this one's on me. Well, me and Mommy." I was fairly sure this was not what Ms. Bishop had in mind when she contributed to this occasion, but it probably wasn't my place to comment.

"So," Sarai started, reaching out to grab Tatiana's hands. "Give me the rundown. How did the thing go today?"

Tatiana rearranged her braids so they all draped over one shoulder. "I'm just glad it's over. For now."

"Me, too," Sam groaned. "I was prepared, but wow. Although—Dzifa, it's so weird she didn't ask you about the whole"—she dropped her voice to a whisper—"wine bottle thing."

I glanced around the restaurant. No traces of B or Avery, but still—this was a little too close to their home for comfort. "I think we probably shouldn't talk about this here."

Sarai rolled her eyes, but Tatiana nodded. "No, you're probably right. That man stays stalking me." *Aren't you stalking him, right now?* I wondered. "I'll debrief you during our next adventure," she promised Sarai, who gave her a double thumbs-up.

"So what should we do after dinner?" Tatiana asked. "Dancing? Bar? Strip club?" She laughed.

I offered a weak laugh in return. "Tempting, but . . . I really would like to stick to the original plan. Just take it easy, you know? It's been a long day."

"Yawn," Sarai quipped. "We should at least do something fun at dinner. What about truth or dare?"

I tried a breathing exercise Carmen recommended, even though I'd explicitly told her during our first session that I had been managing to get oxygen in and out of my lungs for upward of thirty years without anybody in a Free People kaftan telling me how to do so. To my dismay, the exercise she gave me made the difference between, say, indulging an impulse to push somebody out of their chair and not doing so. "I don't know." I shrugged. "Now that I'm thirty, I feel like it's a wrap on those kinds of games, no?"

"Oh, please! I beg to differ," Sam said. "Age is all in the mind." She tapped her temple.

"Okay," I agreed. "Fair enough. But in my mind, I'm about three *hundred* and thirty years old, so . . ."

Tatiana laughed. "Oh, Dzifa. I can't stand you sometimes; I love it. Okay, yes, we *could* play truth or dare. *Or* we could do two truths and a lie." Hadn't we already, though?

The waiter returned with our drinks. I eyed the artfully garnished G&T before me and sighed. "Are you ready to order?" he asked.

"Sorry, we're still waiting on one more person."

"And," Tatiana added, "we haven't even looked at the menus yet. Give us a minute?"

The waiter flashed her a tight smile. "Certainly."

"Dick," Sarai commented as he walked away, loud enough for him to hear. "Okay, two truths and a lie. Who wants to start?"

I spotted a flourish of billowing fabrics and benignly chaotic energy through the window. Zeynep was here; thank God. I was starting to feel like a hostage at my own birthday party.

"Sorry, sorry!" she announced as she approached the table, wrapping me in a bear hug and setting a large, iridescent fuchsia bag in front of me.

"Aw, thank you," I said. "You didn't have to get me anything, though. It's enough you came all the way out here from Philly."

"Oh, no worries!" she said, still standing at the edge of the table. "I was happy for an excuse to escape the ol' parental unit, you know?"

"You must be Zeynep?" Tatiana asked, holding her hand out.

"Oh, sorry! Yes," I said. "Everyone, this is Zeynep. Zeynep, this is Tatiana, Sam, Sarai. Zeynep and I went to high school together." She shook each hand in both of hers.

When she got to Sarai, Sarai surveyed her outfit: an oversize Nine Inch Nails T-shirt, tucked into a tie-dye maxi skirt. "Interesting skirt," Sarai said. "So, um . . . West Coast."

Zeynep darted her eyes toward me. "Thanks?"

"Have a seat," I insisted, gesturing for her to sit on the cushioned bench beside Sam.

"So, Zeynep, we were just about to play—" Tatiana started.

"Uh, should we maybe order first? So we don't keep the waiter waiting any longer?" I suggested.

"That's Dzifa." Tatiana shook her head. "Doing other people's jobs for them, for free. Am I right?" She shot Zeynep a conspiratorial look. Zeynep peered back at her, looking a little confused. Tatiana pressed on. "Dzifa, you just worry about enjoying your birthday, okay? But sure, if it makes you feel better, we can order."

Two rounds of two truths and a lie, three rounds of never have I ever, and several courses later, I ached to go back to the house and sleep. It seemed like Sam's, Tatiana's, and Sarai's energy levels were even higher than at the beginning of dinner, though; they were in perfect extroverted sync, bouncing off one another with quick banter and well-timed gossip. Zeynep was usually just as chatty, but tonight, she was quieter than I was used to, her mouth downturned, her eyes assessing Tatiana.

"Okay, okay, okay." Sam laughed. "We have to do your birthday wishes, Dzifa. What do you want? What are your goals? What's the plan for thirty?" Tatiana and Sarai leaned in; Zeynep stayed uncharacteristically still.

"Uh—that's a lot of questions." I forced a laugh. "I don't know about all that." I could have mentioned the school applications since I'd finally submitted three, but this wasn't the right crowd for that information. "I think I just want to keep trying to live life on my own terms."

"Which means *what*, exactly?" Sarai quipped. "It seems like you're kind of, like, lost."

Zeynep tried to cover her gasp with a final forkful of her now-cold lamb ragu. Sam stared at her empty plate, an eyebrow raised.

"I'm not judging," Sarai continued. "I think it's just that different people have different constitutions. Tati and I talk about this all the time." She tapped her chest, taking a long sip of wine with her free hand. "Me, for example? Everybody knows I started my family a little earlier than anticipated. But I didn't let that stop me from keeping my life together. I have a man, I stay working, we live well, we can afford to travel, my kid has everything she needs. Why? Because I *make* shit happen. You can't just sit around waiting."

"*Sarai*, it's her birthday," Tatiana chimed in. "Don't say that."

"No, I'm trying to help," Sarai said, reaching over the table to lay her palm over my hand. I retracted it, the force of the movement nearly knocking over my empty water glass. Zeynep was quick; she righted the glass before too much of it could spill. Nonplussed, Sarai continued. "Or take Tatiana: She's handling everything like nobody else could. Taking care of her daughter, carrying all this court shit on her shoulders. You think she'd be able to do that if she was sitting around feeling sorry for herself? You can get there, too, but you can't be so *sensitive* all the time."

Under the table, I dug my fingernails into my palms. When I heard Zeynep inhale, I wanted to stop her from getting involved, but somehow my vocal cords were immobilized. Probably proving Sarai's point, demonstrating my weakness.

"That's one way of looking at things," Zeynep started, lifting a hand to signal the waiter. "On the other hand, doesn't the world have *enough* assholes in it?"

"Excuse me?" Sarai narrowed her eyes. "I don't even know *who you are*. Who do you think you're calling an asshole?"

"I didn't say you were an asshole." Zeynep shrugged. "I said I don't think the world *needs* more assholes. Like, I get that nowadays everybody loves to be a cool girl who doesn't give a fuck, but I think we'd all benefit from having a few more people in our lives who *do* give a fuck." She took the last sip of wine from her glass.

The waiter came back to the table with our check. Zeynep, Sam, and I pulled out our wallets. Tatiana, who had seemed frozen as Zeynep spoke, snapped out of it, shaking her head. "No, no, no, I've got this, I told you."

"I don't mind splitting it," Zeynep said. "At least let me pay my portion."

"No." Tatiana stood and grabbed the bill. She slipped her Amex in and handed it to the waiter. "I said I've got it."

"Well, that was fucking random," Sarai muttered. "But . . . cool, I guess. Tati, you wanna get another drink down the block?"

She shook her head. "No, I'm kinda tired. Let's link up this week, though."

"Yeah, I'm ready to call it a night, too," Sam said, quieter than usual. "Happy birthday, Dzifa."

Sam and Tatiana went to retrieve the car while I waited with Zeynep for her Lyft to arrive, the gift bag she'd given me dangling from my gloved hand, reflecting iridescent pink in the darkness.

"Only five minutes," she said, glancing at the app. "Nice."

"Hey, Zeynep—thanks so much for coming all the way out here. And for that whole . . . yeah. Thank you. And sorry about that. You didn't have to do that."

She shrugged. "You know how I am. Crippling self-consciousness but nonexistent impulse control."

I laughed. "That is a profoundly self-deprecating way to phrase *being an awesome friend.*"

"Well." She tilted her head to one side, then the other. "Yeah, I guess." She laughed. "But look, are you going to be okay? I know Tatiana is your friend, but, uh . . ."

"Oh." I looked up the road. Sam's car was approaching. "She's just been going through a lot, and today was super intense. She's usually not . . ." I trailed off. Usually not what? I'd done enough stretching the truth for one day. For a lifetime, probably.

Zeynep's Lyft arrived. "Dzifa? *You're* going through a lot."

I looked at my boots. I'd had them since high school; my mother bought them from the L.L.Bean catalog. They were still intact, only minimally scuffed. Occasionally, her shopping habit benefited me, too. As long as she felt that what she bought me could somehow benefit her.

"Okay, Dzif—I gotta go." She gave me a quick hug, checked the license plate, then opened the back door of the small sedan stalled at the curb. "You're not lost, you know," she said, halfway in. When she was all the way in the car, I closed the door, and she rolled down the window. "That said—*don't* lose yourself, okay? In all"—she gestured behind her to Sam's car, which was waiting at the end of the block—"of that."

We slept in Milton that night. Sam stayed with Tatiana. I lay in the guest bed, fully awake even at 2:00 A.M., then 3:00, then 4:00. I couldn't sleep. I could hardly breathe. I chalked it up to the long day, all the weeks of anticipation leading up to it: the end, I'd hoped, to at least that segment of my daily ruminations.

I slid out of bed, put on an extra sweater and my coat, and crept down the stairs. The blinds over the backyard windows were up; a faint light came through the glass. I squinted through the darkness; Uncle Aman sat outside on the bench. The light came from a headlamp wrapped around his forehead. He was holding a book. Just as I moved to retreat, he looked up, waved. I waved back. *Sorry*, I mouthed.

He stood, set the book down, and approached the door. I grimaced, preparing my apology, or perhaps several. "Sorry," I whispered when he cracked open the door. "I was just, um . . . I couldn't sleep, so I was gonna get some water or something."

"You can come out here, if you want. It helps me sleep when I can't. To get some fresh air."

I hesitated, one foot facing the stairs, the other, the door. "Okay," I said and followed him into the backyard. "Thanks. Um. Seriously, I can just—"

"I'm just going to keep reading, over there." Uncle Aman returned to his spot on the bench, picked up his book, turned the page.

"Okay." I stood by the door for another thirty seconds, then took halting steps to the other side of the grass, where the mural was painted. It was too dark to see the image, but I could see the textures of the mosaic. I stood and looked, even though I couldn't see well.

I glanced over at the bench. Uncle Aman was still reading. It started drizzling. I sat in front of the mural, tugging my coat around me. The longer I looked, the more I could see of the mural. Differently from how I could in the daytime—but like this, it had so much more dimension. It felt alive. I wondered if it felt like that to Uncle Aman. I could ask, but wouldn't. It was such a reprieve to sit in silence. For that to be enough.

When I got too cold, I pulled myself up and waved. "Thanks," I said. "Good night."

"Night." Uncle Aman waved, eyes still on his book as the branches of the tree Tatiana called his sister shielded him from the elements.

I still couldn't sleep when I got back upstairs. But my thought loops began to unwind into open-ended threads: I traced them to the best of my ability. I wanted to believe that our friendship was enough reason for me to stay, that everything that happened in the aftermath of Luca's death permanently sealed it in stone. I thought about Sarai, about Sam, the hours that Tatiana talked to them on the phone, more often with each passing week. I could ask, but didn't want to hear what I already knew—

that maybe I wasn't her best friend anymore, here for a place to stay but giving as much as I took. Maybe, somewhere along the way, I'd become some sort of tragically ineffective death doula who crashed her client's life and refused to leave.

Stomach uneasy, chest tight, I tried the breathing exercise again. Sleep still didn't come easily, but it came.

As soon as I woke, I followed the strange impulse I'd been knocking back since my birthday dinner: I called Esther. It was only six in Oakland, but I knew she'd be up already.

"What is it?" she answered on the fourth ring, the anxiousness in her voice tempered by the forced evenness that standardly permeated her tone. I didn't blame her for being worried; this wasn't how our dynamic worked, not anymore.

"Oh." I bit my cheek. Should have thought this through a little bit more. I shrugged, though she couldn't see it. "I was just seeing how things were going over there."

At least fifteen seconds passed before she replied. "Things are . . . going. How are things going over there?"

My turn to pause. "They're going."

"Mm-hmm," she responded, her voice flat. "Okay. Did you need something?"

I winced. I knew how we'd gotten here, but it hurt anyway. After all these years, there were only ever matters of routine or emergency between us. It made sense; Esther and I were so different, I wasn't sure if we'd know each other at all if we weren't bound by blood. But moments like these, wishful thinking crept in, fantasies of a sisterhood infused with laughter, hundreds of little inside jokes, the freewheeling, casual, messy interactions that signaled unmatched familiarity. The way our eldest three sisters were with one another. The way Sam, Sarai, and Tatiana were last night. Easeful. Tender. "No." I took a breath. "I was just . . . I don't know."

I imagined Esther on the other end of the line, rolling her eyes, tapping agitated hands on her lap. I probably had a good sixty seconds before she gave me an excuse to hang up the call. "So . . . what's your plan?"

Adjusting the blanket draped over my knees, I straightened my back against the wall behind the couch. "Um," I stalled.

"Well, that's a shocker," she drawled.

"Actually." I swallowed. "I applied to a few grad schools."

She mumbled her surprise. "Oh? Which ones?"

"None of your business." It was automatic, a reflex. I wasn't really sorry, though.

Esther sighed. "Okay. Well . . . in case any of your mystery schools are in Oakland, Mom won't be here. So. You're welcome."

I hugged my knees with my free arm. "What? Where is she going?"

I heard a male voice mumbling in the background on the other side of the line. Probably Esther's husband. "I'll be back in a second," she mumbled. "Nairobi. Charity's moving there for work. She helped Mom find something part-time."

"That is"—I searched for the most diplomatic possible phrasing—"very unlike Charity?"

Esther stifled a laugh. "Yes, well, it was a pretty taxing negotiation. Mom's gonna help with Sarah and Blessing," she explained, referencing Charity's youngest daughters.

I shook my head. "And that is very unlike Mom. You sure you're talking about *our* sister and mother?"

"There might have been a touch of bribery involved," Esther deadpanned. "I can be persuasive when I need to be."

As if I'd ever doubted that. "Okay, so . . . she's just gonna . . . move to Kenya?"

"What?" Esther scoffed. "You want her to live in my neighborhood until the end of time? Isn't that why you left in the first place?"

"No." I was surprised by my own response. I took a moment to think it through. "No," I repeated. "I mean, yes, her being there . . . was a hugely motivating factor. But I've been realizing more and more since I've been here, I also just . . . really need to move forward."

"Mm," she grunted. "And are you?"

I glanced around the living room that had become familiar to me over the past several weeks. That was still somebody else's home. That would always be somebody else's home. "I'm trying," I said.

Esther sighed again. "Well, in case you feel like trying harder: I don't know what your situation is in Boston. But part of the negotiation was I took on the title for the house in Maryland."

"You did *what*?" I grimaced. "Esther, no . . . that thing is a train wreck."

"Yes, well," she bit back. "As you know, getting train wrecks back on track is unfortunately a specialty of mine."

My thumbs hovered over the red button at the bottom of the screen. I did Carmen's breathing exercise again. "Ha ha." I shook my head. "What's *your* plan? You gonna move to bumblefuck Maryland? You've never even taken a vacation. You know it would take months to fix that house, right? To make it sellable?"

"I can take some time off in September. Until then, I'll find a new short-term tenant. The family Mom had renting out the place were total con artists. They never paid, and they left a bunch of their stuff all over the house when they fled. There have been a lot of break-ins in the area, so I don't want to leave the place unattended."

I adjusted the phone, bringing it to my other ear. We were silent for a minute, as I digested this information. As I heard the implicit question, or command, in it.

"No thanks," I stated, infusing my tone with as much resolve as possible.

"You have somewhere better to be?" Esther asked.

I surveyed the living room again, wrapped a swath of blanket in my fist, and pressed it hard against my knees. Better? Hard to say. But even the unease of folding myself into Tatiana's family drama had to be better than braving the vastness, and deterioration, of our mother's ill-advised purchase. You're *going through a lot.* I replayed Zeynep's final reminder, still unsure what to make of it, what to do with it. "I can't just leave, Esther."

She replied with a skeptical *hmm*. "Sure you can," she said. "If fixing train wrecks is my specialty, then leaving is yours."

I bit my tongue. “I’m tired,” I finally said. “Gonna go back to sleep now.”

“Fine,” Esther said. Just before I hung up, she continued, “Oh, and . . .” I heard her long inhale, wondered if somehow whatever she wanted to say next was a struggle. “Happy belated birthday.”

“Thanks,” I mumbled and hung up.

PART 4

CHAPTER 22

FOUR MOTHER-OF-GOD-LESS MONTHS LATER | BUMBLEFUCK, MARYLAND

The first week of December, I was driven into the fields I promised myself I'd avoid at all costs, because—and I stood by this reasoning as more than adequate—they looked and felt creepy as all get-out. Too much tall grass, for too long, too wide, too little breaking it up, too much bad history underneath it, fertile and wretched, making the grass keep growing even though nobody was tending it. Cursed grass, I felt.

I was driven into it by boredom, isolation, and regret that I'd agreed to come to my mother's ailing, bloated house to . . . do what? Let my body be a shield or deterrent against intruders? As if I'd know what to do if they showed up. Call the local police who, chances were, would think I was the intruder?

Or was my purpose to clean up the colossal mess, the sea of flimsy black trash bags filled with the most confoundingly useless detritus, which the previous tenants had left strewn across every room in the house? Was it, even, to clean up the mess my mother had made in her determination she could heal her ancestral wounds by buying out the land on which they were inflicted?

I was bowled over by overwhelm those first few days, to the point I started walking, kept going, and at some point found myself far past the outer edges of the property, down across the neighbors' fields, across into some vast, untended grasses I supposed were property of the neighborhood, the state, or, more rightfully, the Piscataway, but that I somehow recalled housed the nearest standing tobacco flat, the one my mother claimed belonged to her ancestors. "Belonged" as in: built by said ancestors to house the crop yielded by them, for the benefit of the land's legal, though not rightful, proprietors.

On an early December evening, the ritual began, as they all do, when I tried something different. It was tempting, in that field, to keep my hands by my sides or crossed over my chest, my shoulders tight, my eyes wide and alert, trying to pinpoint the limitless threats I envisioned through the fading light. But I was bone-tired, convinced no amount of rest would repair it. I relented to my fatigue, sat down in the grass.

It was wet, partially frosted, and crisp in those early days of winter. The earth was hard, abrasive beneath me, but because I was tired, I let the muscles in my thighs, my bottom, my calves, my feet, relax against it. Then, because I was too tired to hold up my own back, I let it sink against the uneven exterior boards of the tobacco flat. Not comfortable, but strong enough to keep me upright, and, as old as they were, soft enough to offer the slightest bit of give.

I sat against the little wooden structure longer than I intended, let it get darker than I was comfortable with. For a moment, I thought to retrace my steps to the house. Wondered if I could do it in the pitch black. My hands decided what to do before my mind did. They crept away from my sides and started mapping the exterior, then interior, of the space. There was nothing but packed dirt, damaged wood, strips of beams dissecting the steepled V of the ceiling, and a sweet, heavy musk. Still, I knew what had hung there for hundreds of years and—eyes closed or open—I swore I could see it, smell it, heavy bundles of dried tobacco, hanging loose like rows of dead bats. Their color stripped back by time, violence, neglected at just the right intervals: stiff enough to sell, just enough moisture retained for fruitful exploitation.

My body shook as I mapped. From fear of the dark, fear of seeing with touch instead of my eyes. Fear of touching so much unknown, fear some part of me knew it well. By the time I'd made my way across the interior walls and ducked out into the black expanse of the field with that musky scent caked into my clothes, the shaking stopped. I could see nothing but walked steadily, reassured by the wet crunch of grass under each footstep. It took longer than it had on my way there, but I found my way back. Astonished, relieved; I'd never had any sense of direction, considered it one of my defining qualities. But I'd made it, somehow, all the way.

The next day, I retraced the journey at dawn, so I could see with my eyes some of what my hands had felt in the dark. The next, I returned at dusk. That time, I mapped not only with my hands but with my back, shoulders, legs, hips, the soft expanses protected by my ribs. Every part of me that felt solid, tender, known, yet to be understood. I returned to that field, that building, every day thereafter, as the day started or as it ended.

My movements bore no resemblance to the kind of dance I learned as a child. But they felt real, devotional, and right. They felt, perhaps, like what I pretended to feel all those years ago at Elmwood, when Tatiana and I spent hours in weekend praise dance rehearsals, trying to get our arms to the correct, synchronized angle, no presence of anybody's god in our bodies as we did. When Carmen suggested I embrace ritual, build routines based on my own needs rather than somebody else's, I doubted this was what she envisioned. Probably, she was thinking yoga.

—~—

The first Monday of March, I did my ritual as usual. I made it back to the house just as the sky faded to black. This far from the city, the stars shone through on a clear night. I started up the long driveway; paused, circled back, past the neighbors' house—a white couple from Washington who'd sold my mom the property—until I reached the base of the hill again.

When we lived in Walnut Creek, my mother loved that our house was on a hill, albeit a smaller one than this. She loved that visitors had to make an entrance from a low place to a higher one to reach her. She liked for them to wait with bated breath as their cars ascended spotless pavement, wound their way up until the house came into view, in all its glory. It surprised me each time she managed to greet guests with a brief, faux-warm welcome as they reached the top of the hill, rather than succumbing to the possibility that seemed to me the more obvious choice: posing in the clean-tiled threshold with arms wide open, tall and tidy in one's newest pair of shoes, declaring, "*Behold.*" Otherwise, what was the point of owning a structure of this magnitude, perched at this angle?

I jostled the rusted mailbox door open. Two big A4 envelopes and three standard-size ones tumbled onto the gravel below. I sighed, scooped them up; it was too dark already to read their covers, but I did wonder at their contents. Could be more bills. This mailbox, like the white metal one we'd had in California, and the digital one on my parents' old voicemail system, and the mailbox in my Cleveland Heights apartment by the time I moved out, was primarily an overflowing storage container for bills that would never be paid. I handled the stack with care anyway; there could be something in it I mightn't be so quick to dump in the recycling pile. I tucked the envelopes under my arm and proceeded back up the hill.

There was no one to behold this particular house except me and the deer who snacked on the twelve decorative shrubs arranged at even intervals in a semicircle at its entrance. It was apparent they were once pruned to fashionably coiffed perfection. Tall, green cylinders, robust curves in their midsections, gentle tapering at each end. Even in the dark, I marveled at their neatness. The deer had managed to choreograph their snacking so there were nearly identical, long half-moon cutouts missing from the house-facing side of each and every shrub.

The house spanned wide, the cream exterior paint surprisingly well preserved. There were two floors aboveground, plus the basement. Though I'd come here to make it clear to any passersby the house was occupied, it never looked so if I wasn't physically inside. As I approached the tall, mahogany front door, I counted, for the first time, the number of windows visible from the front. Six, square, all fitted with thick glass panes and louvered white oak shutters.

I opened the door; the battery-powered sensor light I'd installed beside it came on just in time for me to dodge a stray multipack of balloons I must have missed during my cleanup of the entryway. I picked up the plastic-wrapped package, closed the door behind me, locked it, and toed off my shoes as I crossed to the living room just opposite the entryway. Two carpeted steps down, I sat on one of two wide, cream leather couches my mother preserved from Walnut Creek.

My phone was wedged between two couch cushions. I extracted it, turned it on: 8 percent battery. I assessed whether this warranted a trip out to Esther's old Explorer, which I'd parked just outside the garage after my latest Giant run. I drove there every day; storing fresh food was tricky here. If I went to the car, I'd have more light to read and I'd have electricity to charge the phone in the center console; power was spotty in the house. I aimed the phone at each envelope. Three for the recycling pile, all from banks or PO boxes in Idaho—which probably were also banks. When I got to the two large ones, I saw the two names that had been most on my mind these past months. I held my breath, focusing my eyes on the return addresses: the return city on the lighter envelope read *Boston*. The address on the heavier, more heavily stamped one read *Milan*.

I left the recycling pile and balloons on the couch and brought the two big envelopes out to the Explorer. It took five minutes and several curse-ridden prayers to the deer, the shrubs, or whoever ran things out here before the car started up. I plugged my phone into the waiting car charger and pressed the clunky plastic light on above me. Wedging an overgrown fingernail underneath the envelope flap I nudged the lighter one open, pulling the top sheet out. I did the same with the heavier packet. I sat with one piece of paper on each thigh, looked from one to the other, blinked, tried to steady my breath, failed, and relented, finally, to the heaving sobs that racked my chest, stomach, slumped my head against the steering wheel, the tears soaking the decades-old imitation leather. *Why are you so hard on yourself?* I thought, or said aloud, not sure why I said it, not even sure those were my words.

I had two choices, then, as far as school went. One sensible, one a secret. An April 15 deadline for both. That was all I needed to know for now. It was all I could handle for now. I tucked the top sheets back in, dabbing my cheeks and eyes with my shirtsleeve. I set the envelopes down on the passenger's seat beside me and turned to face the window, though nothing but the stars were visible through it now. It still felt wrong, being in the driver's seat of this car, when I'd always sat in the other position when I was a kid. This was Esther's place, really. But she'd upgraded a long time ago.

I turned off the engine but kept the battery on, stupidly—I'd had to call AAA five times already, in fewer months. My tears had stopped, but my breath was still uneven. I waited for it to regulate. Tried to ignore the rumbling in my stomach and the thoughts that betrayed my want to be uncertain, my sense that uncertainty was more convenient. The thoughts said: *Time to go.* My fingers grazed the envelope sent from the place I knew I'd rather be, couldn't let myself go to. Even though, now, it wasn't a distant fantasy. It wasn't exactly feasible either. But it was less impossible than it had been a year ago, or ten. I hesitated, let my fingers drift to the charging phone. Called Tatiana.

"Oh my God, finally! It has been so hard not to just text you the news, but then I figured—that wouldn't be right. I can totally be patient. But now I can finally tell you! Also hi." She laughed.

"Hey," I said. "I actually—" I looked at the envelopes beside me. "Um—yeah, tell me!"

"Yesss," she cheered. "Just one sec," she said, her voice muffled—I assumed she put the phone down somewhere—"Hey, Mommy, it's Dzifa. Watch Maddie for a sec? Gonna step out front." I heard Ms. Bishop's hum of assent. The sound of the front door creaking open was followed by Tatiana's deep sigh. "Whew! Long day. Okay, so, thanks so much for your patience; I know I've been kind of a tease with the whole 'decision's about to come in' thing. But this legal stuff is very 'hurry up and wait.' Like, everything is a five-alarm fire, but then suddenly, you're in, like, a three-month holding period just . . . bated breath." She laughed; there was a nervousness in her voice I didn't understand.

"Not your fault," I said. "So?"

"So." I heard Tatiana take a breath, hesitate. Her earlier giddiness dimmer. Was she stalling? "So joint custody is the way forward. Legal and physical." She paused.

I tapped my fingers on the wheel.

When I didn't immediately respond, she added, "Which is good! It's good. I mean, I know we were fighting for primary, but . . ."

"No, that's great!" I snapped myself out of my freeze, forced a smile I hoped she could hear in my voice. "That's—right?"

"Yes. Yes," she repeated. "It is great. I mean, ultimately the, um . . . the court decided it was the best thing for Maddie. So. I can deal with that. I mean, it's a little complicated, and we still have to work out the logistics, but honestly? It gives me a chance to kind of figure out next steps with my own life, too. And . . . yeah." Her voice trailed off, quieted.

"That's . . . good. That's good!" I tried for more enthusiasm. "Congrats on—I mean, I know it's not the ideal, but I'm just so glad they didn't do something crazy and, like, give him sole custody or something. Not that that could have actually happened, of course, but—yeah. I'm happy for you." I was, though I was also surprised by how unbothered she sounded. The Tatiana I knew hated to lose a fight, and one of these stakes? How could she be so keen to accept compromise after everything B's family put her through? Then again, I considered, I'd left Boston at the end of November. A lot could change in a few months.

"Yeah, thanks," she said, her voice a little more cheerful. "But that's not even the good news I was talking about. Well, it's not the best part. Brace yourself, and, girl, I hope you have some confetti handy."

"No, but there's a lot of lint in this car, so I could pick some of that up and throw it?" I shrugged.

She laughed. "Whatever you need to do. Okay. So: get this. Brigitte? Outta here. Gone. Done. Finito. Sayonara. Bon voyage. Actually, scratch that last—I hope she has a shit voyage."

My head knocked back against the seat; I winced. "What?" I decided not to ask the question that immediately, involuntarily came to mind.

"Don't worry; I didn't kill her. No—she's just not gonna be in the picture anymore. B talked to her."

My eyebrows scrunched together, I said, "Hm. And—she just . . . listened to him?" This did not compute, if we were talking about the Brigitte I'd met.

Tatiana cleared her throat. "I don't know, girl. They have a weird dynamic. I guess they went to, like, therapy together or something and—look, it doesn't matter; she's leaving Mass, she's ending her leave of absence from work, she's not gonna be involved anymore. Not without my *and* B's permission."

I didn't want to dampen her celebration, but it was hard for me to buy this. "That's . . . amazing. Um, just . . . how do you know she's not going to, like, circle back? Pop up again?"

Tatiana clicked her tongue. "Not everyone is your mom, Dzifa. No offense," she added.

I glanced at the envelopes beside me, then at the silhouette of my mother's house. Esther's house now, legally speaking. Somebody else's house soon enough, I hoped. "Yeah. Totally. I mean—none taken. Here." I paused and actually picked a few pieces of lint from the carpet beside my feet and tossed it over the console. "Throwing ancient car dust as confetti, as we speak."

"I appreciate that." I relaxed at the softening of her tone. "Now. We *have* to celebrate at some point. Just like—the end of a really, really shitty era. Maybe I can finally come visit you soon! Now that things are legally settled and I'll have some free time, I can travel again. I'm so excited to finally see the Haunted Manse."

I laughed at Tatiana's favorite name for the house I now lived in. "You're very welcome. I mean, the house is still not totally habitable, but . . . you already know, I guess. So, at your own risk."

"Girl, calm down," she said. "It's like an hour plane ride, and also, I was in Brownies for a whole year. I may be bougie, but I promise you I can survive whatever you got going on in bumblefuck Maryland for a few nights. I mean, I can survive anything now that Satan—I mean, Brigitte—is finally out of town."

I hesitated. Wanted to ask more questions but felt sidetracked by Tatiana's delivery. Was it evasiveness I detected? "Yeah, I'll bet," I said. I looked at the envelopes again. "Actually, there's something I wanted to tell you, too, while we're—"

I paused at the sound of a door creaking open on her end, someone's muttered voice and Tatiana—phone slightly muffled—saying, "Mm-hmm. Mm-hmm. Sure thing." I drew my eyes away from the envelopes.

"Sorry, girl, I gotta go—movie's about to start. But text me? Or let's chat tomorrow. Then we can start planning our adventure at the Haunted Manse," she teased. "It's gonna be epic!"

"Yeah, sounds like a plan." I exhaled, unsure why I felt so relieved by the interruption. "Talk soon."

I unplugged my phone from the charger and twisted the key, turning off the ignition. I'd call back tomorrow. I would tell her then. I would tell her, at least, about Boston, because that was the only realistic choice, wasn't it? There was no point in opening up about Milan; I'd applied quietly, kept it from everyone. It was just a way, I justified all these months, to assuage the remnants of my teenage self, to give her a gesture of goodwill. I probably wouldn't get in, I'd thought. Even now that I had, I tried to reassure the dissatisfied teenager in me—*Rest easy. At least we actually tried this time.*

I had to stay focused on where I felt safe enough to start again. I had zero regrets about declining the one other acceptance I'd received, a month ago, that would have taken me back to Oakland. I was ready to move on from California, for good. The life I had there was fine, but it never quite fit, even once I reconnected with Zeynep. I was grateful to have her as a friend again; she was a really good one. But I knew she was a friend and not really a sister. I was relieved Esther and I were still cordial enough to attend to this business with our mother's house. She was a sister—a really good one—but not a friend. Tatiana was both. I'd be a fool to leave behind the best chance I'd ever had at a home.

CHAPTER 23

APRIL 10

With the sun up, I feel brave enough to return to the basement. Though I'm no longer as afraid of the dark, I am still daunted by the mess. I'm back to living with battery-operated lights and gallon jugs of spring water instead of the tap. The previous tenants jerry-rigged the electricity when they were living here so they wouldn't have to pay the bill. It works, intermittently, in the basement and rarely elsewhere. I could have called Esther ages ago, asked for help paying for these features to be fixed. I could have chipped in once I started getting more work, even. Something in me resisted fixing the situation, though, needed to have something in my life I made no attempts to fix: one thing, at least, that I could just let be as it was. It gave me a kind of pleasure, the disorder in this house. My mother would never have allowed it, even though technically, this situation was very much of her making.

Heat and mildew blanket the air in the basement: the result of an ill-fated attempt at hanging laundry to dry indoors. The jumbo trash bags the tenants left are strewn across the oblong, half-painted room, some upright and half-tied, others collapsed with their contents spilled against the water-stained walls. I cross the room, checking my barricade at the back exit. Because the house is built on a hill, the front of the basement is firmly underground; the rest is exposed to the backyard. I've done my best to block it with an eggplant couch from the early '90s. I've wedged it, catty-corner, against the doorframe. For good measure, I've taken to placing a plaid armchair on top and pushing it face-first against the glass. I crawl onto the barricade, wobbling as I slide the door open and shut it. The locking mechanism has been broken since I came and remains beyond my fledgling home-improvement skills. If I were Tatiana, I'd have figured out how to spruce up the place with a daily dose of YouTube tutorials on the Fabulous Homes for Fine-Ass Femmes channel, and I'd have single-handedly flipped it for a twenty-million-dollar profit.

Instead, I take my sweet time surveying the damage, address problems as I see them, take naps in between, and hope the strategy to get this place anywhere near sellable will reveal itself. There's not a lot I can do about the structural damage, some of which came with the house when my mother bought it at a heavy discount, some of which was caused by the tenants' various product-manufacturing attempts in various rooms, and the rest of which was caused by my mother herself when she had enough money to get a contractor to demolish a few walls, three of the four bathrooms, and the entirety of the floor in the master bedroom, but not enough money to rebuild.

I step back; the couch is wobblier than usual. I bend down to investigate. There's a notebook with soggy, bent corners wedged underneath one of its legs. I heave the entire barricade up and yank the notebook out. It's damp, dented by a wide circle in the middle. Usually, I place anything I don't think belongs to my mother in one of three gargantuan piles I keep in the sprawling, unusable first-floor kitchen / occasional mouse palace: Pile one, the biggest, is "Bring to a garbage dump"; pile two, the smallest, is "Bring to the nearest Goodwill"; pile three, I have lovingly titled "What the fuck?!" The latest addition to that pile: a bagful of brown-skinned cloth dolls wearing blue felt pantsuits.

Besides my remote data entry job, this sorting is my primary occupation here. It's what Esther needs me to get done by the time she arrives in September. It could be argued I should have finished by now, but I am, at a generous estimate, 60 percent through. I have cleared the upstairs rooms, an uninhabitable construction zone, of trash. But there's plenty more to do. The previous tenants, who were jacks-of-whatever-trade-paid but whose primary occupation, from what I can see, was collecting every object they'd ever stumbled upon, putting it in a trash bag, and dumping it in this house, left me with a formidable task. When I arrived in December, found the spare key, and made my way through the front door, I screamed. The sea of plastic bags, stacked taller than I am, sat imposing, ungainly, like drunken invaders with no intention of ceding their new territory. In some places, they were clustered like bulbous plastic mini-cities. In others, they lay scattered, tipped over and split open, their contents spilled across the old carpet.

I restore the barricade and survey today's crop of bags. My eyes glaze over; not sure I have it in me this morning. I glance down at the notebook in my hand. I'm caught off guard by the even, meticulous script on the front. My mother's handwriting: I've become refamiliarized in recent months. There are, as she promised, boxes full of neatly sorted and labeled family documents, including thirty-seven—not that I counted—drawings I made her eons ago.

I leave the basement, grab my laptop and charger from the bedroom I sleep in, one of two bedrooms near the kitchen—and head to the car. It doesn't start; I call AAA. Someone will be out in a couple of hours. That means, I've learned, at least four hours. Not their fault; it's just not that easy to get out here. It's hard to work here without an internet connection, but I do my best, attending to whichever tasks can be done analog and saved manually.

When I catch the two now-wrinkled school acceptance packets from the corner of my eyes, I wish I could adhere to my usual escapism routine: driving the fifteen minutes to the nearest forest, reading a book from my mother's extensive collection of Italian novels, my jeans rolled up, legs dangling off the stairs of a craggy dock. When I'm there, I sing cheesy throwback ballads and think about what it would feel like to step into the opaque, slushy water of the Patuxent. Probably not great.

Early afternoon, I peel off my clothes and step into the shower next door to the bedroom. I know perfectly well it will not work, but I turn the knob to the right anyway. The metal screeches. A drop of brownish water falls to the tile beneath my feet. I step out of the shower and pick up a plastic gallon jug. It's open. I stand over the sink and take what I once heard my mother call a *whore's bath*. When I've finished washing, I pull on my only pair of shorts and one of her old Harvard T-shirts.

Though my fatigue and depression still crop up, they've abated enough that I've managed surprisingly well with the peculiarities of the house. I attribute this, mainly, to the ample space to walk outside during the day, and the ample time to exist on my own terms. I love being alone. I've always known this, but it always seemed an unacceptable truth. Unacceptable, un-American, unwomanly, un–whatever I thought I was supposed to be that I was insufficiently being. Still, if I'd known Being Unbothered for Long Stretches of Time was a cheaper and more effective medicine than Wellbutrin, that might have saved me a lot of copays.

I pick up the notebook I retrieved from the basement. Scanning the script on the cover again, *Origins—Volume 2*, I open it and fan through the pages. I think it's empty until I repeat the motion, slower, and catch a glimpse of pencil marks on the first two pages. On one, there's a sketch of a young boy with a cloth knapsack thrown over his shoulder. It's detailed, three-dimensional. Lifelike. I didn't even know my mother could draw. Though, if I'm being honest, I have no idea what she does, what she's been doing, all of this time. Even when we were little and she locked herself away. Then, I only saw what she wasn't doing. She could have been churning out symphonies, for all I knew.

I can guess who the boy is by his slightly downturned eyes, the dimple on his right cheek. My mother's father—the only person from her family of origin she stayed connected to, all the way up till the day he died. On the opposite page, she's illustrated what I now recognize as a tobacco flat. Hanging outside of it are two signs she's scrawled in that early-twentieth-century For Sale style: one reads *Tobacco, 25c* and the other reads *Negroes, 10c*.

A motor rumbles up the driveway; I set the notebook on top of the mattress. A tall, white truck teeters to a halt in front of the house. I peer through the top-floor window, checking for three big red A's painted on its side. I sprint down the stairs, gripping the banister just in case, and walk around onto the oil-stained pavement outside the garage.

"Hey." I lift my hand in a lackluster wave as the truck pulls up. The driver pulls a clipboard out of the center console. "Thanks for coming. This is . . . yeah." I throw a thumb back toward the SUV. "How are you today?"

He steps out, glancing at my legs. His face is boyish, smooth skin stretching over high cheekbones. "Morning, ma'am. I'm just fine, thank you. And yourself?" He smiles.

"Oh, I'm okay, thanks. Sweating, but okay."

"This turn of the season is something else; I'll tell you. And it's only getting hotter." I did wonder if it was normal here, for April to feel like what I'd assumed August would feel like. "You from around here?"

I slide one foot behind the other. My big toe scrapes against the hot pavement, and I wince. My Californian accent has diluted over the years, but anyone with half a working ear can tell I'm not from Maryland. "I'm . . . no. I moved here recently."

He tips his head up, scanning the house from the first floor to the roof. "This is a nice house. You live here all by yourself?"

"No, I live here with roommates. A lot of them." I say it automatically. Halfway between an old impulse to never let a man know I was alone and a new impulse to rectify his possible though unlikely assumption I'm a countess, when in fact it was just last month that I stopped receiving food stamps. And it's true enough; I do cohabitate with hundreds of trash bags. On a particularly dull day, I'd even experimented with using the craft store contents of one to attach a face to the outside of another, but then I thought better of it.

"Oh, okay." He shrugs. "Well, let's see what's going on with this . . . What is this, an Explorer? Looks like it's been around for a while."

"Yep. Twenty years. Or something like that." I extend my arm, dangling the keys.

He grabs them gently and opens the driver's door. "And what's going on with it today?"

"The same thing that keeps going on with it, I guess. It won't start."

He raises an eyebrow. "Yeah, doesn't surprise me. Car like this, day like this. You keep it out here all the time, just cooking? I see you have a garage." The garage is where I keep the overflow from pile one so it's easy to locate before a trip to the garbage dump. In involuntary mimicry of my mother, I keep it closed. She would never, not even during a hurricane or nuclear emergency, let a trash bag be seen anywhere outside of its designated bin.

"It leaks. Didn't want it leaking in the garage, so."

"Hmm, okay. Well, I'll take a look, but I'm pretty sure it's the heat. The way they used to make Fords, they'd last a long, long time. But this one came out after all that." He turns the key halfway and looks at the dashboard. "Whew," he whistles. "Two hundred and eighty thousand miles? You do road trips every week or something?"

"Um," I start.

He laughs. "I'm just playing." He tries starting the engine, listening to its weary sputter over and over again. "Yeah, she's worn out. Okay. I'm about to open the hood, so you do me a favor and just pull it all the way open, all right, ma'am?"

When I hear the low click of the hood, I wedge my index fingers underneath the rim and slide them around until I find the ridged button. The hood opens an inch. I force it all the way up, sliding a long, metal jack out of the corner and into its grooves.

"Thank you, ma'am." Did I become a ma'am the moment I turned thirty, or would I have been *ma'am* regardless?

I nod my acknowledgment and step to the side, placing sweaty hands on my hips and fixing what I hope is a knowledgeably quizzical expression onto my face. "So, what's the verdict?"

"Pretty sure it's your alternator, ma'am."

"It usually is." I shrug. "Okay. Hm. So . . . let me guess; I have to buy a new one?" This will be complicated. I need too many new things today to get ready for Tatiana's arrival tomorrow night. A makeshift shower, air fresheners, some form of air-conditioning that doesn't require electricity, food that won't perish. Water. Lots of water. It's Monday; I'm not getting paid again until Friday.

"Tell you what. 'Cause what's happening is, your car really can't deal with extreme temperatures. Hot or cold. And you gotta keep it running, but this isn't safe to drive far. Not just because of the alternator—I see the tires are uneven, the battery is seriously worn. I honestly would go ahead and sell this if I was in your position. It'll just keep eating money until you do."

This is true, and yet it's still my father's name on the title since he was the one to buy it for Esther. It is his to sell. He's unlikely to do so; he's a principled man, and one of his key principles is to hold on to—forever, if at all possible—all things that are irreparable so that they take up space that is urgently needed for more useful objects. I shouldn't disparage this quality; it is likely the reason he's never bothered to officially disown me.

AAA guy walks back to his truck. "Look. I've got a used alternator with me. Good quality, though. Two-year warranty. I'll give it to you at a discount. I see you've been a customer with us for quite some time. How does ninety-nine dollars sound?"

Sometimes, I consider my last stint in California a waste of time and willpower, but at least the twice-monthly roadside calls for my rinky-dink car had one positive side effect. I bite the inside of my cheek. "I'm just going to . . . think about it for a second, okay? I appreciate the offer. Just a minute."

He nods and walks back to his truck. I pick up my phone, take a look at my checking account, nearly depleted. I shouldn't eat out so often, but given the inconsistent power, my only other option would be to learn how to build a campfire. Somehow, I prefer to go broke.

I check my savings next. It's grown steadily since December, but I promised myself I wouldn't touch it, not until I was ready to pay for something school-related. My credit tanked so badly over the years that I had to enter a debt repayment program. It was that or bankruptcy, and that option hit a little too close to home. So, credit cards are out.

I take the five minutes required for my bank app to load its transfer system and move the ninety-nine dollars from my savings, swallowing a twinge of panic.

I exhale. "Okay." I walk up to the technician and hold out my debit card. "Sounds like a plan."

I pace around the driveway while the technician works. He asks me questions periodically, more about my life than about the car, and I give him whichever answers I think are least interesting. I find him attractive, but the part of myself that used to let finding someone attractive be a sufficient reason to do anything about it, or to allow the other person to do something about it, seems to have left the building. There are moments, especially during my nightly patrols, when I think it would be nice not to always be alone. I fantasize, even, about some tall, shadowy figure in a cable-knit sweater sitting across from me at a breakfast table that, in my fantasies, appears to be located at Hogwarts. But I dismiss these ideas as irrelevant to my here and now. The space I am in must be transitional only; I can figure out how to live a fuller life once I leave Maryland.

Thirty minutes in, I hear footsteps intermingled with the rasp of the engine. A middle-aged white couple rounds the top of the driveway. "Hi there." The woman waves, smoothing down her brown, shoulder-length bob as she approaches. She wears starched boot-cut jeans and a fitted flannel shirt. Sensible pearl studs decorate each ear. She reminds me of Brigitte. Maybe a little sturdier. "Your mother told me you'd be staying on when she went back to Africa . . . Guyana, is it? Anyway, I've been meaning to bring by a casserole or something, but it's just been such a busy school year. The kids have been in and out from college, and . . . Well, you know. I think we met you before. I'm Beth. This is Kevin." She extends her hand and nods toward her husband.

I blink, tugging on the hem of my shorts before shaking her hand. Am I supposed to know this person? Kevin surveys the technician with a dispassionate gaze. I step back. "Nice to meet . . . see you."

Beth's smile tightens. "Oh, I'm sorry. It must have been one of your sisters we met. Or a cousin, maybe? You have such a big family." She must have been thinking of the previous tenants, unless my mother had a secret family I didn't know about. Neither Esther nor my elder sisters had ever been here. "We're the Realtors?" she jogs my memory. "We sold your mom this house. We're just next door, see?" She points down the road toward an open expanse of grass. Ah, it was their house I passed on the way to my dawn-dusk ritual. "If you need anything, we're just right over there."

"Thank you." I nod.

"Maybe you need some help with the grass?" Kevin offers in a monotone. The technician clears his throat but keeps his head under the hood of the car.

"I'm sorry?" I look down the driveway at the tall strips of grass that line the pavement.

Beth places a hand on my arm. I try not to flinch. "Oh, it's just that Kevin loves going out on his lawnmower, every Sunday, ten o'clock on the dot. So if you needed help with that, he'd be happy to just breeze on over here. Keep the grass in shape."

"Umm." I look at my shoes. At the grass. At Kevin, who's crossed his arms over a broad, plaid-covered, football-dad chest. "Okay, well, that's nice of you. I'll just . . . ask my mother, I guess," I lie. "And get back to you. Thanks."

"Of course, sweetie." Beth fans her face. Am I supposed to invite them to the porch for some sweet tea or something? "Oh, and if you ever need a ride to town, you just pop on over and let us know, 'kay? Everything okay with your car?"

The technician darts his eyes toward me; I catch his barely raised eyebrow and mirror the expression. I nod. "Just an old car, you know. Going to sell it soon, I think."

"Kevin is excellent with cars," Beth praises. "If you have any more problems, you just let us know, okay? That's what neighbors are for."

"Mm-hmm. Thanks." I throw her a tight smile.

"I'm just about finished here, ma'am. If you want to . . ." The technician stands, stretching his back.

"Awesome, thank you." I shrug at the couple. "So sorry; I'd better . . . but thank you so much for stopping by."

"Oh, anytime. Truly. Don't be a stranger now. Remind me of your name, sweetie?"

I step into the driver's seat. "Dzifa."

Beth squints her eyes and steps up to the open window. I pull back instinctively. "One more time, hon?"

"Jee—fa," I sound out.

"Ooh." She nods, her eyes wide. "That's so interesting; I love it! You'll have to tell me what that means sometime. Okay, you let us know if you need anything."

"Mm-hmm, I will," I say to the dashboard.

"Bye now!" she shouts, steers Kevin away by the elbow.

"Bye," I mutter. I wait until their footsteps fade down the driveway.

I twist the key all the way to the right and wait until the engine roars to life. I hum out a deep exhale. "Thank you," I tell the technician.

"Anytime, ma'am." Before he gets in his truck, he turns and crosses his arms across his chest. "You know, since you're not from around here, I'm gonna give you a piece of advice. Hope you don't mind."

"Okay?" I frown.

He levels his gaze with mine. "Look after yourself. You find yourself somewhere where nobody looks like you, you'd better find somewhere else. You feel me?" He pulls a card out of his pocket and passes it to me through the window. "You need anything, don't hesitate to call. Drive careful, now. Speeding ticket ain't worth it out here."

"Gotcha. Thanks for the . . . everything." I frown, shake my head, pull the gear into drive.

That night, I come back from town; from the trunk of the Explorer, I unpack six small sensor lights, four battery-operated candles, four regular candles and a lighter, a small wicker basket, a pack of face masks and hand sanitizers, two large buckets, and a camping shower. There goes the rest of my checking funds.

At dusk, I do my route to and from the tobacco flat. When I'm back at the house, I charge my phone battery in the car and queue up my check-in with Carmen.

"How are you feeling about seeing Tatiana again?" she asks. "When you mentioned her visit last time, I was wondering if you wanted support navigating any triggers that might come up."

I think about it. "I'm nervous. Things feel different now. I don't know why. I'm having a lot of reservations about choosing Boston, but I'm afraid to tell her. And I feel bad I never told her about the Milan program, but I can't seem to bring myself to do it. It's hard enough figuring out the right choice myself without involving anybody else. Boston is way more practical on basically every level. It's basically a straight shot to a teaching certification, I'd have housing, I even got a partial scholarship . . . A degree in expressive arts therapy won't lead to an obvious career path, I don't know how I'll afford it, I don't know where I'd live . . . the decision is a no-brainer, and yet . . ."

"I hear you," Carmen says. "What is most difficult right now about making the decision?"

"Guilt," I reply, with no hesitation. "I feel like I owe Tatiana's family. Like . . . they really saved me when I was struggling. If I move back there, I could help out. Like, I'd be burdening them again if I lived with them, but then I could help out so Tatiana can rebuild her life, too."

"Dzifa . . ." I can tell Carmen is gearing up to gently read me, because she's doing her quiet but extensive yoga breaths on the other end of the line. "If you owed them—which I would really encourage you to reframe, as even in the most compassionate depiction of what they asked you to deal with there, you helped each other out—do you really believe that denying yourself a future you've worked incredibly hard for is an even repayment?"

I inspect the dirt on the inside of the car window. "I mean, logically, no. But emotionally, yes. I do believe that."

"I see, okay." Carmen let out a honeyed decrescendo sound on her next yogic exhale. "I'm glad you are noting the distinction. I wonder if a more important question is: When you think of what friendship means to you, how you practice it . . . does it involve holding your friends back from pursuing their dreams? Would you want that for anybody you love?"

"No, of course not." I smudge some of the dirt with my index finger, then wipe it on my jeans.

"And do you feel that Tatiana would want that for you?"

I lean back in the seat. "I . . . don't know. No, I guess not."

"Dzifa, what do you want? If there was nobody else you had to think about."

I close my eyes and relax against the worn leather. I twist my mouth to one side, try to conjure an answer. "I'm . . . not sure," I say, dejected.

"That's okay," Carmen reassures me. "It's okay to not be sure. But I wonder," she adds. "Who are you asking?"

"Um . . ." I am, by now, sufficiently accustomed to her therapizing style not to be caught too off guard. But still, there's skepticism in my voice when I say, "It's just me here? So . . . me?"

"Yes," she says, her voice warm. "But which voice in you are you listening to, are you hearing, when I ask you what you want?"

"Carmen . . ." I grimace. "Aren't you supposed to be encouraging me *not* to hear voices?"

She laughs, briefly, then continues, "It depends on the voices. There's a way in which we all are prone—conditioned, actually—to take our cues from all kinds of voices outside of ourselves, whether it be the voices of our family members, religious figures, from media messaging, and so on. Yes, people you see talking to seemingly invisible folks on the sidewalk are experiencing a more pronounced and disruptive form of that—but really, we are all a little bit out of sorts until we start tuning in to our inner voice. Our intuitive voice. The one we may most commonly think of as coming from our gut."

I suck my teeth, considering. "Yeah . . . I get what you're saying. But how would I know which voice is that inner one and which is, like—I don't know, one of my not-so-helpful thought loops?"

"Hm." Carmen pauses. "How does your body feel when the thought loops come?"

I frown, eyes wide. "Uh . . ." I hate this question, but hazard a guess. "I mean . . . when I'm in the loops, I'm not really . . ." I take another moment to pinpoint it. "I don't know. I'm not really aware of my body when that happens, so . . . I don't really know."

"Good," Carmen says, and I roll my eyes—only a little—at her trademark verbal affirmation of qualities and behaviors that are, categorically, bad. I appreciate her whole radical acceptance vibe, but sometimes, it grates. "If you haven't been aware in those moments, that may have been your mind's way of protecting you. Might be healing, when you have a moment, to give your mind some appreciation for its efforts, even as you recognize they may no longer serve you."

She takes another deep, yogic breath. "As and if it feels safe, though, Dzifa: That inner voice? You may try exploring what it feels like for you, personally. For many—for me, I'd say—it's less a verbal thing, more a body thing. It's quiet, still, sort of. When I hear *that* voice, it feels grounding. Thought loops feel destabilizing—my heart rate goes up, I feel unsteady, like I'm on a ship somebody else is steering. When the inner voice speaks, I feel rooted, like I'm part of a root system coming up straight from the earth. When that voice speaks, I'll usually have this thought right after: *Yep, that's true.*"

Her voice light, playful, she adds, "And it's true not because I've combed through hours of evidence or thought through every possible angle. I can simply feel, know, that it's true. Maybe ahead of our next session, you can digest that. Explore, a little, what that inner voice feels like to you. If you hear it. How you hear it. How does that sound?"

"I . . . appreciate you. really, like—I'm listening." I sigh. "But it sounds slightly bonkers, if *I'm* being truthful." My mind drifts to the wrinkled acceptance letters. To Tatiana's arrival tomorrow night. To my future—a swath of thick mist, at this point—unreadable, inaccessible, thanks to my indecision. To my wonderings, how they feel less heavy, less dense, than the thought loops. Then I consider my ritual. My body, moving of her own volition, against the timeworn wood of the tobacco flat. The absence of fear, self-doubt, the way I feel . . . coherent. Whole. "But hey," I relent, "I've already been institutionalized, so I'll probably be called 'crazy' for the rest of my life, whether or not I'm chitchatting with inner-gut voices . . ." I wait for her to laugh. She does not. She continues her audible, rhythmic breathing. "I'll see what I can do."

CHAPTER 24

APRIL 11

I've never done this before. Texted someone who handed me their number, asked them out. When I called the AAA guy—Anthony Dixon, according to his business card—I tried to make it clear, without making it rude, that I was not inviting him on a date. So I said, "Hey, we met earlier today when you fixed my decaying Explorer? I was wondering if I could take you up on getting some more info about the area. No pressure."

He texted back fifteen minutes later with the address of a diner in town.

Tomorrow is my day off. If you like, you can meet me here for breakfast.

I hit the thumbs-up emoji before I could chicken out. My sleep last night was not, as a result, the easiest, but I feel reassured that at the very least, this non-date will provide a distraction, so I don't have time to keep ruminating about Tatiana's arrival tonight.

Anthony's already in the diner when I get there; thankfully, this one's in a part of town where we can both relax. He stands when I approach his table and reaches out his hand to officially introduce himself. I laugh a little at the formality, but return his handshake and pronounce my name, twice.

"Tell you what, Dzifa. I'll give you all the sightseeing tips you want if you tell me how in the hell you ended up here," he teases. He smiles over at the waitress standing behind the counter, and she brings over our menus, large and laminated. "Coffee?" he asks. I accept.

Between bites of biscuits and gravy, I offer the most condensed version of my saga I can manage. It's not easy; I'm sweating not only from the heat—there are two lazily winding fans on either side of the diner, more decorative than functional, it seems—but from the strain of trying to force linearity, cohesion, onto a life that has resisted both. It becomes easier once he reciprocates, and I learn his life has been every bit as winding as mine, if for different reasons, in different ways. Anthony was a military brat, like my mother, like B. Raised mostly overseas, intermittently living at bases throughout the American South. He was a soldier himself, before he moved out here at the invitation of some friends from the Marines.

We talk for nearly two hours. I can't remember the last time I had a conversation like this. Unhurried. Full. Each of us offering plenty, no pressure to say anything at all. No emergency to attend to, no suspected agendas to guard against. Talking has always felt like an obligation to me. Unavoidable. Compulsory. Something to be endured, rather than enjoyed, like getting blood drawn. "Here," is how I've approached conversation, offering up my limp arm, "go ahead and take it." In the rare relief of speaking freely, no particular goal in mind, no particular fear of how what I say will be used, interpreted, misinterpreted, I feel fed. The biscuits aren't bad either.

"Now," I attempt to wrap it up, self-conscious about having spoken so long, "I'm just trying to start over. Without having to completely start over. If that makes any sense. Probably not." I laugh through a grimace.

"But until September, I'm here. Hopefully by then, I'll have left the house in a state my sister can work with."

"Hm." Anthony nods, laying his fork and knife down. "So come September, you're headed across the Atlantic?"

I mirror the motion, frowning. How did he get there? I never said that. "No. I mean, I haven't decided for sure, but I have a couple of days left. And I'm pretty sure I'm headed back to Boston."

He cocks his head to one side, folds his arms across his chest. "That's interesting."

"Is it?" I laugh.

"Yes." He smiles back, tries to hold my gaze before I drop it back down to my plate. "You don't sound like you want to go to Boston at all."

I shrug, focusing on a speck of biscuit crust at one edge of the cracked porcelain. "It's not about where I . . . want to go. It's where it makes sense to go. Like I said, I don't want to start from scratch. Again."

Anthony signals for the check. He pulls a folded black wallet from his pocket and hands a few neatly folded bills to the waitress, waving off my protests and the waitress's gesture to retrieve change. "Thanks, Auntie Mabel," he says.

She responds with a playful wave.

"Oh, that's your aunt?" I watch the elderly woman amble back to the cash register.

"Nah, that's my auntie. We not *related* related, but we're family. Don't change the subject. I see you got all kinds of ways of deflecting. I'm onto you." He smiles.

I sit back in my seat. "I'm not deflecting. If I go to Italy, where I don't know anybody—well, my mother might know a couple of people still, but I don't want to know anybody she knows. I mean, I'd have to start from scratch."

Anthony holds his hands up. "Maybe you and I got different definitions of 'starting from scratch.' Like, one person's 'starting over' could be another person's 'moving forward.' You don't just lose everything from the last place you were."

I consider this, fussing with the fork lying on my plate. Watching the downturned prongs make a slow trail through the remnants of gravy.

He continues, "I can see why you'd think that. I kinda did when I was coming up. My folks were moving us all over the face of the earth. I resisted it for the longest, and my mother's lectures about duty to God and country, and so on, didn't really resonate. I mean, I was proud of my folks." He pauses, lays one arm across the back of the chair. "They both came from pretty humble beginnings. Made a really nice life for me and my sister, made their way up the ranks. But it wasn't until I enlisted myself, got a few years of service under my belt, that I figured it out."

"Okay?" I retract my hand from the fork, fold my hands in my lap.

"I think I was stationed in the Philippines when it dawned on me: There's no such thing as starting over. Even if I had grown up in one place and stayed there, life would still be happening. Change would still be happening. I wasn't at some kind of deficit just because I was changing locations. Maybe I was even at an advantage, because I knew how to roll with it without so much resistance. To see that there's no going back. We move forward, we take what we need from where we were. That's my theory anyway." He shrugs. "So now I'm here; I like it. Life is still changing, even though now I'm a little more still." The corner of his mouth ticks up. He swallows, looks down at his plate. It's much cleaner than mine.

"That's not a bad theory." I take a breath, take it in. Let it sit. "Still, my friend Tatiana? The one I'm picking up tonight? She always seemed so, like . . . I don't know. Sure. Like, the most chaotic, life-altering things could be happening, and she just acts so confident it'll all work out. I always thought it was because she grew up really rooted. Stable. Like, her mom owns this house that's been in the family for generations. And my mom—she's always been trying to have something of her own, but it's like—it never sticks."

"Yeah." Anthony nods. "I feel you. I'm convinced that's kind of our problem."

"Hm?" I fidget with my fork again.

"Our problem." He gestures between us, then around the diner, nodding at the assorted families, couples, individuals, talking, laughing, sitting in silence, eating, being. Not *related* related, but family, I interpret his gesture to mean. It is nice, rare, I note to myself: To see us at ease.

Doing mundane, human things, undisturbed. I wonder if we need a critical mass to achieve such rare pockets of peace. Or if it can be achieved, somehow, even when we are the outliers. I bring my eyes back to Anthony. "I think it's thinking we have a problem."

"Hm?" I repeat.

"A lot of us move like we're broken and tryna hide it," he goes on, "'cause we don't know exactly where we came from. And we don't own as much as we think we're supposed to. Out here paying for DNA tests, tryna pinpoint it. Fighting for people who've been fighting against us, to 'earn' "—he pauses to emphasize the air quotes—"a piece of the pie."

I chew the inside of my bottom lip. "I mean . . . yes. That's . . . I don't disagree." I push my plate farther away from me, a deterrent from further disturbing the now-hardened gravy residue. "But like . . . what else are we supposed to do? If owning something is the way to make it here, aren't we always at a deficit if we don't?"

Anthony holds his hands up, out, tipping each palm up, balancing them like a scale, dropping his arms beside him. "I don't know. I don't have the answers. That's just not what making it means to me. But hey—" He shrugs, a faint smile teasing at his lips again. "I've always been, as my gramma used to say, 'a little touched.' I just don't think I need to own anything in particular, to make myself at home. Land is nice if you can get it, but if you can't?" He shrugs. "Not the end of the world."

I rub my hands on my thighs. "Gotcha. Well—I'm happy you found your home here." I dart my eyes to the window; even the glass is sweating today.

"Thanks." He smiles. "This is a nice place to live. But just to be clear—it's not my home. I am." He drags a hand across the top of his head, his smile dipping into shyness. "Guess I coulda just said that. My gramma also used to tell me: 'Get to the point, Anthony, I'm halfway into the grave by now.' "

A laugh escapes me, catches, escalates, and I draw the attention of an elderly couple in the far corner, who smile and tip their heads in our direction. I tip my head back. "Your gramma sounds like a real one."

"And was." He nods, his smile, and gaze, lingering on mine. "Shall we?"

We stand outside, baking in the unseasonable heat. "What you up to for the rest of the day?" he asks.

I shrug. "Just that airport run. But that's not for a while. Actually—no, never mind." I shake my head, laughing at my own indecisiveness.

"Nah, you're gonna have to tell me. What's going on in there?" He reaches out a hand, pauses to check my eyes. I don't flinch as he lays a cool finger on my temple.

"Okay, then." I allow the coolness of his touch to linger, even when he drops his hand. "So I go over to the Patuxent a lot? Like, through this nature preserve . . . well, you probably know it. Anyway, the water does not look very . . . uh . . . appetizing, but for some reason, I keep having this really strong urge to get in it."

Anthony's full lips curve upward. "So why don't you?"

"I don't know." I laugh. "It just seems like . . ." I consider it and realize there really isn't a good reason. The river isn't even fast in that area; it's practically stagnant. "It's pretty murky."

He waves a hand. "That's just sediment. Nothing to be afraid of. Well, depends on which part of the river you at, but I'm pretty sure wading in just a little won't hurt you."

I narrow my eyes skeptically, playfully, I hope.

"Come on." He beckons me down the block. I look behind me, where the Explorer is sitting.

"But—I'm parked that way!"

"Won't be a moment," he calls back. "We can get to the river from here, too."

I follow him for less than ten minutes, out of the town center and, as he promised, toward the river. As we're walking into a more wooded area, it does occur to me that this very activity is exactly what I was trying to avoid all my life: wandering into an isolated riverbank with a strange man and all. But if, years ago, I would have been frozen in fear, today, I feel even, loose-limbed, curious.

When we get to a good spot, the Patuxent slowly bobbing past, I notice its waters are ever-so-slightly clearer here than they are nearer the house. He takes his sneakers and socks off, neatly folding them, and sets them on a small wooden dock to our right. I do the same. He rolls up his trousers to the knee, exposing lean, strong calves. I do the same.

When he reaches out for my hand, I hesitate. My need to alleviate the heat wins out. I lay my hand in his, which is still cool and dry; mine is a little sweaty, but he doesn't comment on it. Instead, he envelops mine in his and says, "Okay, one, two, three, jump!" and mimes the beginning of a jump. I shriek, and he laughs, straightening up. "Only playing." He smiles. "Here's another local tip for you: These things are better, actually, if you take your time."

We step in simultaneously, my hand still in his. I'm embarrassed by the shuddering breath, the shake of my body as the smooth, cool water hits my feet, my ankles, travels up my calves. I'd be willing to shed more clothes, feel more of my skin brushed by the gentle drift of the river, the beautiful expanse of his skin. Instead, I receive his invitation, whatever it means in this case. What I make it mean is to stand where we are and to feel everything. How it changes, how it's constant, how it's new, and ancient, and, though a little awkward, foundationally okay.

He indulges my standing meditation for a good fifteen minutes, doesn't speak. Finally, he leads me out of the water and sits on the dock. I sit beside him, already missing the embrace of his hand. I don't reach for it again, but I lean my shoulder a little, so that it's nearly touching his. He looks at me, smiles. He reaches up that same hand and rests a finger under my chin. "I'm tempted." His smile grows. "But you really seem like someone who's about to cross an ocean."

I glance down at his lips, then at the sliver of weatherworn deck between our thighs. "I thought that was kind of the dream for men. No?"

He grazes that finger under my chin, then sets his hand back down on the deck. "Depends on the man. This may sound odd to you, but I've been doing this job for maybe . . . five years now? And you'd be surprised how many women have a AAA fetish. It's a little unnerving."

I laugh, my eyes turning away from him and fixing on the river. "I'm not surprised. It's the uniform, and the capability kink. Plus, that big truck. We're only human. But you know, that's not why I called you."

"Right." He raises an eyebrow. "You wanted sightseeing tips."

"No." I shake my head. "I wanted to test a theory I had."

He turns his body toward me, wraps his arms around his bent knees. I lean into his new position a little. He lets me. "What was that?"

"The theory is . . . well, the context behind the theory is, for the longest time, I didn't trust my instincts. And I was super guarded. I thought that's how I had to be to survive."

"You probably did have to be, then, and look—you survived." He tugs a strand of hair that escaped the hold of my rubber band, right at my temple. We both watch it stretch out, spring back into stillness.

"Yes." I nod. "But now I wanna really live. And I figure . . . and have been told by a professional"—I laugh—"that to do so, I'm going to have to learn to trust my instincts again. To let my intuition guide me. And . . . I cannot logically explain why I sent you that message. I didn't have any agenda—or fetishes." I laugh again, then look away, biting my lip. "I just wanted to. So I did."

He stands. Holds out his hand to help me up. I accept the help. "Glad you did. In that case, if you're gonna be around this summer, and you want another fetish-free riverside hangout, or hey—think about the house thing. I know you said it's in bad shape, but if somebody broke it, somebody can fix it. Let me know if you want any help figuring it out."

"Thanks, Anthony. I'll think about it," I say. "Nope," I correct myself. "If I'm feeling it, I'll let you know. And . . . likewise. If you're feeling it, you let me know."

"Sure will. Come on." He laughs. Leads me back into town.

CHAPTER 25

At ten o'clock that night, it's already pitch-black. I head to the airport, the only lights I can see emerging low and hazy from the cars ahead. Despite the mugginess outside, I smack the air-conditioning off to spare myself its noxious stench. I can't prove it's poisoning me, but I also can't prove that it isn't.

There wasn't time to deep-clean the truck after I met with Anthony. I did, however, throw out the many crumpled Dunkin' bags I've come to see as companions. They remind me of Mr. Quartey, my few memories of him. How he decried greasy American food, but then, on his infrequent visits home, we'd find brown Jack in the Box bags stuffed underneath the seats of this same truck, the remnants of Sourdough Jacks leaving their stale, meaty scent for weeks. I love the idea of him caring enough about what we thought to hide the bags, but not enough to throw them away.

I dig inside my purse, fumbling for the iPhone wedged at the bottom of it. When I pull it out, I catch a few pastry crumbs on my fingertips. I really shouldn't text and drive. I type, one-handed.

Almost there. 5 minutes.

The phone vibrates, the screen lit up blue and bright.

No rush! I'm not even off the plane yet.

I let out a breath. My shoulders come down from around my ears, settling somewhere near their natural resting place. My mind drifts to my unmade decision, my undisclosed acceptance, and to Tatiana's caginess every time I follow up about the new custody arrangement, about Brigitte's departure. The latest response when I said, "I still can't believe she just left," was "I don't know, girl, maybe she got tired of being Beelzebub. Can't be a relaxing job, you know?"

When I collect her, she's dressed for a summer party, the same way she used to dress in New York, rain or shine. Her braids are black and blond; the edges are loose. Her skin glows with sweat and highlighter.

We talk about all the usual things on the drive back.

"Should we see a psychic while we're here? Are there even psychics here?" Tatiana always phrases her demands this way, as though they are suggestions.

"Yeah . . . I'm not really into psychics, as you know." Guilt hits me mid-sternum; I soften my pitch. She came all the way here. "But if you want to go, I'll take you."

"Oh, well." She pushes a couple of braids behind her ear and purses her lips. "I mean, as someone who knows a little bit more about psychics and that kind of thing, I've gotta tell you: You can't just write them off. My go-to intuitive in New York was always on the money. Remember? Like, I did *not* want her to be with that last prediction, but she totally was." I can't deny this. I remember that day. The words that, at the time, seemed like a contradiction, when Tatiana asked if she would have a son. "Yes. And no." And so it was. However, this does not in any way entice me to further my dealings with paid practitioners of the occult. It does warm the heart that my betrothal to Hades has yet to unfold, but I don't want to push my luck. The only thing worse than a psychic turning out to be phony is a psychic turning out to be right.

"Totally." I force a smile. "I get it. Like I said, I'm happy to take you to one. I've seen a few down the 301." There is, in fact, at least one whose location I'm sure of. A massive, low-roofed, purple-painted building, surrounded by desolate parking lot. That's all you can really get in these parts: cornfields and psychics. There aren't any prices outside the shop, but all the standard witchy icons are painted on its towering sign. I like witchy things, when left to my own devices. I clear my throat and change the subject to YouTube, hoping to trigger a primer on Tatiana's latest conspiracy theory kick, religious conversion, or lifestyle renaissance. I'm not disappointed; just last week, she bulk-ordered a pallet of ashwagandha elixirs.

As we approach the house, the headlights cast a dim shadow on the shrubs buttressing the driveway.

"Oh my Gooood! I *love* your mom. I mean, I hate her, but I love her taste. It's so . . . me. This place is huge. I thought your parents were broke."

I don't bother to answer; she'll see. Tatiana opens the door and hops onto the pavement. I follow her sluggishly and pull her suitcase from the back seat. She's packed like she plans to stay here for weeks, even though we only have four days. I hit the flashlight on my phone and light the path to the front door. When I turn my key to open the door, I turn my head left and right out of habit.

I apologize, for probably the thirtieth time since Tatiana told me she wanted to visit, for the squalor. I guide her to the best-lit, least moldy bedroom, the one on the opposite side of the bathroom from mine, then go about securing the house.

I flip the broken lock to the garage door and push an old rocking chair in front of it. When I walk back into Tatiana's room, she's standing on the bed, moving her extended arm out at a different angle every few seconds. "What's your Wi-Fi password? I don't think I can get service here. T-Mobile, ya know?"

"Yeah, it's the worst. But, uh, we don't have Wi-Fi, remember? No power, so . . ."

"Oh yeah. Totally forgot." She wriggles her arms for a moment, dropping the phone, and I wonder if she's shaking loose her disappointment. "Whatever. This is like one of those phone detox retreats! I texted Maddie and Mommy on the way, so we're good." She lets herself fall onto the bed and crosses her legs, leaning her head back against the wall. I want to warn her about the spiders lurking behind the headboard, but I feel bad about the Wi-Fi and don't want to make it worse. At least I changed the sheets.

"Cool," I respond, trying not to let my fatigue, or my anxiousness about the state of the house, show. Tatiana idly taps the screen of her unusable phone, and I rack my brain for something to say. "So, your flight was okay?" This is inane; she already told me all about it on the drive. "I mean," I scramble to make it make sense, "didn't you say you brought a book with you? Did you have time to read it?"

Tatiana raises her eyebrows, shrugs. "Yeah, I've been reading it for, like, weeks." She sits up straight and reaches over the bed to her handbag. "Actually, oh my God! This is great, 'cause I've been meaning to show this to you." She holds up the book, purple with old-fashioned yellow script looping up the cover. *Rich Dad Poor Dad.* I refrain from rolling my eyes. "Mommy actually begged me to read this for years, and I totally blanked on it. Then Sam gave me her copy a couple of months ago, and it felt like a sign."

I turn my face away. I'm not sure Sam, having come squarely from Rich Dad, came by her financial security through the book's advice so much as through her trust fund. "You *have* to get into this book," she gushes. "You will never look at money the same way; I swear." Tatiana shifts her muscular legs underneath her on the hideous bedspread. Her floral sundress fans out over her lap, and two battery lanterns give us partial sight. "It's . . . look, I *know* how you're kind of a socialist or whatever, but I'm telling you, this book has already been a total game changer for me. I've had three calls with potential clients this month alone." I assume she's referring to her recent attempts to reinvigorate her old tech career. Similar work, but freelance and, if she has her way, with fabulous clients only. "And they're all women, all high-powered, all arts-adjacent. Reading this, plus talking to Sam about it—me, her, and Sarai have kind of an informal book club going—I realized back when I was coding, then in management, I wasn't playing the game like rich white people play the game. I feel like now I'm kinda figuring out how to play it *right*."

I exhale, extending a cramped leg in front of me. "That's great. I'm happy for you. And I'm not a socialist. I just have these crazy ideas sometimes that, like, maybe we shouldn't actively make life terrible for everyone just to trigger those with an overdeveloped flight mechanism into battling their way to the top while everyone else languishes. Like . . . maybe that's an exciting video game but not so much a good society, you know?"

"Yeah." Tatiana laughs. "Socialism. Anyway, I think you should keep an open mind. 'Cause you have too much potential to keep being poor, my friend."

"I'm not poor." I frown. "I just . . . almost always have very little money." I'm not totally sure about this logic, and as I speak, I spot an open trash bag full of what I'm fairly sure is Monopoly money peeking out from beneath the bed, but I don't backtrack. It's never really been clear to me how long one has to be broke before one qualifies as *poor*. Two decades or two generations? Maybe Tatiana's right and I've already crossed the threshold. Or there never was a threshold.

"Dzifa." Tatiana tips her head down, narrows her eyes. "Just read the first chapter, and let me know what you think."

I finally let my eye roll come through. "Whatever. Sure. Happy to take a look at it."

"Yes!" She claps her hands together, triumphant. "I'm just gonna read you the intro, just to get you started." She holds one of the lanterns above her book and reads.

I tune her out immediately, making sure to arrange my face into an appropriate combination of adulation and intrigue, in case she can see my expression in this paltry light. I, too, have been recommended this book by my second-eldest sister, Faith. "Dad swears by this," she gushed via email after my graduation from Elmwood. That was all I needed to know.

Her performance finally concluded, Tatiana raises an eyebrow and smiles, triumphant. Her smile dims. "Well?" She says it with considerable bite, and I realize my space-out wasn't as subtle as intended.

"Love it. It's great. Yeah, awesome. Thanks for reading." Overkill. I start scraping the dirt out from underneath my fingernails. I don't even have to look at her to know she's rolling her eyes.

"I am just. Saying. You don't have to be an investment banker to get into this stuff. Like, it's just going to help you get off the wheel of suffering and start taking back your life. You've gone from basically being—no offense—kind of a mess, and now you're off food stamps, you live in this giant house, and you're about to go back to school! It's amazing. Don't you want more?"

I force a smile and watch her shoulders relax. I do want more; I just don't want this particular book anywhere near my growth trajectory.

"Of course." I nod. "No, I really do get it. I think it's really cool." When did I become a compulsive liar? It didn't used to be this hard to go with the flow of whatever Tatiana was most excited about; I guess I'm a little out of practice.

I rub my eyes, fighting a yawn, but she catches the motion.

Tatiana clasps her hands together and drops them into her lap. "You know what? I'm kinda desperate to take a shower."

I grimace. "About that . . . you will notice that due to the lack of running water at the moment, there's a . . . Here, I'll show you."

I scoot off the bed and walk into the attached bathroom, smacking my hand over the light switch out of habit. It does not, of course, work, but fortunately before I left for the airport, I put out two battery-operated candles on the white marbled counter, flanking the basket of face masks. Tatiana joins me and peers into the basket. "Ooh! Are these for me?" She picks up a cucumber cooling mask and clutches it to her chest.

"Yeah." I laugh. "I figured it was the least I could do, with you coming all the way here just to stay in what you probably now realize I was not exaggerating about."

She peers around the bathroom, reaching out her free hand to touch the toffee-colored, cowry-studded beaded curtain that separates the toilet and shower room from the counter. Her eyes linger on the art hanging on the other end of the bathroom. It's an abstract painting of my mother when she was eight months pregnant with Charity, her first. I've seen the photo it's based on, and all her pregnancy photos. In this photo, she's laughing, basking in the glow that she's either always had or hasn't left her since that photo was taken. I can't prove it, but I've often wondered if the ultimate skin-care tip for women is to abandon empathy—if not altogether, then at least at regular intervals.

"I don't know," Tatiana says. "I mean, if you look past all those bags of . . . whatever's in them . . . and the construction stuff, your mom has really good taste in decor. In my book, decor trumps functionality, every single time."

"Uh." I raise an eyebrow. "Let's see if you still think that after your 'shower.' " I step through the curtain and pull back the strands so she can see where I'm gesturing. "Okay, I already told you this, but first of all, the toilet situation is a little tricky. There's the gallon jug." I tap the dented plastic container where it rests on top of the closed commode, which is covered with one of the navy-blue toilet seat covers my mother has had since the '80s. I've set out the matching foot mat.

"All righty then," Tatiana quips, though her tone is lighter than I would've expected. "'Tis what it 'tis."

"'Tis indeed." I slide open the old, pebbled glass door to the shower and exhale, grateful that no new insect or rodent visitors have decided to die in here this evening. "And this—is the 'shower.' " I step back and let Tatiana take a look at the contraption I bought at the Dollar Store; the one at the hardware store was too expensive.

She leans forward to peer into the tub and lets out a loud, shocked laugh. "Okay, what? The fuck is that?"

"That is the Dollar Store's very finest discount camping shower, my friend. I'd explain how to use it, but truly, I can't be sure."

Tatiana shakes her head. "I'm sure I'll figure it out, but just for the record"—she laughs again—"this looks less like a shower and more like something women used in medieval times to give themselves abortions."

For a second, I just stare at her. I take another look at the contraption, with its fat, dingy cord, plastic-looking spigot, and the misshapen rubber basin where the water, I assume, is meant to come from. My laugh starts small; once she joins in, I can't stop.

Through a shuddering inhale, I finally say, "I mean . . . I can't prove that it's *not* that. In any case, best of luck to you. Personally, I just take that gallon jug and dump it over my shoulders every morning. And, let's be honest, also every night because you know I'm sweaty even in the tundra."

Wiping tears of laughter from her cheeks, Tatiana nods. "You sure are. But look—I will do the best I can with this, and if I'm not feeling fresh—'cause you know I can't be out here smelling like those psycho environmentalists we went to school with—then I will 100 percent take you up on that gym trial idea."

"Noted." Stepping out of the shower room, I pause at the doorway and find that I'm still smiling. "I'll leave you to it, then. I'm just down the hall if you need anything. Night!"

"Night, Dzifa," Tatiana says, tearing open the face mask pouch.

CHAPTER 26

APRIL 12

"It's so quiet here." Tatiana outpaces me, her pink Converse dodging shallow puddles from the overnight rain. We shield our eyes from the sun. I pull my hand away from my face when we reach the forest. "Although"—she shrugs—"this whole thing . . . it's kind of adorable. Like, quaint. Shabby chic. It's like *Little House on the Prairie*." Her ponytail swings from left to right with every step.

I bring my hands together and crack my knuckles, forcing a laugh. "Yeah . . . well. That's one way to put it. If my mother was here—"

Tatiana halts, does the sign of the cross with an exaggerated grimace. I laugh.

"Probably even Esther, too, come to think of it—either of them would stop at nothing to deep-clean every last surface, fully constructed or not. Which—I don't know." I stop and bend down, yanking the edge of my leggings closer to the line of my socks. "The clean freak in me hates the mess. But this other, weird part of me I don't even really understand is, like . . . grateful for it. Like, the way the house is, is my family's worst nightmare. But now I'm like: Wait a minute, do I actually give a shit? These past few months, I've felt like—" I shake my shoulders as if a spider has crawled across them. "Just—whatever. Who cares if the neighbors think the lawn is overgrown? It's not that serious."

"Yeah." Tatiana nods. "Well, it's definitely not my style, but Mommy's like that. As you know. Me? I'm already saving up for us to each get our own manor, and you'd better believe the lawns will be meticulous. Then, if she really doesn't want to live in hers—no loss! I'll use the extra space for guests at the . . . I'm gonna say quarterly soirees I plan to host." She steps over a lump of dirt.

"I . . . can see that for you."

"It's still so weird to me." Tatiana shakes her head. "How your mom got this house even though she doesn't know anybody out here. Who's still alive, I mean. No offense."

"None taken." I bend to scratch at my ankle, inspecting for a mosquito bite. I don't see one; I keep moving. "Weird it is. Although, we didn't know anybody in Walnut Creek either. We lived there because, at first, that's what was convenient for our dad. Which . . ." I raised an eyebrow. "They just kept hanging on to that property, even when it was literally ruining their lives. I guess because of what it represented to them."

"Suburban glory?"

"Probably." I shrug. "Or just generally a way to say without saying, 'Look! We made it!' But like . . . why is 'making it' being surrounded by people who'd rather we were serving them?"

A bee weaves its way toward us; Tatiana yelps and jumps aside, her shoes sinking into the mud. "Ugh." She waves her hands frantically, thinks better of using them to wipe off her shoes, and proceeds down the path. "That reminds me of what Mommy always says, about 'Go where you're welcome, not where you're tolerated.' But I don't really operate like that. I mean, not to knock your trauma, but I don't think I'd care if I was surrounded by haters. If I'm winning? What's it to me what my neighbors think?"

We find the makeshift dock and sit on the bottom set of stairs. The water is slow and shiny today, bits of leaves and little branches floating along with ease.

"Don't get me wrong," Tatiana says, "Boston is forever crusty. But like—is it actually more racist than where you grew up? You're practically a local by now." She picks a wilted leaf off her jeans and flicks it beside her feet.

I pretend to examine the long, knotted branch arching above us. "Mm . . . it's hard to say. I hardly ever went outside when I was living with you guys. Even when I was in high school, I wasn't paying that close attention the few times I went to the city. But I always found stealth racism way more annoying. Like, the level of just . . . out-in-the-open segregation around here is kind of alarming. And sure, I never got the impression that white people in Boston were *thrilled* to see me. Especially B's family, Jesus. But nobody does stealth racism like Californians and . . . yeah. I just can't deal with that. It's like somebody punching you in your sleep every night and then disappearing right before you wake up."

"Yeah, I get it." Tatiana grimaces. "The schools I went to . . . I guess that was the benefit, though, of getting to come home after a day among the most problematic of WASPs and be around friendlier faces. Like, Boston is for sure racist, but I think people think it's extra racist because there's nothing stealth about it. Even beyond racism, it's just the culture. I've noticed . . . when I'm traveling, I can never tell if people think I'm aggressive because I'm Bostonian, or if it's just straight up misogynoir, you know?" She cocks her head to the side. "I don't think I'm aggressive; I feel like I just know what I want." She pauses. I say nothing. "But Carlotta—from my Abundance Activation training?" she continues. "She's really got me thinking about how to better position myself as a relationship prospect. Like, I don't care if I am aggressive 'cause I know I'm awesome, but if I want to uplevel my life, I'm gonna have to figure out how to appear a little 'softer,' as she calls it. Which reminds me: Hate to break it to you, but high-caliber men won't be into all your feminist diatribes."

I pull my leggings over my socks again and suppress a laugh. No argument there. I steer us toward an alcove that leads down to the water. The water and air are still today. "It shouldn't matter anyway." I shrug. We sit on separate wooden steps, with me closest to the water. Tatiana brushes invisible dust from the wood onto her jeans.

"What?" She frowns.

"It shouldn't matter," I repeat. "If you were aggressive—which you're not," I clarify when she cuts her eyes toward me, "or if you were . . . soft. Or whatever. It really shouldn't matter."

"To who? Whom, I mean." An ant crawls from my steps to hers; she stomps it dead.

"I don't know." I shrug. "Men. White people. The world." I gesture toward the water as if the entire global population is floating by in a single canoe.

"You're so dramatic. I don't care what the world thinks. I'm just tryna have an orchard and twelve bedrooms one day. One of them *will* be a drawing room, whatever that is. This is nothing more than strategy. You know, three months into the marriage, and *then* you show him your natural hair. Wait till the second anniversary, and *then* you reveal your sordid past. That kind of thing."

I run my tongue across the back of my teeth. Deep down, I've always known that the so-called aggression Tatiana claims openly isn't any different from the muzzled bite I carry within me all the time. I'm tired of holding it back. "Right. So is that the endgame with this whole Order of the Divinely Feminine Call Girls business? Get a rich man to buy you a manor, and that'll magically wash away four hundred years of subjugation?" I thought it would feel good letting out what I've been holding back, but my breath catches on the last word, my neck tensing, ears primed, bracing for the impact of her rightful retribution.

She turns away, just slightly—a shoulder shifting farther from mine. I hold my breath in the silence. "Wow." She says it softly, without any ire. But when I look beside me, her eyes are hooded, the muscles around them tense. She's quiet again, much longer than I'm used to her being quiet. "No. That's not the endgame. The endgame is to make sure me and Maddie are set up for success. It's not easy, you know? Being a mother. Sometimes you have to make difficult choices. You wouldn't understand."

It's true and untrue, and I've already stepped in it in ways I can't think how to unwind. I let the silence return, linger, as we, centimeter by centimeter, turn away from each other. We spend another thirty minutes watching the Patuxent sludge its way past. Tatiana takes her phone from her pocket, scrolls through photos of Maddie. I'm not actively looking, but I see from my periphery. Maddie and her, Maddie and Ms. Bishop, the three of them and Uncle Aman, and one I think must be old before I realize it can't be—Maddie looks bigger than when I last saw her—more a toddler than an infant now. Tatiana, Maddie, B, and Avery, posed outside the Museum of Natural History. Maddie, in B's arms, is looking, expressionless, at her mother. Avery offers a closed-mouth grin. The only ones showing their teeth are Tatiana and B.

I descend the remaining steps, remove my shoes, and dangle my feet in the water; Tatiana stays seated at the head of the wooden staircase, arms braced around her knees.

We stop by the local business park for lunch. We're silent on the way there. As far as options in this complex, it's the grocery store, Dunkin', Bojangles, or the drive-through liquor store. "Bo-what-now?" Tatiana's eyes widen when we pass it on the way into the parking lot. "Oh, we're going there."

There's a line around the block in the drive-through, but no other customers inside. There are only four four-seater metal tables to choose from. Tatiana sits at the one closest to the door, setting her Coach purse in the middle.

"I'm gonna get something to drink across the street. You want something?" I stand and pick up my handbag.

She turns her head to the side. Frowning, she faces me again. "At Giant? Why don't you just get something here?"

I shrug. "I have to get more water for the house anyway. And I want some ginger ale. They don't have it here."

The cashier, an amiable Sudanese man, watches us through slightly averted eyes.

"Wh . . ." Tatiana sighs, tugging at the end of a braid. "Never mind."

"What?"

"Nothing," she says to the table.

"Do you want to come with me? Our orders are gonna take like five, ten minutes, so . . ."

"Yeah, but why don't you just wait?" She juts out her chin, turning her head slightly to the side.

I shrug, returning the snide look. "Because that would be inefficient. I have to go to the grocery store anyway, so I might as well go while we're waiting, so I don't have to wait longer." She doesn't move. My temples ache. An unease I have felt every day for most of my life, but from which I've had a reprieve since moving here, creeps up: This feeling teetering on knowing that in every social interaction there is some unspoken yet critical convention, a rule, that I don't know. And that I should know. It's been a long time since I've felt that way around her, though. "Is that a problem?" I follow up.

Her head jerks back; she drops her eyes to the table. The manager remains immobile; I can't even hear him breathe. Is there really nothing better going on in this place? "No, it's not a problem. It's just not how *I* would do things." She raises her eyebrows.

My lips twist into a grimace. "What is there even to do? What is happening right now?"

She moves an inch, like she's considering meeting my eyes. "Nothing. Just go if that's what you want to do."

So I go.

I've picked up some extra provisions with the ginger ale: fresh batteries, four gallon jugs, and a new candle. My bank app alerts me to my excessive spending, as if I don't already know. I'm going to have to live on saltines when I get to school, even with the free rent Tatiana's family is offering. She says nothing on the way back, so neither do I.

"I'm gonna take a nap," she announces when we get back.

"'Kay," I respond, and linger in the car to charge my phone. I check my messages. There's one from Esther.

Status update?

I hold off on replying, since there's no update other than "Still a mess." I'll think of a better reply later.

Next, I see a string of messages from Zeynep. She and her partner got a second dog. Each message has more exclamation points than the last, and a blurrier photo than the last of Zeynep's ear-to-ear grin smushed up against the puppy's face.

Cuuuuute. So excited for you!

Her reply is immediate. I'm surprised; she usually sleeps in till at least noon, and it's only eleven Pacific time.

Let's catch up soon? Sorry it's been a minute. When's good for you? How're things on your end?

I hesitate. I do want to catch up, but I don't want to bank on her time-management skills.

Totally, would love to catch up. No pressure, though. Feel free to call when you're free.

She thumbs-ups the message and replies:

Igualmente!!

I unplug my phone and turn off the car. Midday is a weird time for it, but I'm craving my ritual. I stop by her room, knock gently. I hesitate when there's silence, knock once again.

"Yes?" she says. "Come in."

I open the door an inch. She's sitting in a rocking chair beside the bed, legs crossed, *Rich Dad Poor Dad* on her lap. "Oh," I say. "Did you have a good nap?"

"I couldn't sleep." She shrugs. "Decided to read."

"Gotcha," I say. "Did you want to . . . do something? Like . . . you mentioned going to a psychic? There's one like forty minutes away. Or, we could—"

"I thought you weren't into psychics," she says, eyes still on her book.

"Yes." I clear my throat. "But . . . you came all the way out here. I don't mind going if you want to go. I just won't get a reading."

She frowns. "Well, that's no fun, then." Finally, she looks up, flips the book over, still open, and rests it on her lap. "The whole point of going would be that we both get readings."

I look down at the carpet. Blink. Look up. It's on the tip of my tongue: the response I'd usually give. *Okay, sure; let's do it your way.* I swallow. "Well . . . I don't know if I feel comfortable with that. So . . . I don't know. Do you want to do something else? We could go into Baltimore, or . . . I don't know. I think they have—" I grasp for something that would appeal to her, a peace offering, but my brain feels muddy, sluggish. "An aquarium?"

"What?" She shakes her head. "No, I'm still tired from traveling. So I'd rather chill out here. And to be honest with you, it's just kind of weird to be away from home. Like, I feel . . . weird. I don't know. I'm just gonna read. Let's do something tomorrow."

A bird flies past the window facing the driveway, skimming the side of its wing against the glass. We both jump, then relax once we see the source of the noise. "Okay. That's fine. Um . . . I usually take a walk to this other field nearby. Like once a day. And I was thinking I might go there now. It'll probably take like an hour? Hour and a half? You want to stay here? Or . . ."

"Yeah, we *just* took a walk to a field? So, I'm good." She laughs, joylessly, and picks up her book.

"All right." I nod. "Okay. See you in a bit, then. There's, um—do you remember where I showed you the mini fridge in the basement? There's a few things there if you get hungry, but if you need—"

"Yeah, got it," she snaps. "Thanks."

When I come back, I stop by the car, charge up, and check my messages again. There are two more. One from Esther, a follow-up to her request for a status update, a simple, very-Esther:

I write back.

I'll call you in a couple days. Tatiana's here so it's a little busy.

I don't wait for a response. The next message is from Anthony, though it takes a minute for me to realize since I haven't yet saved his name in my phone. I do so and read it.

Gone for a swim yet? Or is the sediment still keeping you out? ;)

I want to be in the mood to match his playfulness. But there's something familiar and unpleasant dampening the lightness that has been more present these past few months. I keep thinking of Tatiana's coldness when we were at lunch. Can't blame her if it's because of my comment about her Abundance program. But it's not like her to stew over it like this, to refrain from speaking her anger if that's what she's angry about. And what did she mean about feeling "weird" here? I feel weird here, too; I feel weird everywhere. Does she feel that way because of this house, or because it's not *her* house?

I see, then, an uncomfortable parallel: Her unease and detachment as she sat in the rocking chair. The unease and detachment she exhibited, in her texts and video chats, all that time she lived with B. Was it solely due to the goings-on in those spaces, or was it also that she wasn't the person in control of those spaces? I can relate, and I can't. I've always managed to find a place to sleep, but I've never slept anywhere I'd call *home*. Even when paying my fair share of rent, I've always lived with the penitent energy of an unwanted guest.

This house in Maryland isn't mine, but I don't carry myself like a walking apology here. The brokenness, disorderliness of it, the fact that though my sister has taken on the title, it is energetically ownerless, frees me from the practice of tiptoeing through someone else's order, trying not to disrupt it. This house was already disrupted long before I came. It's a relief. And though I feel a little unmoored by Tatiana's presence, by the dissatisfaction she seems to feel about me, this house, or my hosting abilities, it's the first time I don't feel like it's my job to fix it.

It used to feel so easy, accessible: to contort myself to suit other people's moods, to anticipate their needs, to cede what little space I claimed for myself so they could claim all the space they wanted to. So they could occupy the entire universe while I shriveled and shrank deeper inside of myself. My chest aches. I close my eyes for a moment, open them, glance at Anthony's text again. Reply:

Not swimming yet, but did put my feet in this morning. How're you?

I unplug my phone and go back into the house.

Tatiana stays in her room the rest of the afternoon. By nightfall, I've completed an hour of data entry work and sorted through a few more bags. I'm back in my room, contemplating the discomfort of a medium-cold, gallon jug shower when I hear footsteps, followed by two gentle knocks. "Dzifa? You in there?"

"Yep, one second." I open the door. "What's up?"

The flashlight on her phone shines blinding white. Risky move, since when her battery dies, there'll be no reviving it here. "I brought something for you, and I don't want to forget to give it to you." Her voice is even, devoid of its usual pep.

"Oh . . . thank you. You didn't have to get me anything."

"Don't be ridiculous." She holds up her makeshift flashlight and starts down the hallway. "It's in my room."

By the time I get my own phone out and make my way to her room, she's already holding out a blue paper gift bag tied with a bow. The candles I set out are lit along the perimeter of the room, underneath the window that faces the driveway. I see nothing outside but night. I take the bag. "Thanks. This is really nice of you."

"It's not a big deal. Open it."

I untie the ribbon, holding the heavy bag steady with my other hand. The object I pull out feels like tightly packed cardboard. Examining it beside a battery light on the bedside table, I read out loud. "The Nubian Queen: A Black Woman's Tarot Deck." A colorful illustration of a gold-adorned goddess with a poised bow and arrow covers the front. "Wow, this is beautiful."

"I was thinking I could teach you. We can do it tonight if you want."

"Thanks." I set the cards back inside their paper bag. "This is really, really kind of you."

She raises her eyebrows. "You say that like I'm not usually kind."

"Of course you're kind." I pull the tarot deck out again and examine the back. "You and your family are the kindest people I've ever met." I want to believe this is true, though my gut tells me it's guilt guiding the words. I sit on the edge of the bed.

Seated in the high rocking chair, Tatiana's feet barely touch the ground; she lets go and rocks back.

"Thanks—no, we're not." She laughs. "But . . . we'll be glad to have you back." I wonder if she really believes this, feels it. Her tone is light, but ungrounded, somehow. "Uncle Aman, especially," she adds more convincingly. "I feel like you're his dream daughter."

I frown. Her statement is a land mine; given my earlier misstep, I take more time to think through what I'll say next. "I . . . don't know about that." I shrug. "I think he just doesn't know me well."

"That's true." She raises an eyebrow, drops it, smooths her dress over her lap. "Anyway, I kinda can't believe you're going back to school. I always thought you hated it. I always thought you were gonna hightail it out of America altogether, actually."

I bite down on my tongue. Release. Try to breathe. "Um." I make the decision, in a split second. Convince myself: It was never that big a deal anyway. Just a matter of clarifying. Nothing has to change. "Um, actually, speaking of hightailing it out of America . . . I did a thing."

"Mm . . . kay?" Tatiana adjusts her position in the rocking chair. "And?"

"Uh—so it's not really a big deal, 'cause I'm not doing it anyway. But remember when I was first applying to grad schools? When I was living with you guys?"

Tatiana pulls a face. "Yes, Dzifa, that was like five minutes ago. What's the deal?"

"It's nothing." I shrug. "I just sort of threw in a wild card application. For—it's not an education program. Well, not exactly. But it's at this school in Milan I wanted to go to in high school, that I never applied to.

For dance. I mean—" I shake my head. "This time, it's not for dance, per se. It's a program for expressive arts therapy."

Tatiana leans forward as if she's getting ready to leave her chair. She lifts a little, then sets herself back down, leans back, and folds her arms across her chest. "Expressive arts what now?" she says, and a laugh escapes me.

"Are . . ." I clear my throat. "Sorry—I don't mean to . . . are you not mad? I mean I'm not going, obviously." I ignore the pain that shoots through my chest. "Too expensive, not at all practical, et cetera, et cetera, I just did it as, like, I don't know—an homage to my inner child. I don't know." This time, my laugh is forced. "I guess my therapist is rubbing off on me."

"Okay." Tatiana tugs at the ends of her braids. "Uh-hm. Well, that's . . ." She opens her palms, shrugs. "I really don't know. I guess I'm confused? About why you can't go. Impracticality has never stopped you before, has it?"

All the time. "It's not just that," I say, confused myself, about why she isn't angrier. Or even more surprised. "It would mean completely starting over. Again. For like the billionth time. And like—you know, you and your family are so generous to let me stay with you and—"

"Yeah, but"—Tatiana's eyebrows draw together—"is that actually what you want? Because . . . I don't know, Dzifa, but like. That whole Italy dream . . . you've had it for as long as I've known you. Even if it took you ages to really open up about it. Are you seriously just gonna give up on it?"

It's my turn to frown, and fidget. "Do you . . ." It's not the first time I've considered it, but it's the first time I've said it out loud. "Do you not want me to live with you guys? It's okay if you don't," I add, unsure if I mean it. "But just tell me, if . . ."

"Dzifa." Tatiana rolls her eyes. "Of course you can stay with us if you come back to Boston. That's not what I meant. I just mean I don't think you should be so hasty to give up on something I'm *guessing* you're a little more excited about. 'Cause if I think about it, dance is really the *only* thing I've seen you get excited about. Well—that and a good mozza stick," she adds with a weak laugh.

I take this in. Think of Carmen's question, about whether my best friend would really want me to sacrifice what I wanted for her sake. I hate when Carmen is right. But it doesn't matter. I already decided. This is the right thing.

"It's not gonna make me happy to make myself broker, again, and have to start from scratch, again. Like, that is not exciting, at all." I make my mouth stretch up into a smile. "I'm just—sorry I didn't tell you earlier."

"Did you think I wouldn't be on your side?" Tatiana shakes her head. "That's the only thing that makes me mad. You *know* I've always been team 'Get the Fuck Out of America,' for you, especially. Why would that have changed?"

I don't mean to say it; it just comes out. So fast, I don't even know myself quite what it means. "Everything has changed," I say.

To my surprise, she doesn't argue or ask me to clarify. Which is good, because I'm not even sure, myself, what I mean.

"Yeah." She nods. "Yeah, it really has." She relaxes more deeply into the chair, closes her eyes and takes a breath, opens them. "Were you hoping I'd be angrier?" Tatiana looks at me full-on. I see the ghost of a smile on her face.

"Hoping? Definitely not." I laugh. "No. But it wasn't my intention to keep something from you. I just didn't tell anybody about the Italy thing. In high school, I was embarrassed to even be thinking about it. Like, thinking I could do it. And I guess part of me still felt embarrassed. Like I should have grown up by now. Given up on those kinds of dreams. But I wouldn't blame you for feeling angry. You've been there for me through . . ." My mind does a scan. "A lot," I sum up inadequately. I glance at the gift bag. "I feel like I can never repay you. The least I can give you is the truth."

"The truth . . ." Tatiana repeats. Her eyes cloud over. She glances out the window, stays silent for what feels like an eternity. When she looks back, her eyes are sharp again. "The truth is, Dzifa . . ."

I try to breathe normally while I wait for her to finish. Can't manage it, quite. It feels like my words, either this morning or tonight, or hers, either this morning or tonight, have unspooled something that needed to stay intact for our friendship to stay as it was.

"The truth is," Tatiana finally says, "I'm exhausted, girl, so I'm gonna turn in. All this nature is making me sleepy. Was gonna teach you tarot tonight, but let's do it tomorrow, yeah?"

I could draw this out, I know. But our roles are reversed, somehow, and it's unsettling me. I'm supposed to be the one to turn in early; she's supposed to be the one to push me to stay awake, to finish the task at hand or move on to the next adventure. "Yeah, totally," I reply. "You need more water or anything?" I ask on my way out of the room.

"Nope, I'm good," she says, already risen from the chair, her small form disappearing into the bathroom. I nod and close the door behind me.

CHAPTER 27

APRIL 13

The next morning feels charged with some unnameable shift, but on the surface, we keep it simple, familiar. Throughout the day, we keep ourselves distracted with a trip to Baltimore. We visit the harbor, and a tattoo shop Tatiana read about, owned by a Black woman who used to have a reality show. It's smaller than she expects, and there's only one other customer in the shop when we arrive. Tatiana's disappointed in the available gossip.

We leave, pick up lunch on the way back, and I attend to my housework while she wanders around the house taking photos and videos. She catalogs both the oddities she stumbles across and the architectural features she appreciates. "I'm totally gonna have a porch at my summer house," she vows, just as she stumbles across an open bag full of velvet scrunchies perched by the door to the backyard. "Who *are* these people?" She laughs. I'm relieved when I hear the sound, and laugh along. While she explores, I half-ass my cleaning efforts, more moving around bags than clearing them out.

Hours later, it's dark out, and the energy between us feels easier. Hopeful that whatever thread I inadvertently unspooled can be rewoven, that we can somehow get back to normal, I take Tatiana up on her tarot offer. Now that it's spring, the backyard is pretty enough during the day and, shockingly, not littered with trash. But whenever I look at it, I'm hit by a wave of nausea. I have no idea why, and rarely am I interested to find out. But it's too late to go all the way out into the fields I now feel more familiar with.

We grab most of the battery-operated candles and a big plastic lantern I got at the Dollar Store. Tatiana follows me through the living room and out onto the porch. "Just a heads-up," I warn. "If I were you, I wouldn't look around the porch too much. I've seen a lot of little creatures since I moved here, and unless you want to see them up close . . ."

"Ew." Tatiana laughs, doing a flailing dance to shake off invisible—but possibly actual—bugs. I pull an old picnic blanket off the back of a lawn chair and mimic her dance, shaking the blanket as far away from both of us as I can.

We half drag, half carry our tarot setup down the short flight of porch steps and into the long, dark expanse of grass before us. I let go of my chair when we're about halfway between the porch and the shadows of the trees behind the house.

Tatiana spreads the blanket out and sets her chair at the edge of it; I do the same. We set the lantern in the middle, the candles at each corner of the blanket, and in spite of dragging the chairs all the way out here, we end up sitting on the blanket.

"Ahh," Tatiana sighs, fidgeting until she finds a comfortable position with her legs crisscrossed. I'm sitting with my feet on the blanket, my arms folded around my bent knees. "Should we do some sort of, like, circle-opening ritual? I should have brought one of Carlotta's ritual scripts, but we can just make something up."

"Yeah, um—" I shrug. "I have no idea. What do you usually do?"

"In that case, I'mma use something I saw this Black astrologer do on YouTube. Her edges are impeccable, and her readings are always on point." She closes her eyes; I follow suit. "Let's both take a deep breath."

I try to mirror her inhale and exhale, though I'm pretty sure mine is a little rushed. "Ancestrixes and godixes," Tatiana begins, "we—"

Our eyes snap open when the trees behind us rustle. I tilt my phone flashlight toward the forest. "Just a deer," I reassure. We both exhale. I do so fully this time.

"Okay, take two!" Tatiana laughs. "Ancestrixes and godixes, we thank you for this life, for our bodies, our minds, our spirits, our melanin and the shea butter that nourishes it." I snort, lose focus, then squeeze my eyes shut again. "We ask you to guide us in this reading so that we may better understand our purpose, so that we may better serve you. Uh." I crack an eye open again. "Amen? Asé? What are the woo-woo girls saying these days?"

"And so it is," I offer without hesitation. When Tatiana opens her eyes, I shrug. "I'm from California, remember?"

She tilts her head to the side, laughs. "So you are. And so it is. Okay, here we go." Three brightly illustrated cards are laid before me, in a neat row of three. The false flicker of the battery-operated lights makes it tough to make out the picture on each of them, so I just fixate on the colors.

She picks up the first card, holding up her phone flashlight to see it better. "Oh, wait." She puts the card on top of the deck. "First, tell me a little about what's on your mind."

"What? Sleep." I shrug.

"No, I mean, like, what are some areas of your life that you're curious about? Career, school, love, money, world domination?"

"Umm . . ." I tilt my head from side to side as I consider. "Okay. Definitely career. And love, I guess." I mutter the last bit, although she's the only person I'm not ashamed to tell that to.

"Great. That'll help me focus your reading. Let's start with love, 'cause I'm a cheeseball." Tatiana shuffles the deck for a full minute, her eyes scanning the dark backyard. She resets the three-card spread and taps on the first card. "Okay. Basically, what we're looking at is the first card represents your past, the second card represents where you are, and the third one is more . . . not necessarily your future, but it sort of describes the momentum, the path you're on. To understand the whole picture, we have to look at the whole picture." I nod sluggishly, picking at the fabric of the picnic blanket. It didn't register before, but it's one my mother had made out of all of our old T-shirts. She sent one to each of us; my sisters discarded theirs, which means this one must be mine. Tatiana continues; I trace my fingers over a bright turquoise shirt that reads—once I pull my phone closer to it—REDWOOD HEIGHTS CHRISTIAN CAMP.

"So. First you're dealing with the Nine of Wands. She's telling us about your struggle to find love in the past, and your perseverance in not letting heartbreak stop you or break you. Does that resonate at all?"

I frown, pulling at a loose thread in the stitching. "Not really, to be honest. I don't usually think of myself as persevering after heartbreak. I don't think I've ever been sufficiently emotionally invested in anyone I've dated to be heartbroken. I don't know." I roll my head to the side, relishing in the faint pop the movement releases. "What about you?"

"This is your reading." She glares, tapping the cards with her nails.

I freeze for a moment, try a reframe. "Yeah, but I don't really know how to answer yet. And I've always admired how much fun you have when you're getting to know new people. When I think about dating again, even when I sort of want to . . ." I think about Anthony, consider mentioning him. For reasons I feel ill equipped to unpack on the spot, I decide against it. "It feels like a chore. Maybe hearing about how you've persevered with it will inspire me." I want to indulge her, so she can enjoy this activity that feels familiar to her, but there's also a part of me that hopes she'll start talking and forget about the rest of the reading. I'm exhausted by the drive to and from Baltimore, and more than a little bit creeped out by this backyard.

"Well. It's hard to explain. I've just always known I'm worthy of everything that I want. Whether or not other people choose to see it, and even when it doesn't work out right away, I just know it."

Twisting my mouth to the side, I nod. "I've noticed that. It's pretty impressive. Have you . . ." I choose my words carefully, not wanting to activate any more of the pain that resurfaced earlier. "Where do you think that comes from?"

Her head turns toward the porch for a moment. When she faces me again, she says, "Nobody has ever asked me that." She weighs her answer. "I guess I believe it 'cause . . . I've always gotten what I wanted. Or most of the time anyway."

"What? Really?" I bite down on my tongue. Didn't mean to sound so skeptical.

"Yes, really." She shrugs. "Is that so hard to believe?"

"No." I move my thread-picking to the next T-shirt over. This one is white with choppy black lettering. I don't recognize the acronym. "It's just . . . unusual, I think."

Tatiana cuts me an irritated look. "It's not that everything in life goes my way. Obviously. It's more like when I set my mind on something . . . then, yeah, it kind of does tend to go my way." She pauses, frowns, as if whatever's next is a fresh reckoning. "I guess, also, I'm pretty lucky. Mommy gave me everything I wanted or needed. If I wanted to take dance classes, she signed me up. Like, without encouraging me to develop an eating disorder." She cuts her eyes toward me. I shrug. "If I wanted us to go on vacation to LA, or Disneyland, or whatever, we went. What we had for dinner was what I wanted for dinner. You know?" She flicks her thumb and forefinger at the blanket. Another white square: This time, I recognize the name of the dance studio I went to growing up. "Maybe that's a little shaky now, but like . . . even when I decided to keep Maddie, there was never any doubt that Mommy would help me raise her. Not even a little. Whether or not things worked out with B. I just knew it."

There's a lump in my throat. I try to swallow it down, but it sticks. It has never occurred to me that Tatiana was spoiled. Or is what she's describing how parents are supposed to treat their children? As I weigh the thought, I realize she's the first Black woman of my peers, that I know of, who was granted so much room to be herself. Her actual self. My family taught me to keep my head up no matter what, but they also taught me I was a colossal disappointment and that my ancestors almost certainly disliked me. My head is spinning.

"Okay, back to your cards," she interjects. "We have the Empress here in the second position. That's great news for love, family, and creation. But"—she eyes the card next to it—"it came up next to Seven of Pentacles, so . . . you're not gonna like this. You sure you want to hear it?"

"Sure." I shrug, not wanting to admit I'm feeling more invested than anticipated. I feel slightly anxious after her warning.

"Well, what I can tell you is that there will probably be love in your life. The kind of love that was missing for you in the past." She moves her head from side to side. I can't tell if this is part of standard tarot presentation etiquette or if she's really thinking that deeply about the cards. "*However*, it's not gonna happen until you're willing to put in the work it takes to build a lasting relationship. You're gonna need a strategy, especially if you want a high-caliber partner, and you are totally worthy of one."

I frown. "Is that what the cards say, or is that what you're saying? And for the millionth time, what in *Jesus's* name is a high-caliber partner?" I keep my tone light, but my smile feels strained.

"I knew you wouldn't like it, but the cards don't lie." She offers me a faux-apologetic look. "And for the millionth time, a high-caliber partner is one who is well educated, socially influential, and generationally wealthy."

My stomach burbles; I wince. Whether this sensation is a reaction to the bar for male excellence being set squarely in hell or indigestion from all the iced coffee we drank on the road today is unclear. That I want to feel sure Tatiana is wrong is reason enough for me to believe that she's probably right. Just, not for the reasons she probably thinks, and certainly not toward the goals she's set for herself, or for me. If I bother pushing back, she'll remind me that if I just believe in myself as much as she believes in herself, I can expedite my manifestation timeline. But I cannot ignore the evidence anymore: Tatiana has been loved thoroughly, and beautifully, by her family, who have instilled in her an absolute certainty of her worthiness of love, safety, abundance, and anything else her heart desires.

My family made a very different kind of effort, because it didn't occur to any of them that Black children could survive being raised with love instead of fear. Those were our respective foundations, and every self-help book either of us have skimmed or quoted at each other would suggest that self-love is the required entrance fee to healthy romantic relationships, nontoxic family dynamics, and the elusive glory of breaking generational trauma cycles. Yet here we both are, sitting inside my family's generational trauma cycle, Tatiana just a plane ride away from the one she, B, and my half-dissociated deposition to the State of Massachusetts have started anew.

While I have no doubt in Tatiana's ability to make the most glamorous possible lemonade out of her situation, I am not made the same way. She has unshakable faith. In herself, mainly, in a higher power, sure, but most of all in the imminent transformation of even the shittiest of circumstances from unfavorable to completely and justifiably in service to her desires. I lack this faith and most others, though I do seem to have an endurance that surprises even me. Maybe that is the gift my family has given me; they were light on the love, but heavy on what is starting to feel like a useful, if labor-intensive, kind of motivation. It's a motivation to keep going, not because you believe in yourself, not because you believe things will get better, certainly not because you know where you're headed (a particularly elusive knowledge in my lineage). Not even because you take any particular pleasure in existing. You just keep going, because you're already here, and if you're still here, you still can.

This is why I have to leave, I realize as I watch the fake candlelight flicker over the cards. Logistically, Tatiana must stay in Boston for the foreseeable future, yes, but she also can stay. She knows how to make staying work. She could have made staying in New York work, if she'd wanted. I couldn't have. I don't know how to stay, but I do know how to make leaving livable enough. What surprises me most about the realization is how little it stirs me, physically. Where my assertion, till now, that I'll go to Boston, has been accompanied by palpitations, contractions in my chest, my stomach, this realization lands easy, like an overdue settling of something long restless.

I know I could do things the easy way. I could take up the Bishops' offer. I could move back to Boston, live in their lives a little longer. Forever, maybe. Become that auntie everybody has who isn't *related* related but who's family anyway. It would be logical. It would be materially more comfortable. It would be familiar. But I can't bring myself to do it. If I can't break my family's cycle, our shame-laced inability to take root and stay rooted—and I probably can't—I might as well ride it out.

As the unfamiliar certainty opens up space, and breath, in my body, a million snide comebacks float around in my head, a million kind reassurances mixed in among them. I choose neither. "Got it," I state when Tatiana opens her mouth to elaborate on her declaration about my continued lovelessness. "Look, I'm super tired. Let's finish the tarot tomorrow? Before we head to the psychic? I'm setting an alarm for eight thirty." I feel good as I say this; our roles, righted, once again.

She surveys the abandoned tarot cards with a deepening frown. "Okay. That's fine."

"Cool, thank you." I push myself up and start collecting the candles. It's only when I'm back inside, halfway up the stairs, that I realize I've left the cards outside.

CHAPTER 28

APRIL 14

"Whoa." Tatiana steps down and out from the car, taking in the purple psychic headquarters, placed between a Krispy Kreme and an auto body shop with a handmade sign, forty minutes down the 301. The heat isn't letting up, but at least it's marginally less humid today. "It is country AF out here. But I love it, and I know where we're getting a snack afterward!" She bounds toward the entrance—or what looked like an entrance but turned out to be a painted doorway. I'm relieved by her high spirits, reassured that accompanying her on this mission is the right thing to do. And relieved that she's letting me off the hook about getting a reading myself. On the ride over, Tatiana put her phone on speaker and played a TED Talk by her pastor, the same one I saw at the funeral. She spoke on the power of symbolism in daily life; it wasn't a half-bad lecture. "How do we get in?"

"Over here, ladies," a singsongy voice sounds from around the side of the building.

"Uh—" I hesitate, locking the car. "You sure you want to do this, Tatiana? I'm scared." I laugh, but I'm not lying. There are no other cars in the lot, not even outside of the auto body shop.

Her hands outstretched, she traces a very messily painted rune on the painted door. "Oh, we are definitely going in. Come on!" She walks around the building; I scramble to catch up.

The owner, who introduces herself as Queen Kellee, is a tall woman, in her fifties or so, with long, blond goddess braids. The space is bigger than it looked from the outside, but also cluttered with mismatched shelves overflowing with unboxed crystals and incense, and filled with more fish tanks than I feel should be legal. I trip over a pile of books on my way in; somehow, Tatiana is navigating the space gracefully and with glee, skillfully maneuvering through the chaos to examine the available artifacts. When I side-eye the nearest tank, a massive, rectangular structure that contains a baby stingray, Queen Kellee comes up beside me, very close, frankincense and sweat wafting off her multiple layers of robes, and whispers in my ear, "I'm a Pisces." Given her proximity, I don't dare turn my entire head to face her.

My eyes dart sideways. "Mm-hmm."

"I love this," Tatiana gushes. "Love it, love it, love it. Do you do readings? It's been years since my last one, which was spot-on."

"Of course, goddess." Queen Kellee bows her head.

"And . . . how much is that?" I ask, taking a step to the side, away from Queen Kellee.

"For you beautiful ladies, beautiful spirits, let me feel into it—" She closes her eyes and takes a deep breath, so long that I wonder if, mid-inhale, she has perished. "Fifty," she announces, her eyes snapping open. "And I promise you—while I cannot guarantee what I tell you is what you will want to hear, it will give you the clarity to live your dreams."

"I'm in! Dzifa, mind if I go first?"

I shake my head. She can go first and last. It's not that I don't believe in intuitives, and I certainly love myself a good incense. It's just that for me, the allure of witch shit is: It can be practiced in private, non-commercially, and without having to be circled by stingrays while on dry land. At least I have very little faith, so far, that this particular psychic will be as "spot-on" as the last.

Tatiana settles into her seat: a plush, low purple cushion, across from Queen Kellee, who lounges, Roman-style, on a wide, jade-colored faux fur pallet. She reaches out her hands, which, I already know before I see them, are covered in no less than twelve jangling accessories each. "Bring me your hands, goddess, so I can really feel you."

I survey the shop, checking for anyone else lurking in between fish tanks or underneath a pile of spirituality books. After surviving all those years in New York, if this is how we end up getting abducted, I am going to be irate.

Tatiana spares me a lightly skeptical look over her shoulder, but places her hands in Queen Kellee's.

"Mm. Mmm. Mm." Queen Kellee's low hums continue for over two minutes; I take out my phone to verify. "Yes," she finally says, opening her eyes.

"You are very powerful, goddess," she says, shaking her head as if in disbelief. "Very powerful. Smart, too. Slightly devious. But this can be corrected." She releases Tatiana's hands and begins gently shaking her entire body, like she is trying to release something back into the air.

"True, true, and fair enough," Tatiana agrees, not missing a beat. "Can you tell me something about . . . let me see—what should I ask about, Dzifa?"

I accidentally say the first thing that comes to mind. "Is the exit unlocked?"

"Dzifa," Tatiana admonishes with a snicker. "No. Okay. How about—can you tell me if I'm gonna meet anybody, and like—ballpark—what's his net worth gonna be?"

"Ah yes." Queen Kellee nods, concluding her shaking and settling back into her relaxed pose. "Certainly, I can. What you first must understand, goddess, is that the trials and tribulations you have endured will lead you to the—"

I tune out, winding my way through a maze of mini tanks, toward the rear of the shop. There's a small toilet at the back, the wooden door slightly off its hinges. A lopsided bookshelf teeters beside it. I scan the spines, row by row. My eyes catch on a book called *Persephone, Resurrected.* "Nope!" I poke the book with unnecessary force and have to steady the bookshelf to keep it from toppling.

"You okay, sis?" Tatiana calls from the front of the shop.

"Yep," I answer. She and Queen Kellee resume their session. My eyes drift to the floor. I spot a book that fell to the ground when I jostled the case. Small, compact, hardcover. I turn it so the cover faces me. *Intuitive Wisdom: A Guide.* The graphics look similar to the cover of the tarot deck Tatiana gave me last night. I pick it up and open to a random page. There are a few paragraphs of text and an image on the opposite page: a phoenix surrounded, but not engulfed, by flames. I scan the text half-heartedly. My eyes catch on the last sentence:

> Intuition is neither blind impulse nor unintelligent feeling; intuition is your body-mind having synthesized its most deeply assessed, time-tested, collectively known wisdom: ready and inviting you to act in alignment with its whispered truths.

I think of Carmen's invitation to what I've wanted to believe is just a tired cliché about the "inner voice." What I'm now realizing is an actual, physical state. I crouch on the ground, then sit fully, grimacing when I see stale Goldfish crackers scattered a few inches away. I cradle the book in my hands and read that sentence over and over again, feeling how the words wash the guilt through and out of me.

Late last night, after the tarot reading, I had to walk out to the driveway and go a ways down the hill to get enough data to confirm my school selection online. I consider, now, the choice I made. How it never made sense in any way I could explain to anyone else, and yet, it has always been the only choice that made sense.

We stop at Krispy Kreme next. We get a half dozen glazed and sit inside the small, white-tabled dining area inside the doughnut shop. This one is mostly drive-through, so the lack of ambience is to be expected and, after the overabundance of ambience and Goldfish dust in Chez Queen Kellee, I'm grateful for the clinical atmosphere.

We're lucky the HOT sign was on, though Tatiana says it's not luck: It's fate. I shrug and take a bite of the first doughnut, then devour the whole thing in another couple of bites. She takes her time with hers; I don't understand how that's even possible.

"So was that fifty dollars well spent?" I ask.

Tatiana tips her head to one side, then the other. "I mean, to take in all of that crazy? Yes, absolutely." She laughs. "On the other hand, she didn't get as specific as I would've liked. Especially about the net worth thing."

"Well." I shrug. "Maybe you'll have a high net worth yourself and it won't matter as much if your partner does. I mean, I still think it's awesome if he makes more, but maybe it would take the pressure off if—"

Tatiana rolls her eyes, finishing off the doughnut. "You still don't get it. I know I can have a high net worth myself. But why should I bust my behind any more than I already have? In my classes, I've really seen how masculine energy is better suited for that kind of hustle mode. It's not that women can't do it. It's that making ourselves do it is a waste of our true talents."

I frown. "Which are what? 'Cause I'm not sure mine have come in yet."

She picks up another doughnut. I wait a minute, feeling an oversize anguish that if I eat the next one, there will only be two left. "Yeah, well, we can't all be great, like Queen Kellee." We laugh. "But seriously, I just feel like my mom paid her dues, I paid my dues—I've been working since I was *fourteen*—I'm done paying my dues. I'm ready to enjoy my life, and I feel like—I am simply not willing to accept that just because I'm a mother I'm supposed to—what? Submit, again, to being a slave to capitalism? Let some dude be a slave to capitalism—it was built for them anyway, so that's *why* they're better suited for it. Let him pound the pavement, and I will pay forward the freedom that grants me tenfold."

"In . . . sorry, how will you pay it forward?" I ask, trying to keep the judgment out of my confusion.

"Not in sexual favors, Dzifa." She glares at me. "I know that's what you're thinking. And believe it or not, high-caliber men want, and need, more than that. I'll pay it forward by—you know what?" She pauses, shakes her head. "It's one of those things that if you get it, you get it. And I hope you get it eventually, 'cause I want this for you, too." Her expression softens. "Look—I'll always be working on something. You know that. I can't stand to be idle. You know I'm good at making money when I need to, and as much as I want to. My business is already taking off. So this is not about whether I'll have my own money or not. This is about how when a woman is well taken care of—like, really well nourished—she nourishes everyone around her. You don't think so?"

Out of respect, I really take the time to think about it. I finally eat the second doughnut, then the third, and get up to grab a few extra napkins from the counter. I drop a couple next to Tatiana, then take my seat. The skinny teenage boy working the counter is leaning against the drive-through window, staring out onto the empty, hot pavement. "I don't know," I say as my mind drifts to my mother, how she always made sure to nourish herself. Her skin was always glowing, her hair moisturized and meticulously arranged, her clothes tasteful, expensive, coordinated, her closet full, museum-worthy. I feel the weight of her proud remorselessness, at dinner all those months ago. Her recollection of her mother's admonishment. *Soften.* The cage that reminder seemed to symbolize to her, a woman governed by sharpness.

I think of Esther and me opening the large, high-ceilinged pantry, surveying its empty shelves till we found the corner, the dwindling, dented cans of tomato paste, years old, left over from the last time our father was there. These cans were his, from when he was in the mood for light soup or ground nut stew. "I guess it depends on the woman." I look up from my pile of napkins and try for a smile, but it feels a little flat. Tatiana frowns, shrugs. I turn my eyes to the plastic, three-tiered display on the counter, the glaze on the recently made doughnuts cooling, solidifying.

I close my eyes for a moment, seeing my mother's face just after her father died. I see her signature composure breaking, tears streaming, her chest heaving with sobs. The first time I saw the fragile side of her humanity, the flip side of her self-directed vitality. An outpouring, for the first time, of grief rather than rage. A softening, I now see. I'd thought it was the beginning of a new leaf. I didn't understand, then, the nature of people. That we become whoever we believe we must be to survive; we can break from it, deviate in moments that jolt our tenderest humanness back through our systems, but when the dust settles, we are wired to go back to what is familiar, what we know. To break such a pattern and create a new, lasting one takes even more than all the fight we have in us. It takes being able to see that what we've never lived, but deeply crave, is possible.

Maybe I wanted a mother who knew how to pay her nourishment forward gently, gladly, with greater consistency. But if I did, I guess I needed her to have grown up in a world where she'd ever seen a Black woman be nourished. Where she'd seen softness met by softness, where softness like a tender hand rather than a sharp blade was safe enough to be seen, practiced. The world my mother grew up in: A woman was selfless and bound, or selfish, free, and alone, shunned by a society that couldn't stomach her refusal to submit. Maybe I'm no different.

I guess that's why I've always liked to create things. Not for their outcome but for the act of rebellion, the act of faith it is to feel the craving for what you haven't yet seen—some other, more nourishing, way, any other way—and to create toward it, not even knowing if it's possible.

"I'm going to Italy," I blurt out. I want to say more, to explain myself, to apologize maybe, but my voice feels stuck in my throat now.

Tatiana pushes her pile of napkins to the edge of the table. She looks around the shop, then back to me, but her eyes aren't meeting mine. "Yeah, I know. I knew it as soon as you said you'd applied." Her voice is quiet; the sadness in it makes me want to take back my statement, and my decision.

I want to tell her that I made a mistake, that actually, I'll come to Boston and take the scholarship and help look after Maddie while she builds up her life again, exactly how she wants it. I'll keep her uncle's house clean and chip in for electricity. I'll buy groceries every week. But then I think about my birthday, her closeness with Sarai and Sam, and I think maybe *she* doesn't even want that. She didn't seem particularly overjoyed by it when she had it. She seems freer with Sam and Sarai, her exuberance evenly matched, her values and interests, perhaps, also.

"Probably knew it before you did, it looks like."

"I'll visit," I promise, my voice wavering. "I could take the train up this summer, before I go, even. I mean, if you want."

"Yeah," she repeats. "You could do that. You're welcome, of course. Obviously, I'm gonna save up so I can visit *you*, so get ready for that." Her tone is upbeat, but forced. I can see I've disappointed her but am not sure precisely why, now that I've realized my living with her family may not actually have been her ideal either. It feels like we're doing a table read off a script, saying the things we think we're supposed to say without really meaning them at all.

"Yeah, you'd better. Bring Maddie, too. Maybe one day you'll both move to Europe, and we'll practically be neighbors." She doesn't say anything. I guess we've run through the script. "Please tell your mom, though, and Uncle Aman. I really, really appreciate how generous they've been. There's no way I could have made it through everything without them."

Tatiana waves a hand to dismiss my concerns, stands up to collect the napkins and the doughnut box, throws them in the trash. "I want to check in on Maddie. I signed her up for these toddler dance classes a lady from my church organizes, and I wanna see how the first lesson went. I'm gonna call her outside, before we head back."

"Of course." I stand and push both of our chairs back in. "Thanks," I say to the boy at the counter, then follow Tatiana out from the shop, gasping when the humidity hits my lungs.

CHAPTER 29

APRIL 15

Tatiana eats her croissantwich on our way to the museum. It's a thirty-minute drive. We're both too tired to venture to Baltimore again. I considered taking her to the diner where Anthony took me, but wonder if we'll run into him there. I still feel something holding me back from telling her about him. It's not quite like my guilt about having met B or keeping the Milan application a secret; it's not information I owe her, that I'm withholding. It's information that's mine and that I cannot yet see the benefit of sharing. Instead, I suggest the tobacco museum. When we arrive, I join her and eat my sandwich quietly. I take my third coffee of the morning with me; she finishes hers and leaves the cup in the middle console. "Why is it so hot?!" It's the first thing she's said since we left the house. I haven't pushed.

"Yeah, it's pretty disgusting." It was stupid of me to bother dunking a gallon of Safeway water over my body this morning. My T-shirt is already soaked. Tatiana was smart enough to wear a sundress, but she's sweating, too. "I heard this has been the hottest April on record. And I think today is supposed to be the hottest day of the month."

"And we're outside, why?" She fans her face. Lush, green trees surround us, some of their leaves scattered across the dirt.

I raise an eyebrow. "Well, since there's no air-conditioning in the house, it's probably actually better to be outside. Maybe if we walk fast enough, we'll create a breeze."

She snorts and follows me down the dirt path to the visitors' area. It's actually more of a tree trunk with various bulletins affixed to it. I once visited this place when a group of schoolkids was touring through, but I've never seen it busy, exactly. Nobody seems to be here today. Tatiana squints to read one of the signs. "So . . . this is about slavery, or . . ."

"I mean . . ." A fly buzzes around my face. I flap my hands; the fly ignores them. "It's not specifically about slavery; it's about rural life in eighteen- or nineteen-whatever. But it's kind of accidentally about slavery. Also, genocide." We walk down a long dirt path, clinging to the few spots of shade. We pass a tiny log cabin and walk by a blacksmith exhibit. "You don't want to see inside the cabin? I think it was built by this guy who'd been a slave, once he was free. Also, people used to be so short."

"Meh." She shrugs. "I'm still short and do not see the appeal." I follow her outstretched arm to the most modern-looking building on the lot.

"Yeah, this is the one about tobacco." We walk up the steps and enter. It's not a massive building, but all the others are so small that it looks formidable. The ceilings are high and bolstered by long, wooden beams. In the center is a massive sample of a successful tobacco yield. Every time I see it, I jump back a little. It's good news my previous visit to this museum was months after I started the ritual at my local tobacco flat. Otherwise, there's no way I could've braved it in the dark; I'd have seen this display in my mind's eye every single time.

The dried leaves are deep yellow, their hanging shapes mangled and frayed. Along each wall are glossy, blown-up placards detailing Maryland's history with tobacco. I stand before the one card I've read before. It mentions the Indigenous peoples who grew tobacco in the first place, before the invasion. The placard doesn't say *invasion*, but I read between the lines.

"Hm. It's actually kind of well designed," Tatiana says. "I mean, creepy, but hey. The history is what it is, I guess." She peers down at the wooden, dolly-like contraption that holds the dried tobacco display. She continues surveying the room; I step into a smaller one off to the side.

It's partially detached from the rest of the building, and it's dark and dusty inside. There's a placard in here, too, but the light is dim and I don't bother to read it. The ceiling comes together in a V, although I can see that at some point there was a flat roof underneath. Broken pieces of long wooden beams are held up by nearly invisible metal strings. Sinister-looking tools hang from the back wall, and more long, bat-like strands of dried tobacco hang around the perimeter.

At the other end of the room is a wooden structure that looks like an old-timey lemonade stand except instead of lemonade, there's a faded sign that reads *Tobacco 25c*. I wonder if my mother got her inspiration for her drawing here. I sit on the low, wooden bench at the edge of the room and lean back, close my eyes.

"Are you okay?"

I sit up. Tatiana isn't looking at me—she's eyeing the tobacco tools with disgust—but there's no one else she could be talking to.

"Yeah." I snake a hand around the back of my head and crack my neck on both sides. "I'm fine. I was just—I don't know. My mom made this drawing, I think of this display, and—"

"I'm gonna stop you there, friend." Tatiana rolls her eyes. "I don't know if you have Stockholm syndrome through the house or what, but if you're about to tell me you're suddenly having warm and fuzzy feelings about your mom, I'mma bring you to the nearest church for an exorcism."

I shake my head. "Warm and fuzzy, no. Maybe in an alternate universe." I shrug. "No. But I am feeling a little less . . . um"—I search for the word—"critical, I guess. Of certain things. Like . . . at least she tried, I guess? To sort of . . . piece together some kind of legacy. With the house. How it's on the land her ancestors had to work."

Tatiana grimaces. "Yeah, that's a stretch, girl. And even if she was trying to build a legacy, if you think she was doing that for you, you really *do* have Stockholm syndrome. I mean—this is the woman who basically sold you a lie your entire life about where you even come from."

"I—" I frown. "Now *that's* a stretch."

"Is it?" She narrows her eyes. "'Cause first she told you *Dzifa* was a Ga name, which—" She laughs. "You know it isn't, right?"

"I know my own name," I snap.

"And then," she goes on, "she told you that thing about your dad, which—"

"I don't know what she meant by that, and—"

Tatiana laughs. "And you didn't ask why? I'm gonna guess, because you're gonna find out she also lied to you about that. Shit, she probably even lied to you about your ancestors being from here. And about whatever these tobacco things are."

"Tobacco flats," I interject as if that's the most pressing correction to make. I consider gesturing at the placard to punctuate my assertion, but I hesitate. I haven't read it, don't know what it says. I shake my head and continue, "And I didn't ask, because it doesn't matter. My father didn't raise me, regardless. And are you *really* in a position to be criticizing my level of curiosity about my parentage?"

She cuts me a glare, hovers between the bench where I'm sitting and the doorway of the replica. "I'm not criticizing you. And if you are insinuating what I think you are: What a hot fucking take, Dzifa. For the record? I know, and I don't care. Because like you said: It doesn't matter. A father is a man who raises you, whether or not it's his DNA you're made of."

I cannot pinpoint the exact source of my fury, but it boils through me, and out—too big to be contained anymore. "And what is a mother, to you, then?"

She doesn't hesitate. "A woman who does whatever it takes to take care of her children. Whatever it takes." She stops pacing, slows, sits at the opposite end of the bench, lets her head fall into her hands. "And she doesn't need to apologize for it," she says, straightening her back, cutting her eyes toward me.

"Who asked you to apologize?" I ask, bewildered.

"I didn't tell you because I could just—you are so—you're so *fragile*, Dzifa. And I'm not going to apologize for doing what I had to do, how I had to do it."

"What are you talking about?" I ask, trying to catch her eyes.

She pauses so long, I wonder if she's decided to drop it. I weigh my own capacity and the frustration rising in me—my willingness to keep pushing. I'm half-resolved to let it go and leave the room entirely, when finally, she returns my gaze. "There's something I haven't told you about Luca's last night."

My back slumps against the wall; my throat is closed, and I don't even try to speak.

She takes a breath. "I mean, I didn't know about it either. But—" She looks away again, and I wonder what it is she sees in my eyes. "B told me," she continues, fidgeting with her nails, "like . . . a little bit before you left Boston to come here. He told me what his mother did."

I lay a hand on my chest and press down to anchor myself.

"See—" She points at where my hand lies. "Fragile."

I remove the hand, scoffing. "Jesus, Tatiana, what did she do?"

"She'd been feeding him breast milk." Tatiana says it to the fake dirt floor. "She'd been doing it behind my back. Got it from a relative." She shakes her head, eyes wild. "A 'trusted source.' That's what she told B."

I fold my torso down over my knees and breathe there for a minute. When I've recovered, I ask, voice muffled, "Is that? Is that why . . ."

"No," Tatiana says in a low voice. "Probably not. Luca had a weak heart. He was fragile, too." She stares at me, and I cannot tell if it is pity or judgment she regards me with. Probably both. "Even if he had gotten that surgery, he—" Tatiana stops, closes her eyes. "We'll never know."

She opens her eyes again, trains them on the *Tobacco 25c* sign. I'm struggling to breathe, but the harder I try to keep it together, the worse I feel. "But once B finally told me, it was enough to get Brigitte out of the picture. The deal was: He withdraws his claim, makes a positive statement about my character, Brigitte is never anywhere near Maddie again . . . and we share custody."

"I—" I sit up, huff out an exhale. "I do not understand why you would hide this from me. After everything—I call *bullshit* on you thinking I'm fragile. I was strong enough to show up for you in one of the most fucked-up situations I've ever seen in my life. Why did you hide this from me?"

She waves her hands as if the answer is waiting to be plucked from the dusty, stuck air. "At first, you were just going through a lot, clearly. And then—I don't know. Sam said something. About how maybe you were holding me back. And Sarai kind of agreed."

"And you just went along with what they said?" I pause. "Did you *agree* with what they said?"

"I don't really know, Dzifa." Tatiana shrugs. "It's not really about you, okay? It's just—I wanted revenge *so bad*, for what Brigitte did, after how she treated me. But then . . . B and I were talking. It was the first time we talked, actually, since we lost Luca. Since before, if I'm being honest. You know?" She huffs, squares her shoulders. Starts again. "And we just felt like—how much more do we really want to put Maddie through? How many more years would we be tied up with lawyers and courts and uncertainty if we kept going and going—like, what is the point? Is it to get 'justice'? Or is it to raise our daughter? I mean, at the end of the day, that's the only justice I really care about."

She wipes at the tears that tumble down her cheeks, her expression hard, like she can't forgive herself for crying. "But it was a lot. It is a lot, to let Brigitte ride off into the sunset without any repercussions. I didn't want to talk about it because I didn't want to be tempted to change my mind."

I pull at the scarf holding my hair together. Cursing, I untie and retie it as I speak, not even trying anymore, to keep the anger out of my voice. Not trying anymore to comfort her, even as I can see she's hurting. "And you thought I would try to convince you that you were wrong? Tatiana, you have to know that's crazy. That's not me. You know that."

"Yeah, exactly. I wasn't afraid of what you would say. I was afraid I was turning into you."

"Excuse me?" I slide off the bench, stand, face her, my arms crossed over my chest. "And that's, like . . . a *threat* to you?"

"I don't mean it like that," she says, burying her face in her hands again. "But—I want to be myself. And I was afraid that who I needed to be, to be allowed to be a mom, was . . . basically you."

"What does that even mean? I don't even have kids, Tatiana! You just said that the other day. That I don't understand what it's like to be a mother, because I'm not one. What are you *talking* about?"

"Tame, I mean." She stands, shakes her head, her palms open. "Compliant."

I wince. "I am neither of those things." I say it quietly first. Then, "I'm not," I repeat, louder. "And it's really shitty that you don't know that."

She says nothing.

"I'm as wild as you are." I mean to say it straight, but it comes out muffled, sloppy. "I just never had the room to show it."

"Well. Since you're leaving"—she says it like an accusation, her earlier encouragement absent—"I guess you have all the room in the world now."

I regard her quietly, trying to pull the fury back in, struggling, realizing—that's what it is. That's what I have unspooled, cannot seem to rewind. "Let's just go," I say. "I—" I shake my head, tug at my scarf again, stop myself before I accidentally unwind it again. "Let's just go," I repeat.

"Fine." Tatiana shrugs. "This museum sucks anyway."

Tatiana circles around to the passenger door. "Can you unlock it?" When I don't move, she leans a hip against the hot metal and winces, righting herself. "I wasn't trying to be shady earlier, Dzifa"—she rolls her eyes—"about the stuff with your parents. Or about—the other stuff—I was just saying, I wanna be me. That's all."

I unlock the door manually so she can get in, but I hesitate beside the driver's door for a minute.

She knocks on my window from the inside. "Dzifa, can we go? I need something to drink, and I'm pretty sure I have heat stroke."

I climb up into my seat and set my hands on the steering wheel. Briefly, I let my head fall to the side and rest on the window. When Tatiana clears her throat, I twist the key into the ignition. It takes ten tries and a curse to start the car.

My chest is rising and falling so laboriously, I know Tatiana must be able to hear my breathing. I can hear her asking if I'm okay, but I've already retreated so far into myself I'm just going to have to stay here.

I've made it to the entrance of the street that leads up the mountain to my mother's house when Tatiana lets out a frustrated *tsk*.

"What?" I bring myself to say.

"I said I have to get a drink."

"Yes, I left a few on the dining table. You can grab one of those."

"*No.*" She keeps her focus out the window. "It is *boiling* out. I want something cold."

I screech to a halt at an inelegant angle, blocking the road. "If you wanted to go somewhere specific, why didn't you just say so?"

She glances behind us, checking frantically for cars. The road just behind us is full of speeding cars at this hour. "Dzifa! You can't stop here."

My fists dig into the rubbery fabric of the steering wheel. "Please make up your mind—I need to know where we're going to actually get there."

Tatiana snaps her head toward mine. "I just *told* you." It takes a moment for me to recognize this look. It's the same she used to reserve for Brigitte. The same she reserves for anyone who crosses her. I lean back against the window and stare back at her, something in me refusing to turn away. These are Tatiana's eyes, not my mother's, but I can no longer set my bar so low. A stuck place in me—it feels like a taut line of barbed wire, stretched from my throat down to my belly—unlatches, winds with that already-unspooling thread. Strengthens. Revs its momentum. I take in the hardening of her gaze, the one that says, *Fall in line.*

Not even bothering to glance behind me, I hit the accelerator hard, jerk forward, and turn the car around. Tatiana's arms are gripping the windowsill and the center console. Breathing hard through my nose, I spare two looks to either side of the intersection and accelerate out into traffic. I just barely make it between a black, compact car and a giant SUV. Both honk. Tatiana's breathing is loud, her fear apparent in every jolt of the car. I press my foot all the way down and let up only when I've revved the engine as hard as it will go. In this junk Explorer, I know the force will never push the car much beyond the speed limit, but I need the pressure of my foot against the accelerator right now. I can feel it as I do it that I'll regret this later. That this is the worst of who I am, the opposite of who I want to be. I make a hard left into the business park; I don't check for pedestrians, and I don't look over at my friend. When the car skids into a spot in front of Dunkin', I slam the brakes hard. I look to my right and say, "There. Since it's such an emergency."

Tatiana takes a minute of rapid, shallow breaths, her eyes unfocused. Hands shaking, she pushes her way out of the car and stalks off into the store.

I watch her disappear into the entrance. As I turn back to face the steering wheel, a roiling spasm latches onto my rib cage, as if the wire, shaken loose, has gone rogue. Gasping the short, shallow breaths I've learned are the best I can do when taking a full one feels like being stabbed in the gut, I reach under the seat for the little lever that knocks it backward and recline as far as it will go. I pull my bent legs up with me, careful not to change the angle of my spine. My legs are restless, but the upper half of my body keeps me anchored in place.

My eyes facing the grungy carpeted sunroof that I have never once opened to the sun, I press my hands into my shins and squeeze. The pressure doesn't fix it, but it is the distraction I need to stop myself from hyperventilating. When I get used to that pressure, I move my hands down to my ankles and press harder there. When I get used to that, I swivel slowly toward the window in an oversize fetal position and press my entire body against the car door. I grasp for one of the exercises Carmen gave me, to find myself and my breath again.

Before I can shift the sensation back to something benign, a jolt at the back of the car startles me. I swivel around in my seat, yelping from the second spasm that digs into the other side of my gut, to see the trunk opening. I force myself to climb out of the driver's seat, clutching my midsection with a shaking forearm. "What are you—" I pause. Tatiana is standing with the trunk open over her head, pulling her bags out of the car. When did she even put them there? Why did she put them there, a day early? "What are you doing?" I demand. Each word sends a fresh new dagger of pain in the spaces between my ribs.

She waves behind us. An old, black town car pulls up. "I'm going to the airport."

"What?" I stare, slack-jawed. "Your flight isn't until tomorrow night!"

"I got an earlier one, so. I should go."

My back collapses against one side of the trunk, my damp T-shirt meeting the blazing-hot paint uncomfortably. I bring a hand to my cheeks and wipe the sweat, or tears, away. "I don't understand."

She takes a step back. The driver opens the trunk and walks around to set her bags in. "You just seem stressed right now. I'm just thinking of what you told me your doctor said, about how you should avoid stressful situations."

I scoff. "Are you serious, Tatiana? *This* is stressful. You're just fucking bailing because—what? I talk back to you *once* in our entire friendship and you can't handle it?"

She blinks, and again, and I can see now that she's trying to stop herself from crying. "I know. I'm sorry," she says. Why isn't she fighting back?

"So . . . what? You can say whatever you want to whoever you want, you can basically tell me your worst nightmare is turning into me, but God forbid I have anything to say back to you. What the *fuck*, Tatiana?"

"I'm sorry." This time, it's a whisper. Her eyes wide with the same fear I saw for the first time in the car, she ducks into the back seat and waves curtly. The door shuts and the car glides forward.

I stare forward, conscious of the jagged pants I'm passing off as breaths, then look to my right. There's a small crowd observing the spectacle. "What?" I spit out. My feet feel bolted to the pavement; my legs, boneless. As the crowd disperses, I force my way, stumbling, back into the car. It starts up on the first try.

At the house, I idle on the driveway, ignoring my discomfort and parched throat. I spend an hour drafting, deleting, redrafting increasingly caustic messages to Tatiana.

I draft the last; my fingers hover over the Send button. A drop of sweat falls right onto it; I frantically hit Backspace and throw the phone into my bag.

CHAPTER 30

I stand on the porch all the way through dusk, listening to a chorus of cicadas. It feels too early for them. But I don't know if it's the season that brings them or if it's the heat. I can never quite relax into the rhythm of their song. All I think of when I hear their synchronized, chirping roar is how many unseen beings, living and dead, are lying in wait on this land. Right in this backyard, past the porch, before the trees. Beneath the ground I stand on, across every blade of grass, up the towering, ancient trees. This ground, even untended as it currently is, is intended to be palatable, appeased and rebranded by a generation or two of steadfast striving. Of top-tier degrees and admonishments to soften. I know nothing about the actual composition of soil, but I'm convinced: Ground that's been soaked with centuries of subjugated blood can never again be neutral.

I don't know why, but when I go back inside, I use the unfinished bathroom in what was intended to be my mother's bedroom. It's just a toilet on concrete, surrounded by broken beams and industrial canvas bags overflowing with bricks. It doesn't flush. I strip off my jeans and underwear, then my top and bra. I pull a Harvard blanket from the nearest couch and wrap it around my sweat. It occurs to me that Tatiana must have left something—several things, probably. I walk into her room, and it's completely bare, except for the gift bag, which she's retied and set in the middle of the neatly made bed. I peer into her bathroom. All the face masks, minus one, are still there, just as I arranged them before she came. For hours, I sit on the bed and hold the gift bag on my lap.

My phone is dead, so I walk back out to the car to charge it. When it lights up, I open WhatsApp. Wait. Put down the phone. Pick it up. Close my eyes. Open them. Send the message.

Hi. Do you have a minute?

Those three dots appear, disappear, then nothing. I make myself breathe—properly, now. As I do, I remember that I am wearing a blanket. I'm about to shut the phone off to go wash and change into actual clothes when the screen flashes with a new message.

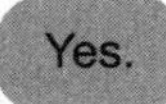

I wince when I see I've pressed the video instead of the call icon. Frantically, I turn off my video but leave the sound on. My mother brings her face close to the phone, her impeccable Afro chignon looming above her. Her eyes are bright, alert. "This is unexpected. Hello? Are you there?"

"Yeah." I already want to hang up, want to take back this call, want to be strong enough, smart enough to make it another decade without talking to my mother. But no matter what that restraint would do for my ego, it would do nothing to change anything that's happened. I'm going to have to let the physical distance, which—aside from the information I called to request—is all I really need from her, be enough. "I mean, yes. Sorry." The amendment is automatic.

"Okay, I can't see you." She taps the screen. "Can everybody else see her?"

"She won't turn on her video," Charity says in the background, amusement in her voice. "Always hiding." My eldest sister is the one I know the least, but she's always been the loudest about her assessments of me.

"Where are you?" I ask, not sure if I'm disappointed or relieved she isn't alone. Relieved, I decide.

"I'm at Charity's house." My mother frowns. "Esther told me you have a visitor. What does she think of my house?"

I shrug, then remember she can't see me. It's for the best; she'd smack the eye roll right off my face if she could see it. But the fact that *that's* her question . . . it takes all my resolve to refrain from chucking the phone out the window. "I don't know. She said you're a good decorator."

"That's very kind of her." My mother nods. "Please convey my appreciation. I do hope you bought some charcuterie for the kitchen, at least."

Whoever's in the room with her besides Charity—her face is so close to the screen I can't see anything else—resumes a conversation I clearly interrupted with my call. Something about plane tickets and inflation. "I'm sorry to call out of the blue," I interject, though I'm not sorry at all. She's done worse out of the blue. "Can I ask you a question?"

Her eyebrows, neatly plucked straight lines, come together in consternation. "I presume you can."

I tighten the blanket around my chest. "What did you say those little house thingies, the ones where they store tobacco . . . what did you say they were called again?"

She pulls back from the phone, the wooden chair she's in creaking as she leans back. Finally, I can see she's in the kitchen. Mary and Faith are there, too, leaning against a long counter. I catch glimpses of Charity's two youngest daughters, eleven and thirteen, milling around in the background. Her eldest two are twins, nearly finished with boarding school. I didn't realize Faith and Mary were visiting Nairobi, but why would I? I'm no longer in the group chat, having given up on the ruse that I in any way belonged in it to begin with. And while Esther may supply the occasional update, I never request one. Several pots boil on the stove in the background. It feels like an age before my mother responds, "I don't believe I called them anything."

My breath catches. I press a hand against my stomach, push on it, forcing an exhale. "Didn't you say they were called *tobacco flats*? Or something? I thought you said they were tobacco flats."

She shakes her head. "I don't recall saying any such thing. Perhaps that's their name. Perhaps 'tobacco flats' refers to the fields upon which those structures stand. I couldn't be certain. Why do you ask?" She tilts her head to the side.

My eyes drift to the biggest pot on the stove. There's a large wooden spoon sticking out of it. I can tell by its shape and the position of the grooves in the handle that it's the same one everybody cooked with when I was little enough that everybody was still there. I remember that spoon and not much else, from that time. "I have to go," I say. "Thanks—um, good night."

I leave a moment for the monotone chorus of byes and hit End, dropping the phone on my lap. The blanket starts slipping again; I tug it secure and pick the phone back up, scrolling down my contacts list until I get to *T*.

I write, then erase, another round of draft texts. I begin writing another, my fingertips aching from the pressure I'm applying to the phone. Again, I hit Delete until my message disappears. On a sharp inhale, I move to the top of the screen, press Tatiana's name, and scroll down until I find Block. My thumb grazes the bright red text, then presses the confirmation notice. It doesn't escape me, the absurdity of blocking someone who hasn't reached out, who, in fact, made a considerable effort to get away from me. I never gave credence, before, to heartbreak as a literal, physical sensation, even though looking back, I've felt it all the time. It bears down on me now. I consider calling Carmen, Esther, Zeynep, anyone. For a second opinion, for a distraction, for some noise, I don't know. I delete WhatsApp from my home screen and climb out of the car.

I adjust the barricade in the basement, put my mother's notebook back inside its storage box. Consider, then bypass, the stacks of boxes beneath it: boxes full of my old drawings, Esther's old dance tapes, all of my sisters' report cards. I retreat upstairs and step into the shower. I've collected all the remaining gallon jugs from around the house. I pour each of them over my head, gasping when the cool water hits my skin. I pour water over my hair, over my feet, behind my back, down my chest. After I've dried off with one of my mother's many monogrammed hand towels from the '80s, I pull on a pair of pajama pants and an old work T-shirt from one of my first café jobs in Oakland. I pull a sweater over the T-shirt and take off the pants so I can pull leggings on underneath. It's too hot for all of this, but I need the layers, the compression, the company.

I kneel by the window, watching for deer, watching for whatever's left of the reception in this place. My phone's internet browser successfully primed, I tell myself, on repeat, *It doesn't matter.* It matters. I type in: "tobacco flat buildings." I check page after page after page. I change my search to "tobacco flats, Maryland," "tobacco flats, slavery," "tobacco flats slavery in the south," "tobacco flats in prince george's county." I find a different browser and wait for it to load. I try again, just "tobacco flats." All that comes up are pages of listings for a mid-range apartment complex, somewhere in Virginia.

—∞—

When I look up from my screen, the rest is automatic. My thoughts move—asking, imploring, how can something that took ten years to build take less than a week to tear down. Hoping, repeating, *It doesn't matter*, cursing, repeating, *It matters.* The thoughts try to loop but can't get a hold like they used to. Not while my body goes about its motions, my heart brisk, but steady. My feet take me back to the basement, hands reach to check bag after bag, until I find the one I'm looking for. I spotted it a week ago but, due to its heft, haven't gotten around to sorting it into one of my three kitchen piles. I don't need the whole thing now anyway.

My fingers curl around the end of the baseball bat sticking farthest out of the plastic bag. My arm lifts it, drops it down so the thicker end rests against my ankle. My feet walk me back up the stairs, through the entryway, out the door, down the driveway, past Beth and Kevin's house, out, out, into the fields. It's the darkest it's ever been since the first time I made this trek. At times, the hand that grips the bat holds it tight against my torso; at others, I let it drag across the ground, the dull *thunk* of the wood on bumpy patches of dirt blending into a soothing rhythm.

When I reach the barn, I stand before it, sweating, my breath faster but steady, and try to make out the shape of it in the dark. It's not easy, even after a minute of letting my eyes adjust. In shadow, it could be anything. A rain shelter. An oversize doghouse. An optical illusion made by low-hanging, sharp-angled tree branches. I clutch the bat tighter. I came here to lift it—my thoughts tell me—to let myself feel the strength in my arms, the weight of the wood in my hands, the power and possibility to destroy, dismantle something, anything. I have always had that power: have been waiting—I tell myself—to use it, have watched, while others used it, have braced, while they used it on me, on others. *It should be my turn*, I think, try to believe.

But it isn't true. I don't think it, but it is known, somewhere else in me. Somewhere I can't quite get to yet. It's known, even as the knowing pushes against the memory of how satisfying it was to press my foot all the way down to the base of the Explorer's gas pedal, to let my foot fully drop instead of hovering it tepidly, unsure, apologetic, calibrating, calibrating. I know, somehow, in spite of the possibility of more of that, more release, more of something, anything besides holding back, that I won't lift the bat, won't wield it, won't destroy the surface of this shadowed, rotting being whose substance—whatever the truth of it may be—can never be erased. It wouldn't be possible.

I could demolish it till it's dust, but—it is known in that place I cannot yet get to—the dust will be welcomed back into the ground, will feed the beginnings of new trees, will become somebody else's relic, ritual, or ruination, in somebody else's time. I loosen my grip, just a little, drag the bat with me as I take one step forward, then another. My knee hits the side of the building.

When I make contact with those old, worn boards, I release my grip on the bat completely. I sink down so my knees meet the intersection of building and ground, shins and feet stretched on the packed-dirt flesh of the field. I sit back on my heels, lift my arms out sideways, lean forward, turn my head to the side, let it rest against the wood. *Doesn't matter what it's called. Doesn't matter what I'm called either.* I wonder if that's true, try to think it till I can feel it's true, but I can't quite feel it. Where I think it, it stretches but can't quite touch that place where if it was true, it would be known.

I change my position. Sit, back against the wall, legs stretched out on the ground, eyes finding their way in the dark. The same way I sat the first time I came to this field, to this thing I thought was, could be, maybe was never, a tobacco flat. I sit and breathe against the wood, out into the night: a full breath. First in ages, first of many.

I sit and ask for the truth of it. I can see—it is evidenced by the bat I carried here but didn't wield, that lies now a stone's throw away, just a piece of wood—that I will not destroy this wall that holds my back. But that's only half the truth. Where is the rest? I feel the weight of it, still cannot name it, cannot find the source of the weight.

If not to destroy it, is it my task to fix it, instead? Is that what my mother meant? To rebuild: bigger, better, on the same or different land to the one where the wounding happened?

What is true? I ask, still cannot feel. Instead, I think it.

I think of Tatiana; I expect a resurgence of rage or betrayal. Neither comes. There is only this recovered breath, and the rest of the truth I strive to think my way into. I think my way a layer deeper than my mind, find that beneath what I think is what I wish.

I wish Tatiana whatever she wishes. If it is her manor, the twelve bedrooms and the chef, the stables, a manor next door for her mother, a partner who cherishes her and amplifies her abundance, then I wish it so.

I wish Esther whatever she wishes. If it's the steadiness of her routines and her spreadsheets and her picket-fence family, I wish her that. If it is release from her own caught breath, if it's time and grace and space to be messy, free, I wish her that, too.

I wish my mother whatever she wishes. If it is a second chance to share her richness, to have it be received in kind by her grandchildren, then I wish it is so. I wish the same for Brigitte, even.

I wish Maddie whatever she wishes. If it is her mother's riches or her mother's richness, or both, then I wish it so. If it is her own riches or her own richness, or both, then I wish it so.

I wish the same, for all. I wish these wishes did not come with such ease, with so little resistance. This layer is a letdown, I think, but I stay in it. Where is the vengeance, the comeuppance, the catharsis and triumph and fanfare? I think so, but stay here. I wish I could hold the rage, or its more blissful counterpart. Some passionate hope or righteous indignation. A flipping of the switch: victim to victor. Loser to queen. *I'll show you* or *You'll see* or *You said I couldn't, and look—I can. You took me from me; look what I have now.* Isn't that what fuels people, I imagine, I wonder, to survive the unsurvivable? Isn't that what fuels us to destroy or rebuild? Are those not, I ask, our only two options? Am I built, I wonder at the wishing layer, for neither? I am built, I test, and sink a layer deeper, to bear witness.

Is that true? I ask this layer. It's quiet here, dark, like the warm, old dirt inches, feet, miles beneath the grass that weaves its way around my legs. Dark and vast, seeing all, judging nothing, like the sky around me. It feels familiar and forgotten. Something I've known, something I've come from, something I've drifted away from. Drifting—that's been my means of survival. Absent the energy to destroy or rebuild, I have drifted.

I'm here now, I say. What is true? I ask and wait. As I wait, I breathe through the nothing, full into the void. I relish this newly replenishing breath, loose and free in the darkness, unencumbered by decades of holding my shoulders taut, my back primed and ready to brace, fight, or fold. The wood holds my back, holds my head, too, my hair a pillow in between. The ground holds my center and lets my legs rest. The air receives my breath, gives me more breath in return.

What is true? I ask again.

It comes. From my belly, from elsewhere. Above my gut, below it, through—I feel it threading, weaving its way through the open space in my heart. Right inside of that long-neglected source: the root of the unwellness, the palpitations, the unfinishedness I've always carried. It's a mistake, medically speaking. *It is not a mistake*, I know, can feel. *It is a mercy.*

I feel it, and: My breath wraps, smooth and facile like tendrils of smoke, around the answer I always wanted to know, the question I never managed to ask.

My mother named me Mercy. I'll never know how she meant it. Not if I ask, not if she tells me, not if she tells me the truth as she feels it, straight from her belly. There is always something lost in translation, in that unmeasurable space between what we intend to give and what is received. A name, a womb, a home, a sanctuary, a decade, a lifetime, ourselves.

What is true? I ask again. What did my mother mean when she named me Mercy?

There is no more waiting. I hear it, know it.

Doesn't matter what she meant. Matters what I mean by it.

ACKNOWLEDGMENTS

There was a village behind the making of this book. To my agent, Alex Kane, at WME: Thank you for believing in this project. I am grateful for your time, feedback, advocacy, and respect for the characters. I cannot thank you enough for the patience and thoughtfulness with which you helped me tend to those early drafts and navigate each round of edits. It is an honor to work with someone who appreciates books as much as you do. To my editor, Chelcee Johns: Thank you for seeing the potential in these characters and helping me shape the story to let them shine. Your guidance was essential to bringing each character's dimensions to the page with greater clarity and impact. Working with you was a gift. Sydney Collins: Thank you for all you contributed to the growth of this book, for your understanding of the characters, and for supporting me through its production and publication. To Annette Szlachta and the copyediting and production teams: I am in awe of the intricacy and care with which you work; thank you for putting up with my punctuation choices. Thank you, Elizabeth A. D. Eno and the design team, for the beautiful cover and book design, and everyone at Ballantine and Penguin Random House for your work bringing this book to life. I've been moved and inspired, witnessing your expertise and dedication to the art and business of bookmaking.

Thank you to Eoin McNamee, Harry Clifton, Ella Gordon, and all who offered feedback on this story's earliest iterations. Much gratitude to

Kevin Power, Carlo Gébler, Sophia Ní Sheoin, Claire Keegan, and all at the Trinity Oscar Wilde Centre who shared their wisdom about writing as a practice and a career. It took time and space to explore how this story wanted to grow beyond its initial concept; the Molly Owen Award provided the resources for me to take that time, and I am so grateful to the award committee.

To the extraordinary Valerie Haynes Perry: Thank you for the courage and community to write, and for being there at every stage of the journey. I am grateful to you for teaching me how to trust my creative intuition, how to communicate with the characters, and how to source connection, vitality, and delight from every facet of the creative process. To all my fellow writing community members: Thank you, thank you, for being with so many iterations of this book. Your support, feedback, humor, and brilliance supported me from the beginning; I'm grateful to be a part of our creative family.

Thank you to my family: immediate and extended, chosen and of origin. Mom, thank you for advocating for my creativity and sharing yours so generously. Dad, thank you for modeling how to create boldly, with care for the collective. Nii, Miishe, and Dwetri: Thank you for cheering me on, sharing your wisdom and humor, and helping me with the Ghanaian naming conventions. To my nieces and nephews: You are my creative icons; thank you for being you. Daniel, thank you for your joyful being and tolerance of all the book talk. To all those whose encouragement, presence, and care have sustained me since I began this novel: I appreciate you. Auntie Beverly, Lindy, Patrice, Margie, Fayola, Alda, Teshone, Hilary, Malik, Nomita, Hanna, Chemeche, Anca, Diane, Susana, Atli, Vicki, Diana, Polly, Faiza, and Elisabeth: I am blessed to know you.

Thank you to the organizers, residents, and local community at Arteles, Gullkistan, NES, and Hub Feenix artist residencies. It is incredibly valuable to have time and space to experience the creative process in all its stages. I thank you all for your commitment to and investment in artists. Thank you, also, to the disability communities and advocates who have been a critical support system throughout the process of writing this book.

The book *Kpele Lala: Ga Religious Songs and Symbols* offered helpful details about Ga spiritual traditions. Thanks, Mom, for recommending the book, and thanks to its author, Marion Kilson, for the vital work of preserving our traditions on the page. Finally, a shout-out to the ancestors, to Oakland, and to the small but mighty nation of Ghana. I can no longer remember if I saw this or dreamed it, but I recall viewing an official-seeming website many years ago, wherein Ghana advertised itself as "the second-friendliest nation in Africa." I love everything about that, and I love us.

ABOUT THE AUTHOR

KAI ALONTÉ is a Ghanaian American artist based in northern Europe. Her work is rooted in a fascination with the dimensions of language. Growing up in Southern California, she found her first creative passions in dance and music. She started writing poetry and essays as a teenager, and later became a food and lifestyle writer. In 2021, she graduated from Trinity College Dublin's Creative Writing MPhil program.

ABOUT THE TYPE

This book was set in Garamond, a typeface originally designed by the Parisian type cutter Claude Garamond (c. 1500–61). This version of Garamond was modeled on a 1592 specimen sheet from the Egenolff-Berner foundry, which was produced from types assumed to have been brought to Frankfurt by the punch cutter Jacques Sabon (c. 1520–80).

Claude Garamond's distinguished romans and italics first appeared in *Opera Ciceronis* in 1543–44. The Garamond types are clear, open, and elegant.